Rope the Moon

AVA HUNTER

A RUNAWAY RANCH NOVEL

Cover Design: Wildheart Graphics
Editing: Lilypad Lit
Formatting: Champagne Book Design

Also by
AVA HUNTER

Babymoon or Bust
For Better or Hearse

Nashville Star Series
Sing You Home
Find You Again
Love You Always
Need You Now
Bring You Back
With You Forever

Runaway Ranch Series
Tame the Heart
Rope the Moon
Burn the Wild

Playlist

Dead Man's Curve | Brothers Osborne
Runnin' Outta Moonlight | Randy Houser
Botched Execution | Shovels & Rope
One Number Away | Luke Combs
Wait in the Truck | Hardy
Tulsa | Elle King
What If I Never Get Over You | Lady A
How Is She | Cole Swindell
Let Me Back In | Rilo Kiley
Summer's End | John Prine
Black | Dierks Bentley
Dust on the Bottle | David Lee Murphy
Greatest Love Story | LANCO
Your Heart or Mine | Jon Pardi
Let's Build a Fire | Cody Johnson
When It Comes to You | Cody Johnson

To the girls who need second chances, small town kisses, and starting over, I got you.

Psst.
The next page contains trigger warnings.
Please skip if you wish to avoid spoilerish content.

A Note from Ava

Dear Reader,

This book contains mentions and scenes of domestic abuse, violence, pregnancy, PTSD related to military service, and anxiety and panic attacks.

If you're sensitive to subjects such as these, please use this warning to make an informed decision about whether to proceed with the story.

As always, take care of yourself. Your mental health matters.

With big love and all good wishes,
Ava

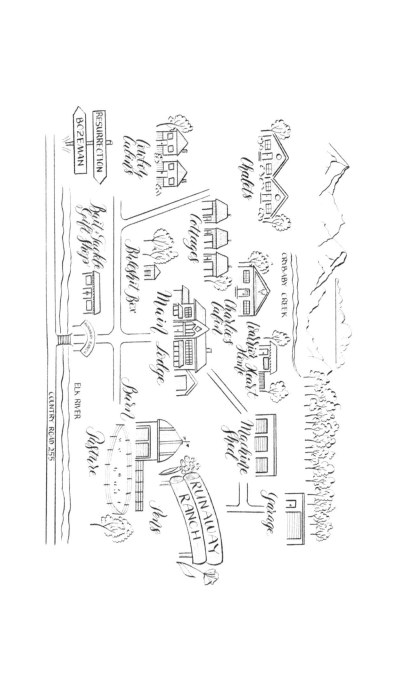

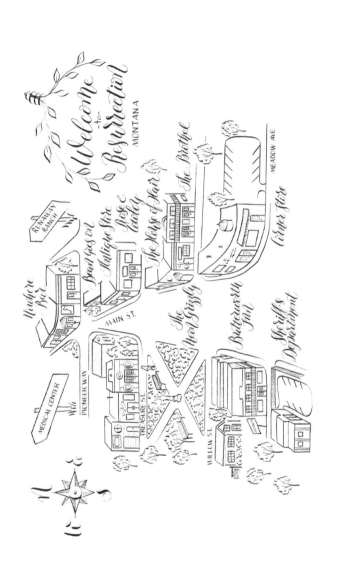

Rope
the
Moon

Two quick knocks signal her arrival. Like kerosene straight to my heart. I glance up from stoking the fire, watching as she slips into the cabin that's been our meeting place for the last six months.

Dakota McGraw.

Resurrection's golden girl.

And my personal goddamn kryptonite.

"Made you something," she says, her voice a husky purr. She lifts a plate in the air.

"I don't—"

"Eat sweets. I know." A sassy eyebrow arch. "But you eat mine."

Damn right I do. This cabin couldn't be situated on a property more aptly named than Eden, because I can never resist her temptation.

With a victorious smile, she lifts the covering on the plate to reveal four cupcakes adorned with thick chocolate frosting. "Brown sugar vanilla cupcakes with chocolate ganache."

I set the poker aside. "You do all that work to make that little thing?"

She laughs lightly. "Yeah, but you'll never forget it, will you?"

"No," I say, my eyes on her face. "I won't."

Dakota grins, desire evident in her expression as she sets her purse and the cupcakes on a small side table. The glow from the lantern illuminates the arch of her back, the curve of her ass, promptly turning my cock into a steel rod.

Her long black hair swishes against her waist, and I stare. It's hypnotic as hell.

Goddamn that hair. That body. This girl. This fucking girl who's healed my wounds, my nightmares, this last year.

And tonight, it all ends.

Every second of today, I've been counting down to this moment.

Fuck, but I'm dreading it.

In two quick strides, I cross the room. I grab her waist and tug her to me. Untie her apron and let it flutter to the ground.

"Hey, Hotshot." With an airy laugh, she launches herself into my arms. I grip her thighs and slide her warm body up mine, her long, lean legs wrapping around my waist.

"Hey, yourself."

My fingertips trace their way up the curve of her ass. I barely get her mouth on mine before she's pulling back, gasping, "How's Charlie?"

"He choked down some dinner tonight, so not a total loss," I say as I kick off my boots. The last thing I want to do is talk about my brother. My broken idiot brother.

Patching a man back together is easy. Watching my brother drown himself in a bottle of Jack has never been more painful.

Mouth on her neck, I back her up to the bed.

A laugh sparkles in her dark brown eyes. "Whatever happened to discipline?"

"Fuck discipline," I growl, tightening my grip on her waist.

I'm a soldier. A man of rules. Secrets. But when it

comes to Dakota McGraw, I've broken every single one of them.

"I've waited all day for this," she whispers, her graceful fingers holding my face.

My entire goddamn life.

"Me too." With that, I slam my mouth onto hers, my tongue tasting every inch of her sweet, sugar-spun mouth. We melt into the kiss, and it lights up the shadows inside of me, the wild, insatiable need for this woman.

Impatiently, I lower her to the mattress. And then she's everywhere. A swirl of wild hair and sweet breath. Cream and honey. Her frantic hands tremble as she works at my belt buckle, my zipper.

She gets on her knees in front of me and swallows me up. I make a sound like a wild animal, the noise echoing through the cabin. Her dark eyes stay locked on me as she works me over. I curl my hands in her hair, tangling it, and a breathy plea rises in the back of her throat. I can see down the front of her dress, those gorgeous breasts bouncing as she sucks me off. It has me ravenous. Has my cock hard as steel.

"Goddamn, Koty, you're so fucking pretty on your knees," I rasp. "Taking every single inch of me." Dakota bats her eyes, and that, plus the combination of her rosy, pouty lips sucking down my cock, has me just about ready to let loose.

I take her arms in my hands and jerk her up. As much as I love her on her knees, I want to be inside her.

"Fuck, but I need it too, baby," I hiss, groaning at how sinfully sweet it is to see the lust building in her eyes.

No longer patient, I strip her bare. Off comes her dress, bra, panties. My gaze rakes possessively down her naked body, across her face. Curves like a goddess. Eyes black like the starless sky at night.

I pull her close and lock her in my arms. My hand drifts, a finger parting the damp, dark curls around her pussy. Dakota moans and twists restlessly when I find her clit. I stroke the sensitive bundle of nerves, her lower body grinding down on my hand. She's so wet, so swollen, so open and unguarded, that my brain goes numb. Her breath shakes, she whines my name, and then she stiffens. Slick sweetness drips down my hand as she comes, her head falling back on her shoulders.

As soon as she's done trembling, I grab two handfuls of her pert ass and spin her around. I get her on her hands and knees on the bed and let loose an animalistic groan. That's goddamn it. I have the best view in the world. Her pussy, pretty and pink and wet, aimed right at me.

If it's even possible, I unravel further. This girl has me by the balls.

With a growl, I fold myself over her and grip her hips, hard, then slam into her slick channel with savage lust.

With a delighted squeal, she throws her head back. I fist her hair and tug. Her long lashes flutter. "Yes, Davis," she purrs. "Yes, yes."

"You feel so fucking good." She whimpers as I drive my cock deeper into her, her muscles flexing around me like a vise. "Fuck. *Fuck.*"

There's nothing but us tonight.

We have to last. Because in less than twenty-four hours, it's all over.

Dakota moans, a husky sound that has me picking up the pace. Skin slapping skin, her breasts bounce as my hips smack her ass. Reaching around, I stick my fingers in her mouth. She takes them deep, sucking on them.

The cabin fills with moans, the smell of sex. I fuck her hard, cleaving onto all that creamy white flesh, savoring these last moments with this girl. It's not enough. It'll never be enough. Not with Dakota.

Tonight, she's mine. I'm taking her. Let her go into the world smelling of my cum and knowing I've been the last one to touch, to taste her.

Dakota reaches back and palms my face. Pressure builds in both of us. I'm already fucking shaking like a teenager.

I grip her hard around the waist and yank her into me. Flesh against flesh, her bare back against my chest. She throws her head back against my shoulder, and I nip at her throat. Arching on tiptoes to get deeper, I thrust harder, working us both into a frenzy. Can't control it. A shudder rolls down my spine and into my cock, and then I'm roaring my release. Seconds later, Dakota's small moans follow mine.

When the quaking between our bodies stops, I gather her in my arms and pull us down into bed.

With a content sigh, she curls into me, all warm and soft like the last light of the evening sky. "I'm not going to be able to walk after tonight," she says with a little laugh.

I grunt. "Baby, you won't be able to crawl."

She's staying in this bed until we run out of moonlight. I'm not letting her go without fucking her senseless. As long as I have tonight, I have Dakota. And I plan on taking my goddamn time.

"Mmm," she hums, tracing a hand up my bicep. Her

wild mane of hair curls around us like a dark cloud of smoke. "Let's hope not."

"Where's your first stop?" I force the question out. Force myself to keep a cool head even if it's the last thing I feel.

"I'm in San Antonio for two semesters. And then…the future…it's wide open." She stretches her arms out over her head, baring her breasts, dark rosy nipples I can't wait to get in my mouth again. "Goodbye, Resurrection. Hello, sweet, sweet freedom."

"Will you miss it?"

"I'll miss my sister. My dad. The mountains." She hesitates, then her gaze drops to my face. "I'll miss you," she whispers.

"I'll miss you, too." Emotion knots my throat, and I tug her into my arms. "Miss kickin' your ass in pinball."

She scoffs and slaps my chest. "Davis Montgomery, I know you're not rewriting history."

I drag a hand over her arm, kiss that little freckle on her lip. I never miss it. I could find it in the dark, blindfolded. "Who's taking you to the airport tomorrow?"

"Stede," she says, her expression flushing with guilt.

No one knows about us. Not her father. Not my brothers. Maybe Ford, my twin, has a clue, but wisely, he's kept his fat fucking mouth shut.

For the last six months, we've been sneaking around, and I hate myself for it. Maybe because the girl in question is the dark-haired daughter of Stede McGraw. A man I consider a father to me and my brothers. Maybe because I should know better, and yet, she breaks every ounce of my self-control.

Don't know how this woman slipped her way past my

cold wall. Intelligent. Disarming. Beautiful. Somehow between the sex, the dreamless sleep, our conversations, she dragged it all out of me. We've only known each other a year, but it feels like I've known her for five lifetimes.

In those blissful hours we spent together, I forgot about my responsibilities. My brother wasn't losing it. My mission hadn't gone to shit. My team was still alive. I didn't have to keep it together. All that exists is this bright force of a woman who's breathed life back into my battered body. Has me feeling more like a man, less animal.

Dakota slips out of bed, and I watch her, my cock resuscitating itself at the gentle sway of her hips and ass as she takes a tube of lotion out of her purse.

I push myself up on my elbows and shake my head. "You don't have to do this."

"Shut up." She slips in bed behind me, reclining me in her arms. "Enjoy it. It's the last time I'll do it."

The singular thought has the power to destroy. My heart hammers, and I look to the window like I can stop the sun from rising. At dawn, she'll be gone, and there's not a thing I can do about it.

Slowly, methodically, like she's done all summer, Dakota rubs the lotion on my bullet wound. I relax into her, wanting to tattoo her touch onto my body. Her graceful hands knead the scar tissue as gently as she kneads one of her breads.

Even a year later, it hurts.

When she met me, I was one arm down. I was focused on Charlie, and she had none of my excuses as to why I wasn't working on it. She bossed and bullied me into doing daily rehab. A year later, except for a numb tingling when it rains, it's back to 90 percent motion.

But that's Dakota. She cares, she gives, and I'm the bastard who takes.

"You take care of yourself, you hear me?" Her soft, soothing hands stroke over my bicep. "Put this on every night."

Reaching up, I cup her face. "I don't regret it."

She smiles. "I wouldn't expect you to. Not you, Hotshot."

Hotshot.

Like I said. She has all my secrets.

When she's finished, she caps the lotion. Her slender arms loop around my neck, and she nuzzles her face against my cheek. My chest burns. I comb her hair off her flushed cheek. Without thinking, I say unhappily, "I fucking hate that you have to leave."

Her breath catches.

Shit.

It's too much. Heat of the moment.

Heart of the moment.

Dakota stares at me. "Davis…is there," she bites her lower lip, swallows, "something you want to tell me?" Her voice is breathy. Hope lights her expression.

Her question knocks me flat. Fucking Christ.

Stay.

I love you.

They're the only words that have ever made any sense.

It's on the tip of my lips and yet…

Her gorgeous face is bright, that daydreamer look in her eyes I've long come to recognize as one of the most stunning features of Dakota McGraw. I won't be the bastard who ruins her dreams. She finally has her chance to get out of Resurrection. I just planted roots here, and she's pulling hers up. It's not like I can offer her a castle and a white horse. All I have is a busted ranch, and a broken brother I'm trying to keep alive.

And Dakota—she has her entire future.

A good girl with her life straight. She'll travel the world, get that bakery she wants, and blow everyone in Resurrection out of the water.

Koty McGraw needs freedom, and I won't hold her back. This girl's born to fly. She deserves the world.

With heroic effort, I give a tight shake of my head, ignoring the selfish bastard inside of me that wants to keep her here. "No. Nothing."

Some of the light dies in her dark brown eyes. Her lips curve in a sad little smile.

Before she can say anything, I'm twisting in her arms and lifting the dog tags from around my chest. I remove and pocket one of the tags, then slip the chain with the remaining tag over her head, clearing hair from her nape as they settle down low between her breasts.

"I want you to take these," I order. Almost hesitantly, she fingers the tag. "Remember, Koty, you need anything, you call me."

Mischief sparkles in her eyes, and her lips pull into a flirty one-sided grin. "Anything? Like alibis, kidnappings, simple beatings?"

"And then some." I softly grip her jaw, forcing her to look at me. "I mean it. Anytime you ask, I'll be there. Five seconds, five minutes, five lifetimes. I will always come for you. No matter what."

The words drop between us, weighted. Our gazes hold for one long beat, the small space between us warming several degrees.

"Promise me," I demand.

Her eyes shutter, then open.

"I promise," she whispers.

Then I take Dakota McGraw in my arms and kiss her until the sun comes up.

1

Dakota

OMEONE ONCE SAID LIFE BEGINS WITH A BANG AND ends with a whimper.

But I think it starts with fire.

Burn everything down to build it back up.

My jeep jostles along the country road, bouncing over a snow-filled pothole, rattling my teeth. Somewhere along the way, I took a wrong turn and now, a sleet-snow rain is coming down in sheets. I'm in the middle of nowhere and cell reception is non-existent.

Desperation fills me as I grip the steering wheel with my good hand, scanning the road for a sign to tell me where I am. After two days in the car, thousands of miles across the country, it's too late to turn back now.

It would be so easy to pull over onto the shoulder of the road and wait for Aiden to find me and bring me back home. But sense hasn't caught up with me yet.

My stomach grumbles. Oh god. How long has it been since I ate?

"I'm sorry, I'm sorry, I'm so sorry."

I don't know who I'm talking to. Myself. My stomach. Tears blur my vision and trail down my cheeks until I'm a salty, sooty, sobbing mess.

I should be in my kitchen right now. It's seven a.m. in DC. The morning rush. I'd be up, hands covered in dough, getting the fast-paced masses to slow down with a simple honeybun.

I glance at the full moon, still burning bright despite the hazy snow-flurried sky.

Rope the moon.

My mother's words blaze a trail to my heart. She never explained what it meant, but I've always interpreted it as *go after what you want.* Make it yours through grit, grace, or gumption.

And I did. For a long time, until I met Aiden, I roped the moon. I moved the infinity out of my life.

Last night, I took it back.

I can do this. Somehow, I can do it.

My jeep smells like smoke, and I feel a flicker of shame, hear Aiden's panicked scream in my ears. *Help me. Help me!*

But I didn't.

Maybe I shouldn't have run, but I saw my chance, and I took it.

But was it worth it? I gave up my beautiful bakery to be free.

With a sigh, I wipe the fatigue and the soot from my face.

Maybe it's another bad decision in a river of bad decisions.

If only it was that easy to leave the past in my rearview mirror. I catch my reflection, wincing at my busted lip, the faded bruise around my left eye. My long dark hair's sweaty and mussed. I'm still wearing my apron from this morning.

Whether the fire bought me any time is hard to know. It'll take the police a few days to shift through the wreckage of the bakery and for Aiden to come up with a story. And when that's done...

Is that when Aiden will track me down?

My hand tightens on the wheel as the tires go into a

skid. On a shaky breath, I steady the Jeep. The rain's coming down in sheets, and I can barely see the road in front of me.

It's too easy, I'm too free. It won't last. Nothing good ever does.

Aiden warned me about what would happen if I ever left.

I want you to remember this moment the next time you think about leaving me. I will fuck with you, Dakota. I will fuck with your family, and I will fuck with your life. And when I find you, I will carve out your fucking heart and feed it to the wolves.

An icy shiver rolls through me. I shake my head, clearing the memory.

My eyes flick to the rear-view mirror. My pulse quickens, like Aiden's behind me on his motorcycle, already anticipating my next move.

Bad idea, Koty, this is a bad idea. Your bakery didn't just catch on fire, so did your life.

And all for what?

To escape?

To go home?

I can't ignore the irony. After spending so many years aching to break free from my small hometown, taking off in a blaze of glory for culinary school, I'm running straight back to Resurrection as my main life hack.

Just yesterday I had my bakery. Milk & Honey.

My blood, sweat, tears. And now…

Gone. All gone.

My mind replays the fire like a fever dream. Our fight. The hard backhand to my face. Aiden screaming. How terribly fast that pan went up in flames. I stared at it, holding my cheek. Mesmerized, hypnotized. The flames licking up the back of the stove to snap at the ceiling. My fingers digging into my purse for my keys like my legs already knew where I was going. Aiden's hand clawing at me, to drag me back, when in the end he stayed to fight the fire. For his money. For his *investment*.

Because Aiden King doesn't lose things.

And he won't lose me.

That bone-deep knowledge terrifies me.

The rage in Aiden's eyes as I ran for my Jeep, hopped in and never looked back.

Because he knew I had my chance.

I gasp when I see the smoke unfurling eerily slow in my backseat. The snap of flame. A monster cloud of mayhem.

No.

I shake my fried brain out if its fatigued daze.

It's not real. I'm imagining it.

My stomach cramps, and I exhale a long breath.

I glance down at my left arm in its dull yellow cast.

How does that feel, Aiden? Someone taking away what you love.

Eyes narrowed, I steer through the sleet. The snow-covered road stretches out in front of me like a never-ending landing strip.

Up ahead, a neon vacancy sign illuminates a motel strip. A sliver of hope fills me. My weary body screams for a bed, for food, even if it is a bag of chips, a coin of Rolos from a vending machine. I allowed myself a short pit stop back in Minnesota, where I napped for twenty minutes at a gas station. Except for that, I haven't stopped driving.

Everything in me aches. I ache for what I've given up, for what comes next.

What I'll tell my father, my town.

Golden girl. Magna cum laude. Homecoming queen. Daydreamer. Chef.

My entire life I have been everything to everyone. Tonight, I may as well add liar to the mix.

The turn comes up so fast I almost miss it.

I slam the brakes and jerk the wheel, but overcompensate, turning weakly one-handed. Gravel flies as the old Jeep spins. My stomach sours, acrid bile hitting my throat. The Jeep slides a few inches forward into the ditch, and then it sighs to a stop.

No.

I grab the keys, turning hard, willing for it to start. But the Jeep stays horrifically motionless.

"You have got to be fucking kidding me," I whisper hoarsely.

There are not enough miles between me and Aiden. Sooner or later, he'll catch up with me.

My palms dampen on the steering wheel. The cab of the jeep fills with the sound of my labored breathing.

I can't let him win. He already took my arm and my bakery, he's not taking anything else from me.

I want to be safe.

I want to live.

I want to be free.

Help. I need help.

Before I left home, my father had pulled me aside under the awning of his old cabin and pressed a hundred-dollar bill in my hand. He kissed my cheek and told me, "Don't be too proud to come back home, you hear?"

Another voice rings in my ears.

Rugged. Deep.

A voice I've clung to the last six years, but foolishly ignored.

"Pull it together," I tell myself, running a shaky palm over my stomach. Reaching over, I grab the dog tag from the broken lock box on the passenger seat and slip the chain around my neck.

I unbuckle my seatbelt, grab my cell phone, and hurry out of the car.

Gritting my teeth, I heft my duffel bag over my shoulder. All my meager belongings, my entire savings that I packed in a frantic haste to get away from Aiden.

I gasp as icy sheets of rain hit me, a chill so fierce I'm shivering even in my thick winter jacket.

Over the deafening sound of my heart, I run up the shoulder of the road. The neon sign of the LIGHTS OUT MOTEL is my beautiful beacon.

I cross the gravel parking lot and stop under the motel eave.

My body goes limp with relief when I see I have cell service.

Then I tense.

I have one missed call from Aiden.

"Fuck," I whisper, wrapping my numb fingers around the dog tag.

I stare at it for one heartbeat. Then two. Then I swipe the notification away and dial a number I've known my entire life.

"Dakota?"

The minute I hear my father's whiskey-weathered voice, relief floods my entire body. I choke on a sob, feeling a little less alone, wondering why I didn't ask for help two years ago.

"Daddy," I choke out.

"Wasn't expecting to hear from you today, daydreamer."

I hate the surprise that stains his voice. I shake off the sting. I can't blame him. I'm well aware I've barely called him over the last year.

"Daddy," I say again. My voice sounds so small, so frightened, that I wince. "Something bad happened."

Instantly, he's on alert. That roughrider who rode bulls and busted broncs and would always do anything to help me. "You need help, Koty?"

"Yes," I whisper, feeling like I've died and gone to hell. I fight down the sob that tries to escape. "I'm in trouble. My car broke down. I'm—I'm—" I search the road for a sign. "I'm in Sioux Falls."

"You hurt, baby girl?"

I look down at my arm, knowing nothing can prepare my father for this. "I am."

"You tell me where you are and I'll make it right."

My father sounds out of breath, huffing. I can hear the frantic jingle of keys, and I flash back to my senior year and the kegger thrown at Lionel Wolfington's house. I called him to come get me because my entire class was drunk off their asses and I wanted to go home.

My father erupts in a series of hacking coughs that have me wincing.

Something's wrong. Something's wrong at home.

"I'm at the Lights Out Motel. I need to come home." I jump clear out of my skin when a stranger sweeps past me. I flinch, hating the way I'm as skittish as a whipped horse. "Fast, Daddy."

"I'm sending Davis."

"No," I blurt. Even though the minute my father says *Davis*, my mind automatically says *safe*.

"Dakota—"

"Please." I move closer to the bright light of the soda machine. "I don't want Davis."

The worst lie I've ever told.

"I can't make the drive, baby girl. For a lot of reasons. I reckon you'll soon know."

Tears spring to my eyes. Panic, sharp and searing snakes in my belly. There's no way I can go back to Resurrection like I planned—calm and collected, pretending I have my life together.

Because Davis Montgomery has always seen right through me.

He'll see all the lies. All my little secrets. All the bravado, all the bullshit. That I'm not strong. Maybe I never was.

Still, hope sings out in my soul.

Desperate, aching, desolate hope.

Nothing can erase the memory of those deep brown eyes and rugged grin. The broad-shouldered Marine I keep telling myself I've forgotten even if all I've done for the last six years is think of him.

Gripping the dog tag around my neck, I exhale. Aiden will come after me. I know it in my bones. He will never let me go.

I need Davis. In the worst possible way.

That man, that unforgettable man who still haunts my dreams.

"Okay," I say with a shudder, feeling like I'm staring down the barrel of a crossroads. "Send Davis."

Because I need a do-over.

Glancing down, I cup the small bud of my belly.

A really, really big fucking do-over.

2

Davis

"**W**HAT'S THE KID'S NAME AGAIN? CALLIE?"

"Cassie," I snap back at Deputy Sheriff Buzz Topper.

Maybe it's the thirty minutes of sleep I got last night, thanks to a god-awful nightmare that woke me up. Or maybe it's the perpetual nasally drone of Topper's voice. Either way, I was wide awake when Sheriff Richter called in *MONSAR*—the Montana Search and Rescue Team—to search for a little girl who went missing on top of Meadow Mountain.

Of course, it has to be a fucking kid.

I glare at Buzz, clench my fists and take a step toward him. "A little girl is missing. At least get her goddamn name right."

Buzz, his chipmunk cheeks pink, stutters an apology and trips over his own two feet to get away from my wrath.

On an exhale, I glance down. The photo in my hand shows a blonde-haired, blue-eyed little girl in pigtails. *Cassie Karr. Two years old.*

"What's up your ass?" Richter booms, appearing beside me. Despite the steady calm in his voice, his black eyes flash. Raised in Detroit, Sheriff Calvin Richter's brought his own form of law to Resurrection. He could have his choice of any big city, but he's here making the town his own.

I respect that.

I pocket the photo and watch Cassie's mother sob on her front porch for so long I have to turn away.

The idea that someone doesn't have their family fucking guts me.

If they don't come home, I don't come home. It's that simple. A motto I live by even if I haven't done right by it in the past.

My gut clenches, but I push through the hollow ache. "Nothing," I say.

Together, Richter and I trek across the frozen lawn toward a group of police officers. The howl of the wind and low conversation are all that can be heard. My SAR dog, Keena, trots impatiently next to me, ready to get to work.

Once Runaway Ranch became fully operable over five years ago, I joined the local sheriff's Montana Search and Rescue K9 unit. I needed something to do other than boss around my brothers. Besides that, free time isn't in my vocabulary. Eating up my days and nights is all I want to do to keep my mind off the past.

Despite its small-town status, Resurrection gets its fair share of search and rescue cases. Lost hikers. Drunk idiots. Dangerous stunts. And I'd take all of them any day of the week over a kid.

As we walk, Keena carefully matches my pace. I flip the collar of my jacket up against the gusts of frigid wind tunneling over the mountain. A typical January winter morning in Montana. Sunshine and ice glints off the trees while shadows dance along the evergreens. Resurrection's beauty takes your breath away. So does the cold. But the windchill doesn't faze me.

After years spent in hellish conditions overseas, I'm

used to the elements. Zone out and focus on what's in front of you. Don't miss a thing. You miss, someone dies.

I scan the icy horizon. Clock entry, exit points. On the trailer's porch, there's a fridge and a windchime frozen in time. A frying pan sits outside, beers in the ice bank.

I stop.

"When did she go missing again?" I ask.

"About an hour ago," Richter says. "She was playing on the porch. Parents didn't think she'd actually leave."

I clamp my teeth together and shake my head. Playing on the porch in the dead of winter. *Fucking ridiculous.*

The crunch of gravel beneath my boots fills the silence.

"We got people in the woods." Richter passes me a light pink sock of Cassie's. "Hoping if she's out there, she stays put." A search team calls her name through the thick grove of trees, and I walk briskly ahead. I want to hurry this up. In a missing person's case, especially a missing kid, time is always of the essence.

"Long as she's got some shelter," I grunt.

"Long as."

With a groan, I sink into a squat beside Keena. My shoulders ease a fraction as I place a palm on her head and look the Belgian Malinois in her eyes.

"You ready, girl?"

Keena's one of the most intelligent dogs I've ever known. A super guard dog, and command trained for voice or hand signals, her climbing and jumping ability never ceases to amaze. Curious, alert and endlessly loyal, Keena doesn't have an aggressive bone in her body. She came to me as a rescue when I was busy training K9 dogs to rehome on Runaway Ranch, and I kept her. We were both in a rough patch and bonded. She trained me back into a human.

She's the best dog in the world. She's got my back and I've got hers.

I rough a hand in her glossy black and brown coat. Watch the determination spark in her black eyes as I pull out Cassie's sock.

This is why I love dogs. They're black and white. There's no gray or ambiguity in life. You give them a job, they do it.

Me—I live for the gray.

"All right," I murmur to Keena. "Let's find this kid."

Her ears prick. Her nose trembles. All the telltale signs of a damn good SAR dog.

I stand, and Richter and I watch as Keena moves toward the house. Frowning, I blink at her unexpected trajectory. I had expected her to make a move for the woods.

Keena, nose working overtime, climbs the porch steps and stops next to the fridge. Her loud whine sounds in the crisp early morning air.

Fuck.

Richter and I both make a mad dash to the fridge. It's old, but the door frame isn't frozen shut like I had expected. Gripping the handle, I wrench it open.

And there she is.

A tiny girl with blonde pigtails swaddled in a purple parka. Seeing us, she lets out a weak cry from her rosebud mouth and rubs her eyes.

"How'd the hell she get in there?" Richter blasts, looking pale.

I grab her up in my arms and hold her tight against my chest. Her small heart hammers next to mine.

"We found you, Cassie," I murmur, cupping her head as she wails. "You're safe, sweetheart. Baby girl, breathe," I whisper into her clammy golden curls.

Sniffling, she lifts her head and gives me a toothy little smile. My heart wrenches. Unable to stand it, I pass her to Richter, who passes her to her mother.

"We didn't have to go far," I tell him, gazing at the trailer.

"Fucking backyard," Richter says, sounding amazed.

Backyards. Most crimes happen in your own backyard. Right under your nose.

I'd call it a goddamn great day that we found Cassie this easy. Most missing persons are hikers who, depending on the time of year, succumb to the elements. Being a local doesn't mean you're immune to the Montana wilderness.

"I'll wrap up here," Richter says, reaching for the radio on his hip. His voice drops an octave. "Make sure the parents didn't have anything to do with it."

"That's a good idea."

"Take your girl and give her a big treat."

"Plan on it. Thanks, Sheriff."

My sharp whistle draws Keena back to my side. I tap my chest, and she gently leaps up to plant her two front paws on my chest. Chuckling, I pet her head. "Those ears work better when food is involved, don't they?"

After a healthy dose of praise, I head for my truck while Keena keeps pace beside me. My skin feels too tight from nerves, and my fists ache for a good session in the gym with the punching bag. Then at least a five-mile walk for Keena.

Inside my truck, Keena rides passenger. I turn on the heat, letting it blast, and crank down a window for my dog. Icy air hits her in the face, her tongue lolling. As my truck winds its way around the sharp switchbacks of Resurrection, miles of snowy wilderness stretch out before me. The crackle of my police scanner spits today's radio chatter.

We pass over Dead Fred's Curve, a narrow stretch of road with blind corners around every bend. Instead of guardrails, there is a multi-thousand-foot drop to the valley below. Posts designating grave markers dot the side of the road. Though harrowing, I prefer to take this route. It's a shortcut back to Runaway Ranch and my time alone to breathe and think.

By the time I get back to the ranch, rays of bright sunlight are streaming through the clouds, chasing away the morning chill in the air.

I exit the truck. With a woof, Keena bounds for the Warrior Heart Home, the kennels and housing facility for my dogs. I chuckle and watch her run. Dog's so goddamn free it kills me.

I scan the ranch and its perimeter. Construction in varying stages is going on all over the grounds to get it ready for opening season. My job, as head of security, is to keep a pulse on the ranch. Keep it safe.

Something I fucked up once.

I won't do it again.

Runaway Ranch has always been Charlie's. Ever since he first set foot on this land to escape the memories of his fiancée's death. His breakdown brought us all out here to keep him together and so far, no one's shown an interest in leaving. Resurrection—just like Runaway Ranch—has become a part of our souls.

And it's become my purpose. Serve my town,

protect my brothers, train my dogs. A simple, peaceful life. Although peace doesn't have much of a chance as long as one of my brothers is around.

"Hoo-wee. I can feel your temper boiling from over here." My twin, Ford, comes loping around the side of the lodge. Shaggy dark blond hair flops in his face. Though all of us Montgomery's are well over six feet, he's got the lean physique of a baseball player while I'm Marine through and through.

One thing we share: we both have damn great aim. I knew stellar sharpshooters overseas, but Ford's fastballs are legendary.

I glance at my brother's Merrill sawtooth hiking boots, then jerk my chin to his pack. "You hit the dome today?"

"Not as early as you." He tosses a bag of powder into his rucksack. "But yeah. I was out and about on the mountain."

Ranch life only works for Ford if he can stay busy. Since he left baseball, he's been spinning his wheels, searching out any small job he can. Ranch hand, bartender, car mechanic, adrenaline junkie. That's Ford. Any adventure, he's game. It's why we call him the wildcard of Runaway Ranch. No one knows what Ford gets up to. Not even him.

His eyebrows lift. "Bad mornin' already?"

"Tough mornin'."

"You find the kid?"

"Yeah. She climbed into an empty fridge on the edge of the property. Keena sniffed her out." I exhale the anger simmering in my gut. The reminder makes me want to punch something. "People and their fucking junk."

Ford follows as I trek across the icy tundra. In the distance, our new barn stands tall and proud. It burned last year after an arson attempt. Thanks to the help of our tight-knit community, we got it rebuilt right in time for winter.

"You okay?" When I hesitate, Ford says, "You didn't sleep last night."

Not since I came home from the Marines. Most nights I'm lucky if I get four hours.

I scoff and shake my head. "Christ, Ford. You and that woo-woo shit."

He flashes a bright white grin. "Maybe so, but I know your surly ass believes it."

I grit my teeth and ignore him. I want to tell him to mind his own damn business, to knock it off with that in-sync shit, but I can't. Because he's right.

I believe it.

So many times, our twin senses have been synced up.

The summer I found him after a gnarly dirt bike accident. One broken ankle, still smiling even as I helped him limp back home.

Christmas, on leave from the Marines, he pulled me from the creek after my horse threw me.

Ford was the first in my family to know I got shot. Before anyone from the higher ups had called my parents, he sounded the alarm and rallied our family.

Somehow, we just know.

I stop, noticing the truck in the gravel drive. "We got company?"

Ford looks back at the lodge and then toward me. "Ruby and Charlie are back."

"Fuck," I mutter. I should have made a quicker getaway.

Ford smirks. "You gonna go hide in the gym or come say hi?"

I grit my teeth, hopes of taking out my restlessness on a punching bag dashed, and head for the lodge with Ford.

Currently, the lodge—or Main House—operates as the epicenter of the ranch. Guest bookings. Chow hall. It's also my place of residence. I live in the annex that takes up the entire third floor. Never needed a place to myself. I don't sleep long enough. So I keep a close watch on the guests when they're there, mind my own business when they're not.

The second I walk up the wide front porch and through the heavy double doors, I'm hit by a cacophony of noise. The brash laughter of my brothers intermixed with a bright feminine laugh.

Bellied up to Bar M are my brothers and Ruby. Charlie and Ruby sit on heavy cowhide stools while Wyatt tends to them, pouring steaming cups of coffee. There's a box of gas station donuts on the counter, no doubt snagged by Wyatt on a trip into town. Boots and jackets strewn precariously in the living room.

My lips twist into a grimace. It looks like a tornado swirled through the lodge. Leave it to my brothers to make a mess, then leave me with the pieces.

Exhaling a breath, I roll out my shoulders. That cleanliness ingrained into me in the military has been damn hard to shake. I try to focus on my family and ignore the clutter.

At least for now.

I clap Charlie on the shoulder, then pull him in for a tight hug. "Too early for a tan, brother."

I haven't seen my brother and his wife in six months, not since they eloped and took off for California where Ruby had surgery to fix her heart. After a detour down south to see family, they're finally home.

Charlie, his dark beard unruly, a smile in his eyes, chuckles. "All that California sunshine."

Speaking of sunshine…

Ruby bounces my way. I catch my sister-in-law up in a big hug, letting down my guard for a second. "How about you?" I hold her at arm's length, sweeping my eyes over her pretty face. "You look good, Ruby."

She beams. "I feel great."

I allow myself a rare grin. I can't help but love her.

This girl died for our ranch. Charlie will never get over it.

And I will never forget it.

Ruby grabs on tight to my arm when I release her. "I've never seen it like this, Davis." Her wide-eyed gaze takes in the place. "The lodge. It's so empty."

I chuckle, leaning back and bracing my hands on the bar. "You're back right in time. Get the ranch in shape before summer."

Ruby flexes her fingers. "I'm ready to do my social media darndest."

Ford wiggles his brows. "Fairy Tale gonna save the day again?"

"Don't need to," I say pointedly. "Business is good."

According to our projections, the lodge is booked for the next two years. And we only have Ruby to thank. After a social media scandal rocked the ranch last year, it was dumb luck that Charlie met Ruby, a social media influencer, and enlisted her help. With Ruby's connections, the ranch took off like a rocket and never looked back.

But it almost didn't happen.

When Declan Valiante, a ruthless developer turned

politician, set fire to our barn in an attempt to take down our ranch, Ruby was hurt.

She almost didn't make it.

And it would have ended our brother.

I'll never forget the sound he made when Ruby wouldn't wake up. That primal, keening wail haunts my memories.

"Left hand still getting used to that ring?" Ford asks Charlie, dipping behind the bar to pull out a bottle of Irish Whiskey.

Charlie lifts his hand, flashing silver, and a big grin. "Day I put it on."

"You want breakfast?" Wyatt asks, shoving a donut in front of my face.

I knock his hand away. "Donuts aren't breakfast." Reckless, loud and smart mouthed, Wyatt's sole purpose in life is to try my damn sanity.

"Same ole protein shake every day of the week, Davis, ain't no way to live."

"My way," I grunt. Dependable. Healthy.

I sit down on a barstool, content to take in my brothers.

"How was Georgia? You survive Mama Belle?" I ask Ruby, temporarily forgetting about the itch to move, to get to the gym.

"I survived," she says, giving her husband a look. She giggles. "I'm not sure Charlie did."

My brother groans and drags a hand down his beard. "Dealin' with Mama is a damn exercise in patience."

Ruby laughs and shoves at his arm as Charlie pulls her in close. "It wasn't so bad." She smiles at the room. "But I'm glad to be back where we belong."

I glance at Charlie and study the dopey grin on his

face. Watch the way he follows around the delicate girl who stole his heart last summer.

Fuck, but I'm glad for him. He deserves it.

He's finally back. Whole. Sober. Alive.

A memory of Wyatt calling me at the Marine bunkhouse pops into my mind. "Charlie ain't gonna make it, D," he had said tearfully. "He's putting whiskey on his goddamn corn flakes."

Real fear had hit me then. My brother was going to fall drunk off a roof before he got over Maggie. Because I wasn't fucking there. I was overseas, recuperating after a special-ops mission with my team had gone to shit. Emergency leave was non-negotiable. I was stuck.

So, I took a bullet on purpose.

Charlie was my mission.

I wasn't putting my brother in the fucking ground. Not another one. Not my blood.

If I couldn't protect my brothers overseas, I damn sure planned to protect my brother at home.

A responsibility my father passed to me. A responsibility I take as seriously as my life.

"Friends are family, but family is forever," he said to me the day our youngest brother, Grady, was born. "Protect those babies."

I took my father's words to heart.

Especially last year.

I thought we settled the mess with Valiante. But early last fall, he came back to the ranch. I caught him at Charlie's cabin, looking for Ruby.

Valiante wasn't getting another chance to hurt someone I loved.

I put a bullet in his brain. Buried him on the far side of the property near Crybaby Falls.

Unlike dogs, black and white doesn't work in Montana. And it doesn't fly on the ranch. We do what we need to do to survive. That includes attacking first.

Men like Valiante can never be trusted. They always come back.

And when they come for my family, they don't get a second chance.

Answering to the man upstairs for what I've done doesn't worry me. What worries me is answering to myself for what I don't do. No sympathy. No remorse. Not for anyone who touches my family.

"Who says we can't charge extra to take 'em out to see the Grunkle?" Wyatt's languid drawl pulls me from my daze.

It takes me a second to realize he's talking about the endangered bird Stede McGraw invented to give the ranch protected status.

I rub my temple. "Can't charge guests for a bird that doesn't exist."

Wyatt rolls his eyes. "I don't know how you can take the most exciting subject and make it boring."

"Idiot," Ford says affectionately, cuffing Wyatt on the head. I smirk, watching a scowl darken Wyatt's face. A big brother's job is to give our little brothers shit at every opportunity.

Ford gets Wyatt in a headlock. Pinned, Wyatt takes a swing at him, causing Ruby to squeak and jump out of the way.

"C'mon, little brother," Ford drawls, tightening his

hold. "You gotta stay on your toes with that big mouth of yours."

"No groups near the falls," I say, holding up my hands to rein in my brothers as they scuffle. Briefly, my hard gaze locks with Charlie's. "I don't want guests out in the back-country unsupervised."

That's when I hear it. The slam of the front double doors. Instantly, the conversation hushes. Wyatt uses the distraction to elbow Ford in the stomach and untangle himself.

King of cowboys, Stede McGraw stands in the door-way. Stetson in his hands. Snow on his boots. His hair is scraped back into thin wisps of silver.

The man's a former bull riding champ and stuntman. As a lifelong local of Resurrection, he was one of the first in town to show me the reins of the ranch before Charlie could take the reins himself.

Blue eyes burning bright, Stede lifts his hat in greeting. "Ruby, honey. Boys."

I sip my coffee, try my best to keep a smile off my face. Though Ford and I both turned thirty-six in December, we'll always be kids to Stede McGraw.

"Hey, old man." I reach for the coffeepot and pour him a full cup. "Good to see you."

"What's going on?" Ford asks.

"I'd like to tell you I'm here to welcome these two back to town." Stede nods at Ruby and Charlie, takes a step closer to the bar. "But hell, I'm afraid my intentions aren't that noble."

I frown. On closer inspection, the man looks like he's aged overnight. Even though he's been undergoing chemo for the last year, he looks beaten down. His knuckles are clenched white around his cowboy hat.

"You okay, Stede?" Charlie asks, brow furrowed.

"You remember my oldest daughter, Dakota, don't you?"

Fuck.

My body tenses like it's in battle. Still, I do my best to keep my face expressionless while my heart slams against my chest like a kick drum.

Remember. More like engraved onto my goddamn soul.

Although, I'd never tell Stede that. Dakota and I are water under the bridge. She came into my life as quick as she left. One year. But it felt like she blew up my entire world.

The memory of her comes in waves. Intelligent dark brown eyes, the color of roasted chestnuts. She always reminded me of the buzz of neon long after it flickered out. Always going. Energy in motion. That was Dakota McGraw.

"Sure, I remember her." I place my hands on the counter to shake off the ache that's already settled and study the defeated hunch of his shoulders. Having spent half my life decoding facial expressions and nonverbal cues, I know without a doubt that he's brought nothing good to the ranch. "What can we do for you, Stede?"

"I'm afraid I need your help," he says grimly. "Koty's in trouble."

"Trouble?"

Fuck.

If Dakota's in trouble, it means I'll kill someone.

Again.

"Got a call from her early this morning," Stede goes

on. "She wouldn't tell me what happened, but she's hurt. Her car broke down. Sounds like she's on the run. From what, she wouldn't say."

"On the run? What the fuck," Ford says, looking bewildered.

"Tell us what we can do," Charlie growls, his arm wrapped around Ruby.

Stede lets out a long, tired sigh. "I'm not too proud to ask…would you go get my daughter, Davis?"

All eyes pin to me. My throat tightens as my mind locks on the promise I made to Stede last year. To always protect Dakota and Fallon. The old man is like a second father to us all. Taking us in. Protecting the ranch by calling in a doozy of a favor when we needed help.

I make a promise, I keep it.

But before I can answer, Stede, shame in his voice, says, "With the cancer, I'm not strong enough to make the drive." Ruby rests a hand on his arm. "And Fallon…"

Wyatt straightens up, blue eyes bright and intense. "Fallon needs help?" he asks over a mouthful of donut. Powdered sugar coats the front of his shirt.

"If Dakota's in trouble"—Stede runs a hand through his wispy hair—"I don't want Fallon tangling with whatever she's got following her."

"I'll go," I announce, feeling all three of my brother's gazes on me. Fueled by anger and determination, I stomp across the floor and grab the keys to my truck. "Where is she?"

"A little town outside of Sioux Falls. 'Bout eleven hours away."

I'll make it in eight.

Ford's eyes are cold. "You need backup, D?"

"No," I grit out.

Only backup I'm taking is my twelve gauge.

I look at Stede. "I promised you I'd protect your daughters and I'll do that. I'll bring Dakota home safe."

I just hope I'm not too late.

3

Davis

I'VE LEARNED OVER THE YEARS THAT HIGH STRESS always equals low logic.

And yet, here I am.

Dead of night, my truck roars down the highway, headlights coasting over flat terrain. I keep my eyes trained on the signs for the Sioux Falls exit and yawn, fighting the urge to let my mind wander.

Good fucking luck with that.

My mind doesn't have anywhere to go except the past. To Dakota McGraw.

My unofficial welcome wagon when I first arrived in Resurrection, recovering from a bullet that sent me home. I was hurting and pissed off at Charlie for not keeping it together.

Sent by Stede, she was the girl next door rumbling down the road in her daddy's Chevy. Dakota came drifting onto the ranch, bringing soups, cakes, and breads. Wearing short shorts and halter tops. Always a dusting of flour on her face. She'd arrange the food in the kitchen, wait for me to storm in and growl at her, and somehow draw me into a conversation.

"What'll it be, cupcake or cookie?" she asked as she arranged food on the counter.

I grunted. "Don't eat sweets."

She mock-gasped. "No sweets?" Her black eyes twinkled. "Then I'm afraid you and I can never be."

Curious, I crossed the room and leaned over her shoulder. Close enough that I could smell her hair. See the plump pout of her lips. "What's in the basket?"

She smiled. "Everything you never knew you wanted."

And she was right.

Slowly that wall I built crumbled. I couldn't stay away from the girl with the big brown eyes.

I told her my secrets, showed her my ghosts, and she never flinched.

She gave me more than I deserved. With her, I re-learned how to be human. She let me talk, never once taking my pissy attitude, always making me laugh. She re-habbed my arm with her massages. I should have gotten a goddamn therapist. Instead, I had Dakota.

She made Resurrection my home.

Any spare time we had; we'd meet. Sneaking around. Hiding it from everyone, including my brothers. Fucking in the cabin, her bedroom, The Corner Store. Ruby-red lipstick streaks left on every inch of my body. I finally found a weakness, and it was her.

And then she left.

I didn't anticipate how much her leaving would ruin me. After she took off for culinary school, I was angry at everyone and everything. I got a dog. Joined MONSAR. Put Charlie to work on opening the ranch. Anything to fill the gaps in my time. Shore up the leaking hole in my chest.

We kept in touch via text the first four years, but out of nowhere, the texts stopped. Those bright bursts of hellos that gave me joy fizzled out like I had imagined them. And when I tried to call her—I found she had changed her number. Iced me out completely. I understood. She had her bakery. She met someone. But goddamn it stung so fucking hard I still have whiplash from it.

Every time I close my eyes, I'm right back in the past. I see Dakota and that last goodbye where I fucked up everything royally.

I didn't do what I should have done.

Ask her to stay.

Tell her I loved her.

It's better this way. The Marines taught me to swear off permanency. Holding things close and precious was a liability. Life. Love. They make you soft. They make you care right before everything is ripped away from you.

Breaking out of my fugue, I check the address on my phone. On the passenger seat is a first aid kit. Stede said she was hurt, so I brought a goddamn pharmacy.

Did something happen at her bakery? Is she having money problems? Was she in an accident? She would have called me if something was seriously wrong, right? The echo of her promise rattles around in my head.

There are so many unanswered questions and all I can do is gun the gas to get answers.

My gut twists as I pull into the lot of the Lights Out motel, feeling the familiar beat of battle. I retrieve my Glock from the glove box and shove the gun into my hip harness while doing a quick assessment of the motel. Gravel parking lot right off the highway. An L-shaped strip of rooms that open to the outside. A gaudy pink neon sign above the office blinks out a VACANCY refrain.

A few feet away, the curtains of a darkened motel room flutter, and then the door opens.

My palms go slick on the steering wheel.

Dakota.

She stands under the eave of the motel, head down, arms wrapped around herself and the oversized hoodie she wears.

Waiting for me.

Heart pounding, I grab the first aid kit and hop out of the truck. My boots stomp gravel. I head toward her like I'm being pulled. Instinct. A primal, powerful urge I've only allowed myself to feel for one woman.

In three long strides, I'm in front of her. "Dakota?"

Without hesitation, she walks right into my arms. "You came," she says, sighing into my chest.

"You called." I exhale, tension leaving my body as I wrap my arms around her.

Another sigh and she's melting into me. Something hard knocks me in the ribs as her hands of velvet wind their way up my jacket and hook under my arms. Delicate, skilled hands. Hands that played pinball with expert precision that entire summer, and hands that changed my bandages when I was too damn stubborn to do it himself. Hands that palmed my broad chest as she rode me like a fucking mustang.

Her scent aggravates my senses. Milk and honey, like freshly baked bread. Unable to help it, I tuck her face against my collarbone. Her face fits perfectly between my jaw and chin.

It takes everything out of me to release her, but I need to see her. Gripping her gently by the arms, I pull back.

The second she tilts her gorgeous face up to mine; I forget everything I've been trained to do. Keep calm. Stay steady.

In the fluorescent light of the motel, I see a bruised cheekbone. Black eye. A busted lip.

Rage courses through me, swift, blinding. "Who did this, Dakota?" I demand, fighting to keep my voice controlled even as my breath comes out in ragged pants. "Who. The fuck. Did this?"

Her eyes flutter closed. "Davis, don't—"

"Cupcake, I'm gonna need you to shut that pretty mouth and let me hold you." It's instinct to call her by her nickname. To tuck that hair behind her ear and pull her into my arms to calm my racing heart.

"Cupcake," she breathes, clinging to me like I'm her lifeline, when all this time she's been mine. Her voice turns watery. "I haven't heard that in so long."

As I hold her, trembling in my arms, I calculate it. Drive Dakota back to Resurrection. Get in my truck and find the motherfucker that did this. Kick in his door. Rip out his fucking throat.

That's when the same hard something hits me in the ribs again.

I glance down to see a light-yellow cast poking out of the sleeve of her black sweatshirt. "Your arm."

Her eyes drop. "It's a clean break."

A clean break. There's so much wrong with that sentence I don't even know where to start.

With a soft nudge, I steer her toward the room, not wanting her out in the open until I find out what the hell's going on. "Let's go inside."

The room's threadbare, the kind of room I'd expect in a cheap motel. Drab, dim, pea-green walls, floral bedspread. On a corner chair is a small backpack like the kind we'd carry on overnight missions. I'd recognize a bug-out bag anywhere.

What. The. Fuck.

After locking the door, I turn on the light. As I shut the curtains, Dakota sits on the edge of the bed. She looks small and fragile. Soft and recently showered.

I set my gun on the nightstand. Her eyes fall on it, but she says nothing.

For a long moment, I stand there, staring down at her like she's a mirage. But she isn't. She's real. Here.

Just as beautiful as I remember.

Her dark, silky hair hangs snarled over her shoulders. Her eyes are the color of earth after a rainstorm. Deep, dark brown against the pale ivory of her skin.

Too beautiful for words.

I'm fucked.

I kneel in front of her and unzip the first aid kit. "Where else are you hurt?"

She shakes her head. "Just the arm."

"*Just* the arm? That's fucking enough, don't you think?" My voice comes out rough. I can't keep it together; I ball my fists to regroup. "Let me clean that cut on your lip."

"You don't have to do that. I'm okay."

"Dakota," I warn. My eyes lock on her face. It looks like someone grabbed her by the jaw and squeezed. Hard. "Don't argue with me."

"Still bossy, I see." Her tone is light yet strained.

I grunt, digging through the kit for some gauze and antiseptic. Gently, I dab at the cut on her swollen lip. As I tilt her head back to check her pupils for a concussion, my vision fuzzes with rage.

I pride myself on having a cool head, a calm center,

but when it comes to Dakota McGraw, I lose the battle. Every fucking time.

She watches me closely like she's been as curious about me as I have been about her all these years.

She leans in, breaking the tense silence. "I like your scruff, Hotshot."

"Is that what we're talking about, my scruff? How about your face?"

She flinches. "What about it, Davis?"

"Tell me what happened, Koty."

"It doesn't matter," she whispers, her gaze skating away from me. "You're here now. I got out. I'm safe."

"It fucking matters," I growl. "A whole hell of a lot."

She waves her hand up her body, stopping at her face. "What do you think?" Bitterness stains her husky voice. "I lived right. I loved wrong. End of fucking story."

My heart stutters at the word love. So this is where she's been the last two years. Why the texts stopped. Why her visits home to Resurrection became rarer and rarer.

Her bruised, delicate jaw clenches. "And now…I'm running." She gives me a crooked, tired smile. "On the lam, something sad and pathetic like that."

"Not sad and pathetic."

"It is to me. I should have known better."

"Who?" I grind out. *Tell me. Just fucking tell me so I can buy a shovel and gallon of bleach.* "Who did this?"

She sits silent. Stubborn.

"Your…husband?" Fuck. I don't recognize the sound of my own voice.

She flinches when I say the words. "No. Not my husband."

Thank Christ.

An exhale rattles out of my chest. It's difficult to imagine Dakota and another man. We moved on. Made no promises and yet…

I don't know how I could lose a good woman I never laid claim to. Just one mistake out of many.

Swearing, I shove up to standing. I want to hold her, pick her up in my arms and tell her it will all be okay, but I'm vibrating. I pace.

I can't decide if I'm going to kill him slow or kill him fast. Break his knees or break his fucking neck.

"I can't pay for that wall if you punch it, Hotshot."

I stop mid-stride, realizing I've balled my hand up into a fist. A chuckle shakes out of me. I hate how well she knows me.

I turn and pin her with a look. "What happened tonight?"

I want all the gory details so I can plan how badly to hurt him. Pain for pain. Eye for an eye. And then I kill that motherfucker.

Her wary gaze falls to the ground.

"You escaped," I prompt.

"Yes." Tears well up in her eyes. "I had been planning to leave for a while. When he realized I wasn't at home, he came to the bakery." She shudders. "It's a blur. We fought. He hit me. There was a pan on my stove. It caught fire and took the stove first, then the ceiling."

I shake my head, horrified at the nightmare she's just been through. "Jesus, Koty."

"He was screaming at me to help him, but I…I ran," she whispers. "I saw my chance, and I took it." More tears drip onto her legs. "I let my bakery burn."

Working with cops, domestic disputes aren't anything

new to me. I've seen nightmare scenarios play out in Resurrection in real-time. Dead of night escapes. Richter shuttling women to shelters. An officer telling a partner to take a walk around the block to cool off and then being called back to ID a body. I know how fast they can escalate. The thought of how close Dakota had come is enough to give me an aneurysm on the spot.

"You did the right thing. You got out."

"I had to," she whispers.

"Who?" I press, fury clawing its way into my veins. "Tell me his fucking name, Dakota."

"Please." There's a hitch in her voice that tells me she's close to breaking down. "Don't make me tell you. I can't. Not now. I just want to go home. I just want my life back."

"How long has this been going on?"

She hesitates, then says, "The last two years."

Christ.

A thought occurs to me. "Would he follow you?"

She nods. "Yes." A shudder of a breath shakes her frame. "He won't stop. He'll kill me."

That fucking piece of shit will be dead before he touches her again.

"Does he know about your hometown?"

"I don't know," she says, hugging her hands tighter into her stomach. "I've spoken about it in passing. In an interview maybe. But I never went into detail." A pink flush stains her cheeks. "I kept my hometown in the past."

Fuck, but I can't pretend it doesn't sting.

So many more questions. But they can wait. All that matters is getting Koty back home safe. And then I plan to never fucking ever let her out of my sight.

She'll be safe. I'll make sure of it.

I cross the room and kneel in front of her. Careful of her bruise, I cup her cheek and stroke a rough thumb over the high arch of her cheekbone. "What else do I need to know? Is that it?"

She looks at me and then covers her face with her good hand.

I nudge her chin up until those dark eyes find mine. "Tell me what I'm missing, Cupcake."

"You're right," she says, the words stilted and soft. "There's something else you need to know." Her hands twist in the hem of her sweatshirt, and she curls into her long body as if she's trying to protect herself.

Fuck.

A knot of panic forms in my gut.

I'm afraid to look. Afraid of what I'll see. More bruises. Cigarette burns. Scars.

I drag in a ragged breath. "What is it?" I swallow, my blood pressure spiking. Wyatt's put a claim on it, but tonight, Koty has the edge "What?"

"I'm pregnant," she whispers.

Her words shoot straight through my heart and leave me for dead.

The world swims.

Fucking Christ. Pregnant.

Dakota's soft voice floats. "Davis? Are you okay?"

No. I'll never be okay again. Never fucking ever.

I blink, managing to grit out, "Are you?"

She chuckles. And that's when I see it. The small swell of her belly hidden beneath that bulky sweatshirt. "Not really, no."

"His?" I rasp.

"Unfortunately." Her voice cracks. "I'm keeping it, Davis."

I close my eyes. "Does he know about the baby?"

Dread creeps into her expression. "No. I haven't told anyone or seen a doctor. I didn't want him to find out."

I scoot closer to her. In another time, another place, my hands would be in her hair, her lips on mine. But not now.

"Look at me," I say firmly. I place a hand on her leg, palm shaping her thigh. "He'll never get near you or your baby. Never again."

"You can't promise that, Davis. If he wants to find me, he'll find me." Her shoulders fall. The look on her face is heartbreaking. "I'm not safe. I'll never be safe."

There's no hope in her eyes right now…only helplessness. That uncontained neon buzz I know and love is barely an ember.

"I burned our bakery. I took his child." Her lip quivers. "He won't let me go."

"He won't have a choice," I promise.

She gives me a sad smile. "Always the hotshot."

"Get some sleep, Dakota. As soon as it gets light, we'll head back to Resurrection."

"And you?" she asks, fear in her eyes. "Where will you be?" Her hands move closer to mine.

"I'll be here." I nod at the corner of the room. "In that chair."

"You'll sit there. All night?"

Before I can stop myself, I lean in and kiss her forehead. "All night."

4

Dakota

"**H**ERE YOU GO. PEDIALYTE AND BREAKFAST tacos."

I start in surprise, tearing my gaze off the truck window's view of bright eight a.m. sunlight. Snow drifts across the freeway. I zoned out when Davis stopped at a gas station to refuel his behemoth of a pickup truck. We left my Jeep on the side of the road. Strangely, I'm not as sentimental as I thought about leaving things behind. It must be my new MO.

"It's no croissant, but…"

"No, it's perfect," I say eagerly, watching as he sets the bag of food and the drink on the console between us. I may be a food snob, but even I know gas station tacos are a win.

He pins me with a look. "You need to eat."

I do. I've been ravenous since I found out I was pregnant. No morning sickness for me, just constant parasitic hunger. My mouth waters as I nestle the fragrant bundle of deliciousness on my lap. I open the silver wrapping paper and tear into a soft-shell taco. A small moan leaves my mouth.

"Better?" he asks, a hint of a smile playing on his lips.

"Yes. Thank you."

I barely get a grunt of acknowledgement before he's peeling out of the gas station.

As I eat, I stare at the bear of a man squeezed into

the driver's side seat. My knight in shining armor is a six-foot-three scowling Marine. Around his neck, his dog tag glints in the sun. A match to mine. My heart launches itself into its typical somersault fashion, as it does whenever I'm around him. It's infuriating that he's still so damn handsome. Even more so than he was six years ago.

Davis Montgomery is as rugged as the leather jacket he wears. Sculpted muscle. Broad shoulders. Tan as buckskin. Close-cropped brown hair. The light scruff on his face frames a strong jaw. Stern brown eyes with crinkles at the corner that exude an intense, ferocious energy. And that soft, southern drawl. Whiskey, honey, and a late-night lullaby all rolled into one handsome country boy.

He doesn't look as haunted as he did when I first met him. Still, the dark circles under his eyes tell me he's running on adrenaline.

Sleep didn't come easy for either of us. I tossed restlessly and woke to see Davis standing at the curtain, gun in his hands, staring into cold blue moonlight.

I remember when we shared a bed, he shared his nightmares. Tortured, tangled in the sheet beside me. I'd draw him into my arms and keep him there until morning.

"You didn't sleep last night."

With his eyes fixed on the road, he inclines his head as if my voice is an unfamiliar sound. "I never sleep."

I swallow the last of the taco and ball up the paper. "Do you still have the nightmares?"

A muscle works in his jaw. "They're not so bad."

"And yet…you don't sleep. Why?"

"Dakota." His voice is soft, but the way his jaw jumps has my chest tightening.

"Sorry. I shouldn't have…" I trail off, unsure how to

end the sentence. Shouldn't have tried to pick back up? Shouldn't have gotten this intimate?

Shouldn't have thought that whatever we once had is still between us?

For all I know, Davis is married. For all I know, he's forgotten all about me.

He scrapes a hand over his crew cut. "No, it's okay." His voice is rough and warm and so damn comforting. I'm horrified when my eyes fill with tears, so before he can see, I turn my face to the window.

I wish we could say more. Wish I could weep in his arms and tell him the absolute nightmare of my life over the last two years. Wish I could tell him what I've been up to pre-Aiden. That I found my mother. That I tried and failed to open my own bakery.

Instead, it's about my face, this baby, and what Aiden did to me.

"How'd it happen?" Davis's grim, demanding voice has me turning his way. There's a storm in his dark brown eyes as his gaze lands on my cast, tucked up into the sleeve of my oversized sweater.

Tensing, I shake my head. Pain floods my memory and darkens my vision.

"I don't want to talk about it, Davis," I tell him quietly. "It doesn't hurt anymore. It'll heal."

I'm not ready. I can skirt the truth, but the traumatic details about my past…

I can't. Not yet. It's too hard. Too heavy. The idea of going into detail to everyone about how badly I fucked up my life makes me incredibly sad.

Davis's brow furrows. "Would you have told me all this?" he asks thickly. "When you came back?"

I keep my gaze on him. "Honestly, probably not."

Last night, there was no time to lie. I had so many excuses prepared, but when I saw Davis, every little white lie disappeared. Because he was safety. He was comfort. He was someone who always knew what to do.

Now, in the harsh light of morning, I realize it's a bad idea. Davis Montgomery is like a dog with a bone. He won't let go until I tell him everything.

And I can't tell him Aiden's name. He'll kill him.

"All the little white lies I would've told. I'd be a legend."

Davis makes a frustrated sound in the back of his throat.

I stretch out in the seat and say gently, "Believe me, sending out some distressed woman SOS isn't exactly the way I wanted to come back to town."

He doesn't smile. Always the same stern, broody face on this cowboy.

Of course, that's the face he's making.

I'm weak. I'm not the girl he knew.

"I didn't know things were this bad," he says with quiet rage.

"No one did." A tear slips down my cheek. "I'm tired, Davis. I'm tired of being good."

I turn my face to the window, feeling sad. Wyoming turns to Montana as we cross the border. "I'm tired of running."

Davis's sharp gaze slides across me, then returns to the highway. "You're not running. You're going home."

Home.

Home to rebuild my life.

At least what's left of it.

Six years ago, I was at the top of my game. A degree in pastry arts. Culinary festivals. Tutelage under Dominique

Ansel. I traveled the country. France. The Keys. The Alps. Budapest. I baked like my soul was a flame and experienced things my small town could only dream of. I ate the world. I never wanted to go back.

Then, three years into my culinary dreams, I met Aiden. And I rushed into it.

He wasn't mine and I wasn't his. At least, not in the way that mattered. He was someone I let into my life. All because the Marine back home didn't want my heart, so I tried to give it away to the first man that would take it.

I tried.

And I failed miserably.

I fucked up.

Because being with Aiden King was like being blind-sided in plain sight.

For the first year, it was good. Then, after I bought the bakery, he changed. Mean. Bitter. Violent. He convinced me I wasn't good enough. *He* was the prize and I couldn't live without him.

Slowly, my world shrank. I left behind my friends, my family, even those bantering texts from Davis that got me through culinary school.

The night Aiden broke my arm was the moment I knew.

Being persistent with the wrong person is death.

But what feels like another death is Resurrection.

Going home feels like failure. Crawling back to a town I rejected. Leaving behind a family I loved. And all for what? Because the past Dakota McGraw wanted to outrun the town she was born? Because I hated how every Friday night football ruled. How our town thought Applebee's and our local chili potlucks were the prime of life.

I wanted culture, the world, and I had it.

Now it feels like I'm being punished for wanting, for dreaming. It feels like Resurrection was right all along. All I have are broken dreams to go along with broken bones.

I cover my face with my good hand and breathe in.

"How am I going to do this, Davis?" My voice cracks. "Tell my father…"

"It'll be okay." His brown eyes spark as his gaze locks on my face and holds. "We'll figure it out. We'll find a solution where you're safe."

I fight that panicky urge building within. "I don't want anyone in town to know about the baby," I blurt.

Davis flinches. I didn't miss the same expression last night. The painful look on Davis's face as he glanced down at my stomach and then up so fast he could have gotten whiplash.

I look down at my stomach, look away. Part of me wants it, part of me hates myself for keeping it. Because it's like letting Aiden win all over again.

Dread pushes against my chest as we get closer to Resurrection. Gray columns of the sugar beet factory rise and meet the horizon. The pale sky of Montana blooms with clouds. At the sight, all my nerves come rushing back.

Home means safety. But it also means questions. Hard looks in the mirror.

A pregnancy, and a baby I have no idea what to do with.

As the late afternoon sun casts its shadows, I pause on the porch outside the screen door that leads into my father's cabin. It feels weird to knock, but it feels even stranger to set foot in my childhood home. My father's bright-yellow vintage Jalopy sits in the drive. Still rusted, still waiting for that oil change. No doubt kittens are living in the engine.

Beside me, Davis lifts his brows in a go-ahead gesture.

But before I can knock, the door is yanked open.

Fallon.

Her nostrils flare when she sees me, her hazel eyes dancing over my black eye, my cast. Then, without a hello, her gaze punches to Davis. "Well, looks like the cowboy cavalry came to the rescue."

Davis crosses his arms over his massive chest and shakes his head.

All I can do is stare.

I haven't seen my little sister in over six years, just brief glimpses of her barrel racing in YouTube videos or on Instagram. She's no longer the feisty tomboy I left behind. She's devastatingly gorgeous. Lean and leggy, with colorful tattoos covering every inch of bare, muscular flesh. Her long caramel hair is loosely braided. She looks fierce, beautiful and annoyed.

"What?" she asks sharply.

"You grew up."

"Astute observation," she says with an eye roll.

Propping the door open behind her, she turns on her heel. "Dad!"

I sigh, feeling awkward and unwelcome, but I follow her inside. What small distance I assumed was between us is a chasm.

Aside from the strange medicinal smell in the air, everything in my childhood home is the same. Antlers, family photos, and my father's framed stills from his Westerns line the wall. The tattered sheepskin rug laid out over the hardwood floor. Across the hall, the kitchen with its white, flowered cabinets, farmhouse sink, and long family table. Down the hall, my old bedroom and Fallon's.

"Is it them? Dakota?" comes the gruff sound of my father's voice. And then Stede McGraw is hustling out of the back bedroom, wiry and disheveled, boots stomping across the floorboards. His surprised, gray-eyed gaze gives me a once-over before he wraps me up in a tight hug.

I close my eyes and let his love surround me. "Hey, Daddy."

"You look worse for wear, baby girl," he says, pulling back to inspect my face once again.

My lower lip trembles. The pity in his eyes is crippling. "I know."

My father gives Davis a tight nod. "Thank you for bringing her home."

Planted in a corner of the room like some brooding bodyguard, Davis's hands fist on his hips. "Nothing's too much, Stede. Not for you. Or your daughters."

Davis's kindness to my father only has my heart beating faster. But just as quickly, realization anchors it. Davis only rode to my rescue as a favor. To Davis, I'm a problem. A pregnant, messy problem who's running back to Resurrection with a baby and a bug-out bag.

My father shuffles to the couch and pats the spot beside him. "Sit here, Dakota, and tell me your troubles."

Troubles. That's a nice way to put it.

I'm opening my mouth to say just that when I notice something new. There's a strange-looking machine next to the couch. Casserole dishes stacked on the chipped countertop. Fallon's bags are in the corner of the room, but I know she has a lavender cottage a few miles down. I Google mapped it when I heard she got her own place.

Sent her a potted viola that I'm sure saw the inside of a trash can.

"Dad?" I ask, my voice weak. "Why is Fallon living here?"

Before anyone can answer, my father erupts in a cough. Fallon's at his side in an instant, fussing, a handkerchief in her hand.

"What the hell is going on?" I choke out.

Davis's jaw clenches, but he remains stoically silent.

A tense silence blankets the room, and a sick feeling settles in my stomach.

"He has lung cancer," Fallon blurts. She grips my father's hand and helps him settle on the couch.

"What?" I blink, a foggy haze settling over me. "Why didn't you tell me?"

"You didn't tell us either," Fallon retorts, cheeks flushed. Her eyes brush accusingly over my busted lip. "Looks like we're even."

Davis looks down on my sister with a scowl. "Fallon, for fuck's sake."

"That isn't fair," I snap at her, frustrated. I look at my father. "For how long?"

"About a year now." My father waves his hand. "We didn't want to bother you. Not when you were getting your bakery off the ground."

The tightness in my chest constricts, the ache in my left arm intensifying. "That would have been the least of my worries. You should have told me."

"It's stage two," Fallon shoots back, handing our father a glass of water. "We have it under control."

I watch their routine, feeling guilty. Left out. It hurts

so badly they kept it from me, but it hurts worse because I know I've been MIA. Fallon's been here, I haven't.

Shame burns a hole in my stomach.

My father pats the seat beside him. "Come sit by your old man. I want to know what's going on with you, daydreamer."

Daydreamer.

My father's nickname for me. I always had my head in the clouds, dreaming of the what-could-be. Fallon was the troublemaker. The one most like my father. I remember even as a child, Fallon was always chasing that adrenaline rush.

My little sister was born fearless.

And me, I was born to run.

After a brief glance at Davis, I nod and swallow the lump in my throat. His steady gaze eases some of my nerves.

I sit on the couch and square my shoulders, my father's hand sandwiched between mine.

I repeat everything I told Davis. My pregnancy. The fire. Our fight. The entire time I explain, Davis stands as still as a statue.

The only thing I leave out is Aiden's name, and what happened the night I broke my arm. It's too awful. I still can't.

When I finish, Fallon hangs back against the wall, arms crossed like some surly high schooler at a dance.

My father sighs. "Sounds like you got yourself into a pickle."

I breathe through the sting of tears and squeeze his hand. "Sounds like it, Daddy."

"Are you in danger from this man?" my father asks, voice tight.

"I don't know." My voice quivers. Just thinking about Aiden causes my emotions to unravel. "Maybe."

Davis's expression turns to granite. "Maybe in my world is a yes. Especially when it comes to you." His voice is deep, gruff, and his dark gaze rakes over my face.

Our eyes lock, the air thickening with heat.

Fallon's voice tears through the tense silence. "As much as I love this fucked-up family reunion, I got a shift at The Corner Store."

"Wait." I stand, reaching out to grab her arm. She flinches at my touch. "You're working at the store?"

She shouldn't be there. That wasn't the plan.

She hits me with a fiery glare and untangles from my grip. "You're not here. Someone has to pick up the slack."

"I can move in with you," I tell my father, desperately seeking some sort of calm and order. "I'm home now. I can help."

"No, you can't." Fallon pauses at the door to whip her head to me. Resentment crackles in the space between us. "You said it yourself, Dakota. What if he comes back? What if he comes for *you*? He can't come to the house. Not when Dad's sick."

"I'm over seventy," my father says with a chuckle. "If I go to jail, we all know I ain't got long. Hell, I'll tell 'em I'm crazy."

"That's not funny," Fallon scolds.

Suddenly, icy terror grips me. "I'll leave if he comes to Resurrection," I whisper. My friends, my family... they're in danger the longer I stick around. "That's my plan. Pack up and run."

"That's a plan that isn't happening." The smoky growl of Davis's voice curls around my heart like a fist.

Fallon rolls her eyes. "Then you tell me, cowboy. What do we do with her?"

A scream of frustration bubbles up in my lungs. I feel like a charity case. Nowhere to stay, no plan, grappling at the wind for a sense of control.

Maybe coming home was a mistake.

"She stays at the ranch." Davis's announcement scorches the air while I blink to make sure I've heard him correctly.

The man stands there, arms crossed, expression fierce. Like he has the final say in the matter.

"I don't think so," I say, my face hot with anger and frustration.

And yet—goosebumps skate across my skin at the thought of close confines with Davis Montgomery.

This is a bad idea. All of it.

Fallon smirks. "Congratulations," she says to me, shouldering her bag. Her gaze drops to my stomach. "Don't expect me to fucking babysit."

I jump at the hard slam of the door. Davis swears hard under his breath.

Heart hammering, I turn my attention back to the problem at hand. "What are you going to do, Davis? Follow me around the next however many weeks until it's safe?"

"Yes." His big, muscled frame stomps forward. I shiver at the bright blaze of protection in his piercing eyes. "That's exactly what I'm going to do."

5

Davis

I F LOOKS COULD KILL, DAKOTA'S FIERY GLARE WOULD incinerate me on the spot.

It was a split-second decision to have her stay at the ranch. Stede can't protect her if her ex follows her to Resurrection. I promised him I'd keep her safe. I intend to do that.

I park my truck in the paved driveway in front of the lodge and shut off the engine. The last slice of light died out an hour ago, and the big Montana sky is now an inky purple-black.

Dakota, huddled in her oversized sweater, sighs and stares out the window. "So, we're here. What's the grand plan?"

"Listen," I say, and her troubled chocolate-brown eyes turn my way. "I'm not locking you up, Koty. We have good security at the ranch. You can come and go. And when you head into town, I'll just…"

"Be with me?" Her words spear through my chest like a knife.

"Something like that."

"And if you can't?"

"There is no *if*. I'll be there."

Her lush lips thin. "My father wanted to call you. Not me."

"Good thing he did. You'd probably be back in that shitty motel, planning to ride a cow back to Resurrection."

My voice is cool, controlled, when all I want to do is wring every ounce of the truth out of her. Remind her of the promise she made, a promise she broke, a promise that scorches me from inside out.

"And who calls it?" Her chin lifts in that stubborn, defiant way of hers. It's almost a relief to see that flash of fire back in her dark gaze. "Who says it's over?"

A vein pulses in my temple. "I say it's over. When you're safe."

I'm already pissed off at her newsflash that she planned to come back to Resurrection without a peep about what happened to her. And now her little announcement back at Stede's that she plans to run if her ex shows up.

Over my goddamn dead body.

Annoyance flickers through her expression. "How long is that?"

"As long as it takes."

A frown pulls at her brow. "Davis, you can't keep me here."

"I don't accept that, Dakota. I won't."

Her laugh is brittle. "Why are you doing this?"

"You helped me back then." My voice comes out strangely staccato. "It's my turn to help you."

"You owe me." She punches the lock on the truck, a soft sheen to her eyes, a wobble in her voice. "Got it."

"Now wait a damn minute." I lock the doors again, keeping her in so she hears me. "It's not pity or obligation. I made a promise to your father that I'd look out for you. And that's what I'm going to do."

"This doesn't involve you, Davis."

I clench my jaw and growl. "The hell it doesn't."

We sit three feet from each other. Me, on the driver's side, Dakota curled up against the passenger door. I'm close enough to her that I can see the rise and fall of her chest, the obsidian darkness of her eyes. Dark enough to rival the night.

"I won't put you in the middle of my mess. Or use you to put my life back on track. I have to do it." Her delicate jaw tilts, flexes in defiance. "I'm not your problem, Hotshot."

It takes all I have in me not to growl in frustration. I don't fucking believe this. She's on the run, in goddamn danger, for Christ's sake, and she's arguing with me.

The fact that it turns me on only pisses me off more.

"You'll always be my problem, Dakota." My breath comes out in a harsh exhale. "And you're not alone. Not anymore."

Her mouth parts, but she stays silent.

I unlock the doors and hold out my hands. "No lock and key, okay? No house arrest. You go and do what you want. And I'll be there."

This time, a hint of a smile plays on her face. "Like a… bodyguard?"

I raise an eyebrow. "I used to do this, you know. I'm good at it."

She presses her lips together, looks down at her stomach. "Right. Fine."

We exit the truck, and I come around to Dakota's side. She stands there for a long second, dark head swiveling as she takes in the ranch, swathed in shadows. The wild howl of the winter. The sting of the winter air. And yet, all I see is her.

Fuck me.

Dakota McGraw is one beautiful woman. In the moonlight's glow, her beauty shines. Full lips, hourglass curves that I long to run my hand over. Her long dark hair flutters in the wind like a raven's wing. My hands clench into fists, my cock thickening at the thought of tangling my fingers in those dark locks, weaving each strand around my—

"Davis?" Dakota blinks at me. "Should we go inside?"

"Yeah." I grab her bag. "C'mon."

Christ, when did I lose control of my facial expressions?

Hands to yourself, Montgomery.

She's not mine. She never has been. She's pregnant, for Christ's sake. Traumatized. The last thing she needs is a man. The last thing she needs is me.

Duty means keeping her safe. Discipline means keeping my fucking hands off her.

We make it halfway to the lodge when I hear footsteps.

My heart trips, and I freeze when Dakota curls a hand around my bicep.

"Davis," she whispers, leaning into me. "Someone's there."

Tensing, I follow her eye line. I hear it again.

The squeak of the front porch, wooden floor boards rattling. The low shuffle of boots. I feel Dakota trembling beside me, the way her breath has picked up, the way her shoulders could meet her ears.

"Breathe, Koty," I say, palming the small of her back, before moving in front of her.

I reach for my hip, cursing under my breath.

I left my Glock in the truck.

Already, I'm fucking up.

Bone-white moonlight dances across the lodge, and a shadowy figure descends the stairs.

I move into a fighting stance, mentally calculating how fast I can turn a duffel bag into a weapon of mass destruction, when there's a hoot from the darkness. "Y'all make it back?"

Fucking Ford. I wonder if my idiot brother knew just how close he was to getting his head bashed in by a duffel bag.

With a ragged breath, Dakota lets loose of my arm. The loss of her contact does strange, herky-jerky things to my heart.

"Goddamn it, Ford," I snarl, my pulse slowing its panicked tripping. "What the fuck are you doin' here?"

Ford gives me a crooked grin. "Gun in the glove box?" Ignoring my under-the-breath curse, Ford's eyes dip to Dakota's cast but all he says is, "Hey, Koty."

"Hey, Ford," Dakota says weakly, mustering a smile. She tucks a lock of dark hair behind her ear. "Good to see you."

"You too, honey."

Ford elbows his way around me. All I can do is watch the affectionate reunion as he pulls her in for a hug. I clock her reaction, resisting the urge to yank her back to me, to make sure she's okay with the contact.

No one will ever touch Dakota again without her permission.

"You back to stay?" Ford asks when he releases her.

Dakota's shoulders sag. "Looks like it."

Ford arches a brow, his expression settling into cool curiosity. Uncertainty. "You staying here?"

I give Ford a shove. "Yeah, she's staying here. Now shut the fuck up and get lost."

With a look that tells me we'll talk later, my twin lopes off.

Dakota sees right through me and tilts her head back to apprise me. "You're the only one who gets to play interrogator, is that right?" She arches a brow.

My jaw flexes. "That's right."

We climb the porch steps. I open the door and let her in. It's pitch black, and I flip on the overhead lights, a great chandelier of antlers that cast a soft glow over the room.

Dakota slips off her parka, and my gaze drops to the small bud of her belly. It's more noticeable without the jacket, and my heart twists. The thought of her carrying another man's baby burns me from the inside until my emotions feel charred.

A selfish, stupid thought. There's no good reason to be acting like this.

I rub a hand over my jaw, getting my bearings. "This is the lodge," I tell her. "For guests. We're off-season right now. Open back up at the end of May."

Her gaze narrows as she looks around the place. "So, this is Runaway Ranch, huh?"

"This is it."

"What made you decide to fix it up?" Dakota brushes her fingers over one of the stained plank walls.

You.

"I needed a project," I grunt, glossing over the real reason for turning the 17,000-acre piece of land into a working ranch. "Charlie needed a life."

"And let me guess, you put everyone to work."

A rare smile tugs at my lips. "Something like that."

"It looks so different, Davis." She takes a step, eyes on the ceiling. "It was just an old building that Fallon and I played hide and seek in when we were kids." She squints at a spot near the stairs. "You ever find that trap door with the slide?"

I chuckle. "We did. Think Wyatt even gave it a spin or two."

She turns toward me. Her bright smile's a shock to my system. "Show me around?"

And I do.

Dakota examines each space with a curious expression, gracefully touching furnishings with her fingertips. There's awe in her eyes as she sees the hard work of the last six years. Timber beams in the cathedral ceiling. Wood plank floors. Cognac couches with plaid loveseats arranged in a U-shape. The massive stone fireplace in the great room. The pine bar with the neon BAR M sign blinking bright pink behind it.

Dakota presses her good hand to her chest. "I can't believe you did all this."

I usher her forward. "I don't know where we'd be without it."

When we get to the kitchen, Dakota freezes.

"It's a chef's kitchen," she breathes.

"It is. My little sister designed it." I step inside but Dakota lingers in the doorway, admiring the expensive stainless-steel appliances Emmy Lou insisted on. "She likes to bake, too."

"Shame." Her soft tone is wistful. Slowly, she follows me in. "This big kitchen just sits empty all these months."

I open the huge fridge and curse at the meager contents. Moldy bags of salad, a ham steak, and a twenty-four pack of Miller High Life. On the large steel counter is a family-sized can of green beans.

I curse again when I see the joint sitting in the ashtray. Fucking Wyatt.

I turn back to Dakota, and my gaze falls to her stomach. Even though we had dinner at Stede's, I ask, "You want something to eat?" Not that there's much I can make for her.

She shakes her head. "No. I'm fine."

I frown at the strain on her face. She's not fine. Her dark eyes dart around the kitchen like she's looking for an exit, and there's a slight tremble to her shoulders. Something has her on edge.

"Can you bake with one arm?" I ask in a low voice.

Dakota glances toward the steel countertop. Another wave of rage crashes over me at the sight of her bruised jaw.

"I don't know," she says in a small voice. "I haven't tried."

I place a palm on the cool countertop, making a mental note to get this kitchen clean for her. "You could try here." I want that spark of fire back in her dark brown eyes. "This giant kitchen's empty. Waiting for your chocolate cake."

She shies away from me. "I changed the recipe. It isn't as good."

"Bullshit."

I never eat sweets. But with Dakota, I remember every pastry, every cupcake, she ever brought me. Her sweets are legendary.

She flinches. "I get the cast off in six weeks. I'll try then. When I'm in my own place."

Alarm speeds through my senses. Whatever happened to her took place in a kitchen. I'm 100 percent sure of it.

I search her eyes, hating the shame I see there. Hating how she's acting like I'm a stranger she can't wait to shake.

Still, tonight's not the night to press the issue. She needs sleep. Her body needs to heal from the hell she's just been through.

"Upstairs," I tell her, pointing at the stairs just off the kitchen. "This way."

Her shell-shocked eyes clear and without speaking, she follows me upstairs.

The attic isn't as much of an attic as an entire living space. We renovated it our second year at the ranch, when I was sick of living in dust and disrepair. It has a kitchenette and an island in the center of the room, with two bedrooms on opposite sides. Built-in skylights across the arched, planked ceiling let in the Montana sky.

"This is…uh, where I stay."

"You live up here?" Dakota roves her eyes around the space. "Like a permanent Phantom of the Opera?"

I bite back a smile. "Ever since we opened."

She tilts her head. "And it's just you here?"

I rough a hand over my scalp, trying to ignore the tug of her plump lip between her teeth. "Just me and Keena."

"Oh," she whispers, her gaze dropping from mine to hit her toes.

"Don't worry, Cupcake. I'll tread quietly." We stop outside of her room. "This is yours."

I swing the door open, revealing a mirror image of mine—a wooden bed, faux-fur throws, wool carpet, and simple white-painted walls. There's a freestanding clawfoot tub in the room's corner beneath exposed timber rafters.

I stand like an idiot in the doorway, watching as she

inspects her room, like crossing the threshold will automatically have us both undressed.

Her in her room, me in mine, is as far as it will ever go. She's mine to protect. A temporary tenant. A dangerous temptation.

She eyes me for a long beat. "And you? Where will you be?"

"Down there." I grunt and point down the hall. The ten-foot distance between our rooms is going to be the death of me. Not to mention my cock.

"Towels are in the bathroom. Make yourself at home. If you need anything, you let me know."

Stubbornness pulls through her expression. "I won't."

"Dakota," I order, frustration getting the best of me.

Glancing over her shoulder, she gives me one of those half-annoyed, half-amused looks. "You growling at me, Hotshot?"

"Do you remember what I told you that night?" My voice lowers, husky, full of the past.

Tell me you remember.

Although, if she does, I'll have a whole other set of grievances. I step forward, planting my forearm above the door over her head, staring down into those gorgeous gunpowder eyes. "The night before you left for San Antonio. What did I say?"

She's silent for so long. An eternity. And I think of every goddamn way I can fill the cursed silence.

Kiss her.

Fuck her.

Beg her.

Crush my lips onto hers, soft, hard, whatever she wants, and back her up and into the bedroom. Kiss her because I can't remember what she tastes like. Kiss her because it's all I've wanted to do for the last six years.

Still, I get myself under control, hands fisting at my side to keep myself from touching her. "Dakota."

She stares up at me with that unflinching, gorgeous face of hers.

She doesn't remember.

But then she opens her mouth and whispers, "'I will always come for you. No matter what.'"

"Always," I repeat.

A tender vulnerability paints her face. "That was a long time ago, Davis."

The tightness in my chest warms. "But I meant it. I still do."

Dakota leans into me, stretching out her hand to brush against mine. An electrical charge explodes across my skin. An ever-present awareness that she is here, back with me, where she belongs.

Easy. So easy to pick up where we left off. The spark. It's still there. Living, humming in my veins every time we touch.

And that's when I fucking see it.

My dog tag looped around her neck.

After all these years, she still wears them.

The sight ricochets through my heart like a bullet.

But before I can say a word, she's plucking her duffel bag from my hand.

"It'll be okay," she says. "It'll all be okay." Her black, haunted eyes flick to mine. "Goodnight, Davis."

The door shuts on me before I can say another word.

6

Davis

I T'LL ALL BE OKAY.

Bullshit. Nothing about this is okay.

Dakota's forced words of bravado do nothing to instill confidence in me. No matter how much she wants to act like she has it handled, she doesn't.

The only consolation I have right now is that she's secure in the lodge, with me on guard.

An hour after the light in her room turns off, I stomp for the Bullshit Box, the place where I run all the ranch's security operations. AKA another place for me and my brothers to bullshit.

I hate leaving Dakota alone, but I need a place to stew. A place to dig.

When I get there, I head for my desk and take a seat. With my gaze on the computer monitor, I type Dakota McGraw into the search engine and scroll through the results.

Does the perfect cupcake exist? Yes, it does. And I found it at DC's Milk & Honey, the boulangerie and bakery owned by pastry chef Dakota McGraw.

Accompanying the article is a photo of Dakota leaning back against a glass bakery case. She's wearing a chef's coat, her ebony hair cascading around her shoulders. On her red lips, a sly smile.

She looks proud. Happy.

She made it. She did it.

This photo isn't new to me. I've looked at it a dozen times over the last two years. A reminder that she was meant to leave Resurrection. That I did the right thing by letting her go.

A rock wedges itself in my throat at the thought, but I clear it and focus on the task at hand.

Leaning back in my groaning metal chair, I keep scrolling until I find what I'm looking for. My attention lasers in on numerous articles from *The Washington Post*.

Fire Destroys Popular DC Bakery, Investigation Underway

Grease Fire at Milk & Honey Bakery Deemed Accidental

No Injuries in Midnight Bakery Blaze

Police Concerned for Well-being of Pastry Chef Dakota McGraw in Connection with Fire; Not Considered a Suspect

I rub a hand over my jaw. "Fuck."

It's good she's back here. Resurrection will let her lie low. She can speak to the authorities and the insurance company over the phone. Because Dakota flying back to DC and being in the same state with the motherfucker who put hands on her is not happening.

If he comes after her, I have to be ready.

People go after the things they want. Especially when they're out for vengeance. I'm not holding out hope that this guy miraculously fades into the ether.

To keep her safe, I have to keep her close.

Which means no surprises. Which means I plan.

Which means I need her entire story. If I know who he is, I can keep tabs on him. Because I already know I'm going to have my hands full keeping tabs on Dakota.

But she has to tell me in her own time. If the Marines

have taught me anything, it's that pushing never helps. It makes you clam up. It makes you run.

"You in here sulking?"

Ford steps through the door, followed by Charlie and Wyatt.

"No," I lie, already wishing I can get back to my quiet evening of plotting someone else's murder.

My twin smirks. "Liar."

"Thought you could use this." Wyatt sets a beer on the desk and heads to the dartboard.

"Thanks." I switch over to the security monitors abruptly and scan the tense faces of my brothers. "What's going on?"

Charlie drops into his chair, scraping a hand over his beard. He glances down at Keena, who's curled up next to the space heater. "Rest of the dogs locked up?"

My skin prickles at the tone in his voice. "Yeah. Why?"

"Some maverick wolf's tearing through the ranches," Charlie says. "Marvin lost a couple of chickens late last night."

I pinch the bridge of my nose and exhale. Fuck. Another goddamn problem. Last year, we had the Wolfingtons. Now we have to deal with actual fucking wolves. "Where? On the ranch?"

"Perimeter." Ford hangs back against the wall, arms crossed. "Near the woods."

"Set a trap," I tell him. "Nothing lethal. We're not killing wolves."

This land belongs to them just as much as us. Our livestock, however, are off-limits.

"How was the rescue?" Ford asks, reaching into his desk drawer and opening a package of cinnamon hard candy. He's been obsessed with them since the major leagues, trying to substitute them for tobacco.

"How do you think?" My words come out stony. "You saw her."

Ford's amber eyes flash. "Yeah. I did."

A muscle jumps in Charlie's jaw. "Take her to Stede?"

I flatten my lips, scanning the room. All of my brothers wear the same look of reckless fury crawling beneath my skin. "Earlier tonight."

One of the hardest fucking things I've ever had to do. Stede kept it together, but I saw it all over his face. The devastation of a man who wasn't able to protect the one he loved.

Ford rolls the candy around in his mouth, then says, "So, she's gonna heal, find a job, and have a baby. Is that what this is?"

I have the sudden urge to drink the beer all in one sitting. "Yeah," I grunt. "Rebuild."

Wyatt whistles. "That's a lot."

"She's got it." I open the beer and take a sip. "She's strong."

"You know who the guy is?" Wyatt asks, flinging a dart blindly at the dartboard.

I sigh, already seeing an ambulance ride in my future. "If I did, you think I'd be sitting here?"

"No. I don't," Charlie says.

I don't miss the harsh darkening of his face. The uneasy glances exchanged with Wyatt and Ford. Anger and adrenaline have each of my brothers in their hold. They want to find this guy just as bad as I do.

I stand and cross the floor to snatch the dart away from

my younger brother before he injures himself or someone else.

"Why's she here, Davis?" Charlie asks.

I sit back in my chair, already tired of the conversation. But I owe my brothers clarity about what's going on. What happens at the ranch affects everyone.

"She thinks her ex will come after her."

"Fuck," Wyatt mutters, rubbing the back of his neck.

A muscle jerks in Charlie's jaw. "Will he?" His blue eyes fall to the security cameras and the screen with his cabin, where Ruby sweeps snow from the front porch.

I harden my jaw. Guilt slices deep. "Trouble won't land here, Charlie."

Ruby was hurt because of my fucking mistake, and I spent the entirety of last fall installing new security measures. I vet each staff member until I know their name and face in my sleep. You are beyond on camera. We monitor every inch of the ranch, except for the tree line and forest. Still, if Dakota's ex plans to come after her, it's dangerous having her on the ranch and Charlie knows it.

I look him in the eye. "And if it does, I'll handle it."

"You've handled enough," he gruffs.

Ford's expression holds none of its typical laid-back attitude. He looks pissy even for him. "So, the plan is she stays at the ranch?"

I nod. "She stays twenty-four seven until she's safe."

A shit-eating grin curls on Wyatt's face. "And what exactly does that mean?"

I scowl. The last thing I need is Wyatt reminding me Dakota and I are going to be in very close confines for the next however many months.

"You focus on the ranch," I bark. Of all my brothers,

I'm the hardest on Wyatt. He and I have always butted heads over rules and discipline. If he only knew it's because I've been losing sleep over the kid ever since he climbed on the back of a horse. My little brother has at least six I-should-have-died-but-didn't stories.

"We open in four fuckin' months and if I'm remembering correctly, you still have a horse to break."

Wyatt rolls his eyes. "Bossy bastard."

"Well, you got us," Charlie says, shoving up to stand. "We'll help. Whatever you need."

With a knot in my throat, I give Charlie a nod of thanks. I don't tell my brothers enough what they mean to me. They're the ones who'd roll up to my house with an empty trunk and a roll of duct tape, no questions asked.

Without another word, my brothers exit the Bullshit Box. Glad to be rid of them, I go back to my computer. After a glance at the lodge on the security cameras, I pull up Dakota's Instagram page.

She would snap my neck with a rolling pin if she knew I was poking into her business. But she's going to have to deal with it.

Find this guy.

It's the singular war cry in my mind.

As I click through the bright, glossy images of Dakota's life, I pick apart the kernels of information I've been doled out over the years by Stede and Fallon, and even Dakota herself before she broke contact. She traveled the world. Earned accolades. Started her own business.

Her photos show all that and more.

Culinary school graduation. Food festivals. Recipes. Behind the scenes posts of her bakery.

There are no tags. No mention of a man.

Is it you, fucker? My gaze narrows on a man standing watch over Dakota as she holds a tray of cookies. The ball of rage in my chest doubles in size.

She may be smiling in her most recent Instagram pictures, but if I look closely, I can see it. While brilliant and blazing, her smile doesn't reach her eyes.

Fear. It's the only word to describe it.

It tracks. Two years ago, is when we lost contact. She pulled away because of her ex.

Now that I have more answers than questions, I can breathe a bit easier. There's enough of the story to at least puzzle it out. I still don't have his fucking name, but that can wait.

Once again, guilt tightens my chest. Guilt that I never followed up over her silence. Guilt that I didn't know anything was wrong.

The only thing worse than knowing I pushed her away is that I pushed her into the arms of someone who hurt her.

"Fuck," I blast.

Rolling out my neck, I scroll back to the past.

An image of Dakota at Lake Cascade with Fallon, me, and my brothers. A day that stands out in my mind as a top-tier memory.

With a wild whoop, she had jumped into the icy water, and like a fool, I followed her in.

The photo hits like a sucker punch.

She's cheesing so hard her beautiful brown eyes looked closed. I can see her nipples through the thin fabric of the skimpy bikini she wears, her tight little ass breaking the surface of the lake.

And then there's a memory that the photo doesn't show.

Me dragging Dakota under the dock and peeling off those thin bikini bottoms. Slapping her tight little ass as she bounced on my cock and rubbed her tits in my face. All while our siblings splashed twenty feet away.

Koty.

My Dakota.

Mine.

Suddenly, it's not just her memory I want, I want *her*. I crave her taste, crave her wild, black hair dragging down my stomach, her supple ass straddling my hips, delicate hands scraping over the muscle of my back.

Dangerous, torturous beauty.

Look, but don't touch.

Duty, not desire.

A ragged groan rips from my chest. I'm hard as a rock, and I loathe it. Loathe what she does to me. Loathe the way I'm giving in, already reaching for the zipper of my jeans.

Helplessly, I grit my teeth.

Before I can stop myself, I'm standing over my desk with my cock out. Pleasure licks its way up my spine as I use my hand to get myself off like I'm a fucking teenager all over again. I stroke myself in a frenzy to get her out of my mind. My veins. My heart.

Wrong. So goddamn wrong.

"Fuck, fuck, Dakota," I pant, hating myself, yet unable to stop the hard milking of my shaft.

She's still in my bloodstream. She's never been gone. Not for a hot fucking second. Never.

Now I'm calling a code-red on my cock all because she's living under my roof.

Goddamn, I don't have a chance.

My body shakes, shudders. Then, with one final violent

wrench of my cock, I erupt. My release covers the desktop as my roar tears through the air, while the security monitors blink red.

Panting, I sit back down and bow my head.

So much for fucking duty.

7

Dakota

SHOWERED AND WRAPPED IN A FLUFFY WHITE towel, I sit on the edge of my bed and check my phone. The text confirming my doctor's appointment has my stomach churning. A favor my father pulled with his connections at the hospital. My small town moves slowly, except when it moves fast.

Just like this baby. It's coming whether or not I like it.

I press a hand against my stomach and just as quickly pull it back. Hot tears sting the backs of my eyes.

Though I fell into an easy sleep last night—sleeping in the big empty lodge never felt more freeing—I woke up at three a.m. My internal clock is always on bakery hours. Finally, when the sun rose, I put my insomnia to use by putting together a plan to feel not so adrift.

I'm determined to get my life back.

Even if all I want to do is lie in bed all day and wallow.

I sigh and change into a sweater and jeans. After towel drying my hair, I add powder to cover my bruise, flinching when I come to the cut on my swollen lip. I straighten up, gauging my weary reflection in the mirror. Does Davis see me as anything other than a woman in distress?

It doesn't matter how he sees me. He's moved on with Keena. Even as jealousy zings through me at his cavalier mention last night, I have no right to be jealous. It's been six years. We were never anything, anyway.

I came back to Resurrection because Davis meant safety. Peace. I don't know how my brain convinced my heart he wouldn't have been the first person I ran to. His arms always had me. Even if now it's like a whisper of a ghost between us.

I return to my spot on the bed. The room is loft-like and cozy. A sturdy desk in the corner. A clawfoot tub set over glossy blue tiles. Slanted windows above the bed let the morning sunlight through.

I haven't unpacked. My bag sits on a corner chair in the spacious room.

Everything about this return home seems so tentative. My baby, my choices, my freedom.

Don't tempt a good thing. Wait it out. Plan.

It's what I did for a week. After I found out I was pregnant, I planned my getaway, and I waited. I had been so careful. But Aiden was smart.

I won't make the same mistake.

Plan.

Otherwise, I might do something crazy like run.

I pick up my phone and scroll through the news reports about my bakery.

Images of the charred wreckage of my bakery bring hot tears to my eyes, taunting me.

The investigators don't think it's arson, but they want to speak to me. An email in my inbox requests a Zoom or a phone call. My heart trips and I stare at the screen for half a second before I turn it off.

Nerves are a grenade of dread in my gut.

How do I explain this? Aiden will never let on that he was there that night. Then he'll hunt me down.

"You fucker," I tell my phone.

Part of me wants Aiden to chase me down. And part of me wants to hole up here at Runaway Ranch. I'm brave but scared. Broken, but whole.

I feel like some yin-yang of a woman.

Pocketing my phone, I exit the room and keep my gaze aimed forward as I walk down the hall, not wanting to run into Keena on my way out.

I pad down the stairs, taking in the great lodge. It's even more beautiful in the daylight. Cognac couches and rustic rugs. Antler chandeliers and wagon wheel coffee tables. It fits the Montgomery brothers to a T—rustic and moody and masculine.

My breath catches as I stop outside the kitchen. It had me transfixed last night and damn if it isn't stealing my heart in the easy light of morning.

Slowly, I walk inside. The kitchen's been cleaned and there's a bag of flour sitting on the shiny steel prep table that wasn't there last night.

The invisible band wrapped around my chest tightens. *Coward. Worthless.*

Aiden's voice is like a gaping black hole following me around. Growing even when I'm out of his dizzying orbit.

Gritting my teeth, I focus on the ball of my fist. The hard dig of my nails into the meat of my palm.

On a shaky breath, I take a step forward.

Just one step.

My gaze returns to the bag of flour. It would be so easy to dip my fingers in the silky texture, add a fine layer to the countertop, and whip up a batch of cinnamon rolls.

When I press my good hand on the cool marble of the countertop, I gasp. Pain zings through my broken arm.

So intensified it feels like it's the first time all over again. My ears ring.

And then I'm back in my kitchen.

Back there. With him.

My tears on the steel countertop. My screams. His threat.

He dipped low, clammy fingers on the back of my neck, his rough voice at my ear. "Remember this, Dakota. I will fuck with your life until you don't have one."

And then—

I blacked out.

A week later, I found out I was pregnant.

And I knew I had to get out.

Shivering, I squeeze my eyes shut and take a breath. My good hand is numb. Chills run through my body as my breath comes out in a shallow ragged pant. I feel like I'm dying in broad daylight.

"Breathe," I hiss through my teeth.

In and out. In and out.

I turn and press my cheek against the cool kitchen wall. The sensation brings me back down to earth.

How in the hell am I going to get my life back together if I can't even set foot in a kitchen without losing it?

Aiden broke my arm that night.

But really, he broke all of me.

I stay like that until the sensation in my good hand comes back, the tightness in my chest ebbs. Wiping my eyes, I look around the kitchen, grateful I'm still alone. Grateful Davis hasn't picked this opportunity to ride to my rescue once again. He can't see me like this. He's already done enough, strong arming me into living on the ranch for God knows how long.

If Aiden came here…Davis and his family could be in danger.

The thought is too awful to comprehend, so I shake my head, clearing it.

After grabbing my parka from the front door coat rack and tossing on a mitten, I exit the lodge through the back double-glass doors.

The morning air is biting and crisp. Exactly what I need to anchor myself in the present.

I step through the light powder of fine snow on the back porch just in time to see Wyatt Montgomery tear across the pasture on a gold-colored gelding. He flashes his trademark cocky grin and tips his Stetson toward me before redirecting his attention to the cowboy in the field.

My father told me Wyatt's been training cowboys in the off-season, including Fallon. I'm surprised she lets him, considering what he said about her. But if I know my sister, she's planning to eat the hearts of all those who have wronged her.

Wyatt's sharp snap of command cuts the crisp air, and the cowboys are off, running loops around the pasture. I shield my eyes from the sun, unable to hide my smile—looks like the wayward Montgomery boys have grown into successful men.

When I turn the porch corner, I gasp.

The ranch. It's even more beautiful than I remember.

Jagged mountains cut the indigo sky. Sunlight sparkles across the dusting of snow.

Montana in its madness. At its finest.

My gaze lands on the protective barricade of forest around the ranch. Fear rolls through my bones. It'd be so easy for Aiden to be out there. Watching, waiting. Coming for me when I least expect it.

That's when I see Davis.

And every bit of turmoil inside of me quiets.

He's yards away at what looks like a small barn or shed. A sign above it reads: Warrior Heart Home. A German Shepherd runs after him, nipping at his boots. Davis lifts a hand and the dog halts in its tracks.

Then he goes and turns his baseball cap around. The single motion upends the entire alignment of my hormones. Hot. So goddamn sexy. The sleeves of his hoodie mold to his sculpted arms, and with his stubbled jaw, and broad shoulders, the effect is devastating.

I take a step toward him, but I freeze when the dog lunges and snarls at Davis. Sharp barks blast the air.

I look around for someone to help before he gets his face ripped off, only I'm stunned when Davis gets down on his knees in front of the dog. Nose to nose. He's calm, no malice in his expression as he kneels there and lets the dog bark in his face. That chiseled jaw of his remains steady as he takes the dog's abuse.

Commanding. Calm. Fearless.

A glimpse of the former Marine curls my toes. I wouldn't want to be the man or dog who faced him down.

His deep voice carries on the air. "We're gonna get you someplace safe, girl. Aren't we? Just gotta get you into shape first."

My heart flips in my chest.

This is why I fell for the man. Kind. Patient. Even with his dark, jagged pieces.

I watch as Davis and the dog engage in what looks like a type of training exercise. They run in tight lines across the frozen grass until they're both panting hard. When they're finished, they disappear into the shed. Not long after, Davis re-emerges. As if he's felt my eyes on him the entire time, he lifts a hand, waving me over.

"Mornin,'" he drawls. His breath makes white puffs in the morning air.

"Morning," I say, trying not to stare. I've never seen bicep definition like that in a hoodie.

"What'd you think of the show?"

"Couldn't miss it." My gaze homes in on the small shed. "What is this?"

"It's the Warrior Heart Home." He puts a hand out like he's about to touch me, then stops himself. "Follow me. I'll show you."

He ushers me across the threshold into the small shed-like structure.

However, once inside, it's anything but. It's a state-of-the-art kennel facility. I take in the beds with plush fleece bedding and the wall-to-wall shelves neatly holding bags of dog food, grooming supplies, and equipment. Skylights flood the interior with natural light. A dozen dogs roam the fenced-in outdoor play yard.

"It's a Marine dog rescue," Davis explains, hanging up a leash on a hook. "I train them, then rehab and rehome them. Dogs I can't rehome live here on the ranch." He shifts when I don't tear my gaze away from his face. "What?"

"It's what I always suspected." I smile. "You are a big softie."

He crosses his arms over his chest. "Dogs are born to do more than serve."

"Sounds like you should take your own advice,

Hotshot." I laugh at the dogs bounding around the fenced-in area. "They're so happy."

"They're safe here," he says with a proud grunt. "And they know it."

This, I realize, is why I've come home. Davis Montgomery keeps those he cares about safe. And that safety is everything to me.

A loud woof has me looking over. A brown and black German Shepherd rushes toward me. In his excitement, he trips over his paws and nearly takes out another dog.

Davis grins. "That's Arlo. He hasn't figured out how his legs work yet."

"I know the feeling," I murmur, drifting around the kennel.

As if it weighs nothing, Davis hefts a large bag of dog food and begins filling bowls. Out of nowhere, a dog with dark fur materializes to stand beside him.

Davis tosses the dog a treat and says, "This is Keena."

This is Keena?

A disgusting feeling of relief sweeps over me. "She's yours?" I ask nonchalantly.

"She comes and goes between houses. Currently, she's at Ford's right now. But she's mine, attitude and all." He runs a massive hand gently through her fur. Keena leans into his touch and I flush.

Unbelievable. I've never been jealous of a dog before, but there's a first time for everything.

"German Shepherd?"

"Belgian Malinois," Davis says, giving Keena an ear rub. I fight a smile. Watching the stern handler from earlier melt over a dog does something warm and fluttery to my insides. "I got her the winter...you, uh, left."

"Oh." An awkward silence falls between us. I sweep a lock of hair from my eyes and study his handsome face. "You did a lot while I was gone."

"Had to," he grunts stiffly. With no further explanation, he returns to his tasks, rinsing off his massive hands in the farmhouse sink.

I shake my head. Forever mute, the man.

While he checks the dogs over, I sink into a squat and look Keena in the eyes. "You take good care of him, girl?"

I stick my hand out and wiggle my fingers in a bid to draw her closer.

If it's possible for a dog to turn up her nose at me, Keena does. She sits there. Her hard gaze as no-bullshit as Davis's.

I don't blame you. I wouldn't want to share him either.

"She doesn't like strangers," Davis says, coming back to us. I stand. "Don't take it personally."

"I won't," I say, ignoring the doubtful glance Keena gives me.

A series of barks erupt from the yard, and I flinch, stumbling into Davis. He wraps an arm around my back and holds me close to his chest. I close my eyes, inhaling his steadying scent of man and leather and coffee.

"Sorry," I whisper into his tense muscles. "I'm jumpy."

"Let's go outside." He steps back and guides me toward the door with firm hands.

We step back out into the chilly morning, and Davis turns, surveying me with a scrutinizing gaze. "You warm enough?"

Before I can answer, he's adjusting my jacket. Butterflies escape in my stomach from our closeness, the heat of his massive frame in my space. The way his big hand slides over my throat as he adjusts my collar.

An image of Davis's hands roaming up my body in the cabin from the last night we were together flashes through my mind, and my heart rate spikes.

"Good?" Davis looks down at me. For a brief second, he winces as his hand grazes my stomach. Pain in his eyes.

"Good," I breathe.

Across the field, I see Charlie stomping down the front porch of his cabin. A small woman appears at Charlie's shoulder, dancing around him as they walk toward us.

"Davis." I grab his arm and he goes rigid at the physical contact. "Who's that?"

"That's Charlie."

Scoffing, I sock him in the stomach. "Stop it. Who is *that*?"

"Ruby," he gruffs, a strange tenderness in his tone. "That's Ruby."

"Oh my god." I stare at their adorable contrast. The tall, broody cowboy with the tiny slip of a girl beside him.

"Yeah." A smile stains his voice. "They got married last year."

"Oh my *god*."

A pleased grunt.

And I know why. Because Charlie Montgomery's a different man than the one I knew six years ago. Gone is the scowl. The darkness. The drink.

Six years ago, Davis and I had taken charge of trying to coax Charlie out of a drunken stupor. I brought a pot of chicken noodle soup; we made him eat and then put him to bed. Davis and I sat in the hallway outside Charlie's bedroom on opposite walls.

"Thank you," Davis said raggedly.

"Food fixes everything." I wiggled my bare toes at him. "Your brother will be okay, Hotshot."

"I mean it, Dakota." He looked across the hallway, wrapped a huge hand around my ankle, and gave it a squeeze. His very touch seared. "I couldn't do this without you."

Warmth in my stomach unfurled. I waited for him to stop touching me, but he didn't. Instead, Davis traced coarse fingertips over my bare leg. Then he gripped my ankle and pulled me toward him like a slow lasso of want. And then I was there. In his arms. And he kissed me.

That night, we went from friends to lovers.

There was no stopping us. I thought he was the most handsome man I ever saw.

Still do.

My jaw drops even further when Charlie picks Ruby up to carry her over a puddle of melted snow. She's glowing and laughing and Charlie can't stop touching her.

"He's obsessed."

Davis snorts. "Doesn't come close."

He's right.

Charlie Montgomery is a man long gone.

There's barely enough time for me to close my mouth before Charlie's stepping up to me. Snow and gravel crunch beneath his boots. "Hey, Dakota," he says, wrapping me in a stranglehold of a hug.

"Careful of the arm," Davis orders.

"Charlie, hi." I squeeze him back, fully aware Davis is watching us with a guard-dog gaze. But I relish the hug. These cowboys are like brothers to me. They never have and never will scare me.

When I pull back, I take a second to study him. Dark

hair mussed, beard trimmed and neat, expression tranquil instead of moody. I squeeze his shoulder. "You look good."

"You too." Charlie grins, but I don't miss the way his gaze dips to my cast. The pity in his eyes.

The pretty girl steps up to me. A hat with a fuzzy pom covers her strawberry-blond hair. "Hi," she chirps and pops out her hand. Her light blue eyes sparkle, a striking contrast to Charlie's deeper blue. "I'm Ruby!"

"Hi, Ruby. Nice to meet you." I shake her hand, already sucked in by her vivacious energy. Her infectious smile does something twisty to my insides.

The wave of sadness hits suddenly. Suffocating. I try to keep a smile on my face, but it feels wobbly.

I wish I looked like that. I *used* to look like that.

Charlie, Davis—everyone's got their lives together. Everyone but me.

I'm a mess.

Charlie tugs Ruby's hat lower over her ears. "We're headed for a ride, but we wanted to come say hi." His eyes land knowingly on Davis, then flit back to me. A gesture that tells me Davis told his brother everything. "We'll see you around, Dakota."

"Bye." Ruby waves at us, and then Charlie's taking her small hand and leading her across the gravel drive to the barn.

"Bye," I echo.

Seeing them go has the crushing weight of my situation bearing down on my shoulders.

So much of my life feels like it's gone forever.

Joy. Security. Love.

Not that I can afford to think like that. There will be

no more following my heart. I have to make wise choices for me and my baby.

"Dakota?" Davis peers down at me, a frown marring his brow. "You okay?"

"I have to go into town," I say abruptly, ignoring his question. "I have a doctor's appointment."

Tensing, his gaze bounces to my belly. Once again, that same pained expression crosses his face. "Everything okay?"

"I don't know, Davis," I grit out. Weary, tired, vibrating with bitterness. "I've never done this before."

His nod is firm. "I'll take you."

Heat consumes my face. "Davis, I can—"

He holds up his hand—all rippling muscles and a perpetual scowl—ending my argument. "Let's get one thing straight, Dakota." The deepness of his voice intensifies. "Here and now. I go where you go."

"Fine."

Turning away from him, I stare into the rising sun until my eyes go blind. My heart pulses angrily against my chest.

One more day. You can make it through one more day.

8

Dakota

THE TOWN THAT USED TO BE MY HOME IS NOW A stranger. It's a different place. Just like I'm a different person.

"Where's the deli?" I ask Davis as we walk up the street to the clinic.

Main Street is quiet in the afternoon light. A Bobcats banner blows in the chilly winter air as I try not to concentrate on the fact our fingertips keep brushing during our in-sync lockstep. The brief contact does something unfair to my heart. A soft, barely there touch of skin. It's enough to have electricity sizzling up my arm.

Davis clears his throat. "Turned to a ski shop last year."

"I remember doing this with you," I muse, taking in a soft pink sign that says The Last Bookshop on the Left. "Showing you around Resurrection when you first got here."

A crease forms on his rugged brow, like the memory annoys him. Maybe it does. Maybe all I am is a burden he's stuck with because of a promise he made to Stede.

Two old men—friends of my father's—are sitting on a porch swing outside Zeke's Hardware. I tug my jacket tighter over my belly. Heat shoots into my cheeks when they look me up and down, but say nothing.

They don't recognize me.

Maybe no one will.

My head swivels as we pass the Neon Grizzly. Even at ten a.m. country music blasts through the windows and every barstool is full.

Right next door is an art gallery. The contrast is staggering.

"The town's gotten so big," I breathe.

Davis chuckles, nods at a passerby. "People still say hello on the street, so not that big."

Resurrection is different. It's not so much gentrified as it is hip. The saloons, antique store, and candy shop from my childhood still exist, but now there's a small-town cool to it. There's hardly a chain-store in sight. Instead, mom-and-pop shops and cute boutiques line the storefronts.

A hollow ache fills me as I take in the sights while we walk.

The soul of my hometown hasn't changed, it got better. But I never wanted Resurrection. I never wanted The Corner Store. Or my father's legacy. Or my sister's wild. I wanted to be perfect and to work hard. Older daughter status that led somewhere. I was a cheerleader and a straight-A student. Homecoming queen and valedictorian. I was Resurrection's golden girl, and I left.

It's clear I'm not one of them anymore. I'm an outsider, an interloper, a deserter.

No one in Resurrection will be happy I'm back. We take off for greener pastures when we should keep tending our own. People invest their life here, so when you're new, or come home, no one welcomes you with open arms.

I had all this hope in leaving Aiden, and now…coming back to Resurrection feels like some perilous journey instead of a hopeful one.

"We should keep moving." Davis's low rumble sends warmth cascading through my stomach.

Then I blink. I've stopped on the street corner and didn't realize it.

The oxygen leaves my lungs when Davis puts a hand out. It hovers over the small of my back, not quite touching it as he gives me a stern frown. A long sigh bubbles up in my lungs before I swallow it down. He keeps doing that. Not quite touching me. What does it say about me that I want him to?

What does it say about him that he won't?

Everything about it is just like the cowboy himself—infuriatingly frustrating.

"Let's go," he says, his voice cool and collected.

We cross the intersection, headed for the end of Main Street. Davis strides ahead, back straight, broad shoulders stiff and on edge. For such a massive man, his energy radiates stealth, calm. His nimble movements are like a shark slicing through water.

Powerful. Dangerous.

I want to complain that he's here with me, but I can't. The truth is, I feel safer with Davis beside me. Isn't that why I came back? Because, deep down, I wanted those five seconds he promised.

Davis holds the door for me, and I step inside the Bear Creek Clinic.

I exhale and square my shoulders, scanning the signs on the wall. First floor. Suite Two. Obstetrics.

A strange mixture of revulsion and fear courses through me. I'm horrified when tears hit my eyes. Even more horrified when I feel the heat from a big, muscled body behind me. The temperature in the room suddenly rises.

I jerk around, put a hand out like I can stop him. "You don't need to come with me."

Still, Davis moves toward me. Worry flashes in those chocolate-brown eyes. "Are you sure?"

No, I'm not fucking sure. I want him there to hold my hand, to take it with me. I want his stern face and that commanding rasp of a voice to tell me it'll all be okay. But I can't have that. I can't—and won't—ask that of him.

I lift my chin and wipe my eyes. "Does it look bad? My face?"

His expression softens, the hard apple of his throat working up and down as he stares at me. And, oh god, this time he does touch me. His big, calloused fingers tuck a lock of hair behind my ear, lingering there. My eyes flutter close at the sensation. The air between us warms at least ten degrees.

"No, Koty," he finally says, his voice ragged. "It doesn't look bad."

"Thank you," I whisper.

"Breathe, Dakota. You got this."

I blink back tears. Somehow, he always has me.

Before he can say anything else, I turn on my heel and leave Davis behind.

⁓

Thirty minutes later, after a variety of pregnancy related tests and a blood draw, I'm reclined on an obstetric table in an itchy gown when the door opens.

"Well, if it isn't little Dakota McGraw. I swear I

couldn't believe my eyes when I saw your name on my chart."

I look up from my spot on the bed and smile weakly. "Lucky you, I guess." Every sigh inside of me is fighting to come out.

My old babysitter, Agnes Winfrey, is now the town obstetrician. And why wouldn't she be? It makes perfect sense she'd be the one to see my vagina after she changed my diapers.

In her early fifties, Winfrey's a woman of boisterous laughter and solemn serenity. I remember her sneaking me Red Vines from her purse when she bribed Fallon and me to get back into bed and leave her and her boyfriend alone.

"What're you doing back in town?" Winfrey shakes her head, her silver locks curling over her shoulders. "Haven't seen you in ages."

"New move," I say, trying for breezy when all I want to do is melt into a puddle. "Back home."

Winfrey makes a snippy little noise of consternation and snaps on a glove. "You know, I left Resurrection once. To get my degree. And then I came back. I swear this town has some kind of alien-beam hold on you."

I stare at the cracked ceiling with fluffy white clouds painted on a blue surface. The cheery scene does little to reassure me. So much for keeping a low profile. Within an hour, everyone will know I'm back home.

"Haven't seen a doctor yet?"

"No," I tell her, ignoring the way her gaze bounces to my cast and back to my face. "I haven't."

A lie. I didn't try to find a doctor.

Aiden finding out was one risk I couldn't take. This baby was my little secret.

Silence lapses for a second and Winfrey clears her throat. "Okay. Let's get down to business, then take a look at this baby."

Winfrey completes her internal exam, snaps off her gloves, and discusses the results of my labs. She informs me I have low blood sugar, but I can fix it by eating frequent small meals and healthy snacks.

"Scoot," she says, slipping on a clean pair of gloves. "Time for that Kodak moment."

I recline on a table and lift the upper portion of the two-piece gown.

Winfrey glances at the door, then pins me with a curious look. "Would the father like to come in?"

"He's not here," I say quickly and leave it at that.

Inhaling a steeling breath, I glance down at my belly. I've avoided looking at myself in the mirror. Like looking makes this real. And it is. Suddenly, there's my belly. My breasts are full, spilling out of my bra.

An overwhelming sort of hopelessness coasts over me.

I need bras.

I need books.

I need prenatal vitamins.

I need so many things.

A job. A home. A life. The heavy weight of responsibility, of happiness.

I squeeze my eyes shut as she squirts a cold gel on my stomach. While the wand coasts over my bump, blood roars in my ears and my heart pumps double time. To calm myself, I grip the cool metal of Davis's dog tag and rub my thumb over the bumpy, raised lettering I've memorized like a prayer.

I wish Davis and his rumbling voice were here to fill

the space inside my head. But he's not. I have to handle this myself.

"There." Winfrey's gentle voice breaks the silence. "There's your baby, Dakota."

Breathe, Dakota. Rope that moon.

I open my eyes and incline my head to the monitor.

A spine, the curve of the skull, a protruding leg. And a heart. Tiny and furiously beating.

A sad smile curves across my lips. "That's it?"

"That's it. Now, let's see…" She does some calculations on the screen. "Based on measurements, you're about eighteen weeks along, which puts you at a due date of approximately June twenty-ninth."

Panic grabs me by the throat. I'm further along than I thought.

All of this is too soon. Too fast.

Winfrey nudges her glasses up on her nose. "Have you felt the baby move yet?"

I squeeze my eyes shut. The roar of blood pounds in my ears. "I don't think so. Is that bad?"

"Not at all. Your little one's tucked in there tight. They'll make themselves known when they're ready."

I swallow, staring at the little baby on the screen.

"Would you like to know the gender?"

"No," I blurt.

Winfrey arches a brow. "Excuse me?"

"No." I shake my head vigorously. "I don't want to know." Guilt heats my cheeks.

I'm not ready. Because if it's a boy, then I have to worry that he'll be like his father. If it's a girl, I'll worry about warning her away from men like Aiden.

All my life, I will hate myself for not being a better example.

Winfrey sets down the wand, her eyes narrowing in a wise way I don't like. "Are you sure, Dakota?"

"Yes," I whisper.

The little flickering heart up on the screen terrifies me. Another life I'm responsible for when I can't even manage my own. It's like that little beat is an SOS signal, a reminder of how badly I'm about to fail.

Tears cloud my vision.

I just want to begin again.

I want to love my baby without sorrow. I want to bake without pain, and I want to learn to love again without flinching or fear.

I just want *me* back.

A sob bursts out of my mouth before I can stop it.

"Oh god." I sniffle, sitting up on my elbows. "I'm sorry."

"It's okay, honey," Winfrey says, handing over a clump of tissues, and I'm reminded why I liked her so much as a babysitter. "It's normal. Hormones."

"Right." I dab at my eyes, tears still blurring my vision.

"Here. I'll print you a photo of that beautiful little blur."

The wand's hung up, the jelly's cleaned off my stomach, and the machine's silenced.

I tug the gown down and take the photo Winfrey hands me. Without looking at it, I shove it into my purse.

A better mother would want this. A better mother would take the sonogram and hang it on her fridge. And then I'm reminded I don't even have a fridge and fresh tears hit me once more.

I don't feel bonded with my baby. I think of my mother

and how she always felt so out of reach. How she'd stand at the kitchen counter and stare out the window at the white moonlight. When I asked her what was wrong, she'd pat my head and send me to bed.

What I understand now is that she wanted to run. And she did.

Like my mother, I'm already running scared.

How can I do this? I've been on my own for twenty-four hours and already I'm crumbling. But I made my choice. I am here in Resurrection. I can begin again.

I can.

"Dakota?"

I gasp, nearly jumping out of my skin as Winfrey's hand hits my shoulder.

Her forehead furrows as she settles herself on the stool beside the table.

"I'm sorry. I'm so sorry." I wipe furiously at my face, wishing I could stop crying, grateful that I can at least blame the hormones.

"Dakota." Winfrey leans in, her wise gray eyes searching my face. "I know Stede's still in town. Fallon too. You ask them for help, you hear me? If things are bad, you ask for help. This is why we have tribes. We lean on them. Even if sometimes asking for help feels like you're jackknifing into a pit of vipers."

"Okay." I sob-laugh, grateful for the moment of peace she's given me. "I will."

"Here." Winfrey rolls her stool to the cabinet, reaches inside a drawer, and rolls back to me. "You still like these?" she asks, holding out a bag of Red Vines.

"Yeah," I say, a wobbly smile finding its way to my tear-stained face. "I do."

9

Davis

"**I** NEED A FAVOR."

A chuckle escapes the whiskey-drenched throat on the other end of the line. "Finally cashing in, Montgomery?"

"Had to sometime." I keep an eye out for Dakota, but the big foyer's empty. So I pace. "I only saved your life, is all."

"So that's how it is. It's been seven years. No 'hello, how are you' just a 'you owe me.'"

I snort. "You do."

"Well, in case you're interested, I got two kids, a mortgage, and a soon-to-be ex-wife with a bad case of cheating-itis."

I needle my brow, not wanting to take a walk down memory lane with Rick Ferraro.

At nineteen, I joined the Marines to get out of my small hometown. I liked horses just fine, but I wanted to be a part of something bigger than myself. It was new and unfamiliar but also exhilarating and powerful.

I knew I could do it.

And I did.

I met Ferraro when I joined the Marine Raider team. A unit that specialized in special ops and direct-action missions that had me gone for months with no contact with the outside world. Dark, dangerous shit that not even my family knew about.

Ferraro snorts. "You're the only reason I got out of there in one piece, so fine, you fuck. What do you want?"

"You still working for that lab?" While others became private bodyguards or law enforcement, Ferraro went to work in a top-secret government agency.

"Damn straight. Sure beats kicking in doors and jumping out of planes." I hear the wicked smile in Ferraro's voice. "What it'll be? Cyanide? Digital revolver? Rail guns?"

I roll my eyes. "Christ, Ferraro, I work on a ranch. No one needs to evaporate a cow." Phone to my ear, I pace to a carpeted waiting area. "That tracking device you invented. I need one."

A long pause over the line.

Then a long chuckle rolls out. "Davis Montgomery spooked. Never thought I'd see the day."

"Yeah, well, that makes two of us."

"Tell me what for?"

"Tell you to go fuck yourself."

"Still a stubborn bastard." Ferraro makes a sound of annoyance. "I'll get it to you. Keep in mind the SullyScan is unlicensed and experimental." He chuckles. "The US government wanted to send me straight to the department of 'the fuck you invented?'"

The tightness in my chest squeezes. "You named it after Sully?"

"Sure did. He's the reason I invented it, so least I could do was give it his name."

"Right," I rough out. Pain lances through me.

Over the line, the shuffle of papers. "You need it, you'll get it. I got your six, brother."

Brother.

I shove the tightness back down, launch into what I need.

Ten minutes later, I end the call. I could have used this favor for anything. A cure for cancer. A muzzle for Wyatt. But I used it for Dakota.

I'm not safe. I'll never be safe.

Her words from earlier haunt me. I need her to understand I've got eyes on her. That I'm here to protect her, and I'll do everything in my power to do so.

Although, if I have to say it, Dakota seems more worried about coming back to town than her ex following her home. As soon as we left the safety of the ranch and stepped out onto Main Street, nervousness came off Dakota in waves.

I heard the small talk between locals after Dakota left town. No matter how far away Dakota was, her memory was an echo I couldn't shake. The whispers of her lingered.

Did you hear she left her daddy and that store?

That McGraw girl is out there, going it alone. Let's see if she makes it.

Shame she ran just like her mama.

She's ready for the big city? Well, let's see how much of a big city girl she is when she sees how much everything costs.

I ached to put a fist through the face of anyone who dared talk badly about her.

Pacing across the floor, my focus shifts from the sterile waiting room to the door Dakota disappeared through. I don't like that she went in alone, but what can I do? It's better if it's just her. It's not my job to go with her.

A door opens.

Dakota walks toward me.

Fuck. She's been crying. Just the sight alone threatens to take ten damn years off my life.

"Hey," I say. "Everything okay?"

She sniffles. Forces a lukewarm smile. "Fine. Healthy. I have low blood sugar, but there's a baby in there."

Dakota glances down at her belly, and I fight the urge to yank her into my arms and keep her there. She looks so damn sad; she's carving out my heart.

"I'm eighteen weeks," she whispers, glancing up at me. "*Eighteen.* It feels like bad luck."

"I don't believe in bad luck." I don't want this kind of thinking for Koty.

She holds my gaze, as if she's considering what to say next, when the lobby door opens.

With the chill of the ice-cold wind, come Stede and Fallon.

Surprise flares in Dakota's eyes. "Daddy."

"Hey, daydreamer." Stede steps forward to squeeze Dakota's arm. "Davis."

I nod. "Sir."

Dakota's dark, hopeful eyes flick to her sister's. "Hi, Fallon."

There's a hesitation in Fallon's guarded gaze. It's been obvious in the conversations I've had with Stede that something chilled between the sisters the day Dakota left town.

Fallon stays silent, giving a cool nod. Dakota's face falls, and I clamp my teeth together to hide a growl.

Dakota takes a deep breath. "What're you doing here?"

"Got treatment." Stede's gaze drops to Dakota's stomach. "How's that grandkid of mine?"

"Had my first appointment," she offers, waving a hand over her stomach, but stopping just short of touching it.

I frown.

"Sure can't wait to meet the little one," Stede says, and Dakota's face softens. Her father's words are exactly what she needs.

Fallon, in a worn army-green jacket, shoulders her backpack. A Louis L'Amour book peeks out from a torn pocket. "C'mon, Dad, we should go."

Dakota perks up. "I can stay with him." She tucks a long lock of dark hair behind her ear.

Fallon looks like Dakota's offered to auction her off in marriage. Her face is a storm cloud. "It's okay. I read to him while we wait."

"I can read too, you know."

I silently swear as Dakota digs in her heels with a stubborn, older-sister attitude.

I take a step forward, wanting to intercept the argument before it starts, but Stede sighs. Blocks me from going forward. "Let it run its course, kid. You're mad for five minutes; these girls stay mad for life."

I look at Stede, the old man's wise and weathered face, and a brick of trepidation lands in my stomach.

Dakota gives Fallon a long, pleading look. "He's my father, too. Let me help."

Fallon snorts. "I've been here since the beginning. You don't know anything about his treatments and you don't get to roll up in here and act like you're some great savior."

"Okay." Dakota's lower lip trembles. "You're mad at me, I get it."

"Do you get it, Dakota?" Fallon's voice rises in the quiet lobby. "You *can't* help. You got yourself into a mess you have to fix. You have to think of yourself. Like you've always done."

Dakota closes her eyes at the verbal hit.

When they finally flash back open, I note the fierce spark of fire in her eyes. "That's not fair," Dakota snaps. "I didn't even know Dad was sick. If you want to act like a martyr because I left town, so be it. But that's on you, Fallon."

Fallon utters a condescending laugh. "If that's the story you want to tell yourself to feel better, good for you."

Fuck it.

I can't stay out of it. I don't want animosity with Fallon, but if I have to choose between them, I'll piss Fallon off every damn time to protect her sister.

"Look." I glare at Fallon, hoping she gets my fucking point, that if she makes Dakota cry, she's going to have a whole other set of problems. "Your sister's been through a lot. Can you give her some grace?"

"Wish she'd give me some," Fallon mutters.

A vein pulses in my temple.

These sisters couldn't be more different. One evokes brotherly love and frustration in me, while the other has my heart full of so many fucking twists and turns I don't know where my mind is half the time. I want to strangle Fallon. Kiss the fuck out of Dakota.

"You know, Fallon, you're pissing me off and acting like a brat," I bark. "Shut up."

Hands on her hips, eyes wide in disbelief, Dakota turns to me. "Don't talk to my sister like that."

"Yeah," Fallon says. "I don't need the likes of you telling me what I ought to do."

I groan, unsure how I'm suddenly the bad guy.

Both sisters round on me. And on my emotions. "One

of us will punch you," Fallon snarls. "And the other will run you over with our truck. Take your pick."

"Enough," Stede roars, hand lifted. His voice cracks from the effort. "This shit stops now."

The sisters freeze.

Fallon swears.

Dakota flinches.

Stede's disapproval coats the room. "I reckon you both got issues, but now is not the time, and it sure isn't the damn place."

Dakota and I share a look. Stede McGraw, pissed as hell, is a sight to see. Never in my life have I seen him raise his voice, and judging by the looks on his daughter's faces, it's been a long time for them, too.

"You girls are my heart, my soul, but damn if you're not breaking both of them the way you're acting."

"Daddy," Dakota whispers, hands clasped to her heart.

Even Fallon looks shamefaced.

"Fallon, you're angry with Dakota. Talk it out on your own fucking time." A mischievous smile ghosts his lips. "And I'll give you the right place to do it, too." Stede looks at Dakota. "You need a job, daydreamer. You come work at the store."

Dakota inhales, sharp.

I drag a hand down my face, swearing under my breath. What the old man is thinking by sticking his daughters together is beyond me. They'll either make up, or they'll destroy the entire fucking world.

"Daddy, no," Fallon says, her face creasing with panic.

Stede holds up a hand, silencing them both. "I love you both. But get it the fuck together."

Fallon and Dakota stare at each other. *Traitor*, Fallon's wild hazel eyes say.

"This way, you two can spend some time together," Stede continues. "Fallon, you can keep your lessons going with Wyatt before you head to Calgary in the summer, and Dakota can work at the store."

Fallon's eyes are now on the toes of her boots, the tips of her ears pink. She stopped taking lessons from Wyatt two months ago. He's been bitching about it ever since she went MIA from the ranch.

It's bad enough I have Dakota to worry about. Now I have to worry about what's running Fallon wild.

"Davis has a job, the ranch," Dakota begins. "He can't—"

"I can," I say. "It's the off-season. Charlie and Ford can handle the ranch. I'll park myself at the station. It's right across the street."

I don't like her being out in the open, but she's right. She can't stay on the ranch forever. If I can give her some normalcy, even for a moment, I'll do it.

Dakota's lower lip sticks out in a pout. She hates the idea. I can see it on her face. Finally, she relents and smiles at Stede. "Sounds like a plan, Daddy."

"I'm happy to hear that, baby girl." He takes a brisk step forward, then turns to amble toward the elevator. "You two are both adults. Figure out what problems you got because I won't be around forever."

"Fine. Here." Fallon shoves a ring of keys at Dakota. When Stede's out of earshot, she hisses, "Fix your fucking face before you come in."

Dakota stands frozen, hands gripping the keys. She

blinks back tears as she turns on her heel and rushes out of the lobby.

"Nice fucking work," I growl, glaring at Fallon.

"Fuck you, Davis." She flips me off on the way to the elevator.

I swear under my breath and follow after Dakota.

These sisters are going to be the death of me.

A pregnant Dakota in tears has my blood pressure skyrocketing.

I catch her as she's crossing onto Main Street. The bright blue sky of the winter afternoon is fading. It'll be dark in less than four hours.

"Your sister's a pain in my ass," I tell her dryly.

She keeps trudging ahead, hand in her pocket. "I can't be sure she isn't a feral gremlin with attitude issues."

I smile. But it soon fades after I inspect Dakota's face. She looks like she's hanging on by her last thread.

"You okay?"

I immediately curse myself. It's the dumbest thing I can ask. *No, she's not okay, Montgomery.* Around Dakota, a word, a touch—it all comes out wrong.

"No." She stops abruptly and leans back to look at me. Tears stream down her face. "I'm not."

On instinct, I grab her shoulders and she huddles into my chest. Warm. Soft. Shaking.

"Lunch," I order, and she lifts her face. Even with the dark smudges beneath her eyes, she's too beautiful for words. "You hungry?"

She sniffles. "I'm always hungry."

"Let's go." Keeping an arm around her slender

shoulders, I steer her toward a red-bricked building at the end of the block.

She hesitates, stopping when we get to the front door.

"What happened to the bakery?" she asks, staring up at the sign that reads the Little Star Diner.

"Went out of business last year. This place is new. No one knows you," I promise her.

My mind's laser-focused on what she told me two days ago when I brought her home. She wants to be on the down low, that's what I'll do.

She smiles. "Thank you."

We step inside the diner and claim a booth by the window. I slide my gaze over the small restaurant, taking in the entry points and exits. Dakota grips the tabletop like it's keeping her steady as she looks around at the walls decorated with old Coca-Cola tin trays.

"How are you feelin'?" I ask gruffly. Nothing makes me more awkward than trying to comfort someone. I have brothers. They get hurt, and I tell them to suck it up and shake it off. But then there's Dakota…

The only person in the world who breaks down my walls.

She leans an elbow on the table, resting her chin in her palm. "How am I feeling? About the fact that my sister wants to kill me, or about the fact that I have a ticking time bomb in my stomach and I have no idea what I'm doing."

"Fallon first," I order.

"She's mad at me."

I grunt. "She shouldn't have said what she said."

Dakota shakes her dark head. "I don't blame her. I left her here." She picks at the Formica tabletop. Guilt edges her voice. "I didn't know she was still working at the store."

"It's a lot for her," I say lowly. "She's struggling to take care of the store and then get out on the rodeo."

Even though I'm pissed at Fallon for treating Dakota like shit, that girl's been working her ass off. Keep the store alive. Keep Stede alive. Keep her career alive. It can't be easy.

"She's right about what she said about my face." Dakota waves a hand around her black eye, the cut on her lip. "I can't go to work until this is gone. Everyone in town will talk if I mosey into The Corner Store looking like Mike Tyson."

Her words hang heavy in the air.

"No one can find out what happened to me, okay?" Her voice cracks. "I mean it, Davis, They can't."

Red stains her cheeks. And it hits me sudden and quick—she's ashamed.

"They won't, okay?" I exhale. A muscle jerks in my jaw. It feels like there's a fire growing between my ribs. "Cupcake, no one will ever know." Anyone says an unkind word about her, I'll hunt them down. I'll fix this. She can't stop me.

A waitress appears to take our order and Dakota keeps her head down, long dark hair shielding her face as we both order burgers and fries.

"The baby?" I ask when the waitress leaves. The words chew up my throat like glass. "How did everything at the doctor go?"

Dakota looks pale and fragile. And then everything pent up from her visit at the doctor's explodes out of her.

"Everything went *fucked*, Davis. I have a baby inside of me. I don't know if I'm going to love it. Or be a good mother. Everything—my entire life—is unplanned." A shudder of a breath rocks her frame. "Babies have schedules. I don't know what timelines to follow or what bottles to buy. All I want to do is eat. I cry all the time. My breasts are huge. I don't have any bras. And I'm…" Her brown eyes flick to mine, drop to her hands.

"What?" I ask, feeling desperate and uncomfortable. The mention of Dakota's breasts sends a rush of blood to my dick and I fight to keep a straight face.

"Nothing." She takes a sip of her water. "I'm trying to survive *the now*. I don't have the bandwidth to plan months ahead."

"And that's okay. You have time." I think about what she said earlier. "Eighteen weeks, that's…"

"Almost five months." She sighs. "Here."

She takes something out of her purse and smooths it on the countertop between us. After a closer look, it's a photo. A black and white blur.

She laughs bitterly. "That's my baby. And I can't even look at it. I don't even want to know the gender. I don't even want to feel my baby move. Because that means it's real. It's happening. Isn't that awful?"

I take the photo and run my fingers run along the image, picking out a spine, tiny toes, a round head. A muscle in my jaw moves over and over again. The idea of Dakota having someone else's child stings, but I'll deal with it because it's bigger than me and my fucking feelings.

"It's not awful," I finally say. "You're going to be a good mother, Dakota."

"How do you know?"

"Because I know you."

How can she not see what a good mother she'll be? She's a fighter, she loves hard, and she's loyal to the core. She gives peace to everyone who meets her.

Her child will be lucky to have her. And if he or she forgets, I'll be around to remind him.

"What if I'm having a monster's baby?"

"Never." I shake my head. "You're gonna look at that baby and not see a speck of *him*. Because it's going to be all of you, Dakota."

She rubs her eyes. "I don't know, Davis. I was so optimistic things in my life would work out. I feel like a failure." Defeat and sadness wash over her face. "I'm not brave, and I'm not strong. I'm not sure I ever was."

Fuck, do I feel that.

I lean forward and take her hand. Dakota stiffens, but her eyes grow soft. "Bravery is being scared and doing it anyway," I say. "You don't have to feel strong. You're allowed to not want this, to be fucking pissed off and sad. But I see you, Koty. And I won't let you fall."

Dakota bites her lip, her eyes wide. "You won't?"

"No. I won't." I squeeze her hand. "Your baby's in there and safe. Now we worry about you. Back on your feet, right?"

She smiles. And damn, she's stunning.

"Right." Dakota whisks her thumb over my knuckle and I fight to keep my face stoic as an unexpected current of electricity slices up my arm.

The waitress drops off the food, and Dakota twists her hand out of mine. The loss of her touch has me fighting to catch my breath.

I take one last long glance and slide the sonogram photo back toward her. "Here."

"No. I don't want it back." She bites her lip. "Give it to me when I'm ready, okay?"

My chest constricts, but I slip the photo into my pocket.

Dakota takes a deep breath and spears her pickle. "Speaking of mothers… I found mine, you know."

My eyebrows shoot up. "No, I didn't. Shit."

"She's a dealer in Vegas." Dakota laughs bitterly. "I ran into her when I was there for a food and wine festival. She left us all those years ago, and that's where she landed. Dealing cards in some shitty casino. She didn't recognize me, and when I told her who I was, it was like one big shrug."

"Fallon know?"

"No." She picks at the corner of her burger. "Just another thing she'll blame me for."

"Dakota," I warn. "You didn't make her leave. And you'll do better than your mother did."

She makes a brief hum of consideration, pops a fry in her mouth, and chews. When she's finished, she says, "You're pretty smart for a man of few grunting words."

I chuckle at that.

"I just…" Straightening in the booth, she presses a palm to the heel of her damp eyes. "I have to get it together. For my baby."

"You will. And until then, you're not alone. Do you hear me?"

Her brow wrinkles in that adorable way of hers. A wrinkled brow means Dakota's beautiful brain is working. So fucking smart. Always a recipe running through there, a kind word for someone, a witty remark. Keeps me on my fucking toes. I've always loved that about her. Her big dreams. Her beautiful brain. A reminder that Dakota McGraw is made for great things. Better things than me.

I spent the last six years torturing myself over not asking her to stay. And now she's back. In front of me like I can have her.

But I can't.

She's not staying permanently in Resurrection. She'll heal, like the warrior she is, and go off to chase her dreams. She's meant for the big city, for new adventures. I have a ranch, my brothers.

Dakota is a job. Keep her safe. Keep my distance.

Her faraway gaze drifts to the window. "What if I'm never safe?"

"You will be safe. Sure as my word, Dakota, I'll protect you. It's my job."

Some of the light dies in her eyes as she looks back at me. "You're such a good guy," she muses, almost sadly.

"Which means...your number, Cupcake." I pull out my phone. A grin tilts my lips. "Gonna need you to unblock me."

She flushes.

"I'm so sorry I blocked you," she admits in one long rush. "You have to know I never meant to freeze you out. I couldn't risk him finding out about you."

My breath stops. The thought never crossed my mind that someone told her to cut off our contact. That she was afraid. That she was protecting herself.

Her long lashes flutter. "It was the same with your dog tag."

"You wore it," I choke out. Unable to help it, my cock swells, and I grip the table.

"I always did," she says, breathlessly. Her darkened gaze lingers on mine. "I never took it off. Until I met A—him."

Damn, but I almost caught her there. The Marine in

me wants to pry the name out of her. But she needs to open up on her own time. Even if it is slowly killing me.

Say his name, baby. Say his name and let me kill him.

She fingers the chain, dulled by time. The look on her face says she's far away, reliving the past. "He was so jealous, so angry it was from another man. He hated it. I had to lock it up. Hide it away, so he wouldn't—" A tiny cry escapes her mouth. She presses fingertips to her lips to smother the sound.

"Koty," I warn, leaning in. Rage floods my system. I close my eyes, dangerously close to losing it. When I find that fucker, every bone in his body will be dust.

"Why didn't you call me?" The question wrenches from my lips. A question I've ached to ask, but dread the answer.

She's quiet for a long minute. "I didn't call you because I was ashamed. I didn't want you to know."

It makes sense. To Dakota, losing control, admitting weakness, is her worst nightmare.

I lean in, pinning my gaze to hers. A growl rumbles up from my chest. "Trust me, Dakota, had I known, I would have come for you. And there would have been nothing keeping me from tearing him apart."

"I know," she whispers, her eyes bright with unshed tears. Her lower lip trembles. "That's what scared me."

Her hand's back in mine. Touching her is my kryptonite.

Dakota's face pokers up. She exhales a long breath and shakes her dark head. "No more questions, Davis. I have to focus on moving forward. Not back."

I grip my water glass with white-knuckled hands.

Back. Something we can never do.

10

Davis

BRAS. BOOBS. BABIES.

Jesus fucking Christ. Is this my life now?

For the last two hours, I've parked myself at my desk in the Bullshit Box, adding strange sounding items like binkies and Boppies to my Amazon cart. I've got a glass of whiskey to my right, and Keena's curled up in her bed near the space heater. Across the ranch, a light is on in Dakota's room in the lodge.

The restraint it's taking me not to go up to her room right now and check on her is crippling.

She didn't have dinner. After we got home from town, she barricaded herself in her room. Has been there ever since. The hunch of her shoulders and the shadows under her eyes tell me today was hard. Harder than either of us expected. The sad cringe when she talks about her baby, the refusal to touch her stomach. I see it all.

Fighting a yawn, I reach down to rub Keena's cool nose. She whines and uncurls for a belly rub.

Dakota's as skittish as the dogs I train. She's a ball of nerves, struggling with trauma. The process with my PTSD dogs takes time. Love and care.

Dakota deserves the same.

I refuse to let her break.

I've reached for the darkness. I know what it looks

like when it reaches back. I don't want Dakota anywhere near that.

She healed me that summer. Which is why I'm determined to help her.

I won't fail her. Not again.

That fiery, stubborn woman's still in there. I have to find her. If she can't take care of herself right now, it's my job to do it.

So, I click through the links. Prenatal vitamins. Body pillow. Bras.

Shit.

One thought of Dakota's full breasts and I'm hard again.

Fuck.

I take a sip of whiskey, letting the sting drown out all thoughts of Dakota. Except it doesn't. All it does is push everything to the forefront of my mind.

I wish I had paid more attention to my mom and dad when they brought another baby home. The memory of changing diapers on Emmy Lou and Grady pops into my mind. Then another of me chasing them around the ranch. One minute threatening them if they didn't listen, another laughing as I hauled them over my shoulders and spun them around.

They're great memories. My family is outstanding. Like all my siblings, I've always wanted a big family, but being in the Marines, I figured it was never in my cards.

Home felt far away from me when I was overseas. Sometimes it still does.

My hand goes to my chest, rubbing at the building ache.

Christ. What the hell am I thinking? Getting too close. Too *in* this?

"Goddamn it," I mutter as I accidentally add two pregnancy journals to my cart.

"Sitting in the dark drinking?"

I glance up at the sound of Ford's voice. "Got nothing else to do."

"I set those wolf traps along the road and back near the woods."

"Good," I mumble. "Hope we scare him off and that's that."

"Yeah." Ford drops into a chair, kicks his boot up and raps the desk, causing Keena to bark. "How's Dakota doing?"

I press my lips together. "She's struggling. She's sad."

Ford hitches a broad shoulder. "Girls cry a lot when they're pregnant. Remember Emmy Lou?"

I rub my brow. "Not that kind of sad."

Ford cocks his head while evaluating me. "You sure you shouldn't be in the gym right now? Because you look like you need to beat the hell out of something."

"I'm fine," I growl.

I go to close the tab on the window, but not before my nosy fucking brother catches a glance of the screen.

Ford gives me a doubtful look. "She's having another guy's baby, man."

My teeth grate in irritation at the reminder. Especially since Ford's the town crier when it comes to relationships. "And your point?"

"My point is how do you feel about that?"

My breath is a harsh exhale. I can feel my skin. On edge. Itchy. "How do you think I fucking feel?"

The knee-jerk snap of anger hits Ford hard, and he arches a brow.

He leans forward, smearing his long fingers over his jaw. "It ain't your kid."

But it should be.

The thought pierces like a dagger.

Dakota having another man's child doesn't stop me from wanting her. I've loved her this long and I won't stop now.

"I don't have time for a relationship," I grunt.

"Good," Ford says and I bristle. "Because you shouldn't get involved with Dakota."

Our gazes clash. "Mind your own fucking business."

There's silence for a second.

Curiosity and worry war in the depths of Ford's amber eyes. "Why are you doin' this, D? Kindness of your heart?" He gives me a crooked grin. "We're gentlemen, but we're cowboys, too."

I glare at him. "Ford. I don't have time for this."

"Fine, you fuckin' lockbox. Keep that shit to yourself. Like always." His eyes meet mine, smug. "Come find me when you put her name on your boot."

I grunt. He doesn't need to know it's been there since the first time I met her. Dumb, horny Davis was an idiot. But he wasn't wrong.

With a weary sigh, my brother reaches into his pocket and uncaps a small bottle of pills. Reaching for the whiskey, he takes a swig and swallows a handful down.

I frown. "What're those?"

He wiggles his brows. "A stash, man."

I make a fist on the desk. Ford may act like the sunniest guy in the world, but years ago, my brother fought his own battles with anxiety and depression. They're either the good kind of pills, or the bad, but I can't get a clear look at the bottle to see.

I shake my head and loosen my jaw to say, "You're the last person who needs a stash."

Poking the past is a risk, but Ford doesn't take the bait.

"Secrets, man," Ford drawls, but his eyes are dim. "You got yours, I got mine."

"Don't fucking quote my own goddamn self to me, asshole."

It's what I told him and my brothers when I got home from the Marines and they asked about the bullet in my shoulder.

With a grin, Ford stands and heads to the door. He pauses on the threshold and nods at the computer. "If you're wondering, Dakota's a 36D."

"Christ." I glare at him. Ford's lifelong superpower is being able to guess a woman's bra size. "I'm going to pretend you didn't say that."

He cackles and disappears into the dark.

I stare out into the falling snow and the darkness that surrounds the ranch. Shadows crowd my head.

Dakota. My family. The ranch.

I can't afford weakness. Can't afford to fail.

Eyes on the security monitors, I reach for the whiskey and take a long, stinging gulp.

For the first time in a long time, I'm suddenly unsure about it all.

11

Dakota

A N ANGUISHED CRY PIERCES THE AIR.
I crack my bedroom door. Listen.
Another shout comes from Davis's room.

Softly, I pad down the hallway. When I reach the closed door, the whimpered moan that follows has my heart dropping.

After a second, I slip inside.

Davis, twisted in the sheets, cries out. I freeze. The sight's so familiar to me.

"No," he groans. Sweat streams down his face. His bare, muscled chest heaves. "Please."

Keena stands beside him. She whimpers, pawing at the side of the bed. A rumpled blanket lies on the floor.

I tiptoe into the room, aching for him. I know all about his nightmares. The suicide mission that killed Davis's team. The bullet he took that got him sent home.

One step, and then a second, and I'm by his bed.

Sitting beside him, I sweep a hand over his broad shoulder. Gently, I shake him. "Davis. Davis, wake up."

Silence. Keena stares daggers as she whirls herself into a frenzy near the open door.

And then Davis jerks so violently, I gasp.

He launches himself out of bed, stumbles, but I catch up with him, grabbing his shoulders. "Hey, Hotshot, hey."

Davis stands there, dazed, wounded. My heart tugs.

"It's okay." I should go. Instead, I wrap my arms around his trim waist. And it's the best idea I've ever had. "It's okay," I say, looking up at him.

"Dakota," he pants, leaning his forehead against mine. His big body heaves as he comes down from the nightmare. Our breath heats the space between us. His bare chest brushes my breasts and my stomach does a slow curl of warmth.

It's nice being held. Feeling safe.

It's been such a long time.

Then his massive, muscled body clenches. Davis pulls back, his handsome face twisted in horror. He looks down.

My wrist is locked tight in his grip.

I never even felt it.

He drops it like I'm on fire.

"You were having a nightmare." Worry clouds my voice. I hate that he still has them.

A ragged breath leaves him. "Christ, Dakota." His brown gold-flecked gaze burns. "I told you *never* to wake me up. I could have hurt you."

Both hands go to his hair as he takes a step backward. Away from me. It stings.

I stare him down. "You would never scare me, Davis. Loud noises, sure. Killer clowns, maybe." Stepping forward, I rest a hand on his tense chest. His heart rapid-fires. "But not you."

"Dakota." He palms my shoulders, and I wait for him to push me away.

"I'm not afraid of you, Davis." I tilt my chin up. "There is one man I fear in my life, and it's not you."

I know what he did overseas. I know who he killed. I know who he lost. And I am not afraid of him.

He swallows, guilt clouding his face.

I reach for him, but Keena intercepts, weaving her way through his legs, until Davis untangles from me to run a big hand over her fur.

"She hates me," I say as the dog keeps her I-will-kill-you eyes on my face.

"She's protective," Davis says, avoiding my gaze. But he snaps his fingers and points at the door. Keena, ears back, slinks into the hall.

I sit on the edge of his bed to take in his room. Davis is still as organized and as neat as he's always been. Nothing out of place. Stacks of records next to a Crosley. Tomorrow's clothes laid out on a bench. A police scanner, a Glock, and a CB radio crowd his nightstand. A small bar with whiskey and scotch against the wall. Three pairs of leather-worn boots all lined up in a row next to the door.

A small smile tips my lips, and I gesture at the boots. "You ready to run, Hotshot?"

"Sometimes it feels like it."

"I haven't unpacked." The admission's out before I can stop it. Shame edges my voice. "Just in case…"

With a sigh, Davis sits on the edge of the bed beside me, staring out the front window that overlooks the ranch. My heart breaks. He looks like a lost little boy. Vulnerable. A person I bet no one hardly ever sees. Except me.

"How often do you have nightmares?"

"Every night," he grunts, scraping a hand over his stubbled jaw.

"About Sully?"

Davis stands, leaving the bed for the bar. I watch how his gray sweatpants slip low on his hips, revealing the top curve of his muscular ass, the dips of his waist. He pours himself a golden finger of whiskey, and I note he didn't answer my question.

I wet my lips, trying to stop ogling him. "I have daymares, you know."

Maybe it's the darkness that fuels my confession. Maybe it's the safety of Davis's room, the cool rumble of his voice. "Right in broad daylight. My arm—I can still see it. Feel it. That snap of bone." I shiver, my voice becomes ethereal. It's my turn to be dazed. "I try so hard to get out of that kitchen. It's like a door I keep stepping through to find the right exit, only it doesn't lead out. It keeps leading back into that memory. That dream."

Davis sighs. "That's PTSD."

"Yeah," I breathe and rub a chill from my arms. "I know."

He pauses, towering over me to wrap a quilt around my shoulders.

All it takes is that quilt, the hit of his smell, and the memories come. Me on Davis's bed. His big fingers tangled in my hair, him swearing, working to unravel the mess, then kissing me, crossing that line, playing with fire, every weekend.

Unable to take the heat from the man hovering over me, I stand. The quilt slips from my shoulders, and I feel Davis's dark eyes follow me as I cross to the nightstand. I open the drawer, and there it is. Same lotion, same brand.

Then, like I've hit rewind, I return and rest a knee on the edge of the bed.

"Sit," I say.

Something in the night must be making me brave. Or foolish. Or horny.

A crease furrows his brow. "You don't have to do this."

"Sit and shut up, Hotshot."

He does.

I uncap the lotion. Then I touch him. His breath goes jagged as he sucks it in, and his body tenses, as if in the grip of another nightmare.

Under my hand, his muscles become clay. Become mine. I massage his arm. His bullet wound like a small, neat pebble. I can't stop my pulse from quickening. My eyes from tracking over his golden and muscular body.

Davis sits there, stiff and unmoving, fists resting on his thighs.

"Your scar looks good." I run my hand along his chiseled bicep, hating how much I love the feel of his solid muscles. "You took care of it."

He tilts his face up, and our gazes meet. That square jaw of his jumps. "You told me to."

Pink stains my cheeks and I'm grateful for the dark. "Bossing the boss man." A small smile ghosts my lips. "Never thought I'd see the day."

"Five siblings. I gotta be bossy."

"You ever stop growling and listen to them?"

His chuckle is gruff. "Think they'd die of shock."

"You listened to me today. Thank you. For grounding me." His gaze holds mine. "You made me feel like a better version of myself, if only for a few minutes."

"I don't know a bad version of you, Dakota," he says in that soft whiskey-soaked Georgia twang of his.

Angling for a better position, I cross in front of him. His knuckles graze my bare thighs. Just one brush and my entire body sparks.

Lust ignites under my skin like an ember.

I hate myself for how badly I want him. How long I have loved him.

"Did you ever tell Charlie your secret?" I ask, my finger lingering over his scar. "About why you really came home?" I've always wondered. It was such a selfless thing he did for his brother.

"No. That's for me to reckon with. Not Charlie." He scrubs a hand over his jaw, his expression wary. Determined. "Some things are better left unsaid."

"Maybe." Once again, I skim a hand over his arm. Restlessness claws beneath my skin. What would happen if I kissed him? Would he push me away with that stubborn heart of his? Would we go back to wishing on stars?

Stay strong. Don't you kiss him, Dakota. He let you go, he let you leave. There is nothing there.

Still, hormones and adrenaline have my body shaking.

After everything I've been through with Aiden, I still want Davis. All these years and the feeling hasn't faded. The men are as separate in my mind as apples and oranges. Good touch, bad touch. And it's been a damn long time since I've had good touch.

I wish Davis knew how long I've been all alone, missing him.

Tonight, I want to be kissed by a man who feels like home. I want comfort. I want Davis Montgomery.

Forcing away my restless thoughts, I rub in the remainder of the lotion, then flip the cap closed. "Still got it," I say with a wry smile. "Even one-handed."

"Your secrets." Davis's sudden growl eats up the dark. "I want them, Koty."

Secrets.

That was our game. How I got him to open up all

those years ago when he stomped into Resurrection shot up and scowling. A game I borrowed from when Fallon and I were kids. Late at night, we'd lie in bed and tell each other secrets. Mostly lies, some truths, but we'd come up with the craziest stories. Sometimes I still don't know fact from fiction.

"It's too late for secrets," I whisper.

He grabs my hand before I can step away. Wide-eyed, I watch as he rises to his feet like some massive sentry. This time, he looks at me dead on. His brown eyes blaze. "Tell me his name, Dakota."

"No," I refuse.

Never.

The muscle jerking in his jaw tells me he's pissed as hell. Still, I dig in my heels.

"He's a ghost. The day I left town, I forgot his name."

"Tell me his name," he demands again.

"No. The memory of him burned up in my bakery."

Just like my past. I have to salvage what I can from this wrecked life. It's the only way to explain it. I want to forget and never look back. Never speak his name again so I can shake the hold he has on me. Because it still hurts too much to confess everything.

The shame, the loathing I feel… I wouldn't wish it on anyone.

I flatten a hand over my stomach, stiffening at the foreign gesture. "My baby will never know him. And neither will anyone else. Let's keep it like that."

His face darkens.

It's not what this take-charge cowboy wants, but it's what he gets.

"Tell me," he says firmer this time, an order. My hand

still in his, he draws me forward. "It's important. To keep you safe."

"I'm safe here." *With you.*

"You're my responsibility."

Responsibility. It sounds so stale. So unwanted. Between Keena and Fallon's dismissal, it strikes a nerve.

"Stop saying that," I snap. "You make me feel like a piece of gum stuck to everyone's shoe that no one wants."

Davis flinches. "Fuck."

Hot, angry tears burn the backs of my eyes. Resentment. Regret.

Davis smears a hand down his square jaw, stands tall and exhales. "Let's get one thing straight. Here and now. You're no piece of gum. You're no burden. And you're not alone. Not anymore."

Not alone. My body fills with oxygen. Sunlight. For one brief minute, I can breathe again. For one brief moment, I believe.

"You'll get your life back, Dakota. I promise you."

A tear slips down my cheek. "It's easy for you to say that. You have control. You're not helpless."

There's a long silence before he responds. "I'm not as in control as you think I am."

"Why not?" I close the gap between us. Like that night at Eden, my hopeful heart pounds. "What do you want, Davis?"

He makes a choked sound in the back of his throat. "I want you to be safe, Dakota."

"I'm afraid." Another tear streaks down my cheek. "I don't want to be alone."

"You're not alone. You're with me." It's a promise. A daydream. A husky breath that threatens to take me down.

I close my eyes and slide my palm up his bare, muscled chest. Just a touch. An impulse. His big palms mold to my shoulders and I wait for his lips on mine, but Davis presses me back, away from him.

Again.

Davis stares at me, his broad chest heaving in the dim light, his face unreadable.

Embarrassment heats my cheeks.

Stupid, horny, pregnant Dakota.

A summer fling. That's all we were. He proved his point when he let me go six years ago.

It wasn't love.

I force a tight smile, my stomach in knots. "I should go."

Davis's mouth is a grim line, strain around his eyes. "Koty, wait—"

Before I can lose my nerve, I spin around and rush for the door, refusing to look back.

"Goodnight, Davis."

And thank you for being a perfect fucking gentleman.

I step into the hallway, my face aflame. Keena prowls near the stairs, and I frown at how unbelievably smug she looks.

When I'm halfway back to my room, I stop.

Fuck Davis Montgomery's walls.

I'm tired of keeping secrets. Tired of keeping my distance.

Heartbeat in my ears, I turn around and walk back to his room. I lift a hand to knock, but before I can, the door's ripped open.

"Dakota," Davis husks, bare chest heaving, muscles rippling.

I wet my lips. "I forgot something."

His throat works, his eyes running over my face, my body. "What's that?"

"Another secret."

"Tell me."

"I miss you," I say, right before cupping that handsome, tortured face in my hands and locking my lips to his.

12

Davis

DAKOTA'S KISS KEEPS BURNING ON MY LIPS LIKE a fire I can't put out.

My muscles scream as I hammer the punching bag. Movement's the only way to keep my mind off everything. "Goddamn it," I mutter, taking a swing that shakes the bag. I can feel the tension of the last three days falling away.

The gym behind the lodge is an old piece of barn we rehabbed. In its center, a punching bag, and off to the side, hay bales stacked for high jumps. Free weights litter the cement floor. It's shit for insulation—running hot as hell in the summer and ice cold in the winter, but it does the job. Gets me out of my head so I don't go insane.

I pause to re-tape my hands. A mistake. My mind goes to Dakota.

I rub a hand over my lips, still feeling her kiss. It was a hundred proof. And against all my bad judgment, I want another round.

After six long years, her sweet taste was heaven. A second chance I never thought I'd get again.

And it has to end now.

What the fuck was I thinking kissing Koty McGraw?

Sure, she kissed *me*. But I kissed her back.

Temptation was the devil on my shoulder, telling me to haul that woman into my room and strip her bare. Tear off those panties and paddle that pretty ass pink in punishment for coming to me while I was in the grips of a nightmare that could have hurt her. Spread those legs and taste every sweet inch of her. Instead, I stopped her. Stopped us. That flash of anger in her eyes almost had me regretting my decision. But she was gone before I could change my mind.

And a good thing too.

I wanted her too goddamn much.

The memory of her soft fingers sweeping over my scar—our heated, soul-baring words—kept me up for the rest of the night. Fuck, how I missed that. Missed *us*. Secrets. Late night confessions. If I have walls, Dakota's my bulldozer.

Forever breaking me down. Getting me to crack.

I only do that with her.

I miss you.

Those words fucked with my mind.

Have me questioning what we are. And it scares the hell out of me.

It's not the time to think about us or the stranglehold this woman has on my cock. It's time to think about her.

She's suffered so much and it feels like my fucking fault.

I never asked her to stay. I pushed her into the arms of some sick fuck who hurt her. If we cross lines and it ends badly, she'll leave, or worse, run. Christ, the thought of her taking off in the middle of the night has my blood pressure skyrocketing. The last thing I want to do is overstep. Her friendship's too important to me to lose that.

Maybe after all this is over, we can talk. I can clear up all the bullshit, say everything I should have said that summer, but…

It's anything but simple. She needs to heal. Focus on that baby.

And me, I have the ranch. With summer slowly approaching, it's going to take all of us to get it back up and running. The lodge needs a fresh coat of paint. The chateaus' need new floors. There're two horses Ford and I have to haul to Missoula. My loyalty is to my ranch, my brothers, and also the promise I made to Stede.

Protect Dakota.

Not fuck her.

The CB radio buzzes, and Wyatt's droll voice rings out on the channel I share with my brothers. "We got the Cupcake headed to the barn with the Fairy Tale."

A growl from Charlie.

I groan at my younger brother's attempt to play dispatcher. "Knock it off," I snap into the radio. "And stop calling her Cupcake. Christ."

That's my nickname.

Through the window, I watch Dakota follow Ruby out of the lodge. Her dark hair's peppered with snow, her jacket zipped tight around her belly.

I grin at my secret weapon.

Ruby.

I asked her to get Dakota out of the house this week, knowing it's impossible for anyone to say no to Ruby.

She needs sunshine, and Ruby and the Montana sky are the best remedies around.

I watch Dakota disappear around the corner, my heart aching.

You're not helpless. Dakota's words from last night float into my mind.

Which couldn't be further from the truth. When it comes to her, I *am* fucking helpless.

I avoided her question last night. My nightmares are no longer about my fucked-up mission. For the last two years, they've been about Koty. The phone call that won't go through. Me, screaming out to a girl who won't answer.

I wish she could see herself the way I see her. Beautiful. Strong. Smart. She has this, even if she doesn't know it, and I refuse to let her wallow. However long it takes to pull her from the shadows into the sun, I'll do it.

Wyatt's lazy drawl rings out. "You got a shit-ton of packages, D."

Gritting my teeth, I pick up the radio. "Where?"

"Bullshit Box."

After one last brutal punch, the bag groaning under the momentum, I aim my boots for the ranch. Keena barrels beside me, romping in the fresh coat of snow covering the ground, snapping at snowflakes.

The sight of the Runaway Ranch sign standing tall and proud in the distance resets my mood.

Charlie and Ford, both wearing Stetsons, load up a rusted Chevy with saddles to be repaired in town. They give me a wave and I hold up a hand. As much as I bark at them, working with my brothers is something I would never change.

I trek through the lodge's gravel lot and head up the deck steps to the Bullshit Box.

Before I can enter, Wyatt greets me at the door with a shit-eating grin. "Girl problems?"

"Wyatt." I close my eyes, not in the mood. "Tell me something productive or get the fuck out."

He gives me a salute. "Packages are on your desk."

It takes me fifteen minutes to unpack it all. I scan what I ordered.

A foam body pillow. Prenatal vitamins. Morning sickness pills, just in case. Bottles. So many types of goddamn bottles.

It's like a bomb of color and cheer has gone off in the Bullshit Box. I blink and look down at Keena, who cocks her head.

I have no idea what Dakota needs, so I got her everything and then some.

I slide a thin book toward me. On the front, in bright yellow script, it reads MY BABY.

I close my eyes for a long second, then open it. My chest feels tight as I reach into my desk drawer and pull out the sonogram photo Dakota gave me. I flatten a hand over a corner, straightening it, then clumsily attach it to the first page, under the words MY FIRST PHOTO.

The tick of my jaw pulses in time with my heartbeats as I stare at the black-and-white blur. I don't know why this is important, it just is.

Dakota needs this. Maybe not right now, but she will.

A flash of light has my gaze falling to Charlie's desk and an overseas priority shipment. One I've been expecting.

"Christ," I mutter, grabbing up the small, steel-looking package. "Idiots."

I break the security seal with a pocket knife to get into the Fort Knox-like box. It had been a gamble reaching out to Ferraro, but it looks like the bastard came through.

Pain lances through me as I stare at the tracking device in my palm, the words SullyScan1700 curving around its side. I exhale and force myself through it.

The tracker/panic button is about the size of a dime, but inside, it's loaded with military-grade software.

A rush of relief spears me. Dakota starts work next week, and I'm antsy as fuck knowing she'll be off the ranch. I need to anticipate everything. Plan for the worst. I can't cage Dakota. I won't.

Especially not after what she's been through.

So, this has to be the next best thing.

I hold the small tracker up to the light and chuckle.

She's gonna fucking hate me.

13

Dakota

DAMN DAVIS MONTGOMERY.

For the last week, baking supplies have appeared every morning. Like ghosts drifting out of the darkness to taunt me with the past.

Today, on the kitchen counter—a warm cup of coffee with sugar and cream. A small notepad. A beautiful ceramic pie plate. Bags of flour—almond and white. Jam and figs. Gold bricks of butter stacked in a pyramid shape.

Recipes weave through my mind. Beautiful, perfect pairings. Scones and jam. Cowboy cookies. Pain au chocolat.

Dares. Evil, delicious dares left behind by a cruel man named Davis Montgomery.

And it's working.

The fucking nerve of that man. He gives me the cold shoulder all week, only to do the sweetest things that make me want to break down and bawl.

And what did I do? Two days into my house arrest and I kissed him. And he tore away from me like I was on fire.

Now? Now he's avoiding me like a plague.

That Marine of iron willpower is a war manual that's hard to read. I'm tired of trying to understand him.

One thing is clear: Davis and I can never go back to the way I want us to.

I'm pregnant. A mess. A liability. A man like Davis is honor bound, duty driven.

I am a job. A favor to my father. A fling from the past. And the past stays in the past.

I press a hand to my heart as I scan the baking supplies once more. My fingers dance over the small notepad, reminiscent of the ones I used to write my recipes. I open the cheery yellow cover and stare at the blank page. A clean slate.

But what about me? Do I get a new start?

That girl who kissed Davis last week was the real Koty McGraw. All confidence and charisma. Someone not afraid of setting foot in a kitchen or taking a risk. Or kissing a cowboy.

Beyond the windows, the darkening sky is heavy with the threat of more snow. The hum of an engine reverberates in my bones as Davis's truck rattles over the gravel driveway. I stare at him for a long second, his black Stetson a shadow against the sun, then tear myself away from the window.

I drift from the island to the counter, frowning when I notice a large box. On the front, is a sticky note with my name. I smile at Davis's chicken scratch scribble. Then I open the box.

My smile disappears.

Inside:

Baby supplies. Prenatal vitamins. Nausea pills. Bottles. One of those happy baby books.

My eyes blur with tears as I stare at the baby book. I still haven't felt my baby move. Something's wrong with me. My baby knows it. Knows its mother is a basket case.

It's hiding just like I am.

Is this why Davis has been in the Bullshit Box for the last week? Ordering supplies for me? Leaving me granola bars around the house because I have low blood sugar? Taking care of me because I can't take care of myself? The thought is as touching as it is horrifying.

I've only been on my own for a week and I feel like I'm failing.

Although, I rallied long enough this morning to take a Zoom meeting with the insurance adjuster. It was hard, but I owned up to running. I told them I left the scene immediately and fled the state because I feared for my life due to my ex. They seemed to believe me, so now I wait for them to conclude their investigation and determine it's not fraud.

At least one thing in my life isn't a complete cluster.

Dutifully, numbly, I reach for the jar of prenatal vitamins. It feels like I'm going through the motions as I swallow one down. It sinks like a lead weight in my gut.

And then, the image creeps.

My entire body freezes.

Fire. Searing heat. Aiden screaming "help me" over and over again.

I ran. I let my bakery burn.

Coward. You fucking piece of pathetic shit.

I shake my head. Squeeze my eyes shut.

No. That's Aiden talking. Breaking me down. Not me.

The back door opens, and I sigh.

Like clockwork, Ruby peeks inside the kitchen, a sherpa hat with furry ear flaps on her head. Her blue eyes light up when she sees me.

"Hi, Dakota!" Ruby chirps. Her genuine, happy face

never ceases to amaze me. She's like the brightest lemon meringue I've ever made.

I force a smile. "Hi, Ruby."

"You want to walk to the pasture today?" she asks, like she's done every morning for the last week. A fact that makes me think Davis has put her up to this.

I very much do not want to walk to the pasture. I want to hibernate in bed for the rest of my life. But the baby in my belly won't let me. Neither will Ruby Montgomery.

Yesterday, we basked in the sun on the front porch. The day before, we met the horses.

I check the time and it's only eight. I'm due at the Corner Store at eleven to help Fallon with the afternoon shift.

Back to the land of the living.

After a week at the ranch, I crave work. Someplace to get away and feel normal. In my bakery, I was up early and down late. Perfecting recipes, negotiating with vendors, mentoring my sous chefs. To be stagnant and feel out of control messes with my mojo.

I can't hide out at the ranch forever. Besides, who's to say Aiden's even looking for me? He could have let it go.

Let me go.

Maybe what was left of us burned up in that fire.

But I know it's too easy.

Too easy for Aiden.

Too kind.

"C'mon," Ruby says, extending a hand. "Let's go for a walk and see how it goes."

See how it goes.

The thought calms me somehow, casting a golden glow

into my chest. Like I only need to put one foot in front of the other to move. It's that simple.

"Okay."

We head out onto the wraparound back deck and down the steps. The morning air is crisp, and sunlight streams through the trees. Ford and Wyatt, on their horses, whistle at us as they load up the horse trailer.

"Today we should see the garden."

I glance over at Ruby. "Garden?" I echo, casting a glance over the frozen earth. No garden has a chance of survival in this barren Montana wilderness.

At my look of confusion, Ruby laughs. "I'll show you."

She links an elbow through my good arm. Barely acquaintances for a week, but already, Ruby's a friend.

Our shoes crunch frozen grass until we come to a spot in the pasture near the Runaway Ranch gates.

"You're right." Ruby's light voice floats. "It's too early for a garden, but it's going to be right here. Sunflowers. They're my favorite." She sinks to the ground and tugs off a glove.

I sink beside her and watch as she scrapes back the snow with her mossy green manicure and digs down into the earth.

"Look," she says, her fingertips stained black. In the dirt, small buds of green grow beneath the melted snow. "Baby blooms."

"Can they grow in the dark?" I ask.

"No." She smiles. "But no matter how dark it is, they always find light."

My heart twists as I study the ground, tracing a finger over the small green buds.

Then we stand.

"Keep going?" Ruby asks.

A wave of dizziness washes over me. I forgot to eat, and I can feel the prenatal vitamin sitting in my stomach like a brick. Still, I force a smile and say, "Sure."

"You run the social media at the ranch?" I ask as we continue our walk.

She nods, glancing down to study my belly. "For now. I want to open a flower shop on Main Street."

I can't hide my surprise. "In Resurrection?"

"There's a shop across from the antique store," she says. "It would be perfect." She gives a little shrug. "Charlie and I are just waiting."

"For what?"

"For my heart. I have a heart condition. But I had a surgery last year that's helped a lot. Now we have the ranch and…" Her light blue eyes fall to my belly, a sadness dimming them. "And other stuff to deal with."

Silence as we walk.

"You own a bakery."

I shake my head. My heart hammers. "Used to."

Every award I earned for Milk & Honey pops into my head. Pastry Chef of the Year. Best New Bakery in DC— twice over. My creations pushed the envelope, and I was the best in the business.

But I don't say any of that.

We continue walking, our breath puffing white as we pass the lodge. We circle behind it and come to a thick grove of fir trees bordering the national forest. It's like a protective barricade around the ranch. A solid iron fortress of frozen wild.

My breath catches. "It's beautiful."

"It is." Ruby smiles brightly and spreads her arms. "It's a woodsy witch winter."

A laugh bursts out of my mouth, surprising me. "Followed by cynical spring and sad girl summer."

We share another laugh, and the smile that curls my lips, along with the warm rumble in my chest, is a strange but not unpleasant sensation.

A sharp bark cuts the serenity of the morning, and we look over.

Davis is tossing Keena a ball, his flannel shirt jacket pushed up to his rippling forearms.

He gives me a nod.

A nod so perfectly platonic I want to scream.

I squeeze my eyes shut. Exhale. Open them.

As I stare into the desolate forest, the hair on the back of my neck stands up.

Aiden.

He could be anywhere.

Fear crawls up my spine. What would he do if he learned about the baby?

I shiver.

He'd kill me.

He'd kill us.

That's when I see the wolf.

The animal darts between the trees. A flick of a white-tipped tail, the snuffle of a gray snout.

Ruby gasps, gripping my hand in hers.

I've never seen one up close before. My father used to tell me stories about wolves. Folklore that he learned from a Cheyenne chief when he lived in Wyoming in his twenties. The duality of their meanings always stayed with me. A symbol of destruction and death? A primal reminder of our wild? Or a powerful guiding force?

The wolf strides closer. Five feet away.

I tense and watch. Searching for food, she weaves her way between two downed logs, cunningly avoiding the trap that's been laid out.

My heart hammers in my chest.

She's frolicking. Free. Brave.

My eyes flood.

Everything I'm not.

Blinking back tears, I stare up at the vastness of the gray Montana sky. Overwhelming hopelessness creeps over me. I try to suck in air, but I can't.

Oh god. My lungs are swampy. Like there's too much oxygen. Like there's not enough.

The world spins. Tunnels.

Ruby's hand leaves mine. She calls for someone, her voice crawling beneath my skin.

I see the cowboy hat, the mirage of a man, a marine, striding my way.

My legs give out, but I don't fall.

"I got you," rumbles Davis's deep voice.

And then I'm in his arms, against his solid chest and being carried. My eyes fall closed and I hold on to him. He smells so damn good. Of earth and coffee and wood. Like a cowboy. Like heaven.

"Talk to me, Koty." The crunch of snow and leaves beneath his boots. His voice sounds urgent.

"I'm okay."

"Need more than that, Cupcake."

"There was a wolf."

"Yeah." Unnaturally quiet. "There was a wolf, Dakota."

"You won't kill her, will you?"

"How do you know it's a female?"

"I just know."

"No," he says finally. "We won't hurt her."

"Good," I whisper, tipping my forehead to his chest.

Then we're in the lodge. Davis sets me on the couch and crouches in front of me. He tips my chin and clocks my pupils. I lean into his touch, but just as I do, he stands.

I frown. "What're you doing?"

"Food," he says, stomping across the room. I swear the man's all broody angst and muscles.

He enters the kitchen, and I sigh, following him. "I have to get ready for my shift."

"You have to eat," he snaps, grabbing a bowl of eggs from the fridge. He sounds exasperated. "Low blood sugar, remember? You aren't taking care of yourself. You're goddamn pregnant, Dakota."

I huff a dry laugh. How is it he remembers things about my pregnancy even I don't? Warmth curls in my core as he stands at the kitchen counter with the tight sleeves of his jacket shoved up to expose massive forearms. The thick veins in his hands are like a road map for my lust.

I watch as Davis reaches into the basket of eggs, a deep furrow of a frown on his face. His big fingers clumsily smash eggs against the side of a bowl. Shards of shell scatter across the counter.

I can't take the massacre of the eggs anymore.

"Let me do it," I say, going to his side. When he doesn't move from the bowl, I shove his brick of a bicep. It's like trying to budge a boulder. "Davis. Move."

He ignores me, lost in his own world, or fuming, and cracks another egg with violent intensity.

I scan the baking and baby items on the counter. Everything crashes into me. Desperate anger I can't ignore.

Frustration. The man's a walking contradiction. Staying away, yet giving me everything I need.

All of my life, I've done it myself. If I let Davis help me, I'm just getting myself into another situation where I depend on a man. What happens when I leave the ranch? When we both move on with our lives?

Losing everything a second time—I can't handle that. Fucking up my life twice isn't an option. I don't have the strength to do it all over again. I don't have dreams anymore.

I have reality.

And Davis Montgomery is not a part of that.

I square my shoulders and lift my chin. "Stop." I drill a finger into his chest.

He rests his hand on the counter. "Stop, what?" he asks, his tone neutral.

"Stop calling me Cupcake and stop leaving me baking and baby supplies." I pace the room and stop to glare at him. "Stop trying to fix me." I flip open the baby book and point at the sonogram picture. "Stop doing shit like this. Stop being *nice*."

His head whips to me. "Someone has to," he growls. "Be nice to you."

"You might be protecting me, but you're not my mental-health or happiness keeper. Do you understand me?"

Slowly, he turns. His body tight and coiled. Then he storms toward me. He cages me against the fridge, my feet touching the tips of his. My senses come alive. Every part of Davis pressed against me feels right.

He looms over me, his chest heaving like a bull. "I know what you're fighting, Dakota. I know what's inside that head of yours. I know what you're running from. But I'm not walking away."

My whole body's vibrating, and his words just shake it even more. "Why?"

"You had to be a fighter for a goddamn long time. You had no choice. Now, you have a choice. Let someone take care of you."

It slips out of my mouth. "Then take care of me." I tip my head back to look at him, arch my body into his.

Davis's hands return to his sides. "We can't do this."

"Why? Because you're so honorable? Because of duty?"

He dips his head, his breath warm in the space between us. "Because the last thing you need is a man pawing at you."

"I wish you would paw at me," I whisper. Honesty's boiling inside of me.

"Dakota." My name falls strangled from his lips.

"You won't even look at me. You won't touch me."

"Touch you is all I've fucking wanted to do since you've been back," he grits out. "But how can I, Koty?"

My lips part. His confession warms every part of my soul. "You can, Davis. But you don't care about me."

An agonized sound rumbles in his throat. "You're wrong there, Dakota. Especially about that."

"Then prove it."

Davis roams broad hands up my body. They linger on my waist, gripping it tight. "This is a bad idea," he husks, gaze blazing.

I grip the hem of his shirt, refusing to let him loose. "It's the best idea."

His eyes close. "When you argue with me, Cupcake, it turns me on. Something fierce."

"Bossin' the boss man."

He leans in, and his hips press me back against the fridge. The muscle of his square jaw pulses as his voice drops to a low growl. "What if I fucked you right here, right now? Spread your legs, yanked those pretty panties aside, and bent you over the kitchen counter."

A tremulous breath escapes me. My sex dampens. My chest heaves. It's all I can do not to whine my approval. I need it. Every atom in my hormone-addled pregnant body craves Davis Montgomery.

"Got news for you, Hotshot," I whisper. "I'm not wearing panties."

He hisses a breath. Desire darkens his face. A big flinger slides into my waistband, all calloused and rough, when we both hear it.

The creak of a door.

A violent burst of barking comes from Keena.

I jump and Davis goes rigid. The change is stunning. Man to machine. His hand goes to his hip, on the gun he keeps there.

I freeze. My eyes dart to the main room.

No.

Footsteps.

Keena's savage barks echo through the silent lodge.

"Who is it?" I ask in a whisper. A feeling of complete blind panic crashes in on me. My heart's a hummingbird trapped in my chest.

"Cupcake," Davis whispers, pressing me back against the fridge. His body becomes a brick wall between me and the intruder. He reaches for the gun on his hip as his lips move against the cool shell of my ear. "Don't fucking move."

14

Davis

" **C**ALL OFF YOUR GODDAMN DOG, DAVIS."

"Fuck." I give a sharp whistle, and Keena quiets, but still paces the floor. My heartbeat hammers in my ears.

Of course, it's a brother. It's always a brother. Giving me grief. Spiking my blood pressure. Cock-blocking my goddamn dick.

Charlie steps into the kitchen, covered in mud and snow, and I can't decide whether to shake his hand or shake the shit out of him. Two minutes ago, I was this close to kissing Dakota. This close to fitting her curves perfectly beneath my palms and fucking her in my kitchen. Maybe he ruined the best thing that could have happened. Maybe he saved my goddamn ass. Either way, it's a chance I won't get back.

"Everything okay?" Charlie asks, his amused eyes bouncing between me and Dakota.

"No," I growl, holstering my Glock. "It's not fucking okay. I could have shot you."

I glare down at Keena, pissed off at the way she flew off the handle over someone she sees every damn day of her life.

Charlie grins. "Payback."

My gaze stays locked on my brother as the memory

of that long-ago hunt passes between us. "What do you want, Charlie?"

"I wanted to talk to Dakota." His eyes move over my shoulder. "A favor."

I bristle.

A soft voice floats. "Down, boy."

I tense as Dakota grabs my bicep and comes out from behind me. The soft sway of her hips, all that tousled dark hair, those pretty flushed cheeks...

The gorgeous sight of her shoots straight to my groin. *Fuck.* I adjust my dick and turn into the counter.

"What do you need, Charlie?" Dakota asks, as she leans back against the island.

"Ruby's birthday is in May," Charlie says. "Seeing as you're in town and all, I was wondering if..." He trails off, his face unnaturally serious even for him.

Dakota smiles. "You want me to make her a cake, Charlie?"

"Yeah," he grunts.

Dakota's eyes flit to mine. "You put him up to this?"

"No." I harden my jaw and glare at Charlie. "She isn't up for it." Annoyance prickles. No matter how much tough love I give Dakota, I don't want her to feel pressured by anyone to get back before she's ready.

"It's okay, Hotshot." Dakota places a palm on my chest. That raging shadow inside of me quiets. "What's her favorite cake?" she asks Charlie.

"Carrot," he says. I have to smother a smile at the goofy grin that creeps over my brother's face. "Cream cheese frosting."

Dakota nods. "A girl after my own heart."

Something flickers in her eyes. Fear. Longing. But she anchors herself. Cloaks herself in steel and determination.

"I can do that," she says after a deep breath. "My cast will be off by then. And I'll make her the best damn carrot cake she's ever had in her life."

Charlie gives her a gruff nod. "I appreciate it." His eyes move to me. "Headed into town. Need anything?"

I cross my arms. "Be there myself shortly."

Charlie gives another look to both me and Dakota before slipping out of the kitchen and leaving us alone.

The forgotten bowl of eggs reminds me I was trying to feed Dakota, not fuck her.

I rest my palm on the counter. "Big promise. Are you sure?"

"No." Her big brown eyes sweep across my face, then the kitchen. "But I think I need big promises."

"Thank you," I tell her. "This birthday is important." At her quizzical expression, I go on. "Ruby has a heart condition."

"She told me."

"But that's not all." I scrape a hand through my hair. "Last year…her heart stopped, and she died on the ranch."

Dakota's hand flies to her mouth. "Oh my god."

"We got her back, but Charlie—he almost lost her." I swallow hard. "We owe her the ranch. We owe her our brother."

"She'll have the best cake, Davis. I'll make sure of it." She heaves a sigh, her fingers curling around the dog tag she wears around her neck. "Now here's to hoping I can bounce back."

I go to her, hating the sad look on her face. "You'll bounce back."

"I haven't baked since I broke my arm."

"He," I correct, my lips curling in a snarl. "He broke your arm."

Her eyes fill with tears. My chest tightens at the sight. "I shouldn't have said what I said to you. To stop doing nice things." She gestures at the baby book. "I like the photo, Davis. I do."

I clear my throat. "I thought you'd want it one day."

She lets out a weak laugh. "I hope so."

"Listen. I know you think I don't care, Dakota, but I do." I tuck her hair behind her ear. Her eyes flutter at the contact. "I care too damn fucking much."

She might not like me anymore after this, but it's a chance I'm willing to take.

With that, I reach into my pocket and pull out the SullyScan1700. I show her the small button perched on my palm.

She blinks. "What's this?"

"It's a tracker. It pairs with my phone, so I always have your GPS location." I affix the tracker to the back of the dog tag. It's small enough to be hidden. "One push and I'll be there. You hear me, Cupcake? I'll be by your side."

She stays silent—or stubborn—and I lean in. "I care, Koty, and never say I don't."

Dakota's face softens. She glances down, analyzing the tracker. "Looks expensive."

I grunt. "Don't worry about it."

Mischief flickers in her dark eyes. Her full lips curve gently. "What if I push it?"

A frustrated growl rises in my throat. "Dammit, Dakota. Don't push me. I can't do my job if I'm worried that you're not safe."

"Your job," she repeats, gaze locked and loaded on my face.

The question heats the space between us, causing my heart to flail madly. "Yes, my job."

It doesn't matter that it means more than that.

It can't.

15

Dakota

FALLON SCOWLS THE MINUTE I STEP INTO THE corner store.

"Davis dropped the leash?" she asks snidely. She's in a worn jean jacket, her long caramel hair in a fat fishtail braid. She looks frazzled and annoyed and entirely too beautiful.

I sigh and tuck my purse under the front counter, shaking off the chill of the winter wind. After a second thought, I keep my parka on. My stomach being the talk of the town is not on today's agenda. "He's parked at the station. He gave me this."

Grudgingly, I show her the tracker.

Amusement dances in her hazel eyes. "Looks fancy. Better not lose it, or you'll have to deal with your babysitter."

Babysitter.

I don't like it either, but it looks like I'm stuck with it. And Davis.

Turning the dog tag between my fingers, I glance down at the tracker. Its red light pulses like a heartbeat.

A thousand emotions run through my veins.

Davis cares.

I felt the hard heat of him pressed up against me. Growling filthy words in my ear that only turned me on even more. He's a stubborn man. I'll give him that. But he's the best man I have ever known. The tracker's a reminder that I am safe. That Davis and Aiden are completely different species.

Aiden would find me because he wanted to hurt me. Davis wants to find me to protect me. There's a difference. One I should have realized from the beginning.

Aiden was never one to take no. He asked me repeatedly for a date when I refused the first time. Waited for me after my shift to bring me flowers. At the time, I thought his persistence was charming. A beautiful man with money who looked like he stepped off the pages of a magazine. Bright white teeth. Tailored clothes. In his perfection, he hid his red flags like bodies. I blinded myself to what was right in front of me until it was too late.

The anxious knot in my gut swells. *Aiden.*

Goosebumps pepper my skin. I remind myself Davis is parked across the street at the sheriff's department. The scare today already scrambled my brain enough. It was only Charlie, but it showed me how much I need to relax.

Although, I don't know what I was thinking when I agreed to Ruby's cake. It was like a dare. I couldn't say no, and now all I feel is panic.

Fallon, wiping down the deli case, says, "Face looks better."

"Not so busted?" I ask and she looks away, avoiding my eyes.

I glance around the store, itching to do something. Then, remembering Fallon's cold shoulder when I offered to help our father, I ask, "What can I do?"

If I have to walk on thin ice to get back to my sister, so be it.

"Stock the shelves." Straightening up, Fallon's gaze falls to my arm. "Think you can handle that?"

"I dressed myself one-handed, think I can fill a cooler."

"Well, get on it, smart-ass," she says dryly.

I make my way to the storage room and grab a cart filled with soda cans and cracker boxes. I push it down the aisles to stock the shelves.

My memory banks swim, high on nostalgia.

The vibe of The Corner Store is a cross between a cowboy bodega and a saloon. It's been in our family for four generations of McGraws. Tucked away in an ancient brick building, it hugs a street corner on downtown Main Street. It operated as a bootlegging still, a mercantile, and then a bank, before becoming the Corner Store. The tin ceiling still bears bullet holes in honor of its wild past.

Nothing's changed. It smells like pastrami, dark dirt earth from bait and tackle, and tobacco. The scene of my wayward youth. Sweeping floors and stealing candy bars with Fallon. Playing tag in the aisles when it was slow. Writing recipes on notepads while Fallon read those cowgirl books she obsessed over.

I peer over the edge of a shelf. Fallon's sharpening a knife at the front counter.

"How long have you been working here?" I ask, remembering what Davis told me. I want to hear more of her story.

"Since you left." Her tone's neutral, but her eyes flame.

I flinch. "But the rodeo—"

She keeps her gaze on the knife. "Dad gets someone to fill in when I'm gone. As long as I'm riding, he's good. Then I come back after the season."

Silence stretches through the corner store and I bite my lip.

I've never seen my sister so still. Calm and order doesn't suit Fallon.

She was born wild. She's a cowgirl. No one and nothing can rope her. Every weekend she was in the field, skinned knees, no tears. She accompanied our father to auctions, while I filled my notebooks with recipes and perfected my take on cinnamon rolls and croissants. Cooking was therapy. It's always been my out. A way to make me different from my sister. A way to take me away from Resurrection.

A wave of guilt sweeps me up.

Going after *my* hopes and dreams tanked my sister's.

I thought by putting culinary school on hold until I was twenty-five that Fallon would be okay.

But she isn't.

The rodeo is Fallon's life. Not the store. It should never have been like this.

Just one more thing I've made a mess of.

"And you'll keep working here until…?" I ask, tilting my head, wanting to drag an answer out of her.

"Why do you care? Not like you'll be around anyway," she says dryly.

Ouch. Fallon: 1, Dakota: 0

I sigh and go back to the shelves.

We work together in silence for the rest of the afternoon. I avoid the kitchen, preferring to refill coolers with beer and soft drinks. We barely get any customers. Most come for the food—our signature pastrami and fries. But the store stays empty.

"It's slow," I venture, wedging a can of Dinty Moore Beef Stew behind another. My attention drifts to a muted *Dateline* episode playing on the corner TV of the dining area.

Beside me, Fallon lets out a slow, withering sigh. Like conversation is slowly pulling at the threads of her sanity.

"It's the off-season."

I give her a look. "More than that."

Fallon smashes a pack of cigarettes onto the shelf behind the register. "We're a mom-and-pop place at the end of the damn block, Dakota. No one cares about us. Locals go to Billings to stock up at Costco. And now there's the Little Prairie Market just off of Main."

I perk up. "What's that?"

"Some fancy indie grocery store from Colorado. Opened in January." Her nose wrinkles in disgust. "They have a little bit of everything. Clothes. Natural foods. You'd think the World's Fair came to town."

I laugh.

A hitch of her slender shoulder. "We're small potatoes. We have all-day pastrami—Dad's recipe. And breakfast. That's probably all that'll save us."

Then why. Why are we still here? I want to ask. But I know the answer. It's all over my sister's face. Guilt.

Fallon's a good girl, a good daughter. She won't leave like our mother did.

I turn to her. "Do you ever think about talking to Dad about closing it?"

The look she gives me could burn fire. "Closing it would end our father."

"I know," I say, feeling chided.

Thoughts spin through my head. I hate the unknown. The ingrained need to game-plan and fix has always been a constant cycle inside of me.

The soft jingle of the door chimes has both of us looking up.

A man about the same age as my father enters the store. He booms a hello.

"You wanted a customer," Fallon says wryly. "You got him."

I smile at the familiar voice. Waylon Wiggins, the local American Legion president and owner of the world-record-setting buck displayed at the Cabela's in Billings, waddles down the aisle to the register. Tall and heavyset, he sports a salt-and-pepper beard and a laugh as big as his belly.

"Wouldn't believe it if I didn't see it with my own two eyes. Little Koty McGraw, come home to roost."

"Everyone's coming to see the runaway girl," Fallon mutters under her breath.

"Here I am," I say, ignoring the sting of my sister's words. "In the flesh."

"You finally come home to help your daddy?" Waylon booms as he bellies up to the register.

I fight a groan. Even the compliments are backhanded insults.

"Something like that." I move behind the counter to avoid his weighted stare.

"You miss Resurrection?" he asks, scanning the shelf to his left.

"Oh, yeah," I shoot back. "Go Bobcats."

Waylon adjusts his suspenders, sucks at the chew tucked in his corner cheek. Then he swivels a fat finger between me and Fallon. "Now, isn't that a sight to see? McGraw sisters back together. Pretty peas in a pod."

Fallon rolls her eyes and disappears into the kitchen.

"How about that bakery of yours? Daddy's pretty proud of you."

Everything inside of me wilts. The last thing I want to talk about is my bakery.

Still, I give the man what he wants. A cheerful smile, a

voice that reflects excitement. Grown up, successful Dakota McGraw. A woman who's come home to help her father. Not a woman on the run from an abusive asshole who knocked her up and broke her arm. A woman with passion, a woman who got out and is still going places.

"He's told me. Thanks, Waylon."

"He said you make huckleberry pies that make the world stand still." Waylon lurches his large frame to peer behind me. "Ain't got any 'round here, have you?"

I chuckle. "Nope. No pies." Time for a subject change that doesn't involve me. "What can I get you?"

"Pack of Copenhagen." He grins down at me. "And toss in a lotto ticket for good luck. And these."

I flinch when he throws a bag of old-fashioned cinnamon barrels on the counter.

Aiden's favorite. Especially when he was angry. He'd put one in his mouth and suck on it, considering all the ways he could hurt me. Like some sick, fucking waterboarding torment. I hated the sound. I kept hoping he'd choke to death, but no such luck.

"You got it," I say, turning away to the back shelves. Quickly, I make sure my CULINARY INSTITUTE OF AMERICA hoodie is loose around my belly. No one in Resurrection knows my business, and I want to keep it that way. Until…

Until what?

Until I make a clean getaway?

Until I figure out what I want to do with my mess of a life?

My back to Waylon, I pinch my eyes shut and try to breathe like a woman who isn't having a mid-life crisis in her early thirties. The urge to give in and palm my stomach, to keep it protected, is a hollow ache in my chest. And yet, I don't touch it.

I don't deserve this little baby and it sure as hell deserves better than me.

"Koty?"

I jump at the boom of Waylon's voice and spin around. "Sorry. One pack or two?"

"Two. But don't tell my wife."

Waylon and I both look over when the door chimes.

Waylon's jowls quiver as his smirk widens. "Well, if it isn't the Wild Witch of West Street."

Amusement and dread grips my chest. Clea Lou Bauer, and her bouffant red hair, hustles through the aisles. She's a local busybody who hosts Monday night book clubs at the library as a secret front for a neighborhood watch program.

I needle my temple. Cast eyes at the sheriff's department across the street. What I wouldn't give for Davis to come charging in and muscle me out the back exit.

But he can't rescue me every time I need him.

I have to do it myself.

"Dakota McGraw, I'll be good and goddamned!" the shrill voice screeches. I force a smile. "What are you doing home? Oh, lord, honey, what happened to your arm?"

Life, I think and inhale a steeling breath as Clea bulldozes my way. *Get it the fuck back together.*

One day, I'll look back at all this and laugh. I truly will, but right now, it's hard to believe that I'll ever fit back into Resurrection, Montana.

Home suddenly seems very far from where I long to be.

16

Davis

SLIPPING IN THROUGH THE SIDE DOOR OF THE
Resurrection Sheriff Department, I glare at the box
of donuts on the station desk and the cops gathered
around them. Doesn't do a thing for our damn image.

"Should be in the break room," I mutter, passing them
by.

"Morning, Montgomery."

"Move," I growl, leveling a finger at Topper, who blocks
the path to my desk. This vantage point gives me a direct
line of sight into The Corner Store. If Dakota leaves the
building, I'll see her. Anyone coming and going, I'll be
ready.

Leaving her alone today fucks with my nerves. She
looked fragile when I dropped her off this afternoon. I'm
not convinced she's safe outside the walls of the ranch. A
fact that renders me utterly fucking helpless. The feeling
is like hot acid in my bloodstream.

Shrugging off my jacket, I settle in at my unofficial
desk. I'm not a cop, but I like having one ear on the hap-
penings of Resurrection. Better to be prepared.

A photo of my nieces sits next to a screwdriver, a
busted old police-beacon light, and a thick stack of folders. I grab up the folders and start sorting them according to the case type. Least I can do is help out around the
station when I can.

"Did you hear?" Topper asks, picking up a donut dusted in powdered sugar. "Gary Custer ran the stop sign at the Shawnee bypass. Slick as snot outside and he started sliding. Mick Anderson tried to miss him but…" Topper chuckles. "He gunned the gas instead of hitting the brakes. Drunk as a skunk."

Small town gossip means nothing to me, yet I glance back into the hallway at the jail cell use to lock up drunks from the bars on Main Street. In the off-season, our tiny force tends to mostly deal with local drunks and car accidents. "When did you turn him loose?"

Topper shrugs. "Never locked him up."

I shake my head at the miscarriage of justice. Topper's an idiot.

At the squeak of boots, I rotate in my chair. "Need a favor," I tell Richter, who's on his way out.

"Fill out a form."

"I need a tail on Koty McGraw."

It's shitty and shady, sending someone else to watch out for her, but I need all eyes on her. No chances. No surprises. Not with Dakota.

"Tailing Koty McGraw?" Richter chuckles, his brown eyes drifting to The Corner Store. "What'd that girl do?"

A chuckle from Topper. "Girl's got you twisted up, Montgomery."

I grit my teeth, resisting the urge to grab the box of donuts and smash it in his fucking face. "Did I ask for your opinion, Topper?"

My dark scowl has Topper blanching.

A smile twitches Richter's mustache. He nods. "Fill out the form. We'll get it done."

"Think you can spare the manpower?" I ask dryly,

arching a brow in the direction of the donut-devouring deputies.

"Alright, point taken, Montgomery." Richter blasts a warning at Topper before drilling a finger at me. "Paperwork."

I grunt, swallowing down my objections. Paperwork will be the death of me. Although, if it's this or running referee between the McGraw sisters, I'd take paperwork any day of the week.

Once again, my gaze drifts to The Corner Store.

The woman makes me insane. Dakota trying to charm her way into one little kiss. The flash of fire in her eyes as she goaded me to touch her. Christ, if she knew what I wanted to do to her, she'd think better of it.

You don't care about me. Dakota's sad voice echoes in my head.

Her thinking I don't want her makes me feel like a fucking piece of shit.

She's wrong.

Because, hell, I've done some scary things in my life, but protecting Dakota fucks with the beat of my heart. If anything happens to her on my watch…

I sigh and drag a hand down the stubble grating my jaw.

The military taught me preparation and calm, but nothing could have prepared me for just how on edge I am. Ever since Koty McGraw sweet-talked her way into my life all those years ago, I've been on edge.

Shoving aside the earlier events of this morning, I fill out the fucking paperwork, leave it on my desk for Richter to sign, and log Cassie's missing persons case into the database. After I check Dakota's tracker, making sure it's working correctly and paired with my phone, I pull up the baby app I've downloaded.

I cast an eye around the office.

Christ, if anyone sees this…

Dakota's twenty weeks today. Her baby is the size of a banana. The fruit comparison makes me chuckle as I scroll through the bright, cartoon images.

It's not my right to get involved. But a little voice inside my head tells me I'm already involved. I couldn't get out if I tried.

By the time I hit the end of the article, the chair in front of my desk screeches across the floor. My lanky little brother drops into it with a huff and swipes the beacon from my desk, turning it over in his hands like a melon.

I place my phone face down on the desk and ignore the eyebrow raise Deputy Parker is currently giving me. "What do you want, Wyatt?"

"Need to report a crime."

I shuffle a few papers around, down the remainder of my cold coffee. At this point, it's basically a race to see whether it's a Dakota or a Wyatt aneurysm that finishes me off first. "Not my circus. Take it up with Topper."

"Theft of my childhood. The night a big brother of mine left me sleeping out in the field."

My head jerks up and I scowl. "That was over twenty years ago."

"Yeah, well, what is time?"

"And I told you that wasn't me. That was Ford." I stretch a hand over my eyes to rub at my temples. Kid still drives me crazy, even at thirty-three years old. "What do you want?" I sound like a broken record.

"We're stocking up on supplies to reno the ranch.

Not like you'd know much about it, seeing as how you're preoccupied."

"I'm busy, but it's my ranch too," I bark, rolling out my shoulders. It pisses me off that my little brother thinks I've let my responsibilities slack. But most of all it pisses me off that he's right. That Dakota's safety usurps any of my concerns about the ranch.

"And why do you need me for this? Ask Charlie."

"Can't. Left Charlie at the hardware store. Lost Ruby in the antique store."

No surprise. My family storming around Resurrection like a wild pack of marauders.

Wyatt folds his hands together, his face growing serious. "That cabin up at Eden—we bulldozing it or what?"

Eden is a property in a hard-to-find area behind Runaway Ranch. While we use the cabin as a bunkhouse for groups or fishing excursions, it's set back in the high forest. The only two access routes are a forty-five-minute drive over Dead Fred's Curve or the shortcut behind the lodge up the old hiking trail.

It's also the spot where Dakota and I started and ended.

Something soft burrows its way into my heart. Bulldozing memories to make room for one more building doesn't sit right with me.

"Not sure yet," I say gruffly. "Let me think about it."

Wyatt shrugs. "If you want, I can handle it."

I eye him shrewdly. "I don't want another chicken shed fiasco."

"What the fuck are you talking about?"

"When you blew up that building. What the fuck do

you think I'm talking about?" I rub my brow at the memory. "Christ."

Wyatt sits up in his seat, eagle eyes snagging on the folder. "Puttin' a tail on Dakota?"

Goddamn it.

I grab up the folder, hit him with it. "Shut up."

He cackles out a laugh, making my blood pressure rise, then sticks the screw driver into the beacon and pops off the battery cap.

"Think I could get one on Fallon? Girl keeps skippin' practice." Though his demeanor is easy, his voice holds a tight strain of tension.

"Ain't skippin' practice," I tell him. Across the street I watch old Waylon Wiggins enter the store. I hope Koty isn't getting put through the small-town third degree. "She's just skippin' yours."

Wyatt's head jerks up so fast I can't be sure he didn't get whiplash. "The fuck. With who?"

It's a big brother asshole move, but if it gets him off my back about Dakota, I'll pull the low blow.

"Not sure," I say, sliding my laptop toward me and opening a case file. "She's acting cagey about it. Don't think Stede knows, so keep it on the down low. Guy doesn't need any more stress."

Wyatt's head tips back to look at me, a sudden storm in his eyes. "I don't know what the hell that girl thinks she's doing," he grumbles. "She's gotta ride in the rough stock days, and she's gonna be out of shape. And when she comes crawling back next year, I'm gonna have a hell of a time whipping her ass into gear."

I snort, side-eyeing him.

Wyatt and Fallon's petty rivalry might fool all of

Resurrection, but they can't fool me. I've been the fucking idiot keeping his mouth shut. I know where it got me, and if Wyatt continues down this stubborn path of denial, I know where it'll get him.

Absolutely nothing.

Wyatt fidgets in his chair. "How can you sit here, man? Makes me itch."

I rasp out a laugh, seeing that little rough and tumble ten-year-old I used to boss around on the ranch back in Georgia. "Patience, brother. It's called patience."

Wyatt has to be constantly on the move, on the back of a horse knocking his front teeth out or training his cowboys, but for me, the quiet, watchful chase is in my blood.

Stakeouts don't bother me. Whether it's taking up post in the dusty desert or in a small-town police station, the objective is always the same—to serve and protect.

This time, it's someone I care about. The mission can't go wrong. Not like the last time.

The void in my stomach opens. My jaw tightens. Shame flickers.

I'm alive. Breathing. I should be grateful. But all I can think of is Sully. My team. The night the earth opened up and swallowed everyone alive. The way I left a piece of me behind in that desert.

I fucked up. And it cost me everything.

It's hard to remember that day. A special-ops mission only my team and my lieutenant knew about. It comes in fragments. Bright colors as loud as the explosion that knocked me away from my team. Panic. Blood. Chaos.

Adrenaline made me move. I crawled through dust and debris to get back to them. I found Sully first.

"They fucking shot me, man," he gasped.

"Oh fuck." Horrified, I took in the four bullets peppered across Sully's chest. "Fuck."

Sully wheezed a laugh. "That's what I said, Captain."

I hunkered next to him, trying to keep my brother's blood in his body. "I know. Hang in there. Just fucking stay with me." I looked to the sky for a chopper. But there was nothing, only that black shadow of helplessness growing inside of me.

Sully swallowed. "Must be a hell of a shot."

"Don't talk," I told him, voice tremulous. I gripped his hand. Squeezed. "Save your energy."

"Save your...speech, Montgomery..." Sully's eyes dimmed. His voice thinned like a thread. "Say your goddamn prayers."

"Fuck. You'll be okay. You'll make it."

But he didn't. Later, I found Ferraro, hunkered down in an old building. We were the only survivors.

That day, the shadow inside me took root.

And it followed me all the way to Resurrection.

"D?" Wyatt's voice hammers like a drill in my head. He gives me a sideways glance. "You okay, man?"

Mustering as much composure as I can, I rise from my chair and move to the window. My heart pounds in my chest. I will it down to a normal level Ruby would approve of.

"Fine," I grit out, curling one hand around my nape.

I can feel Wyatt's questioning gaze burning a hole in my back.

Letting my brothers in is not an option. They don't know or suspect what I've been through. What I've done.

I nearly jump out of my skin when the siren goes off.

"Fixed it," Wyatt announces.

I whip around, hardening my expression.

"Yup, I'm going," Wyatt drawls, picking up on the fact

that he needs to get the fuck out of my vicinity before I unleash big brother bodily harm.

I close my eyes to draw in a long breath.

When I open them, Wyatt and the beacon are gone. So is the box of donuts.

I swear under my breath. It's going to be a long goddamn day.

17

Dakota

CLOCK TICKING TOWARD FIVE, THE SUN DIES A slow death in the sky as early evening shadows creep over the snowy street. First day at the new—well, old—job complete.

Today felt like I was stuck in a freakishly warped version of rewind to the past. Looking for any remnants of that spark between Davis and me, and that sisterly love between me and Fallon. Not to mention, no one in town scowled when I walked by.

My back aches, my feet scream, but I survived.

I can do one day.

On a satisfied sigh, I toss my dusty cloth down and cast my gaze over the quiet store. I've stayed productive—wiping shelves that haven't seen a rag since I left, changing Fallon's TV setting to something less murdery, and reorganizing the coolers by type.

The Avett Brothers' "No Hard Feelings" blares from inside the kitchen, where Fallon's sequestered herself for the last two hours. I stare at the saloon-style door, almost dizzy from the knowledge of what's behind it. My sister. An oven. Dirty counters. Rolling pins.

But I can't be a coward my entire life, so I finally push my way through and enter.

The sight that greets me has me smiling. At the counter, dipped low beside stacks of clean dishes, Fallon's putting on burgundy lipstick using a toaster as a mirror. It softens her, makes her look less vengeful.

"Hot date?" I tease.

She straightens up without answering, only the slow flush of pink over her cheeks gives her away. It always was her damn tell. She can lie all she wants, but those cheeks hold all her secrets.

I wish we could go back. Wish we'd just talk and talk without me having to think of what to say. Wish she felt more like a sister than a stranger. Wish it didn't make me so sad because I know the void between us is my fault.

Sweat dots my brow, but I move deeper into the kitchen.

Fallon's response to my nearness is to slide a dirty rag over the countertop and bang on the oven with the toe of her boot. The oven door slips, crooked on its hinges.

I frown. "This still isn't fixed?"

Fallon snorts. "Oh, we fixed it all right. 'Bout four years ago."

"Well, we should fix it again," I tell her. "I saw the bread you were serving on those sandwiches." I give her a careful look. "It was burned."

Her nostrils flare. "Sorry, *Chef*. I'll get on that right after I take dad to chemo tomorrow."

"I can do it," I offer.

She spends the next minute glaring at me, then says, "No."

A churning sensation twists my stomach to knots. Because, sure, I'm the one who's stayed away all these years. I've earned her hurt. "I don't want to be a problem, Fallon. All I want to do is help if you'll let me."

"You want to know what my problem is? It's you. You

come back to town and everyone thinks you're the golden girl all over again." A toss of that caramel hair. "Must be pretty nice for you. Spin your story."

"Are you kidding me?" My laugh is dry. "They all see me as a loser. You know how this town is." I glance at the oven and scowl. "You get out alive, you get success, no one cares. In the end, all you are is a traitor."

"But you got out, didn't you? And that's what counts. It's what's always counted. Ever since we were kids, you always got what you wanted. You got mom longer than I did. You got into school. Hell, you even got Dad's approval." She scrubs furiously at an invisible spot on the counter, then looks up at me. "Even after all this, he's worried you're in trouble, and still thinks you can do no wrong."

I flinch at the unexpected verbal barb. "I get it. I get that you're hurt."

Fallon lets out a harsh breath. "I'm not hurt. I'm fucking pissed."

I take a step forward.

If she wants to fight, I'll let her get out her frustrations. I'll take her anger, even if it hurts. Whatever it takes to get us there.

"Tell me a secret, Fallon."

At the mention of our game, Fallon sets the rag down. Her shoulders soften. It's been ages since we've played it, but even I don't miss the flicker of nostalgia in her hazel eyes.

I wait with bated breath. Hoping.

Then her shoulders reset. Cold, rigid stones. "You don't deserve my secrets," she says, starting for the door. "Not anymore."

Her words slap and I absorb the blow, resting a palm

on the cool countertop. I'm no stranger to my little sister's stormy moods, but me being on the receiving end is rare. I was her backup. Her protector. Not her target.

"What do you want from me? I'm not this town's sweetheart anymore. I left. That's your job now."

"Must be nice to have the option to leave."

"Oh, fuck off, Fallon. You can't put the blame on me. You always had a choice to leave."

"*Had.* I had a choice. Now, I have the store. I have Dad. There's no other option for me except to stay. Somebody's got to take care of him. Things'll work out for you. They always do."

"You should have called me."

She snorts, a bitter dismissive sound. "And say what? You can barely take care of yourself."

"You know," I sigh, feeling resigned and sad. "I'm trying, Fallon." I gesture at my stomach. "You probably think I can't raise a kitten, but I'm trying here." My voice shakes. "It's not easy coming back home."

"If it's not easy, if you can't hack it here, if you're too good for it, why don't you go back to your perfect bakery?"

It's an atom bomb hit. Any calm I've held on to melts down.

"I don't have a bakery," I shout, and Fallon freezes. "Not anymore. It burned down, remember? It all burned down. I know I lied about my life the last two years. I lied about every fucking thing. I told you and Dad that I was okay, but I wasn't. I was never okay. I was missing you and feeling like a fucking failure on a daily basis if that makes you feel any better." A tear tracks its way down my cheek. "I failed, Fallon. And I don't fail."

Fallon takes a step forward, face twisted into something almost unrecognizable.

A wracking breath rocks my chest. "So, no. I am very far from being fucking perfect."

"Dakota…"

As I shake my head, a glint from the street catches my eye. A reflection bounces off the window. A man strolls down Main Street, hands in his pockets.

Tall. Thin. Longish blond hair, a crisp, tailored shirt. That sly fox-like face.

Aiden.

A cold sweat breaks out over my body. Pain flares in my bad arm, running the length of my cast like muscle memory.

I will fuck with you, Dakota. I will fuck with your family. I will fuck with your life.

I hear him clear as day. A familiar, brutal echo reminding me I'm never free. Maybe I never will be.

Terror trails its thin fingers up my spine. My heart pounds furiously. It feels like everything is over. Like I can't breathe. Like my chest is going to explode.

"Koty?" Fallon says, her voice softer. Smaller, frightened, far off and away.

It's him. He's here.

My vision tunnels, and my knees give out so sharply the impact causes me to bite my tongue. Warm blood fills my mouth. On a cry, I sink to the ground, wrapping my arms around my legs and burying my face in my knees as much as my belly will allow.

"Dakota?" Fallon's hand wraps around my shoulder. She's so close she could climb into my lap. "What's wrong?"

"I can't breathe," I whisper, squeezing my eyes shut

and gripping my dog tag like a life preserver. Over and over again, I jam the panic button. "Davis. I need Davis."

The rush of boots across linoleum. The jingle of the bell above the door.

Silence. Torturous silence because I can't be sure Aiden isn't on the other side of that door.

Then, "Dakota."

I nearly weep in relief.

That voice. Smooth. Safe. As rich and as deep as an aged whiskey. When I raise my head, I find Davis's warm brown eyes on mine, concern etched all over his face.

On his knees in front of me, he settles a firm hand on my wrist. "Are you okay? Are you hurt?"

"No." I tip my head back and blink my wet eyes. "No."

His gaze moves to my stomach, and he spends a long time looking at me before asking, "Is the baby okay?"

My breath trembles. "Yes."

"What happened?"

"I saw him," I whisper.

"Who?"

A moan slips from my mouth. "*Him.*"

Davis whips his head to Fallon, who shrugs.

Storm clouds gather in my chest. "You have to believe me."

"I do, Cupcake." His voice is soft and free of doubt, unlike the cops who told me there was nothing they could do. I shudder out a relieved sob. This man. I may hate him for not kissing me, but I love him to death for believing me.

Despite his calm voice, tension breaks in his face. A lethal kind of focus. Davis shifts, his dark gaze sweeping across the store. "Lock the door, Fallon, and stay inside."

And that's when I start shaking. Shaking like I've fallen

into the coldest part of a lake in winter. Even with my cheeks flushed hot, even with a sweater, I'm freezing.

"Dakota." His voice is so low, but I can hear the desperate edge to it.

"What's wrong with her?" Fallon asks in a small voice. She's frozen against the counter, hands clutched to her chest.

"Panic attack." Davis scoots closer, his eyes still holding mine. "But we got this, don't we, Cupcake?"

I try to wrap my arms around myself to warm the chill, but Davis takes over that duty. His big frame settles beside me and he cocoons me in his arms. *Comfort. Home.* His chest rises and falls and his skin is so hot, but it's still not enough to take away the tremor in my bones.

"Breathe, Dakota," Davis says softly. "You're safe. Just breathe."

I'm unraveling in front of him, but he has me.

Davis is made for this. His eye contact, his body language, everything. He is a safe space that is made for *me*.

"If you could bake right now, what would you make?"

"What?" Caught off guard by the question, I blink.

His big thumb traces gentle circles over my wrist. "What would Dakota McGraw, top pastry chef in the nation, bake?"

My teeth chatter. "I can't bake."

"Pretend you can," he orders. His fingers push a lock of hair from my face. "Pretend you're back in Paris. You finished your shift and now you're texting me at some ungodly hour about the berries you found at the farmer's market."

I close my eyes at the rumble of his voice. Panic ebbs, and just like that, the recipe begins in my mind. The sweetest parts of a strawberry. Ephemeral and delicate batter turned to shortcake sponge. Fresh-cut mint and cream whipped to the highest peaks. A feeling of peace blooms in my chest, exhaling that broken woman I've become.

"Shortcake," I say, breathless. I turn my head, meet those chocolate-brown eyes. "Shortcake with strawberries and mint."

He grins. "Shortcake, huh? Guess we better get you in the kitchen."

A small smile. "Guess so."

"What else?"

"Hot cocoa." My mind floats down from the ledge. "I'm cold."

"We'll get you warm." He cups my cheek, stares down into my eyes. "Hold on to me. I've got you. You're safe."

Safe.

Davis scoops me in his arms and stands. I cling to his rugged body like for once in a long time, I have a home.

18

Davis

I KICK OPEN THE FRONT DOOR TO THE LODGE AND carry Dakota up the stairs. Her head stays buried in my chest. She shivers like she's lost in a Montana blizzard.

Fear and rage sweep over me like a rogue wave. I'm still not over the buzz of the tracker sending my heart into red-alert status. I ran. All I can see is Dakota lying on The Corner Store floor, shaking.

And I lost it.

So much for remaining emotionless.

Instead, a jagged edge of raw want carves me up inside.

I've kept my hands off her and now all I want to do is wrap her in my arms, keep her tucked against me forever, safe from any speck of darkness lurking in the outside world.

Guilt sideswipes me, making my stomach drop. Not even two weeks in and she's hurt on my watch.

I can't even fucking protect her.

This woman who means the entire world to me.

The thought has me letting out a growl.

Dakota looks up at me. "Davis?" she whispers.

I stomp into the bathroom and gently set her on the countertop. Dakota's inky eyes still haven't lost their glassiness. I move to the tub and turn on the shower, crank the heat as hot as it can go.

"What're you doing?" she asks.

"Getting you warm. You're in shock. Anxiety. Chills. You had a panic attack."

Her eyes shutter. "A daymare."

"A daymare."

Steam churns around us. The mirror fogs.

After testing the pelting water, I come back to her.

She wets her lips and slips off the countertop. "Help me undress?"

"Yeah." My throat feels like there are shards of glass in it.

Careful of her arm, I take her clothes off. First the puffy parka, then the oversized hoodie and jeans. She shivers in her bra and her panties, her dark hair spilling down over her slender shoulders and porcelain skin. My gaze drops to her belly. Small, slightly swollen, sexy as hell.

"Let's protect that cast," I say, grabbing a towel and wrapping it around her arm. It'll have to do for now.

Dakota's smile is wan. "Hotshot to the rescue again." She slips her good hand behind her, and before I can say anything, her bra is off.

Fuck.

Fuck.

Perfect full breasts.

I'm glued to the spot. Dakota's a dream. A man doesn't wake up from a woman like this.

She stares at me with those incredible brown eyes, like she's waiting for me to do something, say something. "Well?"

"Dakota. Get in the goddamn shower," I say harshly.

After a frustrated tilt of her chin, she kicks away her jeans, and steps into the shower in a silky, barely there thong. I avert my gaze from the sway of her tight little ass and battle the low groan building in my chest. Because fuck me, it's not okay how badly I want her.

Still, I can't keep my eyes off her for long, because when I glance back over, she's drawing the curtain shut, her balance precarious.

Something primitive and protective courses through my bloodstream.

Has me storming across the tile. When I reach through the sheer shower curtain to hold her firmly by the elbow, she gasps.

"I can do it, Hotshot."

"You're not slipping," I order, holding tighter.

While she soaps her curves and her belly, I grit my teeth and try not to look as the hot water rains over her body. Until one pert nipple drags over the roughness of my knuckles.

I whip my head to her. "Jesus Christ, Koty."

Her coy smile causes my cock to jerk to attention.

So goddamn wrong.

She just had a panic attack, and now she's daring me to do something with the fire building in my veins.

That's fucking it.

With a rough hand, I tear open the curtain and lift her out of the shower. I carry her dripping wet across the bathroom floor, set her down on top of the counter, and cover her with a towel.

Her shoulders rotate back and she stares at me as if she's furious and sad at the same. "I thought you wanted me warm."

I softly grip her jaw and lean in. Her brown eyes

narrow so fiercely I could burn up in their fire. "I won't play this game, Dakota."

"What game?" The slender length of her throat works. "You don't touch me. You haven't touched me since I got here."

A muscle pulses in my jaw. "Dakota, this is not what you need right now."

"I need you." Her voice is an unsteady whisper. "I need you so bad, Davis."

I don't answer, because if I do, it's all over. I've reached a boiling point in my head and my heart. My cock aches to plow through the front of my pants like a bulldozer.

"What if…" Dakota slips off the counter and lets the towel drop. I try to ignore how damn beautiful she looks. Soap suds trail down her breasts, and water glistens on her collarbones. She's dewy and damp, a shy flush tinging her cheeks.

Her eyes glitter as she reaches for the dog tag with one pale hand. She licks her lips—those full, plump lips, that delicate freckle—and says, "What if I pressed it again?"

She does.

My phone vibrates in my back pocket. The shrill alarm that normally would have annihilated me on the spot now has my erection thickening.

"You're abusing your privilege," I grit out, shooting her a warning look.

"What if I want to?"

"It's getting hard to do the right thing here," I growl.

"So don't." Her long lashes flutter, her eyes dark with heat. "You never break the rules, but *we* did. A long time ago, we did. And it was good, right?"

"It was great." On a groan, I shake my head. My heart pumps out a rhythm of self-destruction. "But—"

"But I'm different. I know that." Vulnerability stains her words. She takes a shuddery breath, fisting one hand in the hem of my T-shirt. "I'm not the girl you knew. I know I'm pregnant. I know I'm weak, but I—"

The words have barely left her mouth before I cup her face in my hands and force her gaze to mine. "That's bullshit. You're never weak. You hear me?"

A tear slips down her cheek. "We can't go back. You forgot about me. I get it, but I don't want to be lonely, Davis. I don't want this feeling in me anymore." Her head falls back, a sob tearing at my heart. "Help me make it through the night. Just one night."

Her words—and *my* goddamn dog tag dangling between her full breasts—piss me off. A part of me she's carried with her these last six years is touching her skin and I'm not.

She thinks I don't want her and I do.

Fuck it.

My mouth lands on hers, hard, demanding. The entire world disappears. Nothing's changed. That spark between us is a wildfire.

Her and me. That's it.

Dakota moans, her tongue slipping over mine as her hand slides up my chest. Her nails dig into the hard meat of my shoulder, and she clings to me.

"You think I haven't imagined us together every single day since you left?" I rasp when I pull away from her. My heart pulses in time with my throbbing cock. "You think I haven't been worried sick when you went silent? That's why

I fucking dream at night now. Because I lost you. Because I couldn't find you, and it terrified me, Dakota."

Those dark eyes widen, and she takes in a sharp breath. Too sharp.

I've said more than I should have. Before she can respond, I grab the back of her neck and crush my lips to hers. She tastes like cream and sugar. I drink her in. Eat her up.

A better man would stop this.

But who the fuck am I kidding?

I haven't been a better man since I left the Marines. Since I set foot on the ranch and Dakota charmed her way into my life.

She wrenches at my shirt, her hips bucking against me. "Yes, yes, yes."

Her urgency, her whimpered breaths, her eager hands, slay me. Six years of missing her, of rock-hard want, explodes in my chest. Unable to stop myself, I back her against the counter and yank the strap of her soaked thong, tearing it off roughly.

A delighted gasp escapes her lips.

Fuck if it's wrong. Fuck the promises I made to Stede. I feel like a racehorse who's been holding himself back, and now that I have permission, I'm out of the gate and running. Tonight, I need Dakota. And this woman—she needs me. I'll give her every broken piece of me if it means protecting her.

I get on my knees and look up at her. "Stop me if I hurt you." I tell her sternly. "I can't hurt you, Dakota." My voice is hoarse, shaky even to my own ears.

"You won't," she whispers breathlessly, searching my eyes. "Never."

It's not only her trust in me but also her vulnerability that gives me hope, the tentative promise that we can go back to what we had before. Even if it's just for one night.

Her eyes glow as she stares down at me. A feral, beautiful look has taken over her face. Shower steam rolls through the bathroom, her entire body dewy and slick.

"Open your legs, Cupcake. Let me taste you."

"Yes." Her chest rises and falls rapidly. "Oh, goddamn, Davis."

A low groan slips out of me when I split her pussy with my tongue. Sweet. Swollen. I bury my tongue in her pussy and inhale. Her head falls back on a moan.

"Oh god," she pants. Her fingers grip the sink counter, knuckles white. "Oh. Hotshot," she breathes.

I slow my pace, pulling back to say, "Ride my mouth, baby. Ride it like a good girl."

A half-pant, half-plea erupts from her chest. "Yes, yes."

Dakota rolls her hips, and I lave my tongue across the bud of her clit. She bucks, and I smile at the sound of her cry echoing in the bathroom. Her legs tremble on either side of me.

She clutches at my shoulders. Her nails dig in and make crescent-shaped marks. "Oh fuck," she breathes.

Forcing her thighs wide, I milk that pussy. Juices stream down the inside of her thighs.

"Look how wet you are," I grit out. "Soaked, baby."

"For you," she gasps, trembling. "It's always for you, Davis."

Her words cause a five-alarm fire in my brain. By now I'm fucking primal, my only focus Dakota. As desperate as I am to get inside her, all I want to do is push this woman until she's gasping for air.

Dakota bows back, her breasts bouncing as she lifts her hips to let me in deeper.

I thrust my tongue into her. So damp. So drenched. So goddamn tight. I graze my tongue over the small bundle of nerves and watch the sweat bead on her skin.

Dakota cries out, her walls clenching around me.

And then she comes. Her tight pussy convulses around my mouth and I drink in her orgasm. Steam swells around us as she sobs out my name.

Not just sobs. Screams.

I lap it up. Her sweetness drips down her thighs like a one-of-a-kind dessert. A fucking reward.

My cock strains at my pants, and I stand, grinning proudly like some caveman seeing his girl satisfied.

I pull her into my arms and she all but melts against me. My hands roam over the small bud of her stomach and her breasts. She's stunning and glowing. And extra fucking sensitive. She moans as I cup a heavy breast in my palm.

A haggard groan works its way out of me. I drop my forehead to hers. "How are you real?"

"Oh, I'm very real, Davis Montgomery." Her swollen lips inhale me, her mouth moving to nip at my Adam's apple. "I need more," she gasps, dark eyes glazed with lust. "I'm not done. We can't be done."

Not done.

Never.

My eyes fall closed. My blood roars to life. "Need to hear you say it, baby."

"Fuck me," she purrs. Her graceful fingers skim my waistband before stripping me of my shirt. "Fuck me like you used to."

I lean in, already working at my belt buckle. This

woman's a fucking addiction. "For something so sweet, Cupcake, you sure got a dirty mouth."

"Make it dirtier," she begs, then launches herself into my arms. Smashes her lips to mine.

That's when I notice she's shivering. Goosebumps coat her naked body. I swear at myself.

I'm a fucking asshole.

I tear my gun off my hip, kick off my jeans, and slide her up my body. She hooks her legs around my waist, and the small swell of her belly rests against mine, causing my heart to wrench. She stares at me, heavy-lidded, her focus zeroed in on the muscles of my chest.

"Davis?"

"Shower," I tell her. "Hold on, baby."

We step into the steam and pelting hot water. Carefully, I set her on her feet and maneuver her away from the water, positioning her so her body gets enough to stay warm, but her arm stays dry.

I lean in over her, my body molding to hers. Mouth to her ear, I growl, "Turn around and put your hand on the wall."

"Yes," she gasps, and flattens her good hand over the tile for balance.

I loop an arm high around her belly. Hold tight. "I got you. You won't slip."

Her dark head falls back. Her lips in a pretty pout as she looks at me. "Don't treat me like I'm fragile because of what's happened. Fuck me hard, Davis. I need it hard."

I flatten my body against hers. Cage her against the shower wall so she has no escape.

"You want it. You got it," I rasp. "Hang the fuck on."

No more waiting.

Water beats down on us as I grip her hips, positioning her ass against my cock. And then I thrust into her. She's goddamn dripping, and I slide right in to her sweet, hot warmth.

Dakota mewls, her fingers curling against the tile.

"Ain't gonna last long," I growl into her ear. "Been waiting for you for the last six years, Cupcake."

Her eyes flash open. A small smile lifts her lips. Feline, Ravenous. Beautiful. "Did you think about me, Hotshot?" A whisper of a question. A beacon of hope. An echo of the past.

"Cupcake, every goddamn hour I think about you."

The words hollow me out. If she had no inkling of how I felt, she does now.

Her lips part. "Oh."

Dakota shivers as I fit a palm to her stomach. The smallness of her belly, the curve of it, has an unfamiliar warmth spreading through me.

She pulses around me, hips working in small circles. The rhythmic motion squeezes my cock like a fucking boa constrictor.

Heart pounding, I slam into her. Dakota whimpers and leans her head back against my chest, eyes shut, her mouth open in a pouty O. She lets me hold her, lets me claim her body as mine. Steam covers us in a dewy cloud. I grit my teeth as I work us both into a familiar rhythm. One I never forgot. Hard. Primal. Savage.

I lower my mouth and bite the curve of her neck. Again and again, I slam into her. Some part of me hates being rough with her, but her body and her words tell me she needs it. Wants it. She cries out with each wild thrust, her breasts bouncing, her skin pink from the water.

"Faster," she sobs. Her pussy clenches around me like a vise and I groan. "Oh god, faster, Davis."

"Moan my name, baby." I sweep a thumb over her dark nipple. Pinch. "Take that pretty mouth and put it to good work."

She does. Her squeals echo throughout the bathroom, overtaking the hiss of the water.

"Come for me, Cupcake." My voice is so ragged I don't recognize it. "Don't ever hold back for me, you hear me?"

"No, no, I won't."

She shakes her head furiously. And it's like an unlocking. Dakota goes wild. Her ass slapping off my hips, she fucks me with all she has in her. Friendship. Love. Anger. Grief.

"Davis. *Davis.*"

The husky sound of my name on her lips shatters me.

"Now, Cupcake, *now*. Come with me," I order. Savagely, I thrust, burying myself so deep inside of her my mind empties completely.

Our bodies explode, rocking each other. Dakota jerks against me, gasping, crying out. My orgasm tears through me like a lightning strike. I come so goddamn hard I see stars.

Six years. Six fucking years without this woman.

I'll never get over this night.

I'll never be good enough to deserve it.

Dakota moans, legs buckling as I slip out of her. I catch her high around the waist to pull her limp, trembling body into my arms.

This unforgettable woman. Our flame never burned low. Not now. Not ever.

"Davis," she breathes, twisting into me to wind her arms around my neck.

"You okay, Koty?"

She lifts her dark head, her breathing uneven. My heartbeat steadies when I see her gorgeous face, her content smile. "Better than shortcake," she says, sweeping a hand over my shoulder.

I chuckle. "Glad to hear it." I scan her eyes, her face. She looks happy. It's all I wanted.

After shutting off the water, I grab a towel and wrap it around her shoulders. "C'mon, let's get you out of here."

"Where are we going?" she asks as I scoop her up in my arms and lift her out of the shower.

The words are out of my mouth before I can stop them. "To bed."

Light illuminates her eyes, and the corner of her mouth tips up. She doesn't respond, only presses a sweet kiss to my jaw before laying her head on my chest. My heart squeezes tight, a primal protectiveness washing over me.

I take a deep breath as we step out of the bathroom.

She needed this. I gave it to her.

And tomorrow it'll all go back to the way it should be.

Before us.

19

Dakota

I WAKE IN THE DARK, SORE BETWEEN THE LEGS, AND sigh.

Worn out and worked over. That's what Davis Montgomery does to me.

The air smells like us. Sex and heat and sweat. I roll my head across the pillow to look at the powerful force of nature sleeping beside me in the rumpled sheets. Davis is on his back, one arm crossed over his muscular chest. And the other arm…

His hand lays pressed up against my rounded belly. So large it nearly covers half of it. As if it's his.

My core curls in a mixture of longing and desire. I never thought I'd be in Davis's bed again.

Wildest dreams, right?

The man's still as amazing in bed as I remember.

For one night, we went back. Uprooted everything. I should feel embarrassed about how I begged, how I lost it. But after two years of hell with Aiden, all I feel is re-lieved. My trauma is separate from Davis. Because he is not trauma. He is safe. Strong. Everything I haven't had in so long.

I had sex. I orgasmed. I forgot I was pregnant, that everything in my life burned down.

One night won't magically change anything between us, but it means everything to me.

My heart leaps as I scan my eyes over Davis. I reach for him, delicately tracing my fingertips over the steel muscle of his biceps, before dancing them through the dusting of dark hair on his chest. For once, the man looks peaceful in sleep. No nightmares.

The thought of it hits me like a punch in the gut.

Nightmares.

And I'm the cause.

He was keeping it close to his chest. Only tonight, seeing the taut lines of tension in his face, hearing his choked words...

He thought of me. He missed me. He *dreams* of me.

I roll on my back and glare at the ceiling.

Stop, Dakota.

I've got to stop adding hope to the mix.

I need my life back. And it doesn't include Davis.

A hunger pain slices through my stomach. I hiss a breath and look down at the small bud of my belly. Note to self: skipping dinner for sex isn't the best idea.

Even if it feels like it was.

I kick off the sheets and slip on an old T-shirt of Davis's. In search of a midnight snack, I quietly pad down the stairs to the kitchen.

When I open the fridge and scour the contents, the recipe automatically assembles in my head. I've always seen it like a game of Tetris. But instead of blocks, images slide into place.

With only three ingredients, I could whip up soft-boiled eggs on Greek yogurt with a side of buttered sourdough. Instead, I settle for helping myself to a strawberry yogurt. One bite calms the hunger pains and a content feeling spreads through me.

It's the witching hour. Prime baking time. I can feel it in my bones.

As I eat, I watch the moon through the window.

My gaze slides over the ranch, the large gate in the distance, the snow on the ground.

If Aiden's in Resurrection, he won't make my life easy, but I believe Davis. I trust him. If he says I'm safe, I'm safe.

What I have to do is get it together. I have so much to plan and prepare. Apartment. Job. Sanity. I can't let myself—or my baby—down.

A shuffle of noise behind me has me turning.

Davis, wearing gray sweatpants and a furrowed brow I long to smooth out with my fingers, stands in the kitchen, Keena beside him.

"What's wrong?" he rasps, voice thick with sleep.

"Nothing." I smile and hold up my spoon. "Just hungry." My gaze drops to my stomach. "Or should I say the baby's hungry?"

He takes a tentative step forward, like some massive machine. The bullet wound on his shoulder is a constant reminder of the hero he is. "That's not enough protein. You want something else?"

I drop the spoon into the sink. "No. This'll do it. You were right about me taking care of myself. I'll do a better job. And thank you." Heat creeps into my cheeks. "For tonight. For everything."

A muscle jumps in his jaw. "You don't have to thank me for that."

I wiggle my fingers at Keena, reach for a box of dog treats. "You want one, girl?"

She looks at me, sniffs, then turns and exits the kitchen.

"Don't worry about Keena," Davis says, his arms folded

across his mile-wide chest. "Sometimes she holds a temporary grudge because she's dramatic."

"And I thought Fallon was bad."

He chuckles and crosses the kitchen to run his hands down my shoulders. "What else do we need?"

I blink at him. "What?"

His eyes drift over my face. "In this kitchen, for you to bake."

I open my lips to tell him to stop it, but in his gaze, I see myself. I see him six years ago. Angry. Defeated. Broken. And I see what he's trying to do. Not fix. Push.

"Knives," I tell him.

"We have knives."

I scoff and palm his chest. Revel in the feel of his hot, hard muscle. "Good knives, Hotshot. A knife so sharp I can slice an apple mid-air." I return my attention to the kitchen. "And a mixer. A big one."

"How about this?" Eyes lit with a wicked gleam, he opens a drawer to expose an ancient hand mixer.

I shudder and pin him with a stern stare. "That is an act of war, Davis Montgomery."

The deep, velvet sound of his laughter fills the kitchen. It's so beautiful, so earnest, it loosens the rock in my chest.

"I'll get you all that and more," he says, his smile fading. His eyes are now hard, commanding. "But first, I need to talk to you about what happened today."

I bite my lip, hating to relive today. "I swear I saw him, Davis."

He's quiet for a long second, then he says, "I believe you. I put in a call to Richter. He's going to pull security footage and see if we can spot him."

"What if he's in town?" I step closer to him, expecting

him to pull away, but he takes me in his arms. "What if he comes to the ranch?"

His hold tightens. "Then you pick up that family-style can of green beans and hit him in the fucking face with it."

I laugh.

"He won't get on the ranch. After Ruby—after last year—" Pain and guilt crease his handsome face, and I listen as he tells me about the arson attempt and how Ruby was hurt because of it.

"Our security is fucking Fort Knox," he finishes, his voice dropping to a lethal level. "No one gets on the ranch. No one will hurt you. No one will get close enough to try. And…" His large fingers tug at the dog tag around my neck. "You have this. You have me."

"I have you," I breathe.

But for how long?

One time, right? That's how it goes. One night and definitely not forever.

Davis stares grimly at me. "Be a hell of a lot easier if you told me who he was."

Fear floods my veins and my stomach heaves. "No."

"Dakota." He grips my chin gently with his massive fingers. "Tell me his fucking name."

"Not yet. I can't." I glare at him, hating he won't let me have this one secret. "I have to work my way up to it, Davis."

And also keep Davis from killing him.

The lines in his forehead deepen. "I can't keep you safe if I don't know the details."

I pull out of his arms and shake my head. "Then I'll run." I think of my belongings upstairs, still unpacked, a car I can borrow from my father. "I won't put you and your family in the middle of this."

It's the wrong thing to say.

Davis freezes, and anger reflects in the dark depths of his eyes.

"Help me God, Dakota, you run, you won't get far."

Anger crashes into me. Anger that Aiden can fuck with my mind even though he no longer has any hold on me.

"I will never go back to him," I hiss, stepping backward. "I will die before I let him find me again."

"Don't say that." His features are grave, his voice a low tone of warning. "Don't you ever fucking say that. Nothing is more important than you. Than the life you have. He will not take it away. He will not take you away. Not from me."

From me.

My lips part in shock. I want to ask him what he means, but before I can, Davis says, "Don't run from me, Dakota. Because I'll keep you here."

"I hate him." The words explode from my chest with a vengeance. "I hate him so much."

"I know, baby. Let it out."

I inhale unsteadily.

Hot tears flood my eyes. Blood thunders in my ears.

"I lost everything. My notebooks. My recipes. My investment. My arm."

"What else?" Davis takes a step forward, reaching for me.

Pain wells inside me again, and I squeeze my eyes shut to block Aiden's voice from my ears. "I can't bake. My sister hates me. And I'm scared. I'm scared to be a mom." I whisper it like the baby can hear me. Like he or she will hold it against me for the rest of my life.

"When will I feel okay? Like a human being? Like a

mother? I'm sick of feeling like some broken failure. I'm sick of being strong."

"So don't," he says, low and strained.

"What?"

"Be strong." He captures my wrist and tugs me into his arms, locking me against him.

Shaking my head, I try to shove him away with the heel of my palm, but he holds me tight. Won't let me loose.

"Scream."

"What?" I blink and look up at him, thinking I've misheard.

"Scream. Let it out, Cupcake. Everything. I want this fucking lodge to shake."

My eyes meet his.

Somehow, he always knows what I need.

And then I grab onto Davis's shoulders, dig my nails into the meat of his muscle and scream. The piercing scream rattles my entire body, has my knees threatening to give out, and still Davis holds me upright in his arms.

He doesn't flinch.

He takes it with me. A man giving me a safe place to land.

Tears stream down my face. Power and rage and exhaustion hum through my bones. I feel like a corpse, a shell of Dakota clawing her way out of her exoskeleton.

When the scream turns ragged—as shredded as I feel inside—I crumple in the secure clutch of Davis's arms. I grip his shirt and inhale his scent. Man and earth and leather.

After a few seconds, I lift my face to his.

He brushes the hair off my face, studies my eyes. "Feel better?"

I take a deep breath before I answer. "I do." Everything inside of me feels drained. Lightened. "Surprisingly, that—" I freeze and let out a small yelp. A tear slides down my cheek.

"Koty?" Davis releases me from his arms.

I press a palm over my belly and look down. "The baby," I whisper.

"What's wrong?"

I stare at my stomach, watching tears drip onto the dark navy fabric of Davis's shirt.

"For Christ's sake, Dakota." Davis softly grips my jaw, forcing my gaze to his eyes that are dark and laced with worry.

"It moved." I let out a tearful laugh. "The baby moved. Just like that."

On an exhale, I fully press my hands to my stomach. Every nerve in my hands, waiting. And I feel it. Movement. A rippling pressure. Tiny surface bubbles rising.

I giggle.

"Oh my god." I smile. "It feels so…weird."

"It does?" Davis stares at my stomach.

I bite my lip. "Do you want to feel it?" I ask.

He swallows. "Yeah. I do." He spreads a palm over the side of my stomach and holds it there. We wait. Then I watch his face soften, all his handsome features crinkling in wonder, as there's the tiniest ripple of movement.

"That's your baby," he rasps. An emotion I can't place crosses his face.

"It is." More movement now. A tumbling motion.

"Hi there," I whisper, stroking a hand over my belly.

My baby heard me. He–or–she woke up. Maybe I just did the same thing, too.

20

Davis

"**I**F YOU PUNCH THAT COMPUTER, HOTSHOT, I WON'T be able to patch you back up. I'm a pastry chef, not a surgeon." Dakota sighs while I slam buttons on my computer, logging into the department's database. "Is this really necessary? Don't you have ranch chores?"

"Your personal safety comes first."

"Uh-huh," she deadpans. "My personal safety includes that shower this morning?"

I ignore that.

My frown deepens as I look at her. "This motherfucker is out there walking around, following you, watching you, and I can't do a damn thing about it. And until you're ready and willing to tell me who he is, then this is my next recourse."

Dakota gives one slow nod and stays quiet. Perched in a chair beside me, her gaze drifts to the window of the Bullshit Box, which faces the wooded area across the road in front of the lodge. Wyatt crosses the gravel drive with a vet who's on his way to check on the horses. Charlie and Ruby have already left for town to replace equipment that's long overdue. I should pitch in, but all my focus is Dakota.

It's taken a week to get the security camera footage from Main Street. Richter grudgingly gave it after I threatened to take my dog and walk.

Someone wants to take her away from me. The idea is unthinkable.

And it pisses me off. I need control of my judgment and emotions in a situation like this, and with Dakota in the center of fire, I'm most definitely not.

As I pull up the video from the day Dakota had her panic attack, my police scanner crackles on the desk.

"*Car 59 ready to go. Deputy Topper and Deputy Andrews on duty.*"

"*Dispatch: received 141. You were late to the party tonight, Topper, so you can have the first job. 315 at the top of Dead Fred's Curve. Vehicle is a black Chevy.*"

"Keeping tabs on the town?" Dakota asks with a smile.

"Baby, you know it."

We sit in silence and watch the sped-up footage from noon until five.

At three forty-five p.m., I pause it. "You know him?"

She shakes her head.

"Wait." I lean in. After a long second, I frown. "I know him."

Dakota freezes. "Who is it?"

"Pappy Starr." I point at the man waddling down Main Street. A big-time rodeo agent, who Wyatt and Charlie have avoided like the plague. I can already hear Wyatt complaining now.

I fast forward and freeze it around the time of Dakota's panic attack. There is a man, dressed in jeans and a jacket, walking by The Corner Store window.

Dakota leans closer to the screen. Her pupils dilate.

My heart hammers in fury. "Recognize him?"

"No." A shudder rocks her frame. She folds both arms over her belly. "I don't think so."

"If your ex is in town, how'd he get here?"

"He'd fly." She startles. Grabs my arm. "Davis. He has his own plane."

I give her a look, fighting the urge to get frustrated with her. "That info would have been handy when you got here, Cupcake."

"He has money. Owns properties. He could travel anywhere." A guilty look overtakes her pretty face, and she says, "I call his work every Monday to check in on him. He's been there."

"Again, more news that would have come in handy," I say flatly.

With a small growl that makes me smile, Dakota stands and rubs slow circles on her belly. She's been touching her belly more often, and I drink her in, noting every single detail. She's put on weight. Her hair's shiny and her eyes are without clouds. She looks happier than she has in weeks.

She paces the Bullshit Box, those gears in that beautiful brain of hers turning. "I know I saw him, Davis. I'm not crazy."

"Not saying you are." I push out of my chair and go to her. "I don't doubt that you did. The mind can be a powerful thing." She stares at me patiently, so I go on, the memories unlocking. "The night after my team was taken out, I was cleaning up in the bathroom and..." A muscle works in my jaw. "I saw Sully in the mirror. I threw up. Freaked the fuck out. My bunkmate thought I was losing it. Now, six years later, I still check the mirror when I go in to wash up. Trauma hides, but it doesn't go away."

"Trauma hides," she echoes.

"I shouldn't have told you that," I say with a frown.

Why in the hell did I tell her that? Making her feel better, not worse, is the objective.

"I'm glad you did." She reaches up and cups my cheek. "Makes me feel less alone."

It's a compulsion to lean in and sweep my mouth against her lips.

I hold her close, trying to tamp down the guilt welling in my chest. Temptation bested me last week. In her fragile state, Dakota should have been off-limits, yet I took advantage of that.

What kind of asshole fucks a woman when she's vulnerable?

Me. I'm the asshole.

I told myself she needed it, when I was the one who fucking craved it. And now, I don't know what the hell we are. We're a bad idea, a second chance, all rolled up into what-the-fuck-are-we-doing?

She's living on my ranch, but for how long? Any talk of her moving out leaves me with a hollow ache in my chest.

And yet, I have no rights to her. Dakota needs to heal, not jump into a relationship. All I can offer her and her baby is protection.

Because that baby changes everything.

A chime on her phone has Dakota glancing down. "Oh." Her mouth pulls up in a slow smile.

"What is it?"

"I'm twenty-one weeks today," she says, slightly breathless as she scrolls through her screen. "I downloaded an app. It's all about babies. Today, he—or—she's the size of a—"

"Carrot."

"What?"

Shit.

I scrub my hand over my face. Try to turn away. "Nothing."

She gasps and grabs my shoulder, yanking me back toward her. Her dark eyes contain sheer joy. Disbelief. "Davis Montgomery, are you checking up on me?"

"Have to, Cupcake." I stop fighting it and run my hands over her shoulders, into all the silky dark hair. "Comes with the job description."

"Oh, it does, does it?" There's a playful lilt to her voice. "And what all does that entail?"

I grunt. "Confidential information."

Dakota smiles and leans in for a kiss. Every nerve ending jerks to attention. With a growl, I haul her against me, giving in to the shadows that swim inside my chest.

Touching her is happening now. No way to deny it—I can't keep my hands off her.

Fuck. I already know I won't survive this. But I haven't survived the last six years without her, so I'll call it a draw.

"We're onsite at that 315. Looks like the vehicle skidded off the road while heading north." The dispatch radio crackles. *"Cab has gone over Dead Fred's Curve. We're waiting for an ambulance. One adult male and one adult female. Vehicle's plates are BVD425."*

I freeze, recognizing the plate number. Fear lodges itself into my gut. "Fuck."

A worry line appears on Dakota's brow. "Davis? What's wrong?"

My heart thumps, but my voice is steady. "That's Charlie's truck."

I rush across the office and rip my keys off the table.

Dakota hurries after me. "I'm going with you."

Dread curls in my stomach as I round the bend to see Charlie's pickup truck hanging over the edge of Dead Fred's Curve. Smoke rises from its hood. The left fender crumpled like a tin can.

Dakota gasps. "Oh my god."

With my knuckles wrapped white on the wheel, I do a quick sweep of the scene. Richter, arms crossed over his chest, speaks with another cop. Charlie and Ruby sit in the back of the ambulance. A blanket is wrapped over Ruby's shoulders, her face turned toward Charlie.

"It'll be okay," Dakota says, laying a hand on my arm.

My heart races. I pull over onto the side of the road, cut the engine, and hop out.

Richter turns when he sees me coming, sticking an arm out to bar me from the scene. "This isn't for you, Montgomery."

"The hell it isn't," I snarl and bulldoze past him.

Charlie stands when he sees me. I cup him by the face and search his eyes. "You okay?"

He shakes his head. "No, we're not fucking okay." His voice is frustrated.

"What happened? You hit ice?"

"No. Someone tried to run us off the damn road."

"Start talking," I order. "Now."

Anger creases his face. "We were headed back to the ranch and someone sideswiped the truck. Came out of nowhere. He hit me on the left and it aimed us right at the cliff's edge. I pumped those goddamn breaks, but he came back and hit me once more for good measure."

Charlie pulls Ruby up beside him. He looks more

shaken than she does. And I know why. He almost lost her. Again.

A swear blasts out of his mouth. "Motherfucker tried to run us off the road, I'm goddamn sure of it. I barely got Ruby out before I got myself out."

"Trying to play hero," Ruby admonishes softly. With a grunt, Charlie tucks her under his arm.

A white-hot anger claws its way under my skin. Beside me, Dakota tenses.

"No sign of the other vehicle," Richter says, stepping into the circle. "Guy fled the scene."

"You see the guy?" I ask Charlie.

"Bastard had a trucker hat pulled low." Charlie growls and shakes his head. "I gave Richter the best description I could."

"No other witnesses? Plates?" I ask, glancing toward the smoking truck.

"No. Not even a partial." Richter nods my way, knowing I'm not happy. "His car got it bad too, so we'll be on the lookout for an older Tahoe with front-end damage. We'll find it, Montgomery."

"You need a hospital?" I look at Charlie, not missing his fingers on Ruby's wrist, monitoring her heartbeat.

"No," Ruby says before Charlie can answer. Then, seeing us all stare at her, she draws herself up and glares at Charlie. Her bottom lip sticks out in a stubborn pout. "Cowboy, no. I'm fine."

"Come on." Dakota holds out her arm to Ruby. "We'll give you a ride back to the ranch."

Charlie and I watch them walk off. Then I lean into him. "I want everyone in this family staying close. You hear me?"

"Things are fucked." Charlie drags a hand down his dark beard. His eyes flick in the direction of Ruby. "They have been ever since Koty set foot on the ranch."

I stiffen. "You asking me to turn her out?"

"Fuck you, Davis." A muscle jerks in his jaw. The punch of his finger in my chest rocks me back on my boots. "I'd never ask that. I'm asking you to find this guy. Fix it."

I take a step closer to him. Our gazes clash. "I always fix it." My hand balls into a fist, trying to tamp down the growing shadows. The guilt. "And you goddamn know it."

His nostrils flare. "Then do it."

Richter's loud boom sideswipes the rest of our conversation. "Charlie, a statement."

"Find him," I order Richter, swinging his way. "Fast."

As Richter steps up to Charlie, I walk over to the side of Dead Fred's Curve and stare down over the rocky side of the canyon. The deep crevasse, the terrifying drop. Nausea wells in my stomach.

Ruby and Charlie—they never would have made it.

I stiffen when a hand slides over my shoulder. "This is my fault," Dakota says in a low voice. She leans in, her body warm and firm against mine. "It's him. I know it is."

Feeling the Arctic chill in the air, I tug on my gloves. My breath puffs white in front of my face as Keena's sharp whines cut through the February night.

Need to walk. Need to get that fucked up image of Charlie's truck hanging off the lip of Dead Fred's Curve out of my mind. The cops don't know who did it. No witnesses, no sign of the vehicle. I can't shake the feeling that whoever did this poses a threat to my family. To Dakota.

I want to punch a hole in the side of the lodge. Break stone, break my hand, just to feel something other than the shadows building inside.

That same poisonous combination I carried home with me from the Marines is trying to rise up. Rage. Failure. Helplessness.

I step off the porch, eyeing Ruby and Charlie's cabin. It's lit up with light.

Sleep isn't coming easy for any of us.

The paw on the side of my leg redirects my attention. A pleading whine comes from the dog beside me.

"Listen to me," I tell Keena, who's now in a full-on spin. "We're outside to walk. There's no biting, there's no playing. There's focus. There's no damn time to roll around. You got me?"

Ears pricked to attention, Keena whines once more.

I look up as the back door slides open and Dakota steps out onto the porch, wrapped in her parka. "Late night stroll?"

"Taking Keena for a walk."

She lifts her brow. "At midnight?"

"Never miss."

"Mmm. So, this is the real reason you don't sleep." She steps toward me. "Can I come?"

I shake my head, not wanting her outside. "It's freezing. Go inside, Dakota."

She lifts a defiant chin, hands on her belly. "Exercise is good for the baby."

"You don't listen," I grumble.

She smiles, knowing she's won the battle. "Never have."

Fuck. This woman could play every card in the book and I still couldn't say no to her.

"Fifteen minutes," I say with a sigh. I put my trapper hat on her head, my gloves on her hands, and when I'm satisfied that she's snugly bundled, we step into the yard.

"Hold on to my arm," I tell her. "I don't want you slipping."

She links her arm through mine and my cock jerks like a bobber on a string.

Keena lets out a hearty bark and bolts into the dark.

I sigh, scrubbing a hand down my face. "She makes her own rules."

Dakota bumps her shoulder into mine. "Sounds like someone I know."

Far off, a wolf cries. The sound is distinct from a coyote.

"Is that her?" Dakota asks, curiosity staining her voice. "The wolf?"

I stare into the blackness. "She's close. But she's smart and knows how to stay away from the traps."

"Good for her," Dakota murmurs.

"Yeah. Good for her."

A growl from the woods has Dakota gasping. My senses snap into high alert, and I clinch my bicep to keep her closer. Check the gun on my hip. Keena's growl slowly dies off into soft snuffling, telling me there's no threat.

"The woods scream," she whispers.

I chuckle. "Listen to the woods. They're not your enemy," I say, planting a hand firmly on the small of her back and moving her in the direction of the sound. I point to my right. "They paint a map of where you are. Meadow Mountain and Eden is to the west. The hiking trail near the cabin leads back to the ranch." I pivot her again, this time to the left. Dakota's eyes scan the darkness. "The highway is to the East. You hear the traffic now? Far off?"

She nods. "Yes."

"Trust the land," I say fiercely. "The ranch takes care of us, and I'll take care of you."

She bounces her hip against mine. "And I'll take care of you."

Something cracks in my chest. Sharp and undeserving. "You don't have to make sure I'm okay, Koty."

"Why not?" She turns and cups my face in her hands. "You do it for me. Let me in, Davis."

"You're already in," I admit.

"Oh," she whispers, her eyes momentarily going dreamy. "That makes me happy."

"Good," I tell her. "I like you happy."

Keena bounds back to my side, and we resume walking. A charged silence stretches between us, until I say, "You know, the only time I let someone help me was when I first met you." The cover of darkness is doing something idiotic to my brain, my mouth.

A chuckle shakes out of me. "I loved those cupcakes too damn much."

"Today scared you."

I nod. "It did." The truth has bile rising in my throat.

She's quiet for a long second. "I know you don't want to hear it, but… I should go. He'll destroy what you care about. He's promised me that."

"You're not running."

A sound of frustration. "You can't protect a stranger over your family, Davis. I won't let you."

"You're not a stranger."

"Then what am I?" she asks.

"You're a…friend."

Her hitch of breath is like a knife to the heart.

Fuck, but I'm an asshole.

Heartless is easier. It lets me hide what she means to me.

"I'm not your hero," I tell her and she casts me a sideways glance in the dark. "You've always been able to save yourself." I pull her closer. "But I am your anchor. Because I will always be there when you need something to ground you."

"I like that." She squeezes my arm. "An anchor."

As we walk, her arm in mine, my body hums. A reminder of how we'd talk to each other, how we'd touch each other. Effortlessly. Everything with Dakota is effortless.

Snow crunches beneath our feet as we make our way around the lodge. Dakota's gaze lingers on the woods, the rambunctious approach of Keena, before she looks up at the full moon in the sky.

"My mom always told me dreams are like the moon. Because they are high and bright and brilliant. And sometimes, no matter how hard you try to touch a dream, to bring it down to you, you can't. Sometimes they're stuck. And that's why we needed to rope them. So we could get those dreams come hell or high water."

Dakota bites her lip. Glances at me. "I used to think she was so wise…but now, I think it was probably my mom that was screaming."

I stare up at the moon, wanting nothing more than to pull it out of the sky for her. "You'll get your dreams back, Koty."

"Maybe. Maybe not." She holds her belly, her expression pensive, but not filled with the sadness I've come to expect. "I think that's part of the reason I'm so scared about being back here. I had all these big dreams. And I want them. But I'm unsure how to fit them here in my hometown. They feel scrambled."

A shadow of doubt passes in her eyes. "All I wanted to do was make my father proud. And I don't even know if I've done that." Her voice catches, and I know it's a long-buried fear she's finally releasing.

"Do you remember what you told me the night before you left for San Antonio? You said the future is wide open. And it still is."

Her lips part in surprise. "You remembered."

"I remember everything about you."

She tilts her head, and the cap slips down, making her look like some big-eyed doll. "How do you remember me?"

I chuckle at the memories. "When I remember you, I don't see you as the woman I picked up that night at the motel. I see you at the Roughrider Parade, hurling candy into the crowd. I see you dropping off the best damn banana cake for Charlie, and then sweeping the front porch, even though no one asked you to. I see you as the girl leaping into Lake Cascade in a little string bikini and screaming your fucking head off because it was too damn cold, but smiling the entire time."

Dakota flashes me a smile. "So, what you're saying is I need to jump scantily clad into more lakes?"

A groan tears out of my throat. "You're still trouble."

Keena lurches into view, saving me and my cock from the memory of Dakota that summer. I swear as my stupid dog leaps into a pile of snow and mud. Over and over Keena rolls, her face blissed-out beyond belief.

Looks like that midnight walk is going to turn into a midnight bath.

"She gets the zoomies," I explain to Dakota.

Her lips quirk. "The zoomies?" I clear my throat and she palms my chest. "Under all that steel, you're just a big marshmallow."

"Don't tell anyone."

"Secret's safe with me." A shiver rolls through her slender frame.

"Been longer than fifteen minutes," I tell her.

"Can't go back now. Keena's on a roll." She looks over to where my idiot dog is literally rolling in the snow. "Keep me warm?"

Fuck.

But instead of walking her back to the house, I wrap my arm around her shoulders and tuck her into me. Her body melts against mine. My heart pumps out a hard rhythm, matched only by the throbbing of my cock.

"Is talking in the dark under the moon our thing now?" Her voice comes out slightly breathless.

I kiss the top of her head, inhaling her honeyed scent. "I like under the moon."

"Me too." She beams and every bit of self-control I have disappears. This isn't an itch. Dakota's a need. "Same time tomorrow?"

I should say no. But I can't.

"Wouldn't miss it for the world."

21

Dakota

FALLON'S RINGING UP A CUSTOMER WHEN I EXIT the kitchen, so I hover back and wait until the store clears. Like wildlife, my little sister can be unpredictable when surprised or disturbed.

When she's done, I hold up a jar of Montana huckleberry jam and ask, "Where does this go? Local goods or bread aisle?"

"Local," she says, avoiding my gaze. Her discomfort is so obvious it's painful.

Since our big blow up two weeks ago, we've been walking on eggshells. Making polite, stilted conversation. Running The Corner Store in shifts like two divorced parents who meet in the parking garage to trade children.

It's the way Fallon deals. When she gets mad or sad, she powers down like a robot whose systems are only equipped for wild, never reality. When our mother left, she slept in her closet for two months.

As I move to put away the misplaced item, I graze my belly against the corner of the register. "Oof," I say, clutching my stomach. My baby rolls inside and I smile. I'm getting used to the tiny squish inside of me. We're in it together.

"You're bigger," Fallon says, coming up beside me.

"Tell me about it." I huff a lock of hair out of my eyes. "I'm either bumping into everything with my cast or with my belly."

She gives me her classic droll side-eye. "How long are you planning to keep it a secret?"

"How long do you think I have in this town?"

She snorts. "A month tops." Her left eyebrow lifts. "Won't be able to hide it forever."

"I know," I reply, stroking a hand over my bump.

I'm sick of hiding. My pregnancy. My heart. My dreams.

If Aiden's out there, he better hurry it up.

A smile ghosts Fallon's face. "Or you could just do what I did with my boobs in seventh grade and tape them down."

I bark a laugh. "Somehow, I don't think it works that way."

Fallon's lips press tight as she scans the store. "Fuck it," she says and moves to the door. She flips the sign to closed. It's just after five. "No one's gonna come, anyway."

She stares out into the lavender light of the late afternoon at Davis's truck and taps the glass. "You and Hotshot stop dancing around it?"

My face flushes with heat. An image forms in my mind of Davis kissing me under white moonlight before taking me upstairs to fuck me senseless.

I squeeze my thighs together to drive the image away. "There's no dancing," I say. The words stick in my throat. "In fact, we have a moratorium on dancing."

"Okay, then." Fallon's doubtful eyes flicker to me. "You're not that good of a liar, Dakota." After a second, she crosses the floor and disappears into the kitchen.

My gaze lands on Davis's pickup truck.

Friends, Davis said. And maybe that's the truth.

Maybe that's the problem. Maybe I'm pregnant and horny. And Davis doing sweet things, like buckling my seatbelt over my belly when he drives us into town, sends my hormones into meltdown status.

Maybe all I've done is pin my loneliness onto Davis. It's not love, but sympathy. *Friends*. Friends fucking.

Maybe all it can be is temporary. And maybe I need that. To know there is someone else out there who isn't Aiden.

A good man.

The best man I've ever known.

Brawn and beast. Cowboy and cool. Whiskey and warrior.

The kind of man who makes you feel like the most important, loved, luckiest, and beautiful woman in the universe.

With Davis, I trust him with every inch of myself. I always have.

A part of me doesn't care if it's right or wrong. Doesn't want to understand or fight it.

Because the truth is, I still love him. I've never stopped. I thought being back here would make me realize we weren't meant to be. We changed; we grew apart. That the time we spent together over a year was fleeting, a flash in the pan fling. But the same old feelings still exist for me. He's the same man I loved back then. And it hurts. He's so close, but so far out of reach. For so many reasons.

I need to keep my life easy with simple, attainable things. A man? No. An apartment? Definitely.

Besides, I can't ask a man like Davis Montgomery to take on a hot mess like me, a child that isn't his. I can't put that on him. Who's to say he even wants that?

All I'm taking is his time.

We'll do whatever we do, and I'll be content with that.

For once in my life, I need to sidestep the chaos. For so long, every aspect of my life with Aiden was bedlam. Like a raging static that never shut off in my head. Here, in Resurrection, on Runaway Ranch, I will be in the moment. And, more importantly, I will be safe.

A large crash sounds from the kitchen, and Fallon lets out a string of blazing curses.

On a sigh, I turn and join her.

Inside, my sister kneels amid scattered baking trays, pie tins, and loaf pans. All of which have seen better days. The kitchen looks like it's stuck in 1989. Chaos on multiple fronts—cramped cupboards and never enough counter space.

It has me missing Milk & Honey's sleek kitchen with its gorgeous wood-topped island and kitchen goods like candy molds and egg beaters. A calm, creative space.

Everything The Corner Store isn't. This place needs new appliances and a streamlined work system. My eyes rove, and I frown at the boxes of cigarettes sitting next to the rising bread dough. A container of fishing lures perches next to a slow-cooker of pastrami.

There's a clang as Fallon stacks trays, then shoves them back into a corner cupboard.

I take a step closer to Fallon. "You're doing too much."

She looks up. Scowls. "Do you need something? Other than to boss me around like old times?"

"That wasn't bossing. That was big sistering." I walk around the kitchen space, glance at the recipe board with five lunch specials. "You're doing too much here at the store. You cook, you sell food, you sell worms and cigarettes. You need to pick a specialty and stick with it."

Fallon's fierce hazel eyes simmer. "I guess that's something you'd know about."

"I would." A flare of excitement soars through my chest. The itch to plan claws beneath my skin. "What's your best seller?"

"All-day pastrami. You know that."

"And? You had breakfast." When I started working here, Fallon stopped serving breakfast. At least five locals a day stop in to ask if it's back on the menu.

She avoids my gaze, her cheeks pink. "It does okay. Better since the bakery went out of business."

"Freezer check," I tell her, wiggling my brows. "Let's see what you're hoarding back here."

"No!" Fallon says, pushing back from the counter. Even though she's fast, I see she's limping. "It's a kitchen, Dakota. Of course, we have tons of old shit."

"What happened to your leg?" I ask.

She juts her chin and hurries past me. "Practice."

"With Wyatt?"

Crossing her arms, she sticks her lithe frame in front of the freezer. "Mind your business."

I bump, more like bulldoze her out of the way with my belly. "Move," I order, grabbing the freezer latch and lifting it up. A blast of light and cold air hits me in the face.

"Dakota! Stop!"

"Let's see…ice, ice and more ice." I move aside a pack of frozen peas. "Spaghetti sauce. Bait?" I arch a brow. "Tell me you don't keep Dad's minnows in here." Groaning, I lean down to move a big brick of ice.

She lunges for the freezer, but I'm the older sister and I win, elbowing her back.

"Personal space," she growls, her shoulders tensing, her fists pulled tight.

"Don't make me kick you in the kneecaps," I say as I scrape back the frost on a baking tray.

"That was fifth grade, and you played dirty," she hisses.

"Yeah, and those were my jeans you—Oh my god." Slowly, my head swivels to where Fallon hangs back against the counter, arms crossed, face flaming. "My cinnamon rolls."

I lift the tray and wipe off the lid. I can see swirls of huckleberry and lemon in the frosting. It's my recipe.

Tears spring to my eyes. They're just cinnamon rolls and yet…

They're everything.

Fallon hates baking. My sister would rather chew a bowl of cardboard and milk than attempt domesticity.

"Damn it, Dakota. Don't cry," she orders, eyes darting to my belly.

"You made them," I choke out.

Fallon looks like she wants to light me on fire. "Yeah, well," she says with a hitch of her shoulders. "We needed a recipe for breakfast, so I used yours. Sue me."

"But I never gave you that."

"I found it in the fall issue of *Food & Wine*," she grudgingly admits.

I remember that interview. It was a year before I met Aiden. I was in Paris at a minimalist patisserie that served molten hot chocolate with decadently fluffy whipped cream. I had talked about my new bakery, why croissants are overrated, and the sweet simplicity of the honeybun. But what I left out of that interview was Resurrection.

Thinking back, I credited my culinary school mentor

for my success. But not my little sister for always taste testing all my creations—good or bad. Or my father for giving me the kitchen every Sunday and letting me thrash it with flour and frosting.

Maybe all along I've been wrong. Leaving my past behind, when it was my past that made me.

"I want to try one," I tell her.

She rolls her eyes. "Dakota."

"C'mon." I move over and preheat the oven. "We'll let the dough defrost while we clean up."

And that's what we do while we wait for them to bake. We scrape dirty dishes into sudsy hot water, load silverware and coffee mugs into the dishwasher, and wipe down the counters. I relabel the clear storage containers with neat handwriting, then watch as Fallon, grumbling, pulls the tray of freshly baked cinnamon rolls from the oven.

I sit on a stool while Fallon slathers on the huckleberry frosting like she's carving up a dead body.

She all but throws the plate at me. "Here. Enjoy," she says, her upper lip curling in displeasure. "Or *bon appétit*."

Eyes locked on her face, I break off a piece of cinnamon roll and pop it in my mouth. Slowly, I chew, savoring the doughy texture, the sweet frosting.

I swallow and say, "It's good."

Fallon snorts. "Yeah, right. Critique me. No bullshit. I know you want to do it, and I can take it."

She can. My tough little sister, who gets knocked around by nags and bucked off by broncs, can handle anything.

"The frosting is grainy. And the dough is gummy. You didn't let it rise long enough." I hold up a hand when she snaps open her mouth. "But you did well. For a first timer, I'm seriously impressed."

"Fine. Whatever."

"No way," I say when she goes to clear my plate. "I'm finishing this. Eating for two, remember?"

"Please don't poison your child on my account."

I smile. "Squish."

She wrinkles her nose, and after a second of hesitation, she sits on a stool across from me, elbow on the counter and chin in her palm.

I finish the entire cinnamon roll. It's gloopy and overladen with sugar, but I've tasted nothing more delicious. My sister tried. She tried for me. For our store. That alone is enough to bring tears to my eyes.

A long, withering sigh. "You said you wouldn't cry."

"I'm not." I sniffle. "I'm eating while quietly leaking." As I do, I scan my eyes over her tattoos. Rose bushes up her thighs. Rope–ride on her knuckles. Cowgirls and butterflies on her forearms.

"You got a new one." I point at her colorful forearm folded on the countertop.

"Annie Oakley." She holds her grin close to her heart, looks at me out of the corner of her eye. "The pinup version."

"You and your cowgirls."

"You and your cupcakes." She studies me. "You miss your bakery?"

It's not my favorite topic, but I'll take what I can get from my sister. "I do," I admit on a breathy sigh.

She shrugs. "I remember thinking how much I never wanted this place when we were kids." Her eyes flit to me briefly, then scan the kitchen. "I want to be like dad," she says. "But I don't want the store. I don't want this town. I don't want to die here."

My chest clenches. I can feel her panic, her rush of words fighting against her confidence and cool.

"Fallon, you don't have to do this alone."

"It won't be for long. That store down the block will put us out of business," she says pointedly. "They're better than us."

I inhale a determined breath. "Maybe so, but we'll figure out what our store needs and do it. And if that means closing it…" Fallon pales but hope flickers in her eyes. "I'll be here. And we can talk to Dad together. You shouldn't be stuck with it. And I'm sorry I took that away from you—leaving."

She shifts on her stool, her shoulders tensing. Feelings make Fallon itch. Still, I go on. Even daring to stretch a hand across the table and squeeze hers. "Tell me what you'd do if you could do anything." I smile. "One tiny, little secret."

Her laugh is sad. "No one's ever asked me that. It's all just been…" She makes a fist and rubs a circle around her heart. "Here."

She's still for a long beat.

"I'd leave Resurrection. I'd find Mom. I'd go to Arizona." At my questioning look, she goes on. "There's a camp down south where you can ride with wild horses. Train with Vick Lavoie at his school." A bright blaze of a smile illuminates her face. "I want more than Resurrection. I want the wind. I want freedom."

I stare at her, understanding cracking in my chest. My sister's tumbleweed heart. She's never had any settle down in her boots.

"You made your way. I'll make mine."

"I didn't make my way," I say with a toss of my head. "I built my entire life up only to burn it down."

"No, you didn't." She leans in. "Starting over is okay, Koty. Being alone is okay. What is not okay is staying somewhere where you're hurt or not happy or not safe." Flames dance in Fallon's eyes. "*That* is not okay. Someone hurting you is not okay. And if I ever see that worthless piece of dogshit, I'm going to pound his motherfucking face into the fucking concrete."

My eyes widen. "That's...extremely murderous."

"I only do murder to the extreme."

Fallon cracks a laugh, and I join her. Wild, rebellious laughter, the kind we enjoyed as children.

When the chuckles settle, I grip her hand tighter, desperate for her to understand. "I don't like this, Fallon. I missed you. You're my little sister. You mean everything to me."

"Then why—" She stops, bites her lip.

"Go on."

"Why didn't you tell me?" The look of confusion and despair on her face kills me. "You're my best friend, Dakota. We talked all the time. And then you just stopped calling." She looks down to pick at a thumbnail. "I would have helped you if I had known."

"I know." A deep ache wrenches my heart. "You'd have been there."

"With pliers and a sock full of pennies."

I sigh.

"Fuck," Fallon suddenly blasts. "I'm an asshole. You don't owe me or anyone an explanation."

Even if I don't, maybe talking about it, getting it out is exactly what I need.

My hands palm my belly. "It's okay. I don't expect you to understand. I don't even understand it myself." I pick the words out, pick them apart, still not used to talking about it. Admitting it.

"We were together for a while before it started. And when it did—it was survival. It was like living with a ticking bomb. I focused on work so I wouldn't have to talk about what was happening at home. To my body. I didn't call because I was embarrassed." I wipe my face before the tears start. "I didn't know how to leave. But I knew how to stay. It's like when it's late at night and you're staring at that static on the TV, but you can't make yourself get up to turn it off."

I cast my eyes down, then back up at Fallon. "But you're right. You would have helped me. And I'm so—"

"No," Fallon growls, cutting me off. "If you apologize, Dakota, I will poison your next batch of cinnamon rolls. He did this. Not you."

A tear rolls down my cheek and I wipe my eyes.

"You don't deserve assholes who hurt you. You deserve cupcakes and rainbows and tight-jean wearing Marines." She inhales a shuddery breath and squeezes my hand. "Leaving is powerful. And you are powerful. You had a path, and you made it happen, Dakota. Fuck, I can't even tell Dad I don't want The Corner Store."

I smile through my tears. "We'll tell him together."

Maybe our father was right. The Corner Store turned out to be the best kind of therapy.

I blow out a breath, feeling surprisingly purged, and reach for the tray of cinnamon rolls. "I think I need another cinnamon roll. And I'm going to shove it into my mouth like a lady."

Fallon smirks and grabs a fork. "Fight you for it."

I laugh and the two of us devour the mound of sugary mush.

Food is love. Food is friendship and healing and memory. In every bite, I remember my little sister and that summer our mother left. We still have so much more to say, but we have time.

The muscled body pushing through the saloon door makes Fallon jump. She drops her fork with a clatter.

"Jesus!" She turns her fierce scowl on Davis, who stands in the doorway, his cheeks red from the wind. "Lurk, much?"

"Everything okay?" Davis asks, studying me with his intense stare.

I hold up my fork. "Everything's great."

Fallon slips off her stool. "Gotta go."

"Why are you limping?" Davis's big body pivots to watch her as she passes him. His eyes narrow. "What's wrong with your leg?"

"It's an injury called *none of your business*." Fallon pauses at the sink and dips to grab her duffel bag off the floor. The edge of something powder-blue and lacy peeks over the top of it. "I have practice. Close up, Dakota?"

Davis's hand lands on my shoulder.

"You got it," I tell her, a sweet happiness spreading through my stomach.

At the door, she glances over her shoulder. Gives a cavalier shrug. "I can't take Dad to chemo tomorrow. So, if you want…"

"Yeah," I say, smiling. "I want."

22

Dakota

A BOWL, A BAG OF FLOUR. I STAND AT THE KITCHEN lodge counter, searching my body for the thrill that comes from the chase—the knowledge that my hands will soon create something beautiful.

Pastry chef. I am a pastry chef in the deepest part of my heart.

It's easy to find. It's in my heart. The flex of my fingers. The breath long held that finally comes in an exhale.

Fallon's words from last week have woven through me like a siren song. I dream about them. I wake up to them.

Now, it's time to test them.

I have to bake my little heart out.

The oven chimes in the background. It's ready for me. Rock and roll pulses on the Sonos speaker. Aerosmith, the Rolling Stones. None of Aiden's aggressive metal music.

"You ready?" I ask the big, beautiful kitchen. "Because I am."

I slide the scissors to open the bag of flour. Dip in a measuring cup. Then baking soda. Cocoa powder.

The movements are stiff one-handed, but they're no longer buried. They are not just motions; they are my heart. And I know them. The recipes spill out, some old, some new, as I flawlessly bake the day away.

Slow but steady. That is the name of my game.

I press a finger down, testing a tray of peppermint

bark. The kitchen fills with the sounds of simmering caramel sauce, the soft sighs of cinnamon roll dough. I take a
bite of strawberry jam that has me groaning, has the squish
in my belly kicking with delight.

I hold my belly and laugh.

Joy.

That's the word for it.

I feel joy.

Fucking finally.

My breath catches and releases. The color in the bowl
is bright yellow.

A rope-the-moon color.

An always and forever hope.

As I bake, I picture the Corner Store. What it is and
what it could be.

Yes, I lost my bakery, but I didn't lose myself. That girl,
that woman, that baker, is still in there. She's deep in my
blood, edging out fear, the pain in my arm.

I'm pulling a tray of goodies from the oven when I
catch sight of Davis coming through the doorway in full
MONSAR gear. He's been out on a call to assist in the
search for hikers who went missing near Elk Lake. His
navy T-shirt is stretched tight over his biceps, and I want
to ingrain the heart-thumping sight to memory.

His heavy gaze scans the kitchen, then looks at me, not
bothering to hide his surprise. "You're baking."

His rough voice has my stomach doing a full-on swoop.

"I am." I set the cupcakes on the counter. "I need practice before I make Ruby her cake. I'm rusty."

He rubs his palm across his jaw. "Are you sure?"

"Yes, I'm sure. I want her to have the best cake she's
ever had."

"It's just a cake."

I wag my finger at him. "No, Davis Montgomery. It's never just a cake. It is a bucket list cake." I give him a knowing look. "It's a cake for the girl your brother loves."

His eyes soften. "You want me to leave? Give you some space?"

I smile. This is Davis. Always here, asking me what I need. A safe, constant presence I can count on.

My brow creases in thought and I tip my head. "Will you help me?"

"What're we making?"

"Cupcakes. We can frost together. I need another hand."

He stands beside me, settling back on his boots to watch as I scrape the frosting out of the bowl and into piping bags.

I hand one over. "You squeeze the bag and I'll pipe."

"Fuck," he whispers as one big hand slips, squeezing a ridiculous amount of frosting onto the cupcake.

I laugh. It's funny watching this stoic, strong man do soft things like frost a cupcake. But I like it.

"It's okay. Slower," I instruct. My fingers curl around his. Familiar, steady comfort. Then, with deft strokes, I show him how to pipe a floret.

"Got it." Davis leans in, and his scent fire and spice, the nearness of him towering over me, has my stomach warming.

"You're a natural."

He chuckles. His big hands dwarf the cupcake. "I don't know about that."

We lapse into silence, the soft dabs of the frosting and the turn of the plate the only sounds between us. Our movements are easy and sure. When we've finished piping the silky frosting into dreamy buttercream rosettes, I walk around the island, surveying the cupcake with a sniper's eye.

"Final touches," I tell Davis who's watching me.

The music switches over to AC/DC.

His mouth hitches up in a grin as he stares down at our creation. "What kind is it?"

"It's the Cowboy Cupcake." Pursing my lips, I squint, then pluck a pecan from a nearby bag. I add it to the top of the buttercream for a finishing touch. "It's an ode to the cookies we used to sell at The Corner Store. Loaded to the max with chocolate chips, coconut, and pecans."

Davis crosses his arms. "You know, I don't think I've ever seen you bake before. I didn't know your tongue does this little thing…" He sweeps a thumb over my bottom lip, his eyes narrowing on my mouth. "You quirk."

I arch a brow. "You looking at my lips, Hotshot?"

"Among other things," he grunts.

I laugh and take a stack of dishes to the sink. "Well, let me tell you. There are many things you don't know about me," I tease.

His golden-brown eyes dance in amusement. "Such as?"

"The first time I saw your ass in a pair of Wranglers, I had to take a moment and fan myself." His gaze turns dark as I lick the spoon and drop it in the sink. "I believe in aliens," I say and he groans, breaking into a boom of laughter that has me smiling. "And," I palm his brick-like chest, look up into his eyes. "I made these cupcakes for you."

The muscles in his throat work. "It's been a while since I've had a cupcake."

I pick up the platter, lift it with fanfare. "I know you don't eat sweets, so…if you don't want them, I can give them to your brothers."

He puts a hand on mine and stops me before I can set down the platter. "I eat your sweets." His reply is curt, raspy. His nostrils flare and my heart speeds up. "I don't share you, Koty. Not with anyone."

His low, possessive rumble curls my stomach.

Davis picks up a cupcake with a delicate clumsiness. With his eyes locked on me, he eats the whole damn thing. He chews thoughtfully, like he wants me to see what it means to him. When he's finished, he lets out a moan. "Best damn thing I've ever had."

A happy laugh sputters out of me. "I knew you secretly like my cupcakes." I poke him in the chest. My hand drifts up to his mouth. "And… you are messy," I say, wiping a crumb from his lips.

"Dakota."

His voice is rough as he stares at me, that hard jaw of his working over and over, and then he yanks me into him, his mouth finding mine in a hungry, desperate kiss.

I lose myself in the moment, in this man. Every question about what we are melts out of my mind. His kiss burns like high-proof whiskey, caramel and spice, and my entire body shivers.

"Goddammit, I can't stay away from you, woman," he husks, his hands tangling in my hair before they cup my face.

"So don't," I breathe, pulling back from him. "I'm here. You're here. We both like it. Let's just… be *friends*."

He growls and nips at my lips as if what I've said displeases him.

The place between my legs ache and I step forward into Davis's arms, shifting my hips against him. "Let's be us from back then. Just for a little while." His eyes are dark as they scan my face. "It felt good. It felt right."

"Too goddamn right," he says on a deep groan. He drops his forehead to mine. Then, with one quick move, he spins me around and presses me up against the island.

My self-respect, my determination to figure out what we are, takes a back seat the minute Davis spreads his palms over my hips and whispers in my ear, "Hands on the counter, Cupcake."

"Oh," I breathe, eyes wide.

His long fingers dip to tease at my waistband before they disappear inside the front of my leggings.

I'm panting now, my good hand curled to a fist.

Two of Davis's clever fingers dip into me. Warm mouth on my neck, he groans. "Look how fucking gorgeous you are dripping your need for me."

My breath catches at his words. At the smooth rhythm he creates with his fingers. The gentle thrust and roll has me following it with my hips. His touch reminds me I deserve the brightest light of happiness. Everything good and safe and healthy.

Davis presses himself so tight against me I feel his hardness. His breath tickles my ear as he breathes, "Spread your legs, Dakota."

Like it's a natural, gravitational pull, Davis's free hand moves to my belly. My skin ripples and I hitch a breath. Davis's fingers fan out like he's trying to capture the last of the movement before he unzips his jeans. I swivel my hips, urging him along. So needy, so desperate for this man.

As I glance over the kitchen, a laugh bubbles up inside

me. Dirty dishes forgotten. Frosting smeared across the counter.

I moan and cover my face. "I'll never be able to bake cupcakes without thinking of you," I say, my body pressed down so low I can smell fresh lemon and thyme.

"I know it," he rumbles in my ear. "I want you to fucking remember that, Cupcake."

With that, Davis slips into me.

And everything falls away.

We're those kids from what seems like a lifetime ago. Fucking in the cabin, screwing around under the entire town's noses, me thinking he was the most beautiful man I'd ever seen.

And just like I did back then, I go with the flow.

At least until this baby is born.

Until Davis Montgomery breaks my heart all over again.

23

Dakota

EBRUARY TURNS TO MARCH. I GET MY CAST OFF, leaving my arm pale and withered. The snow melts and the first buds of spring unfurl on the apple trees. I go into my twenty-fifth week. My baby's now the size of a head of lettuce and he–or–she rolls around in there like a tumbleweed. I restock The Corner Store with cinnamon rolls and fill notebooks with new recipes. I work on Ruby's cake, but it's still not perfect.

I call the insurance company, ask about my claim. They're still working on it. I call Aiden's work. Every Monday, he's there at the agency. With that comes relief. He gave up, he let me go.

It seems too good to be true.

But I'll take it.

For a long time, it felt like I couldn't wake up. But with no sign of Aiden, I feel like I'm slowly easing into life. A better life that could be mine if I only let it.

One Friday after my shift at The Corner Store, I stroll down Main Street, a box of bread loaves in my arms for our local food bank, Beartooth Cupboards. The baby kicks and the box against my belly bounces as I head inside.

"Hi." The woman at the front desk slides a sign-in sheet toward me.

In return, I slide the box of bread onto the counter. "Hi. This is for you. Donation."

"Need a receipt?" the woman asks, giving me a head-to-toe scan.

"Nope," I say, shifting away from her eyes on my belly. Soon, I won't be able to hide it.

I exit the food bank and stop to glance at the store next door. Resurrection Real Estate. I look up, following the red arrows and lettering that reads APARTMENTS FOR RENT.

When I was a kid, I always loved the old brick buildings on the main drag in Resurrection. I always pictured brick walls, wooden floors, and old gas lanterns, even though I know now what a terrible fire hazard it would be.

I give my stomach a rub like it's a good luck charm and enter the office, where I schedule an appointment for a showing at the end of next week.

The sky's a crisp blue as I walk back toward The Corner Store, a bounce in my step as I pass the biker bar next to the lingerie store. I'm only ten minutes away, but I can feel Davis worrying. Watching. My body can't shake his eyes. It can't shake a lot of things. Like, the fact we're sneaking around like old times.

There's no naming what we are, no expectations or commitments, just sex on the sly.

Permanently wrinkled bed sheets.

Stone-cold secrecy.

We're beating the heat we had that summer. A heightened awareness lingers between us, our hands and lips magnetized for each other. Every time he buries his face in my hair and growls, a delicious ache forms in the pit of my stomach. It's like instead of backing away from whatever's between us, we jumped in head first. Unleashed it.

What that is, I wish I knew.

It's a wonderful feeling to have him back in my life,

but also so terrible because it will end. I've loved him for so long, but I have bigger life problems than to tell him how I feel.

Especially right now.

This will end when the baby comes, if not before that, and I have to be okay with it.

Before I cross the sidewalk, my gaze flicks across the street to the Little Prairie Market. Beneath its minimalistic sign, a cheery red strip of metal with silver cursive proclaims, *Farm and Family Focused.* With its white shutters, shiny red façade, and garage style doors, it's like nothing I've ever seen in my town.

It's beautiful.

I bite my lip, guilt and curiosity crawling through my veins. Do I dare?

Yes, I dare.

I narrow my eyes and cross the street, hustling past the town terror, a ferocious-looking Pitbull named Hungry Hank. I want to see this store Fallon's been complaining about, but first, I reach for my phone in my back pocket and fire off a text to Davis.

Me: Wanna get frisky?

Davis: Dakota.

I smile at the stern message. My heart thumps as I watch those three bubbles appear, disappear. Falling back into our bantering texts feels right.

Davis: What do you have in mind? Should I bring handcuffs?

I giggle.

Me: Well, it does involve nudity.

Me: I need new bras.

Davis: What?

Me: I want to check out the new market. You're my bodyguard, right? C'mon, Hotshot. Move those boots for my boobs.

Me: Can you come?

Davis: For you, always.

Davis: Be there in five.

Mission accomplished, I pocket my phone and head inside the store.

∽

"I'm a traitor," I hiss to Davis, skirting the aisles like I'm hiding from a sniper. "Fallon will kill me."

He chuckles as his dark eyes rove the store. David Bowie drifts over the speakers, giving it a kind of eclectic cowboy cool. "I have to admit, it's impressive."

Impressive is an understatement. Little Prairie Market is everything Resurrection needs. Charming. Innovative. Accessible. And a bigger supermarket chain means no more driving to Billings or Bozeman to stock up—everything is local.

They're not the devil Fallon painted them out to be, but they're not doing The Corner Store any favors.

"How can we compete?" I ask Davis. "Dad can keep the store open and bleed money if he wants...but Fallon... she's wasting away there."

A thoughtful look crosses his face, and his hand moves to the small of my back. "Maybe you don't compete?"

I arch a brow. "That's...helpful?"

He grins and grabs a cart.

I give a cursory glance around. Under the bright lights of the market, it feels hard to hide. From Resurrection. From my stomach.

There's a handful of people with baskets strolling past a mural of Billy the Kid painted on a crisp white wall. I marvel at the displays of fresh-caught seafood. As I meander through the aisles, Davis behind me, my brain turns his words over and over. *Maybe you don't compete.*

Maybe we don't.

Maybe we change.

The Little Prairie Market has everything we don't. But we have a restaurant, and the one thing the town doesn't have—a bakery.

I gasp when I turn the corner and find myself in the home goods section.

More specifically, the baby aisle. Cans of powdered formula, funky wooden rattles, and organic baby food surround me. I find myself pausing, taking in the tiny onesies and plush blankets.

"Holy shit, they do have bras," I say, lunging for a rack with greedy hands. I unzip my jacket, then push on my chest, my cleavage in upheaval. I moan at the relief. "They're huge now."

Davis's face reddens. "Jesus Christ, Dakota." His voice is anguished.

I hide a smirk at this big cowboy coming undone. Davis's appreciation for my breasts knows no bounds. With a flirty smile, I lean into his chest and purr, "But you already know that, don't you?"

Eyes turning dark and feral, his hand slides to squeeze the curve of my ass.

I drop a bra into the cart.

"I'm going to check out the baking supplies." I swat at him when he makes a move to follow me. "Stay here. Guard the bras," I say, enjoying the look of panic on his face.

The last thing we need is the entire town gossiping about us. Even if I can't get the thought of two earth shattering orgasms from this morning out of my head.

He rolls his eyes, but stands near the aisle endcap, arms crossed, looking like some overprotective bodyguard on baby aisle duty.

Briefly, I let my eyes linger on the sexy sight, then head for the dairy aisle.

"Oh my God," I say on a breathy sigh.

It's better than anything I've ever seen in my life.

Coolers stocked with the most decadent essentials of ingredients.

French grass-fed butter flaked with sea salt. Crème fraiche. Organic eggs. A hopeful giddiness rises inside of me. I'm already envisioning Ruby's birthday cake. A carrot cake as tall as the Rocky Mountains. As sweet as the girl I've come to know.

"Never thought I'd see it," a raspy voice says from behind me. I turn, stifling a groan. Sheena Wolfington slinks around a display of soup cans, looking like she's been lying in wait. "*Goodbye Girl* on aisle three."

I take a step back from Sheena and yank my jacket shut. But I'm too late. Her wolfish eyes lock on my stomach. "Don't you have better things to do than lurk in dairy aisles, Sheena?" I ask, squaring my shoulders.

Best friends in grade school, bitter rivals in high school. We fought over head cheerleader, prom queen, and Sam Bailey. I came out on top. But from the delighted look on Sheena's face, not anymore.

"How's that big fancy job of yours?" Sheena sneers, waving her blood-red nails in the air. Her black hair, once a long tumble of curls, is cut into a shaggy bob, and she has too much makeup on her angular face. She's a forever buckle bunny chasing cowboys, getting her entire personality from a rattlesnake.

Humiliation flames over my cheeks. "I'm home. You can probably figure that out for yourself."

"Restaurant didn't work out, huh?" Sheena's lip curls. "And now the golden girl's back. Knocked up. Without a man. Never thought I'd see the day."

She gives me a long, satisfied look and I flinch.

My heart twists and I cover my belly protectively. My baby doesn't deserve this.

She makes a sour face. "Thought you'd do things differently, didn't you? Thought you were so great, and now, look who's come crawling back."

"You're in the big leagues of petty, Sheena," I say, feeling sad and exhausted. I glance at the end of the aisle, and Davis is nowhere to be seen. Great. Now I have to extricate myself from Sheena's claws.

"Get on the bench, baby." Sheena advances. "Everyone's talking."

A flicker of the old Dakota McGraw rises in me. A memory surfaces of me knocking her on her ass in eighth grade for calling Fallon "trailer park pretty." You can take the girl out of Montana, but you can't take Montana out of the girl.

Head high, Koty. Rope that fucking moon.

I lift my chin, ball a fist. "I'd rather be talked about than be the miserable bitch doing the talking."

"But talking's fun. So, who's the father, Dakota? We're all curious."

The question stops me cold.

"I can't wait for this." Sheena crosses her arms, the glee in her voice unmistakable.

My chest fills with panic. So much of my skin is tight, chilled. I want a way out, an escape hatch, but all I can do is sink.

"There you are. I've been looking for you." The boom of a voice makes both Sheena and I jump.

Davis strides my way, his gold-flecked eyes fierce and flashing.

Before I can say anything, a massive hand slides down my ass. Davis cups it. Squeezes. I squeak and lurch forward, but he grabs me back and locks me to his body. Then he stares down into my eyes and plants his mouth to mine.

I go limp. Molten.

The kiss is soft and sweet, his lips sweeping over mine, his tongue playfully tangling. When he pulls back, he keeps me firmly in his grasp, refusing to let go.

I squirm, wanting to get out of the public gaze. Two aisles down, Chet Hill, an old fishing buddy of my father's, double takes.

"Davis." I gape up at him, clinging to his broad chest. I try to shove him away, but he refuses to budge. "What are you doing?" I whisper.

Eyes searching my face, he tucks a lock of hair behind my ear. "You ready to go, Cupcake?"

Sheena, her face sour, recoils. "Are you two—"

"Yes," Davis growls, his expression murderous.

And then it softens as he looks at me and places a broad palm on my belly.

A message so obvious I want to cry.

If Sheena's jaw could permanently unhinge, it would be on the floor.

My knees are jelly. Every ounce of fight dissipates as I go pliant against Davis's rugged chest.

Sheena clutches her grocery list in her fist. "I don't fucking believe it."

Davis's face turns to stone as he whips his head to Sheena. "Didn't you learn your lesson with Fallon?" he growls in a tone that no sane person would argue with.

Sheena's screech of colorful curses echoes through the market as she walks away.

Davis tilts my chin up to meet his concerned gaze. "You okay, Cupcake?"

"Why'd you do that?" I ask, dazed, still clinging to him.

"Because," he grits out. He gives me a scolding look, steers us forward to retrieve the cart. "I saw that fist you were ballin', baby. No fighting. Not in your condition."

"But…" My mind cartwheels. "Everyone will know, Davis. Everyone will think you're the father." I rapidly blink against the warm sear of tears, Davis's possessive arm around my waist. "Oh my God."

Davis curls one hand around the cart handle and guides us forward. Amusement creases his handsome face. "That's kind of the point, Cupcake."

My jaw drops and I process his words as we head to the checkout. I'm vaguely aware we've reached the register when Davis passes over the bra, a stuffed blue bear, and a baby monitor to the clerk.

"Hey, Pete," Davis says.

Pete Perry's eyebrows slant low. "Damn, Montgomery, you got a baby on the way?"

Davis chuckles, hands over another stuffed bear. Pink this time. "Sure looks like it."

My entire body turns to a puddle, and I grip the conveyor belt to stay afloat. Oh, this man. Protecting me in so many other ways than just bodily.

Davis pays for our items and by the time we walk out the front doors and into the snow, I've regrouped. Indignation curdles my stomach.

Grabbing his plastic sack-clad arm, I back us into the alleyway and narrow my eyes at him. "Davis Montgomery. You do not have to keep saving me."

His stare is stoic. "What's wrong with that?"

My mouth opens, closes, then his warm rumble of a chuckle washes over me. After letting the bags fall to the ground, he takes my face in his hands. "You can save yourself. I know that. I've known that since the minute you walked onto my ranch and force fed me a cupcake. I'm just here to keep you steady."

I nod, hot tears filling my eyes.

"Steady," I whisper. "Right."

It feels like that. No longer adrift. Not anymore.

"No more small-town drama. That isn't your focus. I don't want you worked up." His hand falls to my belly, and I melt into his gentle hold. "I don't want anyone asking you questions you're not comfortable with. This cuts out the bullshit." A rare grin graces his handsome face. "They won't talk shit about you with me."

"And why is that?"

His eyes flash. "I know how to kill a man."

"Because you were a Marine?"

"Because I have a little sister." On a low growl, he takes my chin and holds it forcefully but gently between his big fingers. His voice a stern, yet, soothing command. "No one in Resurrection knows your story but you, Dakota. You get to tell it. Change it."

He's right.

The truth about my child's father doesn't matter. What matters is what people believe. That I have grace from my past here in Resurrection.

Still, for him to do this. It asks a lot. Davis treasures his sanity, his privacy.

"I just—"

His eyebrows lift. "What? What is it?"

"Won't it bother you? People talking?"

"People are already talking," he says, leaning down until he husks it against my lips. He smells of pine and coffee, his massive body providing a barricade from the wind at the mouth of the alleyway. "At least now they'll talk about us."

Us.

That's all there is to say. The wind blows my words away, and I fling myself at Davis, crashing into him like he's a stone wall.

Davis smiles, eyes crinkling at the corners, and grabs me tight to him, his muscled arms wrapping around the center of my back. My belly nestles against his.

I brush my lips against his and whisper, "Davis. What are we doing?"

"Cupcake, I don't fucking know," he says and kisses me breathless.

24

Davis

TOUSLED HAIR. TANGLED LIMBS. DAKOTA IN MY bed.

For the last seven days, every night, every waking moment has been us. We haven't stopped having sex since we got back from the Little Prairie Market. Barely leaving bed except to refuel, rehydrate, and repeat.

But now it's time to face reality. What the fuck was I thinking? Me claiming Dakota's baby as mine in front of half the damn town makes things even more complicated. But when I saw her taking Sheena's attack with a stubborn chin and tear-filled eyes, the shadows inside of me raged. I couldn't stop myself from stepping in.

The last thing she needs is any small-town drama. So, I kissed her. To make them shut up. To take that sad look off her face. Dakota told me she didn't want people to know the truth, and this way, the truth is ours and ours alone.

No one will disturb the peace Dakota's created in her life. Especially not the bastard who put his hands on her. He's mine. He just doesn't know it yet.

The late morning sun shines outside my window and my ears pick up the distinct sound of tractors puttering around the yard.

"Shit." I glance over with a groan. Dakota's buried beneath the rumpled sheets, so deep all I can see is her mound of dark hair and a creamy white leg tossed over the covers, tangled with mine.

A wave of primal protection crests over me. In a single action, I've claimed her. And her baby.

Everything is different. The way we breathe. The way we move. The way we fuck. There's no more distance between us. And it has me realizing I have to be honest with her about how I feel. What I want. We're good together, and I want more of that good.

But first, there's work to be done. Work that takes me away from the gorgeous woman in my bed.

I press a kiss to the top of her head. "Cupcake, I have to go."

For the first time in years, I've shirked my responsibilities on the ranch. Even as a kid, I was the one rounding up my brothers for farm chores. The ranch can run on autopilot with Charlie around, but it's damn duty that has me dragging my sorry ass out of bed to go help my brothers.

Facing them is inevitable. By now, everyone knows about me and Dakota. I've gotten no less than ten texts from the boys at the station. The kicker was a text from Stede yesterday that simply said: *Let's talk, son.*

Christ.

The man's going to kill me.

I owe it to him to have a sit down. Soon, too.

Dakota peeks her head above the blankets, her dark eyes sleepy as she burrows into my chest, causing my cock to jerk like a puppet on a string. "Stay." Her scratchy morning voice rasps against my skin. "Don't make me beg."

A smile tugs at my mouth. "What if I do?"

She tips her head back, sticks out her tongue. "Then no kisses. No cupcakes."

"But I like your cupcakes." Impatient, I devour her mouth. Our lips lock together, warmth rising in the sheets between us.

Fuck the ranch. All I need is Dakota.

And I'm the damn fool who took this long to realize it.

I lick and kiss my way down her neck until my teeth graze the dark pink bud of her nipple. She moans, a content exhalation, and I pull her closer.

Her belly kicks me in the stomach, causing me and Dakota to freeze. We laugh, and I surf my hand beneath the covers, resting it on her bump. "Squish's got the timing down pat."

She feels her ribs, stroking her palm over the moon of her belly. Softness is etched across her pretty face. "Hmm. Squish is killing my lower intestine."

"Be good to your mama," I tell her belly. After a second of hesitation, I give in, pressing a soft kiss to her stomach.

I feel the hitch of her breath, and her hand lands in my hair, her graceful fingers dragging over my scalp.

The pain of knowing Dakota's pregnant with another man's child has slowly ebbed. Whatever happens, I'll be in her child's life. She and her baby aren't alone anymore. They have me. It's that easy.

But I can't lose sight of what's on the line. Their safety. Her ex is still out there, and I can't afford distractions. I need to be operating at 100 percent. Even if the distraction is gorgeous as hell.

I kiss the freckle on her lip and sit up.

"I need to go see about the ranch," I say, grabbing my clothes off the corner chair. "Check in with my brothers."

"I can help with chores." Dakota sits up in bed, and the sight of her smile renders me motionless. She looks stronger, happier than on the day I picked her up at that motel.

Pride flares inside me. My girl. My goddamn girl.

I run a hand up her shoulder and through all that dark silky hair. "I want you to rest."

She fingers the dog tag around her neck. A teasing smile tugs at her lips. "What if I need you?"

"Baby, you press that button and you're going to give me a one-way ticket to a heart attack." I slip my shirt over my head, grab my CB radio. She's still staring at me with those dark, stubborn eyes. "You want to help, feed Keena. Take her for a walk."

She laughs, rolls her eyes. "Oh, sure. Give me the fun job."

I plant one last kiss on her lips before dragging myself away from her.

This woman's a distraction, interrupting all my best laid plans.

And I fucking love it.

On my way out, I lock the lodge and straighten up on the front porch. It finally looks like spring. The low-hanging gray clouds that loomed over the ranch are gone. Chased away by bold, bright sunshine. I take a breath and get to work.

Two hours later, after checking in on my dogs and running them through a series of training exercises, I make a stop at Charlie's cabin.

"Well, look who rejoined the land of the living," Charlie says, glancing up from his cup of coffee and running his eyes over me.

Ford, sitting at the counter, snorts, ignoring me in favor of the beer in front of him.

"Coffee," I demand as step I inside and glare at Charlie.

I'm not in the mood for an asshole pile-on session from my brothers.

"Hi, Davis."

At the bright chirp of a voice, I halt in my boots and look down, about two seconds away from barreling over Ruby, who sits cross-legged on the floor. Three mewling kittens crawl across her lap. What the hell do they plan to do with three kittens? Strike that. There are four. Another one claws at the front of Charlie's shirt. He looks big and awkward holding the small bundle of fur.

I smirk at Charlie as he passes it down to his wife.

He jabs a finger at me. "Not a word."

My brother's a goddamn sucker. But for once in a damn long time, I understand. I think of the stuffed bears I've been buying for Dakota's baby. I don't have a fucking chance.

"You want one?" Ruby asks. The kittens sound like slowly deflating balloons with their imploring squeals. "They need homes."

I grin. "Keena would love her."

She gives me a chiding look, then says, "We rescued them from the woodpile." A calico kitten casually eats Ruby's hair while she cuddles it. Her pretty face turns solemn. "Because of the wolf."

"Wolf?"

Charlie says something in a low voice to Ford and that's when I notice a pile of trash and bones on the kitchen table.

I scrub a hand down my face, turning to Charlie. "What did I miss?"

"The wolf's still getting onto the ranch," Charlie says, sliding a cup of coffee my way. "We took those cattle off the public grazing land up at Eden and moved them closer in, but the wolf followed. Killed a heifer last night. She's sneaking onto the ranch somehow."

"She's a wolf," Ford says with a shrug of his shoulders.

Charlie's eyes darken. "Chuck Gibbons said his granddaughter was almost attacked. If he hadn't had bear spray with him, it could have ended differently."

"Jesus." Annoyance flares beneath my skin. Not knowing what's going on with my family chaps my ass. "Why didn't anyone call me?"

Ford cocks an eyebrow at me and picks up his beer. "Been busy."

I move to stand with my brothers at the island. Cross my arms. "Not too busy for my family."

Ford just stares at me.

A white-hot frustration boils under my skin. Ford likes to piss me off. Normally, I find it amusing, and give it back as good as I get it. Today, I'm damn close to dumping the entire pot of coffee over my twin's head.

"Speaking of family…" The edges of Charlie's lips twitch. "I hear congratulations are in order. You and Dakota being in a family way and all."

Ruby giggles and stands, gently cradling a marmalade kitten in her arm.

"Christ." I groan. "Who else knows?"

"I reckon the whole damn town after what y'all did at the market."

A grin appears on my face before I can smother it out. Fuck, but I want the whole town to know what I do. That Dakota's devastation is everywhere. My disheveled hair from where her hands have been. Scratches down my back. My rumpled shirt carries the scent of her perfume that not even ranch work can chase away.

Ford's sullen voice carries across the room. "Just because y'all are humping like bunnies doesn't mean you can forget about the ranch."

"Don't fucking start," I growl, swinging his way. Next to me, Charlie tenses. "And I haven't forgotten about the ranch."

"Bullshit." Ford shakes his head. "We got problems here, man. And you got too many distractions. Too much girl drama."

"Yeah, you'd know all about girl drama, wouldn't you?" I say, my voice low and dangerous.

Ford's eyes flash. "What's that supposed to fucking mean?"

"Easy, we're all in this," Charlie reminds us.

A charged silence falls over the kitchen as both of my brothers stare at me. One confused, the other pissed off.

They don't understand the history between Dakota and me. If I finally opened up to them, would it make things easier? I'm a rock, but it's not doing me any favors. They're my brothers, and by holding back, I keep them at a distance. Every day I don't tell them the truth, I push them away.

That changes today.

"Dakota and I…" I drag a hand through my hair, unused to letting my guard down. I face my brothers. "We were…screwing around back when I first came to town to help out Charlie."

That gets me dropped jaws from Ruby and Charlie. Only a scowl from Ford.

On an inhale, I set my mug down. I'm holding it so tight it's a wonder it hasn't broken into a million pieces.

"I was depressed, okay?" I grit the words out, meet Charlie's eyes. "I was going through some shit. Nightmares. PTSD. And she helped. She was there for me in a way no one's ever been, which is why I'm here for her *now*. And I'm not walking away."

I need my brothers to understand that this matters. *She* matters.

"Christ," Ford says in exasperation, slugging down his beer.

"We're picking up where we left off. I care for her. I've always cared for her. So, since you're giving me the fucking third degree, there's your answer, you fucking assholes."

"Well, shit," Charlie says, opening his arm to Ruby, who slips beneath it. The marmalade kitten has made a nest between her hair and collarbone. "That's a long time, Davis." He cracks a grin, but his eyes are soft. "Sure can keep secrets, man."

"So you're what?" Ford demands. "Dating? Fucking?"

"Not your business," I tell him.

"Don't do the no-label thing, Davis," Ruby says, her eyes big and beseeching. She moves to clamp my bicep, and the kitten scampers up my arm. "You have to tell her."

Ford's jaw tightens, and he swears. "Whatever happened to not having time for a relationship? Whatever happened to priorities?"

"Priorities change," I growl and pluck the kitten from my neck to hand it back to Ruby.

"Priorities." He snorts. "Thinking with your dick's your priority."

Ruby squeaks.

"Okay." Charlie lifts his hands. "Let's just keep it above the belt."

"You got sense, D," Ford says, sounding aggrieved. "Why are you fucking with Stede's daughter? She's pregnant. She's gonna have this guy's baby and split."

"Careful," I warn. Ford's skating on thin ice. Anyone shows the slightest interest in love, a relationship, and he gets a goddamn attitude.

"You're my brother. I gotta look out for you." He twists on the barstool to glare at me. "We need to get the ranch ready for the summer. We can't have distractions. Not after last year."

My eyes flick to Ruby, back to Ford. "Fuck you for using last year against me." It's a low blow, and he knows it. "Is this what you did with Charlie?" I snarl, anger slowly burning inside of me. "Warning him away from Ruby, telling him she had her secrets, and he was going to get hurt?"

"You're an asshole," Ford snaps.

"And you have to get a new MO, Ford. You have to get over the past and stop bringing everyone down with you."

A contrite look crosses his face as his gaze flicks to Ruby. Her hurt blue eyes are pinned to the ground. "That's a bullshit move," he hisses. "And you know it."

It is. But I play dirty when it comes to Dakota.

I drill a finger. "You don't bring up Dakota again. Especially not when you don't have anything fucking nice to say."

"Fuck you," Ford mutters. He slips off his stool, goes to Ruby. "Honey, I'm sorry," he says softly. "You're the best thing that ever happened to my dumb little brother. Us too. We couldn't get along without you."

"It's okay," Ruby whispers.

Charlie watches her, worry tight on his face. He told me last week he caught her crying in the stables. Ruby has a sweet heart and when she hurts, we all feel it.

Ford tilts Ruby's chin up. "I'm sorry, Fairy Tale."

A glimmer of a smile lifts Ruby's lips. "Make it up to me. You can take a kitten."

Ford balks.

Ruby hugs the marmalade kitten tight. "They need homes."

"Take a fucking cat, Ford," Charlie barks.

"Fine. Fuck." Our brother scowls, then leans down to curl his large hands over a bounding black kitten. Its tiny mewls fill the air as he lifts the furry bundle high and scrutinizes it. "This is the stinkiest bastard of the bunch," he tells Ruby.

Ruby swats at him. "No, don't be mean."

Ford grins and tucks the squirming kitten in the front pocket of his flannel. "See ya, honey."

Without a second look at me, he's out the door and pounding down the porch steps.

"What's wrong with Ford?" Ruby asks, drifting to Charlie's side.

I rub the knot brewing in my temple. The urge to go after my twin and kick some sense into him is tempting. "That's what I'd like to fucking know."

"He's going through something," Charlie adds. He glares at me. "You both are."

I grumble. "He's acting like an asshole."

"Then you two stay the hell away from each other." Charlie grins. "Or you settle it like you did when y'all were kids. Fists out in the cornfield. Either way, fucking focus. We got shit to do."

We do.

I leave the house, intent on dealing with the wolf, but Ruby's words repeat in my head.

You have to tell her.

The thought hits me in the gut.

What the fuck am I doing sneaking around with Dakota again? Acting like we're faking it, when for me, it's never been fake.

Maybe Ford's right, maybe I am distracted by Dakota, but I don't give a shit. She makes me feel like I deserve my life, instead of trying to hide away from it.

I cross the ranch in whip-quick speed, my heart damn near beating out of my chest when I enter the lodge.

Dakota's in the kitchen, putting her newest sonogram photo on the fridge, and I'm hit by an undeniable feeling about how damn right it looks there.

Hearing me, she turns. Her smile lights up her face. "I hope it's okay," she says, gesturing at the photo. "I'll get my own place soon, but for now…"

"Better than okay." I band my arms around her waist and drop my mouth to hers. When I pull back, my gaze catches on the glossy pages of the *Resurrection Review* out on the counter. "What's this?"

"Apartment hunting," she says, and the breath leaves my lungs. "I have a tour set up next week. One of those lofts on Main."

I frown. "Cupcake."

She shakes her head, reading my mind. "I have to go sometime, Davis."

"I don't like it." At this point, there's no way in hell she's moving out. If I have my way, never.

I tighten my grip, pull her closer, running a hand over the curve of her belly. "I like *this*. You here, against me."

Her lips part, those stunning dark eyes widening.

"Whole town thinks we're dating. Stede too," I rasp against her mouth. "Might as well make it official."

"Oh, yeah?" she breathes. "Fake it for the town?"

My heart pounds, but my voice is sure. "No. It's never been fake for me."

Dakota freezes in my arms. "Then what was it?" She sounds breathless.

Love.

Always has been.

Still, I hold my tongue. Too soon. Dakota needs slow.

I kiss her forehead. "We can spend time worrying about rumors or we can worry about us."

Her smile widens. Breaks my heart in the best kind of way. "Us?"

"Yes. Us. There always should have been an *us*, Dakota."

"Maybe we're just better as a secret," she whispers, her brown eyes damp. "As friends."

"No." It's a growl that ends any further arguments. I cup the back of her neck and stare into her eyes. "No more secrets. No more hiding. No more friends. I'm taking all of you, Dakota. And I want the town to know it."

25

Dakota

"**Y**OU READY TO GET YOUR ASS KICKED?" DAVIS asks, holding the door open for me. The electronic clacks and dings of the pinball machines are music to my ears.

"Uh-huh," I deadpan. "If memory serves me correct, I was usually the one kicking your ass, Hotshot."

The minute we step into the neon lights and lasers beams of the Rose and Cowboy Arcade, the place goes quiet. Heads turn, gazes direct our way, and I wince. The whole town believes I'm pregnant with Davis Montgomery's baby, and even though my brain screams it's an idiot plan, my heart says otherwise. I'm pregnant. Does it matter who the father is?

I step closer into Davis's body, into all those muscles that have me drawing from his strength. "Everyone's looking," I whisper.

He drags in a breath, nostrils flaring. Then he takes my hand and leads me across the floor. "It's okay. I got you."

I square my shoulders.

He does.

Ignoring the attention zeroed in on us, I roam my eyes around the Rose and Cowboy Arcade. An arcade-slash-pool hall with a retro Wild West vibe. It's the hot Saturday night thing to do in Resurrection that doesn't involve falling dead drunk off barstools at the Neon Grizzly or drag racing down Dead Fred's Curve.

I fell in love with the arcade and its neon lights the second it came to town. When we were kids, Fallon and I would beg our father for quarters and play the afternoon away.

It's the place I had my sixteenth birthday. I took my first Jello-O shot with Patti Ann behind the Street Fighter arcade game. It's where I took Davis when I met him at the ranch. He asked me what I did when I was bored in this town and I told him I'd play a game of pinball.

I glance down at my stomach, cup its low swell, then look over at Davis and smile. "Baby's first pinball," I tell him.

And according to Davis, our first official date. Since he declared no friends, no secrets, my head's been spinning. After months of dancing around it, we're finally moving in a direction that feels dangerously close to what I've always wanted.

Us.

God, I hope we last.

I can survive Aiden, but I can't survive Davis letting me go again.

Davis grins and steps closer, fitting his warm palm to the small of my back. "Where to, Koty?" The steel in his voice, the way he possessively cups my back, has me hot all over.

He cares. And it's been a long time since I had that.

I scan the room, seeking out familiar machines, one in particular. It's a long shot, though, because the Rose and Cowboy trades out the machines every few months to bring in new ones.

I squint through the crowd, aware Davis is waiting for an answer. "I don't…"

"Over here," he says, taking my hand. He leads me to a darkened corner of the room, and we stop in front of a bright bubblegum pink pinball machine. *Cowgirl Coven.*

"Oh my god," I breathe. "They still have it."

I grasp the plunger, test out the flippers, and run my eyes over the colorful machine. Fallon and I always loved the cheesy '80s storyline. Cowgirls battle the devil in a Wild West apocalyptic showdown that's part zany hijinks, part psychedelic mushroom trip.

Unbidden tears spring to my eyes. My favorite machine's still here. Existing. Like even though things have changed, some little part of my life is still around.

Davis scruffs a hand over his face, stares at me like I'm killing him dead. "Koty."

"I'm okay." I wipe my cheeks and sniffle. "It's just…it feels hopeful that it's still here. Not everything changes. I know this is stupid. I'm crying over a pinball machine."

A half-smile touches Davis's lips. "Cupcake, you cry your beautiful eyes out. And when you're done…" He pauses, leans in. "I'll kick your ass."

I sob-laugh. "Bullshit." I grab the flippers and hope the need for competition will dry up my tears. "I wonder if our high scores are still there."

Davis drops a token in the slot and the blaring banger of a theme song—dueling banjos and electric guitar— drowns out the sound of every other machine in the arcade.

"You ready for an ass kicking?" I taunt.

There's a rumble of a chuckle from Davis. "Going from crying to ass kicking? That's what I'd call underhanded diversion tactics, Cupcake."

I scoff. "Let's play."

"You're on," he says as he wraps one massive hand around the plunger.

"Outta my way," I tease, elbowing him aside.

We play token after token. Long and loud into the evening. Even with my weak arm, I kill it and beat my best score. Squish kicks in my belly like he—or—she is keeping rhythm with the bright noises of the arcade.

"Damn skill shot," I mutter. "Damn bitch, multi-ball," I growl as three balls come out of nowhere. My game's ended with a deafening "yeehaw" and the crack of a whip.

"Shit," I whine. "I almost had that." Then I look at Davis, our scores, and lift a brow. "Still beat you, Hotshot."

It makes his lips curve, and I relish the sight.

"There she is. The Koty I remember." Davis encircles me, his broad, rough hands slipping over my backside. I gasp as he spins me around to cage me against the machine. My senses are consumed with him—my breasts crushed against his powerful chest, the vibration of the pinball machine, the electric arc of our bodies. Heat and heart and soul.

Davis dips his head, his voice a husky rasp against my ear. "My sexy little trash talker."

"You're one to talk." Brazenness zips through me, and I palm the front of his chest. "I never knew you had such a filthy mouth under this uptight exterior."

His eyes flash. "Uptight, huh?"

"Oh, very. Davis Montgomery. Boss of brothers. Broody super soldier. Cupcake eater. And—"

Nothing else gets past my lips.

Davis silences me with a kiss so mind-melting my knees nearly go out.

We sway together as I drink in his heady taste, my arms twined behind his head.

The arcade gets louder, the lights brighter. My cheeks flame. But I tune it all out.

I tighten my grip on the man in my arms.

What Resurrection thinks doesn't matter. What matters is I am kissing Davis Montgomery in public. What matters is I am alive. What matters are all the tiny glimmers of happy I've collected this last month.

Maybe this town is still mine.

And maybe so is Davis Montgomery.

∽

Margaritas drunk: 0.

"Remember how those poolhall margs just hit different?" I ask with a sigh. I gaze longingly as a fishbowl-sized margarita gets delivered to a nearby couple, two straws for the win.

"Remember how they hit you," Davis says, giving me a full-wattage grin that has me melting.

"The dancing." I cover my eyes and groan. "I remember the dancing."

We've claimed a sticky high-top in the middle of the room, and despite the clang of arcade games and the clack of billiard balls, conversation has been effortless. A reminder of yet another reason the muscled Marine claimed my heart.

"Drinks?" the server asks. He looks bored, the typical small-town kid working a Saturday night shift to scrounge up some extra cash to get the hell out of this town. The bolo tie around his neck looks as frayed as he does.

"No. Nachos," I tell him. My palm finds my stomach

as a small cramp settles in my right side. Squish and I—
we're both starving.

"Kitchen's closed until six."

Davis looks at him with a frown. "Come back at six,"
he warns. "On the dot."

"Sure thing," the kid says before hustling away.

"Stay here," Davis says, slipping off his stool. Before I
can say anything, he heads outside and returns with a box
of granola bars. When I say nothing, only stare at him, he
goes on. "You get hungry. Low blood sugar's dangerous for
you and the baby."

I arch a brow, my heart free falling. "And you just happened to have a stash in your truck?"

He gives me a look. "You gonna eat 'em or interrogate
me?"

I grab a bar and tear at the wrapper. "Maybe I like to
interrogate you."

"I'll give you three questions." His eyes are dark with
humor. "Ask away."

"MONSAR," I say and take a small bite of granola
bar. "Do you like it?"

"I do." A muscle rolls in his jaw. "It helped with the
PTSD, after you left." He exhales, cradles his beer between
his palms. "The ranch is Charlie's. MONSAR, the dogs,
they feel like mine. Even if I used them to run away at first."

"They helped you."

He nods, his face unreadable. "They did. I hid myself
for a long time. From what happened overseas. From what
I did for Charlie. I've seen things that make monsters out
of men, and I didn't want that for myself. I didn't want to
be helpless, so I fought through it."

As I listen, I see him so clearly. I always have, but more

pieces fall into place. Those Fort Knox-like layers of him peel back and reveal why he takes my protection so seriously. Why he's a hard-ass around his brothers. He pushes people away even when he wants them to stay.

"It gets hard when it's a kid on the front lines, but…" Davis inhales. "I goddamn love it. I do."

My heart squeezes at the thought of a baby or a kid in trouble. "I couldn't imagine," I say softly, cupping my belly.

Davis watches me closely. "Nothing will happen to your baby, Dakota." The words come out rough and determined. "I swear it."

My smile fades and I fight a shiver at the sudden dangerousness etched on his handsome face. "You think he's here, don't you?" I try but fail to hide the note of fear in my voice.

"I'm not sure," he says grimly. "I wish I were."

"Is it stupid to hope that he's given up?"

"No." He takes my hand. His fingers, warm and rough, curl around mine. "Hope's not stupid. It keeps you going."

I smile. Leaning on Davis doesn't feel like taking a step backward anymore. It's accepting support.

"What else? Interrogation, remember? Still got two more questions," he says with a lift of a dark brow.

Elbow on the table, I prop my chin in my hand and think on it.

Maybe it's the neon of the arcade or the baby in my belly, but a sudden braveness overtakes me. I sit up straight, even as my stomach flutters with what I'm about to ask. "Has there been anyone else, Davis? While we were apart?" I bite my lip as he stays silent. "Not that I have a right to ask, but I…I just wondered."

Muscles tense in his broad shoulders, those impenetrable brown eyes flickering. "No. There hasn't."

My heart pumps hard, dangerously close to giving out. The answer's close. So close.

"Why wasn't there anyone else?"

"Because I couldn't have you."

For a moment, his simple truth stuns me into silence. The warm edges of a flame flicker against my heart, and I look at him under lowered lashes. "I don't need a date to know I like you, Davis. I've liked you ever since I met you. I don't think I've ever been so happy as the summer we spent together."

A shudder rocks Davis's body.

Emotions knot my throat, but I go on. "In fact, all these long years, I've been the very best at missing you."

Dark, smoldering eyes stare back at me, crackling with intensity. This time, he draws my hand closer, his lips sweeping over my knuckles. "As far as I am concerned, we aren't starting over."

My lungs constrict. "We're not?"

"No." Emotion slashes across his handsome face. His next words come out unguarded and raw. "We're picking back up right where we left off. I'm not wasting another minute without you."

Oh. Oh god.

And just like that, my heart's on the moon.

"Last question," I announce, trying to hear myself over the hammer of my heart. "What do you want in life, Davis? Like really want?"

Before he can answer, a piping plate of nachos is dropped on the table with a clatter. "Six on the dot," our server says flatly, setting down silverware roll-ups and appetizer plates.

A growl rumbles in Davis's throat at the interruption, and I can't help but laugh out loud. My soul feels so light.

The baby turns over in my belly, causing another cramp, and I gasp. No more time for questions. The truth will have to wait.

"Bathroom," I say to Davis. "Squish is massacring my bladder."

"Like I said, kid's got perfect timing." But he's grinning as he stands and carefully helps me off the stool.

Without another word, I'm off in search of the bathrooms.

Halfway there, a thought crosses my mind and I backtrack to stop at the customer service counter.

Gus Sanders, sporting a pornstache and a bowtie that has him looking like a human version of Roger Rabbit, glances up from his phone. "Hey, Dakootie McGraw. What can I do ya for?"

I roll my eyes at his old nickname for me. "Still got the bowtie, huh, Gus?"

"Never stopped."

"That machine…" I point to *Cowgirl Coven*. I'm already picturing it in my new bakery. "If you ever plan to get rid of it, will you call me? Sell it to me?"

"Can't." He taps out a message on his phone, looks up. "That thing ain't going nowhere. It's already been bought and paid for. With strong instructions to never move it from the premises unless we, uh, 'want our asses beat.'"

I frown. "What? By who?"

He jerks his chin. "You're sitting with him."

My eyes rush to Davis, sitting at the high-top, arms

crossed, stern and stoic. He bought our machine. My heart gallops as I turn and head to the restroom.

Giddy. It's the only way to describe how I feel. This perfect moment, this night, this man. That life that once felt so out of reach seems so close all over again.

It's a step forward.

We're a step forward.

Us.

26

Davis

TONIGHT WASN'T JUST A DATE.

We've flirted, traded trust, confessed secrets. I've already said more than I should have with Dakota's interrogations. But the woman's a beautiful addiction. A vice.

There's no more hiding us. After tonight, the entire town knows she's mine and mine alone.

I meant what I said too.

I'm not wasting another minute. I wasted the last six years. It's a miracle she's back in my life.

I won't lose her again.

I scan my eyes around the arcade, check the time on my watch. The bright dings and pings of the pinball machine don't compute with the darkness clouding my head.

Something's wrong.

She's been gone too long. Fuck. It's my job to stay close. What if she slipped out? What if he got to her?

My fingers tighten around my beer bottle.

Get it together, Montgomery. Her ex didn't shimmy down the drainpipe and crawl in through the window.

What if he did, though?

Fuck it.

Dakota can call me overprotective all she wants, but I won't apologize for keeping her safe.

Hand on my holster, I slip off the stool.

I'm halfway across the floor when my phone vibrates.

The tracker.

Fuck.

Heart in my throat, I bolt across the arcade toward the bathroom.

I slam into the women's restroom, scanning the space. Only one stall door is closed.

I step up, muscles coiled with tension. "Cupcake, you okay? You in here?"

The toilet flushes, and her hollow voice sounds from the stall. "Davis."

The edge in her voice sends all my senses snapping into high alert. "What is it? What's wrong?"

"Everything," she whispers breathlessly. "I'm bleeding."

The air's sucked from my lungs. "What?"

The baby. The thought's a rock in my throat.

The stall door opens, and Dakota, pale and trembling, emerges. She squeezes her eyes shut, sliding one hand down to cup her belly. "I'm having a miscarriage. I know it."

My chest goes cold as fear bubbles up inside of me.

"Don't say that," I tell her.

She stares at me with pleading eyes, shimmering with heartache. "What do we do?"

On instinct, I pick her up in my arms and fight the urge to panic as I rush her to my truck.

Death. It's been my one constant shadow.

On the ranch, in the military, it's a part of life. I've walked the fine line that comes with the shadowy part of my past. Faced it down when Sully was killed, when I was shot, when my brother lost his mind.

And I fixed all that. I survived.

But this…

This I can't fix.

Utterly fucking helpless.

I pace the small, sterile room, then go to the back of Dakota's table to help her into the thin paper-like gown. It's not the first appointment I've been to, but it's the first time I've been inside the room with Dakota. My gut clenches when I see the blood on her balled-up jeans.

"I don't want to lose my baby," she says as I help her lie down. Her eyes are wide and bright with tears.

"You won't," I rasp. I lean in close, resting a hand on the hard ball of her belly. Hoping to feel the reassuring thump of Squish, but there's nothing.

Dakota sniffles. "This is my fault. I didn't want the baby in the first place and now…" A shudder wracks her body. "Now it'll be taken away from me."

"Stop," I demand. "Don't say that. Don't think that way."

My heart's in my goddamn stomach. I'm just as afraid as she is. I want this baby as much as she does. I want it for Dakota.

For us.

Christ, it's like the rational part of my brain has turned off. Instead of feeling a duty to keep my hands off her, my heart out of it, it's been replaced by a duty to step up.

I love this woman, which means I love her child.

It's as simple as that.

"You bought the pinball machine." Dakota's soft voice tears me from my thoughts. She gives me a teary smile. "Gus said you bought *Cowgirl Coven.*"

I slip my hand around hers. Not long after she left Resurrection, I purchased the machine. The thought of it disappearing like Dakota did left me with an ache in my soul. "It's my favorite piece of memory in this town. Because it reminds me of you."

Her laugh is husky, sad. "Thank you. It means so much, Davis."

She reaches for me, but as she does, she hisses a breath and grips her stomach. Worry flashes over her face.

"Where's that damn doctor?" I growl, on the verge of storming back into the waiting room and demanding someone get the fuck here now. But I don't need to. The door opens and inside steps a woman with long silver hair.

"Hi, Dakota."

Dakota sits up on her elbows. A stream of tears streak down her face. "Hi, Dr. Winfrey."

"I'd say it's good to see you, but the circumstances aren't ideal, are they?" Her gaze flicks to me. "This must be the father."

"Yes," I say.

Dakota goes still, turning her face up to meet my eyes. I keep my hand in hers, keep my eyes on the doctor.

"I understand you're having some bleeding," Dr. Winfrey says as she washes her hands. "Tell me about it."

"We were out tonight and when I used the bathroom…" A tremble wracks her. "There was blood. Not a lot, but it was dark red. That's bad, isn't it?"

"Any abdominal pain, cramping, fever, chills, or contractions?"

She winces. Fresh tears fill her eyes. "A small cramp. Earlier tonight."

Please, Christ, let something go right in her fucking life. Let her have something good.

After running a series of tests, Dr. Winfrey snaps on a monitor and wheels it close to the bed. Within minutes, she has a glob of goo squirted on Dakota's belly and a wand in her hand. "Let's have a look at that gorgeous baby."

Dakota grips my fingers tight, like it's her only lifeline. Her breathing grows choppy, and I stroke a hand over her hair. "Breathe, Koty."

My heart rate doubles, watching as the doctor slides the wand around. My shoulder muscles are knit so tightly it'll take a week on the bag to get the tension out.

Then the room's filled with what sounds like the hooves of a stallion on Montana earth.

"The heartbeat," Dr. Winfrey explains.

The screen fills with the shape of a baby, and I suck in a breath and stare, feeling like I've been sucker punched.

A sob escapes Dakota.

"Found you, sweet pea," Dr. Winfrey announces.

The shape moves. A little squirm that has me chuckling.

"Oh my god," Dakota gasps. She lifts her chin to get a better look. "Is it—is the baby okay?"

I frown when there's no answer.

"Tell us," I demand harshly.

"I don't see any placental abruption or premature labor." Doctor Winfrey squints at the screen. "A small amount of spotting is normal during the second trimester. Having sex or even vigorous physical activity can cause it."

Dakota tugs on my arm. "Davis, this morning."

Fuck.

I drag a hand down my face, remembering Dakota's hands gripping the headboard this morning, magnificent ass arched, as I slipped inside her and pumped until we both came hard.

Guilt winds up in my chest. If it's my fault, I'll never forgive myself.

Doctor Winfrey chuckles. "Rest assured, sex is normal, Davis. Especially when pregnant. It makes the world go round, you know."

"Christ." A relieved breath shakes out of me. I grin down at Dakota. "Never touchin' you again, Cupcake."

She laughs. "Don't you dare." Eyes fastened on the monitor, Dakota asks, "So…the baby's okay?"

Doctor Winfrey looks at me, then back at the screen. "Everything looks fine, but I'd like to keep Dakota overnight just to be safe."

Dakota thins her lips. I intercept before she can argue her way out of it. "That's a good idea," I tell the doctor, shooting Dakota a warning look.

Bossy, she mouths.

I give her a quick kiss. "Get used to it."

Dr. Winfrey snaps off the monitor. "And that's my cue."

"Wait!" Dakota says when Dr. Winfrey rises to go. "I want to know…" Tears leak from her eyes. "I want to know the sex."

Dr. Winfrey pauses, smiles. "The two of you have a healthy baby boy."

Dakota chokes out a sob. Her fingertips go to her mouth.

A boy.

A son.

I clear my throat of emotion. "Thank you."

"Sit tight," Winfrey says. "I'll get you admitted and then be back."

Dr. Winfrey exits the room.

I sink beside Dakota, take her hand. "Thought you didn't want to know."

"I didn't, but…" She sits up on her elbows. "I didn't want to be attached, but I do now." Her lower lip trembles, juts out in that defiant stubbornness I love. "At first, I didn't think I could do it, but I can. And I want the chance. I want this baby."

"You have him." I squeeze her fingers. "Your son."

Fire lights up her eyes. "I don't want to feel bad about my past. Blame myself or my baby. I want to move on. Live. Be happy." She laughs, cradling her belly with both hands. "I want him so much, Davis."

I clear my throat. Shift my weight. There's no stopping it. Won't talk myself down. Not anymore.

"You asked me back in the arcade what I wanted in life." I look into her eyes. "And I never got to give you an answer."

Her eyes widen.

I trace a line over the high arch of her cheekbone, and say, "This is what I want." I drop my hand. "And this." I cup her belly.

Tears fill her eyes. "I can't ask you to do that, Davis."

"Do what?"

She wraps her arms tight around herself. "Saddle you with another man's child."

"Saddle me." It comes out gruff. Resolute.

She blinks. "What?"

"Cupcake, I want you." I lean in, meeting her eyes. "That means I take him, too."

Her chin quivers and I rub my jaw, smothering a grin. By now I'm used to my girl crying. Goddamn adorable, is what it is.

"Are you sure?" She sounds breathless.

I drop a kiss to her mouth. "So damn sure."

27

Dakota

S THE SNOW MELTS COMPLETELY, BRINGING WITH it the bright blue skies of April, as only Montana can do, so do my thoughts of Aiden. My son grows low in my belly. Life consists of The Corner Store. My baby. Davis.

I've accepted his words for what they are—a claiming. Some tentative, happy, love-drunk space. For once in a long time, I'm not worried Davis will come to his senses and realize he's crazy for taking on a pregnant woman, another man's son.

I have hope. Hope I don't have to run. Hope we will work out. And though neither of us have said those three little words I've long felt, I'm at peace. With what we have and where we are.

The words will come.

Like all the light I've found over the last few months.

Finally, I see clearly. I see Resurrection. Maybe it's how I should have always seen her, but I see her now. Sometimes you have to leave home and come back to find things you never knew you had.

And best of all, I see The Corner Store.

Our old country store has good bones. It can be something so much better. All it needs is a second chance. And I can breathe life back into it like I've been doing to myself these last few months.

It's a Friday afternoon, and I'm pulling a loaf of sandwich bread out of the oven. As usual, The Corner Store is dead. The only sign of life is Fallon. She's leaning over the counter applying lipstick using a butcher knife as a mirror.

It's hypnotic. The juxtaposition of her sharp angles. Her beauty and her anger.

"How's the arm doing?" Fallon asks, without looking at me.

I flex my pale arm, testing it out as I thump the bottom of the golden-brown loaf with my knuckle. The hollow sound tells me it's done. "Pale and scrawny, but ready for the world."

"Silly putty," Fallon notes, straightening up. "Use it to strengthen the muscles."

I give a nod, upturn the bread onto a cooling rack. "Here." I slide the moderately chunky loaf Fallon's way. "Try this. It's a new recipe."

My sister tears off a hunk, her pearly candy-pink nails glittering in the harsh kitchen light. She chews, then closes her eyes and says over a mouthful, "Fuck. I think I'm closer to God, Dakota."

I laugh. "I got good." I'm still a long way off from baking with two hands, but with the cast off, I'm getting close.

"I'm serious," she tells me. "You got *great*." Her face darkens as she stares at me. "And I hate that man who took that away from you."

I smooth a hand over my stomach and smile. "He didn't take everything."

Fallon's phone lights up. *Danny* it says on the screen. She scrambles to mute it, and I pounce on it.

"Who's that?"

"No one."

I follow my sister into the store, watching as she busies herself at the till.

I arch a brow. "Are you seeing someone?"

Fallon lets out a strangled laugh. "I'll tell you tonight."

"What's tonight?"

"Girls' night," she says without enthusiasm. "Me. You. Ruby. Nowhere."

A Friday night at Nowhere, Resurrection's rowdy local dive bar, is asking for trouble, but if it means spending time with my sister, I'll take it. The invitation has my heart soaring. Another glimmer of us. The little sister who hung out and opened up to me.

I pull out my phone. "Yeah, I just have to—"

"Text your bodyguard with benefits, I get it," she says dryly.

My cheeks heat. "Fallon."

I text Davis a quick *Going to Nowhere with Fallon and Ruby* and pocket my phone before I can see his reply.

She lifts a cool brow. "Well? That's what you two are doing, isn't it? Knocking boots. Especially now that you're having his baby?"

I laugh and cover my face. "Oh god."

"I knew it," she says with a smirk. "That big, handsome cowboy wanted more than just your cupcakes back in the day."

I snort. "You're the worst." But she's not wrong. Sometimes cupcakes and cowboys are all a girl needs.

Fallon crosses her arms and tilts her head. "It's sweet what Davis did for you."

"Yeah." Flushing, I finger the dog tag around my neck. "It is."

"If only all Montgomery men had common sense." She

dips down, hefting the gym bag she keeps under the front counter. Peeking out of the poorly zipped side, riding boots and heels. A helmet and a pair of leather gloves. I frown. Fallon never rides with a helmet. Another one of her ways she defies death.

"You living out of suitcases these days?" I ask.

She zips up her bag, hooks it cross-body style. "Something like that."

⌐∕

Twenty-eight weeks pregnant and bellied up at Resurrection's local dive bar on a wild Friday night with my sister and Ruby.

The night's never felt more perfect.

The jukebox pumps at unholy decibel levels, the neon so bright I could get a tan. Peanut shells and spilled beer cover the floor as we cross to the bar.

"What do you want?" Beef, the bartender, grunts. His long black beard trails the sticky bar top as he wipes it down.

"Tequila," Fallon says. "And something pink for Ruby, and water for Dakota."

"Hi," Ruby chirps with a wave.

He lifts his chin at her, and his scrutinizing eyes slide to me. "Dakota."

I give him a nod, smiling at his bad attitude and tattoos. To me, he'll always be that sweet boy who took me to homecoming my sophomore year. "Beef. You still got the band?"

He straightens up. Pride crosses his craggy face. "The Turbofuckers? Hell, yeah. Still rocking in my garage." His big hands drum the counter. "Glad you're home, Koty."

"Thanks."

Another grunt and Beef's gone.

Fallon settles onto a barstool with a happy sigh. "God, I already feel drunk and I just sat down."

"Place hasn't changed," I add, roving my gaze around the neon lights.

"It's where I met Charlie," Ruby says. "Bar fight."

Beef hurls down our drinks. A tray of shots, a gaudy pink drink in a tall, curvy goblet with a big bendy straw, and a large water with a cherry on top.

Fallon grabs my drink and leans over the counter. "Beef, if you put booze in this, I'll knock your ass up to your receding hairline."

A raise of Beef's middle finger. "Stop bitching at me, Fallon, and suck it."

I watch as my sister sips my drink before passing it to me. The sweet act of protection makes me smile.

She looks at me suspiciously. "What?"

"You love me."

Her cheeks turn bright pink. "Shut up."

I laugh as my stomach bumps, then I groan. "Ugh, it's like a squirrel going sicko mode inside my body."

Fallon tentatively splays a hand out on my belly like it's an alien about to burst. My sister has zero maternal instinct. It would not be abnormal for her to eat her young.

"Kid's doing barrel rolls," she says with a pleased grin.

Ruby wiggles on her stool, adjusts the hem of her sundress. "Have you thought about names, Dakota?"

"Shockingly, no."

Fallon slugs down a shot, reaches for another. "One more minute of baby talk. Then I'm cutting you off, Ruby."

Ruby stirs her drink with her bendy straw. "You have to have a baby shower."

"Would you believe I'm taking it one day at a time?" I admit.

Fallon barks a laugh. "I don't believe it." Her gaze flits to Ruby. "My big sister treats planning as an extreme sport."

I elbow her. "Excuse you." Ignoring Fallon's grumbles about my pointy elbows, I turn back to Ruby. "But she's right. I used to have plans. Order. I could do it all, and I didn't need help. I could bake the fuck out of a croissant. And now I just have a baby."

"That's not a bad thing," Ruby says, her eyes falling to the bar top.

I smile. "No, it's not. I love my little Squish."

"What about Davis?" Fallon interjects. "You have your Marine."

I prop my chin in my palm. "Maybe. Maybe not. We used to fuck in secret, now we're just…fucking in public."

Ruby giggles. "Oh, I think we've all done that."

I stare at the shots. Is it possible to get a contact high just from looking at them? "How many would it take to forget I admitted that?"

"It's girls' night." Fallon's gaze is shrewd. "We gonna bullshit or be real tonight?"

Ruby and I both look at her like she's an all-seeing wise witch.

"Well? Truth or bullshit?"

I take a deep breath and debate. She's right. So I clear my throat and let it out. "I don't know what Davis and I are doing. I just know it feels right. It feels normal. Is that so bad to want something simple?"

"No," Ruby says, her eyes as large as saucers.

"I don't know where I'm going," I say. "I just know there's no one else on earth I want to be with." The words build in my chest. "I've built a life before, and it all burned down. But instead of being afraid, I'm up for the challenge. To do it all over again and hope maybe I get this life right." I inhale. "I am someone new now and that is okay."

There's a long silence, and then Ruby speaks up. "Before my surgery, this would make me sick," Ruby explains, pointing at her pink drink. "But I can do stuff like this now. Charlie worries because he's Charlie. I can do a lot. But I can't do everything." Her eyes flicker to my belly. "And I'm still trying to be okay with that."

"Goddamn." Fallon exhales like Ruby's words have taken a toll on her.

I look up at Beef. "More water."

Ruby dips her head and hoovers the rest of her pink drink.

Tequila and secrets. Apparently, that's where girls' night has gotten us.

Fallon's three shots in when the stomp of cowboy boots rattle the floorboards.

I glance over at the door.

My knees go weak at the sight of Davis.

Davis and his brothers stand in the mouth of the bar. Broad-shouldered, broody, intimidating cowboys. Half the bar has their heads on a swivel.

"Here comes the parade of assholes," Fallon drones dryly. Then she scowls. "So much for girls' night."

Davis's dark eyes rake over me. My stomach curls as I drink in the sight of his dark hair and rough stubble. A tight US Marine Corps T-shirt. Biceps. Oh god.

"Uh-oh," Ruby whispers. "Here they come." She secretly sounds delighted.

"Oh, hell no," Fallon complains, hopping off her barstool. "We're not letting big, dumb men interrupt our night." A wicked smile appears on her face, and she leans in conspiratorially. "You want to see the quickest way to clear a room of four tough cowboys?"

She waits until Davis and his brothers are within earshot and says, "Tell me about pregnancy, Dakota? Have you lost your mucous plug yet?"

All four pairs of boots instantly beeline in the opposite direction.

Fallon snickers.

Beef passes Ruby another pink drink, and she feels blindly for it, staring at Charlie like a woman long gone.

I smother a smile, watching Davis redirect his brothers like they're children instead of tough cowboys.

Turning to Fallon, I arch a brow, run a hand over my stomach, feeling the little pepper of feet. "Mucous plug?"

She gives a cavalier shrug. "I did some research." She lifts her glass in the air and loops her arm around my neck. "Welcome to the Weird Cowgirl Club. It's you and me now, Koty, no take backs. No secrets."

"No secrets," I echo, ducking my head so she can't see the tears that have sprung to my eyes.

Ruby stirs her drink, a bright pink clashing of liquors while the Montgomery men claim a table in the room's corner. Davis gives me a nod, tugs his hat down low and settles in like my personal attack dog.

"God," Fallon groans. "Are they always so—"

"Morally gray cowboys with killer tendencies? Yeah. They are," Ruby breathes, watching Charlie from above the rim of her drink. She looks enamored. Lovesick. "That's my cowboy."

"Really leaning into this wild honky-tonk lifestyle, aren't you?" Fallon says to Ruby.

Ruby sips her drink, slurping as she reaches the bottom of it. Her cheeks are bright pink. "Oh, yes."

I point my straw at the brothers. "What do you think a pack of them is called? A murder of Montgomerys?"

"Welcome to the dating pool in Resurrection," Fallon drawls with a flick of her hand. "Your options are a douchebag from California with mommy issues who won't date you until his psychic reads your aura, or a cowboy with busted boots and a dusty attitude who is prepared to antagonize you even through a zombie apocalypse."

At that, Ruby and I share a wide-eyed look.

"Wow," Ruby breathes. "So specific."

"No more about me." I twist on my stool toward my sister. I can feel Davis's intense gaze burning a hole in my back. "Let's talk about you. And this guy you're seeing."

Ruby squeaks.

On Fallon's lips is a rebuttal, but I shake my head and grab her hand. "One secret. Tell me." I give her a hard look. "We can be real tonight or we can bullshit."

"Real," Ruby echoes.

"Ugh, god. Fine." Fallon puffs her chest out and exhales. "He's just some guy I met at the stock show in Butte."

It all makes sense now. Fallon wearing lipstick, nail polish, sneaking out of work early. Her duffel bag full of lacey undergarments. My fierce, independent little sister has a boyfriend. She was never an idealist about love, especially after our mother left. Usually, she was quoting Elizabeth I's speech on avoiding marriage and cursing men.

"When was this?" I ask.

"Over the winter," she says, downing another shot. Her fifth or sixth of the night. By now, I've lost track of counting.

I slide a glass of water her way, hoping she takes the hint. I don't want a repeat of graduation night when I held back Fallon's hair while she threw up Four Loko. "Well, don't stop there. What's his name? What's he like? Tell. Me. Everything."

"Relax, Dakota. It's not a relationship or anything." She cocks a brow. "We're casual. It's something fun with someone who's not a cowboy. Who doesn't live in the hellscape that is Resurrection." A smile softens her face. "We've been on maybe six or seven dates. Had sex in a Pinto. Girl's gotta get laid."

A groan-laugh pops out of my mouth. "I'm happy for you and didn't need to know that."

Ruby wobbles on her stool, grips the bar to steady herself, then clears her throat. "But what about Wyatt?"

Fallon scrunches up her nose. "What about him?"

Ruby casts a confused gaze at me, but I stay quiet. Fallon's beef with Wyatt started long before they ever competed.

"Shit," Fallon mutters, glancing at the Budweiser clock on the wall. She stands and grabs her duffel bag tucked beneath the stool. "I gotta change. Metalhead concert in Missoula." She wiggles her brows. "With Danny."

Ruby's mouth falls open.

Fallon holds up a finger. "And before you ask, no, you can't meet him."

Ruby and I stare after her as she hustles to the bathroom.

Grin on his face, Davis crooks a big finger and motions us over.

Ruby clasps her hands to her heart and looks pleadingly at me.

A ghost of a smile plays on my lips. "Fine, let's go."

28

Davis

I PUSH BACK FROM THE TABLE AND WATCH AS DAKOTA and Ruby cross the dance floor like it's their own personal catwalk. I'm tense, on edge. Especially since that text from Dakota. A pregnant Dakota in a rowdy honky-tonk is enough to give me a goddamn aneurysm. Leave it to Fallon to pick the most dangerous bar in town. The same bar Ruby nearly got trampled in last year.

I get that Dakota needed a night out—time with her sister—and I would never stop her. I planned to lurk in the shadows, watching over her like the overprotective bastard I am. But I never could steer my brothers away from cold beers and Fridays. We've been doing it since we moved here, and we won't stop now.

Ford rolls his eyes. "She's across the room, man. No one's gonna get her." He reaches for another beer, looking like he'd like to crack it over my head.

"You want to back off?" I say, clocking how much he's had to drink. If my twin wants to get a pissy attitude, he can do it on his own damn time.

I glance back at Dakota, tracking her as she pushes her way through the tight crowd. I don't know what they put in that pregnant water, but goddamn. Dakota looks sexy as fuck. Big brown eyes. Hourglass figure. The tight dress she wears shows off her belly, her hair falling in glossy dark waves around her shoulders. Happiness radiates off her in waves.

Every man's wildest dream.

But she's all mine.

I have to fight the urge to storm across the room and brand my mouth to hers. Every eye in the bar follows her. Because she draws people toward her.

Resurrection's letting her back in. She doesn't even have to work for it.

"We're combining tables, Cowboy," Ruby drawls as Charlie pulls her onto his lap. He kisses her, and she wraps her arms around his neck and hangs on.

"Don't have such fond memories of this bar, Sunflower," Charlie murmurs. He has Ruby pulled so high on his lap I'm damn near ready to tell them to get a room. "Not when you're in it."

I stand and reach for Dakota. I tug her close, loving how she arches into me, like she's made for me. My. Perfect. Fucking. Girl.

"Checking up on me, Hotshot?" Dakota says, a smile teasing those full lips of hers.

"Damn straight." I press a hand against the side of her stomach and breathe her in. "Don't want you out unprotected." She shivers as I rough the words into her hair.

"So chivalrous," she purrs, her cheeks flushed pink.

I pull out a chair and help her sit.

"She ain't unprotected," Wyatt says, finally coming up from his beer. "Don't you got a tail on her?"

Dakota arches a brow, leans away from me. "Excuse me?"

"Wyatt," I snap. "That's private information."

"Not anymore," Ford mutters.

When I sit down beside Dakota, she's shaking her head in amusement. "Really, Hotshot?"

"Really." I scoot her chair closer to me and lean in. "Cupcake, that might be the tightest dress I've ever seen." I give her a grin. "Hope you wear it all the time."

Her lashes flutter. "For you, I will."

"You're makin' this hard, Dakota," I say, so low only she can hear. "Making me want to lay you down on this table and fuck your gorgeous brains out. Show you how a real man treats you."

Surprise and desire flare to life in her eyes. "Davis." It's a whisper.

"I want everyone to see us." I run my hand up her bare thigh, between her legs, and trail a finger over the damp spot on her lace panties. "My name on your lips. My hand up your fucking skirt, making you come. End of the night, this entire town will know you're mine."

She whimpers and it nearly breaks me. It takes all my control not to take her outside to my truck and fuck her.

"Drinks?" Beef booms, passing Dakota an ice water. My dick throbs painfully in my pants and I briefly consider using it to cool off.

"More fucking alcohol," Ford orders.

"Pink drink," Ruby hoots, sticking her glass up in the air.

"How boring is that water?" I ask Dakota.

She scoffs. "Keep talking. Soon as I give birth, I'm wrestling you to the ground."

A series of pings from my phone has Dakota glancing at me. She giggles and leans in, her bright smile warming the coldest parts of me. "He's an eggplant."

Our gazes meet and I run a hand down the curve of her stomach. "Bigger every day," I husk.

"Why do you have a fucking baby app on your phone?" Ford cuts in.

"Because it matters to Koty," I snarl at my asshole brother.

He scoffs, tucks his hands under his armpits. "Y'all livin' in dreamland right now."

Dakota's eyes go wide.

A five-alarm fire licks in my chest. Next to me, Charlie cocks an eyebrow at Wyatt.

"You're out of line, Ford," I say, my voice low and dangerous. "Watch your fucking mouth when you talk to her."

Combustible. That's the only way to describe the space around us. A Luke Bryan song plays on the jukebox as I glare at my twin. Something tells me I'll have a boot up his ass by the end of the night.

"It's fine, Davis," Dakota says in an unbothered tone. "It's not worth it." She shifts in her chair and rests a hand on my arm. Her touch is all I need to unclench my jaw. "Don't let it ruin our night. Besides, you owe me a dance."

"Whatever, man," Ford says, glancing up as Beef returns with more drinks. He takes a shot and opens a beer. "Y'all wanna play house, by all means."

"Way it's gonna be from now on," Wyatt warns Ford. "Get used to it. Broads and babies."

Ruby glances down at the floor, and Charlie leans in to whisper in her ear.

"Not me," Ford drawls. "Lifelong bachelor right here."

I roll my eyes.

That's when Dakota gasps.

"Baby, you okay?" I ask. My gaze immediately finds her belly.

She doesn't answer, and I look up, following her eyeline. We all do.

"Holy shit," Charlie says.

Fallon's breezing out of the bathroom. Duffel bag slung over her shoulder, she wears thigh-high cowboy boots and a jean skirt. Her shimmery halter top, cut off at the midriff, exposes a tan, toned stomach. Her hair cascades untamed around her shoulders, and the shade of her bright pink lipstick matches her flushed face. She looks like some dolled-up cowgirl.

And Wyatt looks like a hand grenade waiting to explode.

Even Ford's tongue is on the floor. "So Fallon does own a skirt." A wicked grin tips his lips.

"What the fuck?" Wyatt blasts. He jolts in his seat, nearly upending his beer onto his lap. "Since when is she dressing like that?"

"Since she met someone," Ruby says softly.

Wyatt goes stiff.

"Girl's wilding out," Ford cackles.

"Well, look at what crawled out of the trash and into our lives," Fallon says as she takes the seat next to her sister. She squints at me, then looks at Dakota and Ruby. "I leave you alone for five minutes…" A shake of her head. "Traitors."

"You're the one going out tonight," Dakota murmurs with a smile.

I keep a close watch on Wyatt. There's not enough alcohol in Resurrection to get me through this meltdown.

Ford lines up the shots in front of us, shooting two back in quick succession.

Ruby's worried eyes flick to Charlie.

"You're really going out with some random guy?" Wyatt asks hoarsely.

Fallon straightens in her chair. "Not that it's any of your business…but yeah. I am."

Ford sails a shot toward Fallon. "Let me tell you something, you're a little fucking bulldog, but you polish up real nice."

Fallon floats him a grin, takes the shot. Her smile's feral. "Thanks, Ford. I'd say the same about you, but I'd be lying."

"Hell, I feel bad for the guy already," Wyatt rasps.

Fallon shoots Wyatt a fire and brimstone glare.

"Don't you fucking start," I warn him.

But he does.

"Should focus on your horses," Wyatt mutters. "I saw you ridin' the other day. Your form's sloppy."

"My form is none of your business," Fallon snaps.

Down goes one shot, then another. By now, between Wyatt and Ford, the bottle of Jack is half empty.

"Christ, the least you could do is put a shirt on, wear a pair of fuckin' shoes," he grouses. "Goin' out dressed like some buckle bunny, that ain't you, Cowgirl."

Fuck.

Dakota looks me dead in the eye as if to say, *Are you fucking kidding me with this shit?* Even Ruby's frowning.

"Wy," Charlie says, settling a big palm on our brother's shoulder. A signal to cool it.

Hurt creases Fallon's sharp features, and she blasts out of her chair. "Fuck you, Wyatt."

"No," Dakota says, twisting to snag her sister's hand. "Don't go."

I smear my face with my hands. "Fuck."

"Sorry," Fallon tells her sister. "I need a twenty-four-hour intermission from this fool." Eyes blazing, she takes two steps away from the table, then backtracks to wheel around on Wyatt. "And by the way," she hisses. "I fucking hate you."

"Feeling's mutual," he says hoarsely, but I don't miss the wince that crosses his face.

After stopping briefly to squeeze Dakota's shoulder, an action that has Koty's face softening, Fallon stalks out of the bar.

Ford whistles. "That girl's a whole lotta outlaw."

Wyatt just sits there, and Charlie leans in. "You want her to sleep with the guy?" he growls in Wyatt's ear.

"She's doing it for him." Dakota's soft voice takes me from my watch on my brothers.

I take her hand. "I know."

Christ. I wish my brother would wake the fuck up. I don't know why they can't get it right, but it has me realizing everything I need to do to make things right between Dakota and me. Tell her I love her. If I don't, I could lose my chance, and the past will start over. She'll go, move on with her life, and I'll be the sorry son-of-a-bitch who let her leave.

Not again.

Never again.

True North. Dakota and that baby.

A loud groan has all of us looking over. "Jesus. All y'all lovesick bastards." Ford drums his hands on the table. "I told y'all once and I'll tell you again. You gotta keep your head on a goddamn swivel when it comes to a woman."

"Would you cool down?" Charlie growls, removing the beer from Ford's grasp. "You're being a massive asshole."

Ford slaps Wyatt on the back, rocking him forward. "You gonna cry, cry into your tall boy and keep it the fuck down for the rest of us."

I'm horrified to see tears welling up in Wyatt's eyes. He looks miserable, throwing back his second round of doubles.

I clench my jaw, level a finger at Ford. He's gonna get his teeth kicked in if he doesn't watch his fucking mouth. We all like giving our little brother shit, but Ford knocking Wyatt down when he's clearly miserable is taking it too damn far.

"Knock it off. That's not a request."

"You sound like a fucking babysitter," Ford says, before turning his attention back to Wyatt. "Face it, little brother. Sometimes you're second place."

"I don't get fucking second place," Wyatt shoots back. Then, face crumpling, he erupts from his seat and tears out of the bar.

"Take his keys," I tell Charlie, who promptly plucks Ruby off his lap and races after Wyatt. Charlie's the only one who can talk Wyatt off the deep end.

A charged silence falls over the table as I glare at Ford. "Get your shit together. I mean it."

"Yeah, okay, Dad," he says, his tone dripping with sarcasm. "I didn't know we had a complaint department on the ranch."

Ruby, God bless her, is there to intercept.

"Ford, you want to dance?" She hits him with a full-wattage grin and tugs him clumsily out of the chair. Her concerned eyes flick to me as she leads him away, and I give her a grateful nod.

"I love your brother so much, but why does he have to be this tragically dumb?" Dakota says softly, watching as Ford and Ruby hit the dance floor.

I shake my head. "Tonight's not what you needed."

"Can't control everything," she says, a wry smile on

her lips. "My sister, your brother. What're we going to do with them?"

"Put them in sacks, drop them in the river," I say, deadpan. She laughs.

I shrug. "They gotta figure it out. We did." I take her hand. "You want to dance, Cupcake?"

For three long minutes, the chaos falls away. My eyes lock on Dakota, hers lock on me. Peace. We sway slowly to an old George Strait number on the crowded dance floor.

Like I said, peace.

And then that peace is quickly shattered.

The song on the jukebox changes to the sounds of George Jones singing about loving a good woman until he dies.

My boots screech to a halt. "Fuck."

That song. It's the equivalent of dropping an atom bomb on Ford's heart.

Dakota freezes like a doe in a clearing. "What's wrong?"

Quickly, I scan the bar. "Where's Ford?" Jesus, I need tracking devices for every goddamn person in my family.

But I'm too late. The second the chorus hits, there's the smash of glass. I rip around and watch in disbelief as Ford puts his hand through the jukebox.

Fuck.

Nowhere loves a fight, and the bar erupts into mayhem.

Boots and hats and flying fists. A sea of chaos explodes across the dance floor.

Ruby, trying to help Ford, gets caught up in the surge. Someone grabs her wrist and tugs her onto the dance floor. Ford tries to help her, but a leather-vest wearing biker gets a fistful of Ford's shirt and shoves him into the wall.

"Cover your eyes," I growl. I may be pissed at my twin, but the second anyone touches one of my siblings it's fists out.

Dakota squeaks. "What? Why?"

"You're about to witness a double fucking homicide."

Dakota grabs up a beer bottle from the nearest table.

I give her a look. "You planning to swing that or drink it?"

"Go," she says, eyes glittering with mischief. "Help Ruby. I got this."

I glance down at Dakota. I hate to leave her, but the way she's holding that beer bottle reminds me she was born and raised in Resurrection. I kiss her temple. "Hang tight. I'll be right back."

It's with those words that I stomp into the melee.

I don't start the fight, but I fucking end it.

I close the distance and grab Ford off the jukebox, put a fist through the biker's face. Before I can drag Ford's ass out of here, he's right back in the chaos.

This bar doesn't stand a chance.

I'm looking around for Ruby when I see Charlie.

I shake my head as Charlie pins a guy to the wall with a violence reserved only for someone who fucks with his wife. When Charlie drops him with one quick punch, I turn back for Dakota.

My heart trips.

She's trapped in the surging crowd. I catch her flash of dark hair, her frightened eyes.

The crowd surges.

It's turning bad, fast.

Dakota's arms drop to her sides. She cradles her belly protectively, flinching as a circle forms around her.

I curse. She's surrounded on all sides. If the crowd keeps pushing, she'll be crushed.

"Davis!"

The panic in her voice has the dark shadows inside me snarling.

I sprint toward her, smashing my way through the crowd, until I'm in front of her. I cover her with my body. "Let's get the hell out of here."

She wraps her arms around my waist, pressing her front to my back. "What about your brothers?" she shouts above the din.

I give a last glance at Charlie slinging Ruby over his shoulder, and Ford cackling like a damn maniac. "They started it, they can finish it."

Holding her close, I shove our way through the crowd. We're almost to the door when Dakota is tugged to a stop. With a growl, I whip around. Some drunken idiot has Dakota's wrist and is trying to tug her back into the fray.

Bad mistake.

A snarl rises in my throat and I have my hand on the guy's neck so fast he barely has time to squeak out a protest. "Drop her arm or lose yours."

He does.

I pull Dakota to the side of the bar, skirting the wall, and finally throw open the front door. I get her in my truck and then we're whipping out of the gravel parking lot.

There's a long silence and then—

Dakota laughs, long and loud. Her silvery peals of laughter ring out as she holds her belly.

"Well, that escalated quickly," she breathes.

My knuckles are white on the steering wheel. Looking her way, I quickly scan her for injury. "That could have been bad, Koty. Christ."

"I know. But it wasn't."

I stare out the window, jaw locked. The trust she gives me. I don't deserve it.

"Check it out," she says and unveils a golden bottle of whiskey. "Nabbed it on the way out. Like a true local."

I chuckle. "Bootlegger babe."

"Just like my daddy." Her eyes scan the dark road. "Where are we going?"

"Home," I grit out. I want to speed back to the ranch, but there's precious cargo beside me, so I force myself to drive slowly.

"I don't want to go home. Not yet. Not tonight." The warm hand on my thigh stops me from turning left. Dakota leans back against the seat, her eyes glowing and heavy-lidded. Voice husky, she says, "Take me to Eden."

I jerk, her words like a fire.

Eden. Our spot. The cabin in the woods where it all began.

I eye her belly. "It's late."

She rolls her head across the seat. The sly grin that illuminates her face has my dick jerking to attention. "Best time to do some damage, Hotshot."

I grin. Gun it. "Hang on, Cupcake."

"Faster, Davis." She sticks her arm out the window. The wind whips her hair like a raven's wing, slicing the night sky. "Faster."

29

Dakota

WHITE MOONLIGHT. THE RUSH OF THE WIND. Woods and farmland for miles around.

Davis and I sit on the tailgate of his truck. It feels like we're the only two people in the world. I stare at the tiny cabin where Davis and I would meet six years ago. Frantic, fumbling, starved for each other.

I point at a bright orange stake in the ground. More are scattered back in the trees. "What're are those?"

"Boundary lines," Davis explains. "We own the land all the way back to the falls. Land we've let sit for a good ten years." He rubs his jaw. "With the ranch finally making some money, we could put it to use."

I frown. "Knock it down?"

"Not sure yet."

"We're in the north," I say, remembering what he told me about the direction of the cabin. "And the ranch is…" I incline my head to the left. "That way."

"That's right." Davis's deep voice is hypnotic in the dark. "You want to go inside?"

"No." I smile when there's a rustle of fabric, and Davis drapes his jacket around my shoulders. "Tonight is a night for secrets."

He eyes me with amusement. "You sure Fallon didn't slip you a shot?"

I laugh. Heat warms my chest. I feel alive. Breathless. Becoming.

Squish rolls in my belly, and I press my hand against the patter of his little feet. My son.

This night. Freedom.

There is something in the air, a rush of brave.

A rush of me.

"Secrets, then." Davis exhales and I watch those big shoulders of his relax. "Okay. You start."

I smile in the dark. "Pregnant woman goes out to a bar and has a great time."

Davis grips my thigh with his brick of a hand. The steady brush of his fingers provides a comfort. "Man on the verge of killing every brother he has."

I laugh. "You'd never."

"Don't tempt me." He sighs and removes the whiskey bottle cap to take a swig. "Ford was out of line."

"He was, but…we can bullshit or we can tell the truth." At my words, Davis arches a brow. "It's something Fallon said tonight," I explain. "And I think she's right. I think what I've been doing ever since I got back here is bullshitting myself that I can get back what I lost. And I can't."

Davis looks at me, but stays silent, carefully scooting closer.

I blow out a shaky breath. "I realized tonight that the girl I used to be is not coming back. And that's okay."

Tears prick my eyes. I study the outline of the gnarled and twisted trees in the darkness. Scenes out of a horror story, but with Davis beside me, I'm not frightened. I am safe. And it's why I came back, isn't it?

To have something, someone to hold on to—strength.

And Davis is one part of that strength.

But I'm the other part.

"Aiden King," I say.

Davis hitches a breath.

Saying it out loud is like releasing a poison.

"That's my ex's name." My stomach knots as Aiden's face flashes in my mind, but I push on. "I met him when I worked as a pastry chef at La Rêve. He made me feel special, visited me early in the morning while I prepped my kitchen. He became my lover. And then my investor. He was charming, handsome, rich. Holy trinity on paper." I chance a glance at Davis. His face is tight, emotionless. I know it'll never be easy for him to hear this.

I take his hand, then say, "I was stupid, I suppose. Some girl from Montana who thought she could make it, who thought she found a light." I sigh. "I never saw what he was until it was too late."

"No. Not stupid." Davis strokes my arm. "Dakota, you're not a bad person for looking for a good love."

My heart pinches at the memory. "When we moved in together, after the bakery was open, that's when I knew something wasn't right. The dynamic changed. He was off. Annoyed when I'd leave to go to work. He'd come to the bakery and sit at a table all day until I went home with him."

Davis's brow furrows.

"Aiden was good at the long game. Lying in wait. Making me feel fucking crazy when I was talking rational. Taking inventory on just what exactly he wanted to diminish about me.

There were all these tiny put downs. Critiques of my skills. He was an investor, but he wasn't a chef. I wouldn't listen to him." I chuckle. "Aiden trying to keep me down

only made me work harder. I got better. Bigger. And he…
he couldn't handle it. He got angry."

"Because he knew you deserved better," Davis growls.

I nod and cross my arms.

"Three months after opening the bakery, I was closing
up for the afternoon. And like always, Aiden was there. He
was counting the money in the till, complaining that we
were in the red. I told him he was crazy. That it was too
early to worry about money. And then he…"

I pause and look into the dark.

"Tell me," he says gruffly.

My eyes flick to him. "He slapped me across the face.
Just once. Told me it was his responsibility to take me
down a peg. I was so surprised I just went back to closing down."

In the dark, Davis's face is a mask. But that strong
jaw of his is clenched, and I recognize murder in his eyes.

"There were other things," I whisper. "Cutting me off
from you. My father. Fallon. And I let him. I couldn't just
leave Aiden. He wouldn't allow it. He'd hunt me down.
He'd take my bakery. I felt like I had so much at stake, and
Aiden King doesn't lose. I didn't want to accept the truth."

Silence stretches through the darkness like a heavy
cloak.

"I thought I could compartmentalize. That maybe,
somehow, we'd just dissolve. And it worked. Until the night
he broke my arm."

Davis tenses. His fingers dig into his biceps.

"We were alone in the bakery one night. And out of
nowhere, he started making all these angry demands. Sell
the bakery. Stop working. I couldn't help myself. I laughed
and told him to fuck himself. And it was like I flipped that

switch." I close my eyes. "It was the real Aiden. The violent temper. The rage."

The night sky stretches above us. Stars blink in and out. And then I whisper—

"He broke my arm with a rolling pin."

Davis swears. A dark, violent sound.

He's suddenly on his feet, pacing in front of the truck, as though he'll combust on the spot if he stays still. I can practically hear the gears of his jaw grinding together.

My fingers shake as I trace them over the small scars on my arm. "He pinned me to the counter, and he brought it down. And then I passed out."

The ground crunches as Davis moves to the front of the truck.

I slip off the tailgate. "Where are you going?

His eyes look wild, crazed. "To get on a fucking plane to DC and kill the guy."

"*No.*" I hook my arms around his massive frame, stilling him. "You stay with me. I need you here. *We* need you."

I feel the rage melt out of his body. Davis heaves a sigh, and then he turns, crushing me against his chest. He's shaking. "Jesus, baby," he murmurs, his chin sweeping the top of my head.

I sniffle, burying my face in his chest.

"What happened then?"

"He took me to the emergency room. I knew if I said anything, it'd just end in more of the same. I was in pain and hysterical. All I could do was let him take me home."

I look up. Silent tears slip down my face. Seeing them, Davis reaches to wipe them away, but I shake my head, wanting them to fall.

"He apologized, but in the same breath, he told me it

was my fault. Told me if I ever tried to leave him, he'd kill me. He'd find my family. He'd make me pay."

A shudder rocks my frame, but Davis holds me tight.

"Aiden's the perfect monster. Calculating and charming. You never think…men like this…"

"He's not a man." The frozen rage in Davis's dark gaze steals my breath. "He's a piece of shit. A coward who tried to manipulate a strong woman because he was never good enough for you."

I let his words settle. Let my breathing steady. Then I say, "The next week I found out I was pregnant."

Davis swears.

I look down at my belly. "Squish woke me up. He saved me. I stayed with Aiden for another week, getting my things ready. And then we got in that huge fight and… well, you know the rest. It all burned down."

His hands shift to my shoulders, holding me closer. We sway in the headlights, under the glow of the moon. That last unfinished dance from Nowhere. "Tell me," I whisper against his broad chest. "Are you mad at me? Do you think less of me for staying with him?"

"I'm fucking furious." His voice grates out.

I look up, feeling vulnerable, but when I see the fierce flash of protection in his eyes, warmth spirals through me.

"I am fucking livid that a man thinks he has a right to lay hands on you. To take that happy from your eyes. I hate myself for not being there and protecting you."

Tears sting my eyes at the raw rage in his voice. "I didn't love Aiden."

I swear he stops breathing. His massive body goes still, fingers clenching tighter around my shoulders.

The weight of his gaze on my face singes as I go on. "I

thought I did, during those first few months. But it wasn't love. It was something to fill the space. Your space."

His big hand curls around the back of my neck. "That's because you never should have been his."

Butterflies explode in my stomach. "And why's that?"

"Because you're mine," he says gruffly, and my heart tumbles. "And I'm the fucking fool who let you go."

"Why did you?" The words wrench from my very soul. I'm aching to know, even if it hurts.

He stares into the dark and says, "I wanted to make you happy, so I let you go." This time, he looks at me. His throat works. "I let you go because I love you."

I gasp. "What?"

"I love you, Dakota." His hands move to cup my face. "I've loved you since that summer before you left."

Tears fill my eyes. The aftershocks of his words ring in my ears. "I never—I never knew. You never said it."

"And I'll damn myself until the end of my days for that." A tortured groan wrenches itself from his mouth. "I know I fucked up and lost you. I know I—"

I let out a sob. "No, you didn't fuck up." I search his eyes, push him back when he tries to take me in his arms again. Because it's my turn. "I love you too. I have always loved you, Davis."

For a long second, he looks stunned.

On a roar, he slams his mouth on mine, devouring me as he lifts me off my toes. Our tongues battle for control. I slide my hand up the chiseled wall of his chest and hang on for dear life.

Davis's mouth leaves mine long enough to murmur, "I love you, Dakota. So fucking much. I can't breathe without you. So fucking long, I've been lost without you."

I whimper. My heart wants to explode out of my chest. Those words. My wildest dream.

He loves me. He loves me.

"Take me to bed," I demand, opening my mouth for him again. "I need you, Davis."

The entire world spins. Hands on my ass, Davis lifts me up, pinning me tightly against his muscled frame. His mouth seeks mine as he walks us backward and into the cabin, straight to the back bedroom.

Gone is my tight dress, leaving me in a bra and the lace panties Davis decimated earlier. Greedily, I tug his shirt over his head, my hands roaming over the chiseled lines of his chest. When I've had my fill, I reach for the zipper on his jeans. After stepping out of them, Davis pauses long enough to turn on the bedside lamp and fan out a clean sheet on the bed.

But I'm already on him, running a hand around his velvet shaft. I lick my lips. "I need you, Davis." I don't care that the cabin is dusty and decrepit. All I see is *us*. All I see is Davis. Whiskey and a rebel soul. Duty and destruction and rough hands.

"Fuck, baby," he rasps. A bead of sweat rolls down his brow as I stroke his cock over and over. "Later. Tonight, I'm going to fuck you."

I obey. What Davis commands in bed, I go willingly.

Calloused hands press me down on the bed. He drops on his knees in front of me, and his thumb parts the lips of my sex. As he strokes over my clit, warmth spirals through my body, rising like a flame reborn.

"This pretty pussy drives me so fucking wild, Koty."

I nearly combust, my back arching off the bed. This man and his filthy mouth.

He gives me a devilish grin. "My little sweet cupcake. Made for me." I watch him nip the inside of my thigh.

"Yes, yes."

Warm mouth. Long fingers. My brain zones out the second Davis runs his tongue over my clit. My legs fold sharply. A shiver rolls through my spine, and then I turn to jelly, a puddle of lust and love being lapped up by this hungry man.

A full body moan rips its way through me as Davis eats me like a last meal.

His tongue laves over me, his broad hands gripping my thighs, spreading them open like he can't get enough. He alternates between slow and fast, love and lust, causing my mind to melt down.

"Davis," I gasp, and wrench at his hair, riding his face. A desperate, all-consuming need has my body arching. Higher and higher.

"Come on my mouth," he orders. "Then you get my cock."

"B-Bossy," I say, my mind barely able to focus.

"Baby, you have no idea."

Davis dives deeper. This time, his skillful fingers find my clit. His fingers and tongue match a perfect rhythm. Each breath of mine comes sharper. My legs and spine straighten hard. Vibrations rock my pelvis and I buck. Davis holds steady, holds on, riding my pussy as the buzz of the orgasm rockets through my toes to my core. Warmth. Everywhere. I come undone. My scream shakes the cabin. Tears stream from my eyes.

I lie breathless, my mind swimming in bliss.

A low chuckle before Davis licks his way up my legs,

kissing over my belly. His massive hand finds my face, turning my mouth to his. Our kiss is ravenous, coarse.

"I'm still hungry," I say when he pulls away.

"Granola bar?"

"No. For you." I run my hand over the cut muscles of his shoulders. "Need more," I say, heavy-lidded.

His lips curved in a pleased smile. "My girl doesn't wait."

Rough hands pull me on top of him. With a whimper, I sink onto his thick penis. Davis lets out a guttural groan, and my fingers flatten on his steel chest. My body responds to him instinctually. I feel him in my cells. He never left. We have always existed.

"Heaven," he pants, sliding one hand up my stomach to cup my heavy breast. He stares up at me, brown eyes glazed with love and lust. "You like that?"

"Yes," I breathe.

I squeeze my wet thighs against him, riding his cock. I remember things about my body when I'm with Davis. Things Aiden took away from me. The way my stomach clenches when his thumb strokes my clit. The way my nipples tighten when he runs a firm hand over my breast.

Everything I thought I lost, brought back because of this man.

"This is how it's gonna be," he rasps. His hand kneads my breast, a primal growl rising out of his chest. "Me buried inside of you. Every night, Dakota."

There's nothing sexier to me than watching Davis—steady, disciplined Davis Montgomery—fighting for control. His ridged muscles rippling, the hiss of air between his teeth. Hooded brown eyes glazed with lust.

A man whipped wild beneath my hands.

A man who's mine.

The powerful thrust of his hips has me rocketing up, but I hang on. My knees shake, my thighs ache. Another thrust of his hard erection has me gasping for air.

"Dakota." My name's a plea on his lips. His fingers stroke over my nipple. "Never letting you go again. You hear me, Cupcake? Never fucking ever."

A hot tear slides down my cheek. "Davis," I whisper.

"You and that baby—I'm going to spoil you fucking senseless. Love you both so damn hard. Protect you until the end of my goddamn days. I swear to God."

Tears leak from my eyes. They're the most beautiful words I've ever heard. My son and I—loved.

Safe.

This man has no idea what he does to me.

"Say it now," he growls. "So there's no doubt. Not anymore. You're mine."

On a broken sob, I gasp. "Yes. I'm yours, Davis."

Satisfaction flares in his dark eyes "Goddamn, Dakota, you break me."

I angle my hips, and Davis goes deeper. I pulse around him and a hot wave of desire builds in me, exquisite and forceful.

"Davis!"

His grip tightens on my hips. Bruising. Claiming. "Milk me dry, baby," he growls.

His words light a fuse and I go wild on top of him. He stretches me open and I surrender, filling myself with all of Davis. I ride his hardness until we're both panting like we've scaled Everest.

"Mine," he grits out, eyes locked on mine.

"Yours," I say breathlessly.

Davis powers into me. I throw my head back and grind against him. He tenses beneath me and then we both come apart. Davis unleashes, spilling into me. Our release sends us into a shattered realm—six years' worth of secrets, of love confessed in a single night. There's no going back. It's just Davis and me and an endless sky of stars.

Our cries echo throughout the cabin. Moonlight falls through the windows. Nothing between us now. Nothing to keep us apart.

30

Davis

I WAKE TO THE BEST VIEW IN THE WORLD. AND I'M not talking about the jagged mountains cutting across the morning sky. It's Dakota in my arms.

This is how it should be. Koty in my arms every goddamn morning.

This is how it *will* be.

Only Dakota in my bed. For the rest of my goddamn days, it's this woman. It's always been this woman. Her and no one else.

All these years, I never imagined Dakota felt the same way I did. Had I known that, would I have stayed away? Would I have told her earlier how I felt? It doesn't matter. We have a second chance. It's all I've ever wanted.

Not fucking up. Not letting go. Never again.

There's time for us.

But first, Aiden King.

I have the bastard's name now. I'm on the offense. Already my mind lights on a game plan. Get his picture. Call in every contact. Every favor. And if he sets foot in Resurrection—beat him so goddamn hard he won't even be recognizable as a carcass. Black and white has no meaning for me anymore. There's only gray.

Only Dakota and that baby I love.

Nothing can happen to them. I wouldn't survive it.

Dakota moans sleepily and buries her face in the

pillow. Her black hair spills across her porcelain skin. Ebony on ivory.

I splay a hand over her swollen stomach, feeling the tumbling of movement inside. The wave of primal protection cresting over me has me by the throat.

This changes goddamn everything. This woman. This child. They are what I want.

The very fact that someone could touch her, lay a hand on her, has me livid. That fucking piece of shit who took Dakota's light and then tried to destroy exactly what made her shine. I'm going to destroy the bastard.

Dakota's story is a nightmare.

But from now on, she'll only live in a dream.

I'll see to that.

With quick, gentle fussing, I spread the blanket over her and take a second to stroke my hand down the curve of her spine. Then I pull on my jeans, grab my phone, and creep into the kitchen.

"Shit."

Five missed calls from Charlie and one text.

Charlie: Wyatt went HAM last night.

Christ.

I text my brother back and pocket my phone. Annoyance slices through me as I scan the small kitchen. It's a disaster, no doubt thanks to Ford. Wrappers from the fancy cinnamon candies he loves to eat lay scattered across the counter. I sweep them into the trash and hide away his fishing knife and tackle box. In the cabinet, I find a small packet of instant coffee and a jug of water we keep in case of emergencies. I mix the cold coffee, take a swig, then get back to Dakota.

I stare at her stomach, wrapped tight in the cotton

sheets. "Cupcake," I say, stroking a finger over her cheek. "You up?"

She stirs. "Best sleep ever."

I chuckle. "Yeah, it was."

On a yawn, she stretches out in the bed, her stomach sharking beneath the sheets.

"Listen, baby. I want to get back to the ranch as soon as we can."

She sits up, eyes flashing. "Aiden?"

"I'm gonna head to the station, dig into it." I scrape a hand over my scalp. "At least see where this bastard's been."

"You think he's here?" Her hand goes to her belly, cradling it.

As a Marine, I try to rein any emotion back. Her words from last night unsettle me. *Aiden plays the long game.* Vague threat or truth? I can't be sure. That's why this can't wait. Because what if he's already here? What if he's been here?

The thought has a cold sweat slicking over my skin.

The idea of her getting hurt or taken is unthinkable.

"You're safe on the ranch," I tell her. "I'm going to get eyes on King. If we can keep tabs on him, we have the upper hand."

Defiance flashes in her eyes. "I hope he comes after me."

"No." The word is sharp, causing her to still.

"I hope I kill him."

On a growl, I pluck her from where she sits and settle her on my lap. "He will never lay a hand on you again. I need you to understand that, Dakota."

She tries to press against me, but I tighten my hold, refusing to budge.

So damn stubborn. She scares the hell out of me.

"You told me his name. Now, trust me to protect you." I nudge a finger beneath her chin, force her gaze to mine. "I won't lose you to this."

She sighs and curls into me, resting her head against my collarbone. "And to think this whole night started with secrets."

Secrets.

There's one I haven't given her yet.

"Listen, Cupcake. There's something I have to tell you."

She sits up, her hands going to my shoulders. "Another secret?"

I grip her tighter, terrified she won't understand. "Another secret."

I close my eyes, my chest heavy and tight. I've told Dakota more than I've ever told another person in my life. She's heard about the darkest parts of me, and still brings me into the light.

"I killed a man."

She smiles, amused. "You're a Marine, Davis."

"No. This was last year." Her lips part in surprise. I go on. "The man who tried to take our ranch, who started the barn fire, who hurt Ruby…he came back. He came back to hurt us."

Her fingers sweep over the soft scar on my shoulder. "And you killed him."

It's said so calmly that for a second, words fail me.

The knot in my throat refuses to budge. "I did."

She stares at me without fear, and says, "They're your family. You just got Charlie back. I would have done the same thing." She says it simply, as if it hasn't set off an atom bomb in my heart.

This woman's going to be the death of me. She knows

what I went through with my team. She knows about Charlie. And she knows this. And she isn't afraid.

This strong, fearless woman.

This woman who is *mine*.

"He's buried on the ranch," I say. "It's a protected reserve. No one can dig without getting tied up for years in permits. They'll never find him."

A contemplative nod. "Good. That's good."

"What do you say, Dakota?"

"I say...I love you, Davis Montgomery." Her voice cracks. "And I'm so honored that you let me see you."

"Only you." The words wrench deep from my soul. I cup her cheek, stroking a thumb over her full bottom lip. "All these years, baby, I've been careless with your heart. Forgive me."

She flashes me a grin. "Nothing to forgive, Hotshot."

I kiss the top of her head, my heart still aching. "Never again. Rest of my life you'll know where I stand."

"And where's that?"

"In love with you." I lay her down on the bed and devour her mouth.

She gasps out a laugh and winds her arms around my neck.

At the ping of my phone, I growl impatiently.

Charlie again.

Dakota arches a droll brow. "The ranch calls."

Groaning, I fall to my elbow beside her. Kiss her lips. "It does. I have to get back. Straighten out some things."

"Like what?"

A muscle pulses in my jaw. "My brothers."

Dakota rolls her eyes. "You know, you could bark at your brothers, Hotshot, or you could try to listen for once."

A chuckle vibrates in my chest and I blow out a breath, considering it. With Dakota, she makes everything sound so easy.

My hand drops to her belly. "Could be good practice."

She leans into me and smiles. "The best practice."

⁓

Charlie's in front of the stables saddling up Winslow when Dakota and I pull into the drive. With laughing eyes, she mouths, *Listen*, and disappears into the lodge.

Gritting my teeth, I stalk up to my brother. "What's the damage?"

Charlie squints into the morning sun and loops the rein over the saddle horn. "Caught Wyatt puking in the bushes this morning. Kid tied one on last night."

"Shit. Where is he?"

"Bullshit box. Working his way through a bottle of bourbon." Charlie drags a hand down his beard. "Ford's in the garage. Took him to the ER last night. He's got twelve stitches and a fucking attitude."

"Christ." I feel like a goddamn high school principal as I run an assessing eye over my brother. Cut eyebrow. Bruised jaw. "You okay?"

"Got Ruby out of there in one piece, so that's all I care about." He hitches a broad shoulder, a smile ghosting his face. His dark blue eyes scan my rumpled appearance. "Looks like you're doin' better than me, man," he says, punching me in the arm.

I reach out and squeeze his shoulder. "I appreciate that. Listen, we gotta talk later," I say grimly. "I know the motherfucker's name."

Charlie's face turns to stone. "You got it."

Temper and concern fueling me, I stomp to the Bullshit Box. I had my confession with Dakota. Now it's time for a come-to-Jesus with my dumbass little brother.

Wyatt sits at his desk, his head in his hands, a half-full bottle of Jim Beam beside him. Clear as day, my brother's licking his wounds.

"Wyatt," I boom.

"You don't have to yell. Decibel levels, man."

I snort when he lifts his head. On his face, a pair of sunglasses with one lens missing. "I feel like shit," he groans.

I pull out a chair, sit beside him. "Don't think it's the bourbon that's got you hurtin', brother."

Wyatt squints real hard at the bottle, then with a sigh, takes off the sunglasses and rubs his eyes. My little brother has that same lovesick look on his face I only associate with the McGraw women.

I decide to cut to the chase. "You and Fallon?"

"No. I don't know." He holds his head in his hands. "I fucked it up. It's my fault," he says mournfully. "Using Sheena last year to make her jealous. That's why she's doin' all this." An unhappy growl rolls out of him. "I bet this guy she's seeing is just some average fuckhead who doesn't give a shit about her."

He's trying to play it off, act like it's no big deal, but those shadows under his eyes tell a different story. Wyatt's brave enough to take on Fallon McGraw. Maybe he already has. One thing's for certain—my little brother's gonna fuck up what he never had before he even has it.

Which surprises me. Ever since I can remember, Wyatt's been wild, free. No strings. Maybe he finally found the one girl who won't give him the time of day. Because Fallon McGraw hates his guts and he's still working for it.

"Listen." I fold my arms across my chest, sit back in my chair. "If you're lookin' for a one-night rodeo, don't do it with Fallon McGraw. She's like a little sister to me. Not to mention, she's my responsibility. I promised Stede I'd look out for her, and that includes when it comes to you, too."

Wyatt glowers, straightens up. Defiance flashes in his blue eyes. "Yeah, but she's my—"

"What?" I look at him hard. "She's what?"

A muscle in his jaw works. "Nothing."

"You finish that sentence, you mean it." I reach over and pour myself a shot so I'm on the same footing as my brother. "Don't fuck with her heart. Because I won't hesitate to kick your ass."

Wyatt flinches. "I swear, you always think the worst of me, man." He twists his hands in his hair, keeps them there. "I'm never gonna be like you. I'm not perfect."

Fuck.

The lecture I was about to deliver falls out of my mind. I see that little kid from Wildheart, running across the field to me because he had fallen from his horse. And I picked him up, and I told him it would all be okay.

I'm still that brother.

"I'm far from perfect." I clear my throat and exhale. "And you're right. I don't give you enough credit, Wyatt. You're not me and I'm not you. And I'm sorry for last year. Not believing you with the Wolfingtons." It's an apology that's long overdue.

"Hell." Wyatt looks stunned. "You hit your head last night?"

"No," I grunt. "I didn't."

I look toward the window, at the sky that's turning

pink and purple with the sunrise. Then, I say, "I love you, Wy. And I'm proud of you."

Wyatt's mouth falls open.

A chuckle rumbles out of me. "That shuts you up?" He says nothing and I go on. "I've been looking out for you since you were yay-high," I say dryly. "You gonna listen to me or not?"

"Yeah, yeah."

"Do I know everything about women? No. I can't pretend that I do. But I know about not taking the chance when you have it. I did that with Dakota. I fucked up when I let her go. Six years of agony. I don't want that for you, Wyatt."

He nods, and I can see the pain break in his eyes all over again.

"But I also know that you have no right to ask Fallon to sit it out if you won't commit." I hold his cloudy gaze, making sure he understands. "You can get jealous all you want, but asking a woman to wait around for you when you ain't ready...you got no claim. Simple as that."

Wyatt takes a heavy breath. "I know," he croaks. "I'd play her game if I thought I could win."

I give him a look. "Who says you can't? You're no quitter."

He grins and sits up, caps the whiskey. "You're a damn good brother. Even if you are a bossy bastard."

Snorting, I reach out and loop an arm around his shoulder.

Wyatt tenses. "What is this?"

"I'm hugging you, asshole."

"Oh." He awkwardly pats my arm. "Thanks, man."

I bark a laugh. "Eat a fucking sandwich and sober up. You gotta ride tomorrow."

With that, I exit the Bullshit Box, looking toward Ford's shop.

One brother down. Another to go.

$$\backsim$$

The reverberation of the impact wrench hits me as soon as I step inside the garage. The scent of oil and gasoline hang heavy in the air. Tacked to the particle-board wall are posters of Babe Ruth and newspaper clippings of the Braves. The black cat Ruby pawned off on Ford sunbathes on a workbench.

Pulled up alongside Ford's mallard green Dodge Dart Classic is a vintage John Deere. Like Wyatt rescues those horses, Ford rescues scrap metal.

I watch my brother's shaggy head of hair flop around until he looks up from the hood of the Dodge.

When he turns off the impact wrench, silence lands. Heavy and tense.

After clocking his bandaged hand, I meet my twin's gaze. "You put your fist through the jukebox, Ford."

"Sure did," he says evenly. He steps away from the car to wipe his good hand on a rag.

"Last night, that shit you pulled with Wyatt…" I glare at him. "You put him in a headlock as much as you want, but fucking with his heart, that's a dick move."

"I know."

Our gazes clash. We've been in our fair share of arguments through the years, fought over girls, horses, and chores, but there's been nothing we haven't gotten over.

We'll get over this. I just might have to tie him to my truck's hitch and do a few donuts in the pasture first.

I step up to square off with him. "Look, this whole doomed relationship act is getting old. First with Ruby. Now Dakota." I shake my head. "Ford, if you ain't happy with your life, fix it. You can't go back to that place. I got one brother back; I'm not losing another."

"It was that song," he mutters.

That goddamn song will be the reason Ford gets admitted to the psych ward.

Ford's face screws up. "Every time I hear that song, I think of Savannah. And when I think of Savannah, I think of that goddamn kid. I can't hear that song without wanting to put my fist through something."

Ford picks up a baseball and tosses it up in the air, then catches it again. There are things people never heal from. Ford's taken more than his fair share of heartbreak in life, and I'll never forgive the woman who broke my brother's heart.

"Savannah…"

He flaps his hand. "Me and Savannah could have gone either way, D." A hard edge laces his drawl. "She wasn't the one." He looks me in the eyes and exhales. "You don't gotta fix me, man. I'll be okay."

"You drink too much."

"I reckon I do," he says easily.

"Whatever you're goin' through, get right," I tell him, jabbing a finger. "You're not pushing us away by acting like a prick, but we sure as hell won't take your bullshit, either."

He snorts. "Yeah, I figured that out pretty damn fast when Wyatt punched me in the kidneys this morning." His mouth curves up at the corner. "Kid's got an arm."

He sobers and reaches over to scratch his black cat. "There's no excuse," Ford says. "I'll make it right with Wyatt and Dakota."

"See that you do." I cross my arms. "Because she's not going anywhere."

"Your girl, huh?"

"Yeah. My girl." The words feel right in my mouth. Fucking perfect, in fact.

"She's good for you." Ford moves across the garage to his '57 Chevy and swipes something off the hood. "If you buy a goddamn ring without telling me, I'll kick your ass."

I grin. "Count on it, brother."

"Found this." Ford comes back to me to slap a severed metal tube into my hand. His gaze is grim. "From my Chevy. Cut brake lines."

I freeze. "When? On the ranch?"

"No. In town."

Fuck. Panic grips me by the jugular.

Ford lifts his brows. "What're you thinking, D?"

"Bullshit Box," I growl. "You, Charlie and Wyatt. Fifteen minutes."

Then I haul ass across the ranch, desperate to get back to Dakota.

Classic rock and roll hits me the minute I step through the front door of the lodge. The Rolling Stones sing about brown sugar, and I smile when I see my clean kitchen messy as hell. The soft movement of Dakota and her belly is slowly becoming my favorite sight.

I'm ready for it. All of it.

Too damn beautiful for words. Barefoot, she's changed out of last night's clothes and into a long slip dress. Her belly's hugged by a blue apron. Dark hair rolled in a messy bun. Golden April sunshine falls through the window, bathing her in an ethereal glow.

I watch her size up a big bowl of batter before reaching a hand toward the lip and getting a hard grip. At the contact, she closes her eyes. A tear slips down her cheek, and her knuckles go white as she lifts the bowl, using her healing arm to boost its bottom. A sob slips from her mouth.

But there's no tentativeness, no recoil.

I want to go to her, but I stand my ground. She needs to do this. There's something in her face, in her rigid shoulders, that I haven't seen since I picked her up at that side of the road motel.

A shaky little breath puffs out of her and then she comes alive. She carefully pours the batter into cupcake tins and returns to the flour. She cuts butter into chunks. One-handed, she sprinkles flour on the counter, adds milk and yeast. Armed with a spine of steel, she measures every ingredient with a sniper's precision.

She's slow, but she's sure.

Steady.

Strong.

I've never been more goddamned proud.

Meeting my gaze, she nods her head at me.

I drop the wires on the counter and stride toward her until she's in my arms. She smells of warm dough and cream. I cup the back of her head and bring her sweet mouth to mine.

"You knocked me loose, Hotshot," she murmurs against my lips. "I couldn't wait."

I run my hands down her body, her soft curves fitting perfectly against my palms.

When we pull back, I stare at what she's created. She

hasn't just baked. She rose from the ashes. Left her past behind in a mess of dough and flour.

Dakota exhales a shaky shudder. "I'm free," she says, gesturing at the mess. Her hand cradles her belly, leaving behind a white flour handprint.

Fear twists my heart.

My gaze moves from her to the cut brake lines lying on the table.

Dakota's ready to fight. And it scares the ever-loving fuck out of me.

Because he's here.

Eventually, he's coming.

And she knows it.

31

Davis

I SIT AT RICHTER'S DESK, TRYING NOT TO LET RAGE consume me. Across from me, Richter carefully sifts through the flight records of Aiden King.

"Looks like he's been using his plane every other Friday night for the last three months," Richter says.

I lean in, ignoring the crackle of the police scanner. "New York City?"

Richter nods. "That's where it says he's going." He sits back and runs a finger over his mustache. "He registered the craft with the FAA, but that doesn't mean he's not forging his location. Or he knows someone who can delete flight logs."

"Smart." I shuffle through the papers, move on to the still images taken around town. Dakota opening the Corner Store. Wyatt down at the rodeo grounds. "He'd be on the security cameras."

Richter studies me. "They don't get every nook and cranny in this town. You know that."

I do.

I also know what Dakota told me.

Aiden plays the long game.

If he can wait a year into a relationship to lay hands on his girlfriend, then he sure as hell can lie low in Resurrection.

"You have enough to g___ ___" asks after a long sip of cold coff___

"Unfortunately, no."

"We could open a case down in DC, ___ how that'll go."

It'll go right into the trash.

There's no police report. No photographs of her bruises. Nothing other than Dakota's word against King's. Certainly nothing that will have the cops in DC wanting to take the lead from a small town.

I glance at the files spread across the desk. An unofficial case file Richter's opened for me. It's been three weeks since Dakota sprung the name Aiden King on me. Since then, Richter and I have worked tirelessly to dig up anything we can on him.

Other than going missing for forty-eight hours on the weekends, it's all we have on him. He's up to something. What that is, fuck if I know.

I could fly to DC, put a bullet in his goddamn head, and end it, but I don't want to leave Dakota alone. Don't want to risk us crossing paths. Besides, it'd be a deadly mistake that could cost me everything. Dakota. Our future. The thought of getting caught is enough to make me play it safe. Play it smart.

At least until King sets foot on my turf.

Richter rubs his chin and waits. "Should you be messing with this guy, Montgomery?"

I glance at the blown-up photo of Aiden King pulled from the website of his equities management firm. Arms crossed, he leans back against a brick wall. Pretty-boy attractive with rough stubble and a sharp jawline. Smug fuck.

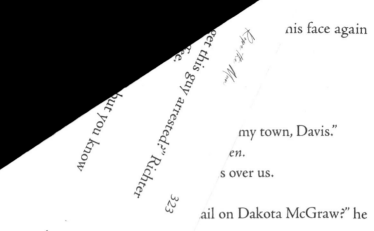

his face again

my town, Davis."

en.

s over us.

...per this guy arrested?" Richter

...but you know

...ail on Dakota McGraw?" he asks.

It makes my s... n churn to ease up on Dakota's safety.

Crossing my arms, I glance out the window to The Corner Store. Dakota's new Jeep shines in the parking lot. She's twenty feet away, and her nearness is intoxicating. She's the center of my gravity and every second I'm apart from her, I feel like I'm falling off the face of the earth.

As irritating as he is, I consider Topper's question. She has the tracker, and she's barely out of my sight. Maybe it's enough. Still, it has me anxious to think of taking eyes off her, especially now that I know King's pulling the disappearing act every other weekend. I also can't underestimate Dakota's stubbornness. She won't let me keep her under lock and key forever. Plus, that baby's coming soon. Our life won't know what hit it.

Because that's what this is. Our life.

My son. My girl. No doubt.

"No," I tell him. "A few more weeks."

Richter eyes me. "You think about becoming a cop?"

"I got enough on my plate with my brothers." I slip the photo of King into the manilla folder.

"What you want with that?" Richter demands.

"Target practice."

Aiden King's photo is going up on the Bullshit Box's dartboard. I want to ingrain the asshole's face in my memory, so if he comes to Resurrection, I'll know exactly where to aim.

My phone vibrates.

DAKOTA: ALONE IN CORNER STORE. PREGNANT. BORED. HORNY. SEND HELP. OR BETTER YET, A MARINE.

I chuckle. The thought of a naked Dakota pressed against the kitchen wall of The Corner Store has me hard already.

Folder in hand, I shove out of my chair. "Appreciate your help," I tell Richter and turn for the door.

"Montgomery." Richter's boom of a voice stops me. "You don't have a badge. Remember that."

My hand fists.

Richter swears under his breath. "I'm breaking rules for you, Davis. Because you're a good guy. But my station, my town, comes first."

I give a nod. "I understand that, sir."

Richter won't have to break his black-and-white rules. But I will. When it comes to my family, gray is all that matters.

I'm halfway across the parking lot when the sputter of an engine has me turning.

Fuck.

Stede McGraw.

Our meeting flashes through my mind.

A meeting I've forgotten.

Quickly, I tuck the folder containing King's photo

under my arm and redirect my stride from Dakota to Stede.

But the old man misses nothing.

Stede's bushy eyebrows rise. "My daughter safe?" he asks as he wanders toward me.

"She is."

"I like to hear that." He motions toward his truck. "You want to talk? Let's talk."

We settle inside his dusty pickup, twisting to face each other.

The scent of coffee and sawdust fill the cab of his truck. A photo of Dakota and Fallon as little girls peeks out from the underside of his visor.

"I don't like rumors, Davis. Not in my town." Stede's tone is no-bullshit. "And when I hear rumors, I like to get to the bottom of them."

"I understand that, sir." I harden my jaw and look Stede in the eyes. "That's why I wanted to talk to you today. It's about Dakota."

Frowning, he puts his hand up. "I told you to take care of my daughter."

Fuck. I swallow hard. The man may have cancer, but I have no doubt he'd take me to the mat for his daughter. Especially if he knew I was just on my way to fuck his daughter raw. "That isn't what you meant; I get it—"

"No, son. It's goddamn exactly what I meant." A smile cracks his craggy face. "It took you two long enough."

The tightness in my chest loosens.

"My daughter's strong," Stede says. "She's a fighter. She makes me the proudest father in the world. And you're the one she needs."

"Pretty sure I'm the one who needs her." I rub my jaw, then come out with it. "I want to marry her, sir."

It's the only thing to say. I need a ring on her finger like my last breath. Rope myself to this woman until the end of time.

"Every blessing you want—they're yours." His grin widens. "This saves me time and saves you time. You want to marry her and raise that boy as a Montgomery, then you do that. And remember what I told you."

"And what's that?"

"Be true. It's all I ask. Otherwise, I got a shotgun with your name on it."

"Always." I grin, my heartbeat jumping all over the place. "You should tell your daughter you're proud of her, sir. I think she'd want to know."

The old man's gray eyes go misty. "Giving me advice?"

I chuckle. "No, Stede. Just sticking my nose where it doesn't belong."

Stede holds out a hand, and I take it. "Welcome to the goddamn family, son."

32

Dakota

"**Y**OU GOT MORE THAN THAT BUN IN THE OVEN, Dakota?"

I laugh and wag a finger at the grizzled man peering into the kitchen. "We have fresh cinnamon rolls on Tuesdays, Lou, and you know that." Balancing on tiptoes, I reach for a container of Skoal behind the counter. "You should quit this if you know what's good for you."

He looks both annoyed and embarrassed.

A crash of cans from the beer aisle has me looking up. "Hamm's is two rows from the top, Clyde."

Lou takes the can, pays, and hitches his jeans. "Be back Tuesday for those cinnamon rolls."

I give him a wink. "Be sure to save you some."

Lou shuffles out of the store, making way for Clyde and his six-pack. After that, the store is quiet. Fallon's called in late, so I make myself useful, whipping up a batch of cinnamon rolls and letting the dough rise.

Finished, I exit the kitchen and cross to the big window overlooking Main Street. Warm. Sunny. Spring's in the air. Shops and boutiques and restaurants are all getting ready for the tourist season. When the ice melts in the pass, that's the sign our small town is open for business.

My gaze flits around The Corner Store. Nostalgia sweeps over me. But also change.

I reach in the back pocket of my jeans and unfold the

check I got this afternoon—the fire insurance claim payout for Milk & Honey. A nice sum that has me marveling at all that money.

I can see it all. The realm of possibilities. My bakery. A place with warm coffee and caramel rolls. A place that opens with the sun and closes before the day is done. That grows with Resurrection, not against.

For so long, I thought it was all about escaping my hometown and moving on to bigger and better things. But finally, I see Resurrection for what it was: a place to leave.

And I see it for what it is now. A place to be.

And I shouldn't feel bad about that.

That's what second chances are for.

That's the life I make.

I had to grow out and grow up first.

Because sometimes there is no place like home.

I glance at the police station where I know Davis is watching and fall just a little harder in love.

My core warms, and a familiar throbbing between my legs makes me sigh. I smile at the memory of Davis's hands running over my body, and *I love you* on his lips. It feels like a fever dream. I've wanted him for so long, and now... he's mine.

Since we officially said *I love you*, calm has settled over my soul.

This life I am building, this baby, Davis...it suddenly doesn't feel so nebulous. It feels real. Hope's a bright flame burning in my chest. I both crave and fear it. Because it means I have something I cherish. Something I can lose at any time.

I'm still terrified Aiden's lurking somewhere in the

shadows, still unsure about where the future will lead, but as for me and Davis...

We are the right-now. And I'm all-in.

I slide a hand over the curve of my belly, then deposit the check back in my purse. I'm making shit happen. Making my life right for me and my son.

The door opens, and Fallon slinks in. "Sorry, I'm late," she says, avoiding my gaze. "Late night."

"Lot of those lately." She's been noticeably absent from The Corner Store, calling out of her last two shifts to work the rodeo circuit in Round Up. She's been keeping ungodly hours and coming to work tired as hell.

Fallon gives me side-eye. "Planted at the window like some war wife? Let me guess...daydreaming about your Marine?"

I laugh. "Not much to do. You could have stayed home. But since you're here," I say, trying to sound casual. "I wanted to talk to you about The Corner Store." She's the first one I need on my side if I'm going to talk to our father about taking it over.

"What about it?" Fallon hisses a breath as she sinks into a squat. The back of her shirt rides up as she stuffs her duffel under the front counter.

That's when I see the bruises.

Up and down her back, spattered like war paint. Yellow tells me some are old, but there are fresh ones.

My pulse skyrockets. "Fallon," I croak. "What happened?"

My sister gives me a strange look as she stands. "What do you mean?"

"Your back."

She busies herself at the candy counter, making me even more anxious. "Nothing."

"Bullshit. That's not nothing. Look at me."

Shoulders stiff, she slowly turns. Oh god. Her right eye is black and blue. I recognize the attempt to disguise it with concealer.

My body freezes and revs up at the same time. Alarm races along my spine, and it's the moment where I remember who the fuck I am.

I take a step toward her. "The guy you're seeing. Did he do this?"

Fallon's eyes dart to the door. Fear flashes across her face, her ice-queen routine disappearing briefly. "Do what?"

"Cut the shit." I grab her arm. "Did he do this? Did he hurt you?"

"What?" She squirms in my grip, but I tighten my hold. I fist my hand in the hem of her shirt and yank it up. My eyes widen at a large bruise on her right side.

"God, Dakota," she complains, struggling to pull her shirt down. "For a pregnant woman, you have actual insane strength."

"What's going on?" My voice borders on hysteria. I feel rage building in my chest. Rage for my sister. For myself. I think of her late nights, her duffel bag, her strange, secretive boyfriend.

"Tell me now," I demand, not bothering to let her loose. My heart feels like it's in a vise. If I have to tattle to Davis to keep her safe, I will.

She holds up one hand. "It's not what you think."

"Talk to me," I demand. "I know I left you, but I'm here now. *I'm here, Fallon.*"

"Stop. *Stop*," Fallon hisses, using the leverage I have on

her to pull me in closer. She holds my cheek with her free hand. "You don't have to do this, Koty."

"I'm the older sister with anger issues," I growl. "I protect you."

Fallon's face softens. "Dakota, it's okay."

"No more secrets," I beg. Tears hit my eyes. "Tell me. Now."

Fallon gives a big, dramatic sigh. "Fine." Then she grins. "I'll do better than that. I'll show you."

~∽~

I can't watch.

But even as I'm on the verge of absolutely losing it, I do.

My gaze is glued to Fallon on the back of a raging black bull named Man Killer.

"Rope the moon," I whisper as Fallon jerks wildly. I wince as her muscular body gets thrashed for a full three seconds before she flies off the bull.

She tucks and rolls, landing flat on her back in the pasture and the dirt. She lies there a long second before she slowly pulls herself to standing. A cowboy lopes up to her and helps her brush herself off.

We're at Old Cowhand Farms twenty minutes south of Resurrection. Owned by rodeo agent Pappy Starr and an old-school rodeo cowboy named Jerry Malone, Fallon's been taking bull riding lessons for the last six months. The reason for all her secrets. And her bruises.

At the crunch of grass, I lower myself off the fence and turn to see pearly whites and a Stetson the size of Texas. Pappy Starr, stopwatch in his hand, swaggers his big belly up to me.

Instantly, I don't like him.

He's going to get my sister killed.

"You know," he begins. "I clocked that girl from a mile away, coming up to me with a dream and a dare. And I thought to myself, plucked from obscurity. That's how I'm gonna tell the story of how I found this pretty little girl."

He clicks his stopwatch, narrows his beady eyes at me. "Dakota McGraw. The saner of the sisters."

"Sane, but no less murderous," I warn. "I don't want my sister hurt."

"I don't want her hurt, either." He turns an eye toward Fallon, who's disappearing into the bunkhouse. "God help her, she's got a horrible fucking attitude, but she's got a face that means money. She better take care of it."

I point a finger at him. "You better take care of *her*."

Pappy looks down at the stopwatch. "2.3 seconds. Time isn't good enough."

"She's good." I can't stop the bite in my voice.

Pappy cackles, his belly bouncing. "We'll see about that."

Fallon comes limping out of the bunkhouse, changed into fresh clothes. "How'd I look?" she asks, breaking the ensuing silence.

I open my arms to her. "Absolutely crazy."

She laughs, pride alight in her eyes, and then throws herself into my hug. I squeeze her tight. When we pull apart, Pappy is sauntering toward the bunkhouse.

"I don't like him," I announce, shaking my head.

"No one does." With that, she hooks her arm through mine and leads me to a picnic table in the middle of the field.

I open the small cooler of waters and beers we've

brought with us. "He's using you to make money, Fallon. He doesn't care if you get hurt."

She shrugs. "So? I'm using him for the same reasons."

"Why are you doing this?" Even as I ask it, I know why.

I see myself in her face. Her eyes. Eager. Hungry. Fierce. She wants out of Resurrection as badly as I did.

She pulls one knee up to her chin, letting her other leg dangle. "I want to be the best."

"You're the best there's ever been, Fallon. And I mean it."

She shakes her head and twists the top off her Coors Light. "I've won every other event. I want to win this. I want to ride bulls with the boys. I want to win the PBR Championship. Like Polly Reich. I want a million dollars."

I inhale a breath. "It could kill you."

"Everything will kill you." She wiggles her brows. "That's why you gotta choose something fun."

I groan at her absurd logic. "I don't like that, Fallon."

"I know...but...Lawless needs surgery with cash I don't have. I have to *move*, Dakota. I have to make it out. I want to find Mom. I want those wild horses in Arizona." Her eyes take on a faraway glaze. "Staying here...it'll be worse than dying on the back of a bull."

I remember a fortune teller at the State Fair telling Fallon she had nine lives, and she's believed it ever since. Since then, she's been counting down. Defying death multiple times. Jumping off cliffs into the lake, drag racing on the back roads, getting trampled by her nag Lovely. And from then on came a never-ending list of injuries. Broken wrist. Shattered clavicle. Two concussions.

It all started after our mother left. That reckless search for something she hasn't yet found.

I don't want this for her.

But she wants it.

"I have a secret," I say and bite my lip. "I found Mom."

Surprised, she blinks at me. "Where?"

"Vegas. She's a dealer at a shitty casino off the strip. At least she was three years ago."

Fallon picks at her label, her eyes on the chipped wood of the picnic table. "Did she—did she ask about me, or anything?"

I debate lying to her. Then, my heart aching, I say, "No. I'm so sorry, Fallon, she didn't." I reach out and squeeze her hand. "She barely knew who I was."

Fallon nods, then takes a long hit of her beer. Her fierce hazel eyes shimmer with anger and sadness.

"I want you to know I'm staying in Resurrection."

She shakes her head. "I don't want you to stay for me."

"I'm not. You can leave because I'll be here. I want The Corner Store," I announce and she looks up in surprise. "I want to turn it into a bakery. I want to call it the Huckleberry. We'll be that one shop—a destination. But not just for tourists, for our town. The best bake shop. We'll be open from five a.m. to noon. I'll have the best lemon bars this side of the Mississippi, and when the rodeo comes to town, I'll have a booth. And I'll serve hand pies and make everyone pitch in, even you, when you're in town. Except in the summer."

"What happens in the summer?" she murmurs. Fallon has her eyes closed, lulled by my rambling fantasy.

I smile. "In the summer, we'll sell soft-serve ice cream and stay open past nine p.m."

"Hmmm," Fallon says, cracking an eye to look at me. "That's the dream."

"That's the moon."

We both turn toward the setting sun. I lean back, warmed by its rays, thankful for this time with my sister. I feel breathless, victorious. I'm safe here. I belong here.

And I'm happy here.

"I'll talk to Dad," I say, looking over at her.

"We both will," Fallon says, giving me a rare smile.

"I missed this." I can't stop the rock lodging itself in my throat. "I missed you. And I'm proud of you. I don't want you to do this, but I understand why you will."

"You're sappy when you're pregnant."

"Deal with it."

Fallon considers me. "Be real or bullshit, right?"

I laugh through my tears. "Right."

"Then..." Exhaling, Fallon slugs down the last of her beer and sets it down. "You are my best and first friend, Dakota," she says, looking straight into the sun like she's willing it to blind her so she doesn't cry. "You are my absolute heroine. My big sister. My Calamity Jane. And I'm proud as hell of you for burning your entire life down and coming back." Fallon smiles. A brilliant, beautiful smile that lights up her face. "Our mom couldn't mom...but you will. You're gonna have a kid and be the best mother that's ever fucking lived."

"Yeah," I say breathlessly, turning my teary gaze to the sunset. "I damn sure will."

$\backsim$

I dip a spoon into the cream cheese frosting and taste it. It's bright and sweet, like the first bloom of good love. Setting the frosting aside, I wrap the cake halves in plastic wrap to keep in the fridge until Ruby's party this weekend.

I hum along to the Eagles as I move back and forth between the fridge and counter. With each sway of my movement, Squish kicks. "You and me, huh?" I smile and caress a hand over my stomach. "We got this. Don't we, Squish?"

Outside the windows, the evening light is a dusky hint of purple as it settles over the ranch. Tomorrow's May, and in eight more weeks, my son will be here.

A shadow in my periphery has me freezing, but my heart rate stays calm. I feel his steady presence and I turn.

Davis stands in the kitchen, sweaty and dusty from ranch work. That blue T-shirt I've come to love is stretched tight over those bulky biceps. Keena skitters beside him, her expression wary as she regards me.

Stepping around the island, I hold out a hand to her. "Hey, girl."

Keena whines and leaves the kitchen.

I arch a brow. "Still chopped liver."

Davis chuckles. "She'll get there."

I lift the spatula in greeting. "How goes the ranch?"

"Ranch is good. Finished getting the summer pasture ready. All that's left before we open is redoing the sign." He strides toward me, a force of rippling muscles. "Hi," he says, pulling me in for a kiss, one big hand cradling my belly.

"Hi." I press a kiss to his warm mouth, his whiskered jaw.

He drops his forehead to mine. "You happy?"

I squeeze him around the waist. "Uh-huh."

Davis stares at me. With a bemused grin on his face, he taps the smile on my lips. "Who did this?"

"Fallon."

He arches a brow. "That's new."

"We talked. Had words."

"Dakota," he growls.

"First...the good." After drying off my hands, I reach into my purse and pull out the check from the insurance company. I exhale and slap it on the counter. "I got my claim from the fire. I'm going to buy The Corner Store."

"Okay," Davis says slowly. Thoughtfully.

"And I'm going to turn it into a bakery."

He looks me in the eyes. "Tell me what you need."

This man. This beautiful man.

"Nothing. I am going to live and bake and be happy." I wiggle my brows. "You want to do it with me?"

His gaze darkens. "Every goddamn day."

"I'll talk to my dad soon...and I'll do it. I did it before, and I can do it again."

"You can."

I hold out the spatula. "Taste."

He does, satisfaction in his expression. "It's outstanding."

"Now...the bad." I cover the bowl of frosting and head for the fridge. Davis moves, following me. I stare into the fluorescent light of the fridge and say, "Fallon's riding bulls."

"Christ."

"She's all banged up. Black and blue." I shut the fridge and turn toward him. He looks none too happy. "I'm worried, Davis. She's working with Pappy Starr, and I don't think he has her best interests at heart."

He shakes his head. "I'll talk to her." The way he looks out for my little sister like one of his own warms my heart.

"You won't sway her," I tell him. "I tried but..."

"What is it with you McGraw women?" He sighs, dragging a hand down his face. "When you don't listen, you argue."

"Stubborn."

"I'll still talk to her."

"Talk," I order. "Not boss."

"Fine," he says, but a grin tilts his lips.

Before I can get back to my work, he snags my arm and pulls me back against him. "How's Squish?"

The raw husk of his voice scrapes along my spine, warming my core.

"Squish is good."

Davis puts a massive hand on my belly, applying light pressure to move the baby's feet out of my rib cage. Squish likes Davis's broad palm on my belly and his rough rumble of a voice.

My baby has some of the best sense I've ever known.

I sigh, tilt my head back against his chest. "You're so good with him."

He smiles. "You want to put me to work?"

"Nope." I turn to face him. "I'm done. Just need to frost and assemble it the day of. Besides, you're one of the worst sous-chefs I've ever had." I pinch his ass and laugh. "But you're sexy as hell in these Wranglers, Davis Montgomery."

His eyes flare. "I like this. You, here with me."

I nuzzle against his throat. "The baby's coming," I whisper. "There's so much to do. I don't even have a crib for him."

He makes a growl of disgruntlement in his throat. Tightens his arms around me. "I know."

"Are you sure?" Hand on his chest, I look up into his eyes. "About us?"

"I've never been surer about anything in my life." A haggard breath shakes out of his tall frame. "I can't move slow anymore. Not with you. We'll get you a nursery. Get you everything our son needs."

Our son.

My eyes fill with tears. "I get to love you," I say breathlessly. "And that's all I need."

I kiss him in that kitchen filled with hope and sunlight and love.

And at least for now, it's all perfect.

33

Davis

"WYATT, YOU SNAP ANOTHER FLOWER, I'M GOING to wring your fool neck."

Charlie stomps across the floorboards and snatches the bouquet before Wyatt can unceremoniously dump it in a vase. I smother a smile as I watch my brother prowl around the Lodge like some birthday bodyguard.

Wyatt lets out an annoyed laugh and looks at me. "He been actin' like this all week?"

I lift a brow, hitching fingers through my belt loops, content to watch the madness. "Pretty much."

Between getting the ranch ready to open to guests in less than a month, and actual ranch work, Charlie pulled together a surprise birthday party for Ruby.

My brother's gone all out. Everywhere you look, there are flowers and feminine touches to the big masculine lodge. Light yellow streamers and gold twinkle lights. Balloons. Colorful linens with sunflowers. We moved the big table from the chow hall into the main room. The margarita maker sitting on the bar was Wyatt's idea, an impromptu rental from Zeke's hardware.

Wyatt swears when the crepe paper gets tangled around his hands. I pull out my knife and slice off the end of a ribbon.

"Look, I don't know what the big deal is," Wyatt

complains. "Ruby's had birthdays before. She's had cake. She's had flowers."

"She needs this," Charlie says, fluffing the flowers with more violence than necessary.

My eyes flicker to Charlie. "Everything okay?"

A muscle jerks in his jaw. "We had an appointment with Ruby's cardiologist. He still thinks even with the procedure…it's not a good idea for her to have kids."

Wyatt's face sobers. "Fuck. Sorry, man. I'm just a dumb shit who doesn't know anything."

"You knew that," I say to Charlie.

"Yeah," Charlie says. "I did. We both did. But I think she thought…" He breaks off, brow creasing, then clears his throat. "How's the cake coming?"

I clap my brother on the shoulder, feeling for him. "Cake will be ready, Charlie. Dakota's on it. Relax."

The mouthwatering fragrance of vanilla and sugar fills the entire lodge.

Wyatt looks around. "Where is Fairy Tale, anyway?"

"Sent her out for soil for the garden," Charlie says.

"You sure she's comin' back?"

Charlie glares at him. "Help me or get your ass out of here."

"You do it like this," Wyatt grouses and jerks the string of lights away from Charlie.

I roll my eyes, letting my brothers argue.

Wanting to give one last look over the ranch, I walk away, pass Dakota in the kitchen, and exit the front door. Bright May sunlight filters through the clouds. Crybaby Falls will soon receive the melt-off from the snow-dusted peaks of Meadow Mountain. Already, it's unreasonably warm. If it keeps up at this pace, it'll be boiling by the time June rolls around.

In three weeks, the first batch of guests will arrive.

Runaway Ranch is ready.

Still, there's a nagging feeling in my gut as I scan the ranch.

But there's nothing. It eats at me and I don't know why.

The familiar rumble of Fallon's engine catches my ear. She circles her old Chevy around the parking lot, lets it sputter to a stop, and hops out.

I sigh. One more woman I have to wrangle.

"Need an extra hand?" I ask, coming to a stop beside her truck.

She shakes her head, plucks a purple-wrapped present from the passenger side seat. "I got it."

"Where's Stede?"

"Cattle drive in Bixby. He finally feels good enough after chemo, so he couldn't pass up this chance. He sends his regrets."

"Can't keep him down."

"No, you can't." Pride shines in her hazel eyes. "Not my daddy."

Hefting the package on her hip, she takes a step toward the lodge, but I put a hand out, stopping her. "Listen, I want to talk to you about something."

She sighs. Shields her eyes against the sun as she looks up at me. "Let me guess. Dakota squealed."

"You're riding bulls, Fallon. Why?"

"Ugh, don't go all overprotective-old-school-cowboy on me," she says testily.

"It's not safe," I tell her gruffly. "If my brother were doing it, I'd sit him down, too."

Her nervous gaze flicks to the lodge. "This doesn't involve you, Davis. Or Wyatt."

"That's where you're wrong. It involves me." I nod her way. "You're Dakota's little sister. I promised your father I'd look out for you, and I intend to do that. No matter how much you want to fuss and fight."

She stares off into the distance, caramel hair whipped by the wind, expression unreadable. "And what about Dakota?"

"What?"

"What about my sister?" she demands. "She's pregnant. She's staying in Resurrection. What are you doing with her?"

I scowl, wondering when she turned the interrogation tables on me. "I'd prefer to talk about you," I mutter, gripping the back of my neck.

The explanation's simple. I love Dakota. Always have. There will never be another, and loving her is as natural as breathing. She's everything.

But Fallon isn't waiting for my answer. She jabs a nail into my chest, staring coolly back at me. "You hurt her, and I run my truck through your lodge." She shrugs. "It's already red, so your blood won't make a difference."

I fight the smile ghosting my lips. "Is it you or me giving the lecture?"

"Screw my daddy liking you. I like you. So, you might as well buy the ring."

"Already got it."

Her eyes widen, and she gnaws on her bottom lip like she's considering whether to believe me. "Show me."

My stomach in knots, I pull the ring out of my pocket. A round diamond solitaire with tiny diamonds on the side.

I bought it yesterday in Bozeman with Ford along as moral support.

"What do you think?" Though my voice stays steady, a nervousness I've never felt before courses through my veins. But it's not at the thought of asking Dakota to marry me. It's at the thought of her becoming my wife.

Fallon's silent for a long beat, but a smile tips her lips. "It's not big enough. But…she'll love it."

I rough a hand over my hair, go on. "I love Dakota. I've loved her the last six years and haven't stopped. I don't need time. I don't want to date her. I want to marry her and make her son mine."

"Well," Fallon sniffs. A bright sheen coats her eyes. "I guess you're all kind of chivalrous, aren't you?"

I chuckle, shake my head. "I want to be good with you, Fallon. Because you're family. You *will* be family."

A long silence falls, and we stare out at the ranch. Across the sky, a golden eagle soars through cotton ball clouds.

"I'm riding because I want to, Davis," Fallon says, breaking the quiet. Her face is angled toward the sun, away from me. "I want to be as good as Stede. I want to get out of Resurrection."

I nod, thinking of what Dakota told me about Fallon's broken dreams. Battered and bruised isn't enough to scare Fallon away from what she wants. I can't stop her. Or the yearning in her eyes. Fallon's a raging river that no man can divert.

I close the space between us and curl my hands around her shoulders. Surprise creases her face as I turn her toward me. "Let me break it down for you, Fallon. There's simply only so much time until you're hurt. No matter how good you think you can ride. It's inevitable." I look her in the eyes and say softly, "You'll get hurt. Maybe die."

She nods slowly. "I understand."

"Okay. Make sure you do." I take the present from her hands and head toward the lodge.

"Davis, wait." She follows, her lower lip pulled between her front teeth. "You won't tell anyone, will you?"

I arch a brow. "Anyone mean Wyatt?" At her silence, I say, "He'll find out. Sooner or later."

"Will he be angry?" she asks, her eyes unguarded.

"I couldn't tell you, honey. I don't know."

With that, I leave Fallon. She has her own demons to battle. Whether she listens to me or not, I said my peace. And I'll be there for anything else she needs, whatever happens.

My boots carry me straight for the kitchen.

My truth north.

My girl.

Dakota's putting the finishing touches on Ruby's cake. Beautifully piped buttercream sunflowers unfurl over the cake like a blooming garden.

My heart pounds against my chest.

With her hourglass figure and bump riding low on her belly, Dakota's fucking flawless. That pregnancy glow surrounds her like a halo. She shimmies around the kitchen in a sexy little dress that stops mid-thigh, and all I want to do is slide it up her curves and see what she's got on underneath.

"What do you think?"

I stride toward her. "Think it's the carrot cake to crush all carrot cakes."

Dakota squints at the cake, lips pursed. "You think?"

"Baby, Ruby's gonna lose her damn mind." Which is what I'm close to doing.

"Think you can sacrifice one of those muscles to have a slice?" she teases.

I band my arms high around her waist and ease her back possessively against me. Sugar, milk, cream. Her scent goes straight to my cock, and it flexes.

"Think I wish I were that apron wrapped around your hips."

"Goddamn it, Davis," she swears as the cake rocks. "If you make this cake fall, I'll kill you," she growls, shoving sweaty hair off her brow. Her face flashes fierce, that no-bullshit look she gets when someone's in her kitchen. Fuck, it turns me on.

I take her arm and haul her back toward the pantry.

"Davis," she gasps, shoving at my chest, but I see the flames of excitement leaping into her eyes. "Everyone's out there."

"We got thirty minutes," I rough against her throat, pulling her into the pantry. "Ford's always late. Wyatt's hanging a pinata, and who's to say Charlie and Ruby ain't doing this same damn thing."

The corners of her red lips turn up. "You're playin' reckless, Hotshot."

"With you, baby, always."

Our bodies slam together like rockets, hearts screaming, nerves on fire.

Blindly, I press her up against the door, kissing her deep and hard. No need for lights. I know Dakota in the dark. Every inch, every curve of her body. Mine.

I drag the top of her dress down, kneading her breast in my rough grip. "Fuck, Davis," she moans.

Her breath picks up. Her delicate fingers toy with the waistband of my jeans.

"Let me take care of you," she breathes.

And then she gets on her knees.

My senses scramble. I grip the corner shelf to hold myself upright and get a goddamn grip on sanity. Too many fantasies are coming true at once. Dakota on her knees in front of me. Dakota for the rest of my life.

It's then her warm, wet mouth closes around me and my mind goes blank. She sucks my cock into her mouth so deep that I almost come. The gentle drag of her teeth, her hands cupping my balls, have me groaning, agonized.

"Suck me off, Cupcake." I wrap a fist in her hair and give it a gentle yank. "Take all you can with that pretty pink mouth."

I can feel her smiling against me. She milks every long stroke, no rushing. She takes her time, gives me everything I don't deserve and then some.

"Fuck," I curse. Sweat beads on my brow.

Unable to help it, I buck and thrust my cock deeper into her mouth. Her nails dig into my ass. She holds me against her, sucks me deeper. There's no holding back. I come so hard my ears ring. She takes all of me, drinking me in.

Dakota pulls back, looking triumphant.

"Your turn," I rasp.

"We don't have time," she whispers, her wild eyes darting to the pantry door.

I look down at her and grip her jaw with my hand.

"I always have time for you. You never accept no. You never *deserve* no. If you need something taken care of, you tell me. If you need to be taken care of, you tell me. Do you understand me?"

Those black, starless eyes darken and she nods. "Yes, Davis."

"Your turn," I repeat. Need has me reaching down and yanking her back into my arms. I grab a handful of that spectacular ass and hold on. "Now bend over."

She obeys, leaning forward and gripping an empty shelf for balance.

I slide up her dress, exposing a thong with red cherries on it. That combined with the heels she's wearing feels like I'm in the Garden of goddamn Eden.

This time, I slam on the light, not willing to miss out on the sight of Dakota ready to take all of me. Her puffy pink pussy and tight round ass are positioned at a gorgeous angle that makes it hard to breathe.

I spread her legs open and slide a finger through her wet channel, tugging those panties to the side. She's wet. Swollen. The pulse of her core around my finger fires every nerve ending in my body.

"Davis," Dakota whispers, looking over her shoulder at me. She rolls her hips impatiently and it sets me off.

I fucking line myself up with her entrance, grip her hips and slam viciously inside.

"Davis!"

Dakota's squeal of delight makes me grin.

Breath coming in short bursts, she dips lower, giving me the most exquisite angle. Deep. I'm so damn deep. Her slender fingers fan out on the shelf as I power into her over and over again.

"Tell me if I hurt you," I growl.

"Never," she gasps. "You'll never hurt me, Davis."

Her trust is devastating. Decimating. The burn in my chest intensifies. So do my thrusts. In and out. Hard and fast until she's gasping for air. Until she's holding onto the shelf for dear life.

"Oh, God, *Davis*."

"That's it, baby. All of me."

I should go slow, but I can't. I fuck her how she deserves to be fucked. All my attention, all my love, Dakota gets it.

"Made for me, baby," I say, digging my fingers into all that creamy white skin. The velvet feel of her tight pussy break me into a million pieces. "You're fucking made for me."

"Yes, *yes*," she cries out. She's shaking as a sob escapes her lips.

I fold over her, finding that swollen bundle of nerves between her legs and stroke. I fuck her with my fingers. Fuck her with my cock. Dakota gets the best of me. And she'll always have it.

The scent of sex. The sound of skin against skin. Dakota's breathy whimpers as she writhes and begs without words. It's too much.

"Come for me, Dakota." I press a kiss against her silky back. "Come for me, Cupcake."

I grit my teeth, desperate to release my load. But I wait for her. I'd wait six more years for a chance with this woman. Her and that baby are my light, my soul. The best thing that's ever happened to me.

"Davis, Davis—"

That's when Dakota's entire body tenses. My cock's frozen inside of her as her pussy tenses and ripples around my shaft. And then she's shuddering, weeping, closing her eyes and burying her face in the crook of her arm as the orgasm rockets through her.

I explode. Violently. Earth-shattering tremors rock my body, and a bellow tears through my throat. I reach a hand around and cradle Dakota's stomach, pulling her closer to me to absorb the jerky motion.

When we come down, I withdraw and yank up my jeans. Dakota rasps a shaky laugh, her eyes fluttering as she tries to rein in her breath. I adjust her thong and straighten her dress. And then she's back in my arms where she belongs.

Dakota moans and buries her face against my chest. Her heart races against mine. When she lifts her head, beautiful dark eyes peer up at me from beneath dark lashes. "You, Davis Montgomery, are a pussy crasher."

I chuckle. "That's right, baby, and don't you forget it."

With a wicked grin, she grips me by the shirt collar and brings me to her lips. "Now let's go out there, throw a fucking party, and eat the best damn cake you've ever had in your life."

34

Dakota

"**G**ET NAKED," CHARLIE ORDERS GLEEFULLY.

"Assholes," Davis growls.

I smother a smile as Davis swallows his bourbon, then stands and takes off his jeans.

Fallon raises an eyebrow and looks at me. "Briefs, huh?"

Davis sits back beside me with a long-suffering sigh. "Why's everyone picking on me?"

Ford grins. "Because we get to harass your bossy ass for once."

I lean into him. "And you keep taking my turn."

"You're pregnant," he grunts. "No one but me sees you naked."

I smile. I'll never get tired of his possessive mouth.

"We're too old to be playing this," Davis grumbles, wrapping an arm around me to kiss my temple.

"You mean, you're too boring," Charlie drawls.

Ruby giggles, sweet and stunning as the birthday girl. "Davis is like the responsible dad of the friend group," she amends kindly.

I laugh. "Then consider me the tired mom."

The lodge doors are thrown open, Chris Stapleton plays over the speakers, and we all sit at the long lodge table, playing a chaotic game called *Truth, Dare, Drink, Underwear* that Wyatt invented one summer.

Charlie's down to his boots and boxers.

Ruby wears my apron over her underwear, and a long white ribbon in her hair.

Fallon's in her bra and boy shorts.

The birthday party has descended into madness. The cake still needs to be cut. Keena circles the table, a frenetic pace that has me dizzy. Unwrapped presents and wrapping paper cover the floor.

"Your turn," Ford says, looking at his twin.

"Truth," Davis grunts.

"Same question as before. One last chance." Ford's eyes narrow. "You don't answer, you're naked as the day you were born. Did you or did you not kiss Lucy Vale in fifth grade after I professed my love to her on the schoolhouse steps?"

Davis goes still, but his gaze is on his brother. His strong jaw is dusted in scruff, the firm set of his mouth gives nothing away. I love this side of him. Relaxed, enjoying his brothers, having fun.

"Kissed her and enjoyed it too."

"Fucker," Ford swears.

Davis tilts his head back and laughs. A deep and joyous boom that has the room erupting into howls.

I look around the room and smile.

This is my home. Family and found.

This is the start of everything I have ever wanted.

I suck in a gasp as Squish does a tumble that could get him to the Olympics.

"Everything okay?" Fallon asks.

"He's definitely your nephew," I tell Fallon, rubbing a hand over my belly. "Wild."

Davis places a hand over mine. Brown eyes pinned on my belly, he says, "Son, you have to take it easy on your mama."

The entire room stills. My breath catches. The pump of my heart is so loud I'm sure everyone can hear it.

Because everyone heard Davis's words.

Son.

The thought has hot tears filling my eyes.

Ruby stares at us and squeaks, her hands wiping fast at her face.

Keena whines and paces the room. She stops by my side, tries to put her paws on my lap, only to get shooed away by Davis.

"Is she okay?" Ruby asks.

"She's been doing this all day," I say, using the table as leverage to stand. Instantly, Davis is beside me.

"Sit down, baby." A broad hand claims my hip while the other slides over the curve of my ass. "You've been on your feet all day."

I rub my stomach. "I need to walk. My back's killing me." I scan the room, unable to resist the urge to move. "You need a drink, Ford?"

"Nah. Not drinking." He lifts his glass of sweet tea to me. "Me and you are in it together for a couple of weeks."

I smile at him, but I don't miss the look that passes between him and Davis. The proud nod Davis gives his twin.

Davis glances at Wyatt, who sits sullenly in a chair with his arms crossed. He's barely said a word since the party started. "Your turn."

"Don't want to play."

His words are stiff—short.

Fallon's eyes flick to him.

"Cake then," Charlie says, his gaze on Ruby's face.

Davis and I get the cake, safely sequestered in the kitchen. We collect plates, forks, and candles and move the party into the living room. Everyone curls up on the spacious dark leather couches. Champagne glasses are filled and Davis brings a bottle of sparkling grape juice for me.

Ruby stands and watches in delight as I stick elegant gold candles on top of the three-tier cake. I watch Charlie grin, his blue eyes fixed on her panty-clad butt showing behind the apron.

Ford, leaning back against the wall, sucks on a hard candy. "Standing around naked, cutting cake. Who'd have thought?"

Fallon shrugs. "Done weirder."

Ford snorts.

"This must have taken so much work, Dakota," Ruby breathes. She dips low, inspecting every inch of the cake. A frosted confection of dreamy goodness. Nothing better than a homemade birthday cake glittering with candles. It's the incredible power of pastry. Bringing joy, bringing people together.

Straightening up, Ruby dabs at the corner of her eye. "I really appreciate it."

I smile and give her a hug. "Of course. I loved doing it."

We sing. We pour champagne and lift the glasses high in the air.

"Speech, speech, speech," Fallon chants. She nudges Charlie with her boot. "C'mon, big guy, get those words out."

Charlie stands, a sudden softness settling over his face. Ruby, wide-eyed, gazes up at her husband. The muscles in Charlie's jaw work. All his attention is on her. "Sunflower, you're the brightest thing in my life. Happy birthday to the reason I'm breathing. I love you, baby."

And then he kisses her. We all watch as Ruby all but collapses into his massive chest.

Ford smirks. Fallon claps.

"Charlie," Ruby gasps when he pulls back.

"I think it's time to cut the cake," I announce. I slice thick slabs of carrot cake and Davis hands them out. I glance over my shoulder at him and grin. "How domesticated are you, Hotshot?"

He leans in and whispers, "Take me back in the kitchen and I'll show you." My stomach flips at the ragged husk in his voice. Demanding. Devouring.

Cake cut, everyone relaxes on the couches, plates on their laps.

All of this is a perfect rope-the-moon kind of day.

Keena whines and nudges her nose at the back of my legs, nearly propelling me forward. Davis makes a quick grab and holds me steady.

"Dog's trying to kill you," Fallon quips as I settle back into our little circle.

Davis shakes his head and grabs Keena's collar, pulling her away from me. "Keena. What the hell's gotten into you?"

"Most attention she's ever shown me." I laugh. Keena retreats to the corner and watches us with dark eyes. With my fork, I break off a piece of cake and lift it up. "Look," I tell Davis. "The crumb's perfect."

"Actually, hold up." Wyatt's lazy southern drawl rings out. He's sitting in a rocking chair, arms crossed, long legs kicked out. "I got somethin' for the game."

I freeze, the piece of cake perched precariously on the tines of my fork halfway to my mouth.

"Fallon's turn," Wyatt says, and all eyes swivel to her. "Truth, dare, drink, underwear."

My gaze slides to my sister, who's gone still like an animal caught in the headlights. I wonder if she'll back down, take an out. I pray she does.

"Dare," Fallon says icily.

Wyatt makes a buzzer sound with his lips. "Try again."

Nostrils flaring, Fallon tips her chin. "Fine. Truth."

Nobody moves. It's like one of those ASMR videos. The only sound is cutlery clanking awkwardly.

"Your new trainer," Wyatt begins, and my stomach tumbles. Davis tenses beside me. "Who is it?"

Fallon and Wyatt stare at each other. A kind of manic energy radiates between them.

"Let's just eat the fucking cake," Charlie growls.

For a brief second, Fallon's panicked eyes meet mine. But she swallows and says, "Pappy Starr."

A soft muttered shit from Davis at that.

Wyatt blanches. "Bullshit. He doesn't—"

"Rep girls," Fallon interjects with an eye roll. "And yes, we know all about your chauvinistic male standards, so please spare us the theatrics."

Ford's frowning. His long fingers run over his jaw in quiet contemplation. "He doesn't work with barrel riders, cowgirl."

"I know it." Fallon steels her spine. "I'm training with Pappy to ride in the PBR."

Silence. One second. Two.

Wyatt rockets to his feet. The veins in his neck charged with anger. "The fuck you are."

"That's funny." She scoffs, her eyes grinding him to

dust. "I mean, I can't think of anything you have a say in less than my life."

"You don't support this, do you?" Wyatt demands, wheeling to me, to Davis, to the room. He rips a hand through his hair, grips the back of his neck.

Charlie's pale, trading a concerned look with Ford, who stares at Wyatt.

No one likes it, but it's Fallon's choice. No one can talk her out of it except herself.

"It's her decision," I say, and Fallon flashes me a grateful glance. I back my sister. Always.

"Wyatt, sit the fuck down," Davis orders in his scary Marine voice.

But he doesn't.

I watch Fallon flinch as Wyatt thunders toward her. Which is strange because my sister doesn't flinch. Not when a horse runs at her full throttle. Not when she falls off the back of a bull.

It's not fear.

It's something…dangerous. Powerful.

Something *else*.

Oh no.

Oh shit.

God, it's so painful I can't look away.

Wyatt sticks a finger in her face. "You ain't got no damn business ridin' bulls," he snarls.

Fallon's nostrils flare. She grips her fork like she's about to stab Wyatt in the leg. "It's not your problem."

"You're wrong. It is my problem. And when you die, it's going to be everyone else's problem because of your selfish, stupid antics."

I eye them with worry as I stand and move to the

cake to cover it with a damp towel, not wanting it to dry out. Then I throw Davis a pleading glance. *Say something. Anything.*

Keena nudges my knee.

"Wyatt, this isn't your party to ruin," Davis says, standing to move Keena away from me. Or at least he tries. Keena darts away from him with a whine. Davis growls at his dog, then turns his attention to our siblings. "You're making Ruby cry, so cut the shit."

Ruby sits there, a huge slab of cake on her lap, her eyes wide and wet. Charlie looks pissed, reaching out to take Ruby's hand in his.

Fallon shoots off the couch. "I'll save you the trouble, Davis. I'll go."

"Oh no," Ruby says, her small hands going to her mouth.

"Oh, for the love of Christ," Ford groans, burying his face in his hands. "Would you two just—"

Two shots cut the tense air.

Glass shatters.

Ruby screams.

Davis roars my name.

Two paws land on my back, the force pushing me to the ground. Twisting onto my side, I shove against the furry powerhouse that is Keena, but she won't let me loose. I look up and realize Wyatt has tackled Fallon and pinned her beneath the coffee table. "What's happening?" I gasp.

Fallon shakes her head over and over. "I don't fucking know."

Davis's voice booms across the room, hitting us all with force. "Everyone, stay on the fucking ground."

Another shot rings out. Somewhere across the room, Charlie swears.

Keena whimpers, her nails skittering across the hardwood floor as she flattens me down like a pancake.

"Keena," I gasp and wrap my arm around her neck. The dog lies on top of me, her wet nose in my neck. She's trembling, her warm body like a calming blanket. I squeeze my eyes shut and hang on to her for dear life.

My heart is in my throat. I can barely breathe, barely think, except for one singular, terrifying thought.

Aiden's here.

35

"**P**UT THE SUITCASE DOWN," DAVIS GROWLS, pushing into my room. His gaze burns into mine, his posture tense and coiled.

"I have to go, Davis." I race across the room, stuffing socks, bras, and T-shirts into the duffel bag I once dared to unpack. It feels like a rewind to that long strange runaway road back to Resurrection. Intent to stay, to dream. Now all my hopes smashed to smithereens. I feel like a madwoman.

"You're pregnant. Where are you going, Koty?"

"I don't know. I don't care."

"You're not going anywhere." Davis takes a step toward me. At the sudden, slight raise of his voice, he's blocked by Keena. The Belgian Malinois puts her body between him and me. Fur rippling, teeth bared, she stares at him.

His face softens, and he puts a hand out. "Easy, girl. You did a good job today."

I look down at Keena. She hasn't left my side since the shooting. "She protected me."

"She did." He roughs her fur and Keena settles. "And I'll owe her the rest of my life."

A shiver slides through me, and I turn back to the task at hand. When I catch a glimpse of the bassinet in the room's corner, the cache of baby supplies collected by Davis, my eyes well with tears. "I was an idiot coming home. All I brought was trouble. If he's here…"

"Dakota, baby…" The duffel bag is torn from my hands. Davis takes my wrists and I'm gently but forcibly stilled.

"It was a couple of hunters in the forest behind us. They were trespassing and claimed they were trying to hit the wolf. Richter's taking their statement now."

My mind's spinning. "Do you believe that? Do you?"

He's silent for a long second. "I don't know."

"It doesn't feel right. Nothing does." I thrash my head. "You have a hole in your fucking lodge, Davis. Weeks before you open."

Davis closes his eyes. "Dakota—"

"It was supposed to be Ruby's perfect day. It was the best dessert I've ever made, and he ruined it." My lower lip trembles. "No one even got to eat the cake."

"They'll eat the cake," Davis says, his dark brown eyes fierce. "We'll eat the cake. And everybody'll goddamn like it. I'll drag them out of their beds at midnight, Dakota, if it'll make you happy."

I sob-laugh, the weight of today easing somewhat.

Yet, just as quickly, my smile fades. The consequences of today feel too heavy. "Ruby could have been hurt. My sister. Your brothers."

It's that thought that calls me back, lights a fire inside. I untangle myself from Davis's grip, steel my spine, and move for the bed. "I have to leave."

"Stay."

I go still. My heart's ripping in two. "Davis," I whisper.

"*Stay.*"

The floorboards thud behind me and then I'm in Davis's arms. I squirm against him but he locks me to his chest. "I won't let you run. Not anymore." The vibration of his voice rumbles through me.

"You have to," I gasp. "What if he hurts my family? Yours?"

His big fingers take my chin to move my gaze to his. "If you go, I will chase you. I will find you and bring you back home. You belong here. With me."

"I'm scared," I say, holding onto his solid body, his strength.

"He will never get near you or our son. You hear me?" His voice drops two octaves deeper. I shiver at the frozen rage in his eyes.

Rugged. Violent. Protective. And he's mine.

He cups my face with his rough hands. "Cupcake, I need you to trust me. I will not let this monster win. I won't let him chase you off. I want all of your years, Dakota. I lost six of them. I won't lose any more."

I wince. His words hurt.

Davis's massive chest heaves. For a long second, only the sound of our breathing.

"I love you and this baby," he says. He closes his eyes like he's in pain. "My biggest fear is you being taken away from me. I won't let it happen, Dakota."

"But, Davis…" I look up into his eyes, asking him to tell me the truth. "This doesn't feel—"

"Right," he cuts in. "I agree." He roughs a hand through his hair. "With what happened with Ruby and Charlie, and then Ford."

I pull back, narrow my eyes. "What happened to Ford?"

He wraps his arms around me, sighs. "His brake lines were cut in town."

"Oh my god."

My mind spins. Aiden is fucking with us. Slowly. I would bet the ranch on it.

"How do we move on if this is never over?" I ask.

"I know one way."

"What?"

One hand on mine, he lowers himself to a knee. With the other, he digs into the pockets of his jeans. "Fuck, but this isn't how I wanted to do this."

My heart's in my throat. "What are you doing?" I ask nervously.

"Getting on my knees," he says, voice serious.

"Davis—"

I gasp when out of his pocket comes a ring. A stunning diamond on a silver band.

He takes a deep breath. "I'm doing what I should have done the night before you left. Beg you to stay until the sun came up. Tell you how goddamn bad I need you. Want you. Love you."

I hiccup and shake my head.

"I have Stede's blessing. I have Fallon's." His dark brown eyes sear mine. "Stay with me. Marry me."

Tears blur my eyes, slide down my cheeks.

"Let me protect you and our son. Let me make you happy. Let me love you for the rest of your life."

An unholy sob wrenches out of my mouth.

And then Davis is standing, watching me with careful eyes. "What do you say, Cupcake?"

I throw myself into his arms and pepper his whiskery jaw with kisses. "Yes, yes, yes!"

Yes, to the easiest question anyone has ever asked me.

He slips the sparkling ring on my finger. "My wife," he whispers, his voice breaking. "My Cupcake."

I palm his face. "Yours."

"I love you, Dakota," he says gruffly.

"You," I whisper. "I love you."

He kisses me. Hard. Hungry. Squish kicks between us and suddenly, terror has no place here.

Despite today, I have hope.

Because I have love.

And that has to be enough.

It has to be.

36

Davis

"**H**OW IS THIS SO FUCKING BORING?" WYATT grumbles as he runs coarse-grain sandpaper over a sign post. It's our last tick off the to-do checklist before we open for the season—sand and varnish the log posts, coat the metal Runaway Ranch entrance gate sign.

Charlie chuckles. "We're opening in T-minus twenty days, you better get ready to work."

"That's because you're doing it wrong," I mutter, resisting the urge to rip it from his hands and do it myself.

"Careful," Ford warns. He's high in the air on the front-end loader of the tractor. "D's about to run this shit like the fucking Marines."

Ignoring him, I turn my attention to the ranch, unbuttoning the cuff of my sleeve and beginning to roll it up.

It's been a long three days since the scare at the ranch. That night, after proposing to Dakota, I checked in with Richter. Aiden's plane never left DC. Flight records confirmed it.

I still don't know if I believe it was a couple of hunters with a magnum flashlight and a .308. Either way, it was too close of a goddamn call.

After checking the tracker on my phone that shows Dakota in the lodge, I turn to my brothers and ready a breath. "Dakota and I made it official."

A stunned silence falls.

"I proposed," I clarify.

"Whoa. When did this happen?" Charlie demands.

"And we didn't know about it?" Wyatt grouses, irritated at being left out.

"After the gunfight at the O.K. Corral, got down on one knee and said some sappy shit?" Ford drawls, unhooking the metal Runaway Ranch sign.

I shake my head. "I asked her to marry me. Wasn't the place to do it, but…"

Dakota deserved a proposal with flowers and moonlight, but I couldn't wait anymore.

Wyatt groans, swings a finger between me and Charlie. "Man, y'all both are whupped. Both of you makin' grand confessions of love when shit hits the fan."

Charlie and I share a grin.

"Only way to do it," I tell Wyatt, slapping him on the shoulder. "We ain't cowboys if we're not on our knees in front of a good woman."

I'm lowering Ford and the sign to the ground when I spot the sander shooting out of Wyatt's hands. It lands in the pasture, sputtering. He and Charlie snicker.

"Jesus." I jump out of the tractor and toss my black Stetson on the ground. "Can't we have one day on this ranch that doesn't end in bodily injury?"

"You're the one getting married," Wyatt says. "You're signing up for bodily injury on a daily basis."

Ford hops out of the front-end loader. "So, when's this big shindig happening?"

I help my brother lower the sign to the ground. "Soon as we can."

"And Stede didn't kill you?" Ford asks.

"Stede doesn't know yet. We're telling him tonight. At Family." I take a deep breath, ready to share more news with my brothers. "I want to talk to y'all about another thing. Eden."

"Anything up there anymore?" Charlie asks, using the extension cord as a lasso to pull the sander back to us.

"Just Ford's old smokes." I give my twin a look. "Hard candies."

"Hey, man," Ford says, holding up his dusty hands. "Not me. Gave that shit up."

I rub the back of my neck, squeeze it. "I know we decided we're not selling the land, but what if Dakota and I moved out there?" I've been thinking about it ever since the night we spent up there. Build Dakota a home, give her the biggest kitchen in Montana. "It's the perfect place for our family."

Charlie and Ford blink.

"We can't live in the lodge forever. With the baby... we could build a place up there. I'd still be around for the Ranch. I just wouldn't be—"

"Up everyone's ass all the time?" Ford says dryly.

I give him a look. "Up everyone's ass all the time."

"Well," Ford says with an easy shrug. "Gotta stay close seein' as we're gonna be uncles and all."

I cut a grin at my brothers as joy takes root in my chest and spreads.

No more shadows.

Only home.

After my conversation with my brothers, I tackle training exercises with my dogs and head back to the lodge. My job as a Marine has prepared me for some mentally tough situations, but nothing braces me for the sight that hits me when I step inside. Dakota sprawls on the big leather couch—maternity jeans rolled down, shirt pulled high, hands over her bare belly—crying. Keena stares from her nearby position on the floor.

Panic seeps through me. I'm on my knees beside her faster than I care to admit.

"Baby, what is it?" I ask, fanning a hand out over her stomach.

"I was just thinking…" She sniffles, rolling her head across the couch cushion to look solemnly at me. "What if Squish and I were on the Titanic and I couldn't save him?"

Christ, that's it?

Relief fills me as I smother a smile. By now, I'm used to Dakota's crying fits over the smallest thing. It tears me up inside, but damn if she isn't adorable.

I chuckle softly. "If you were on the Titanic, I'd be your personal life boat."

"Really?"

"Really."

She sniffles.

I reach for my back pocket. "Granola bar?"

A smile tugs at her mouth. "You're like a walking vending machine, Hotshot."

"Only for you." I curl my hand around hers and search her wet eyes. "You okay?"

"I am the most tired woman in the world," she admits. "I am tired when I get up. I am tired when I sleep." She sighs. "My brain is soup. My feet are busted biscuits. My breasts are watermelons."

"I love your biscuits." I sweep my thumb over her cheekbone. "And I especially love your watermelons."

"I hit my stomach on the kitchen island corner." Fresh tears fill her eyes. "Squish is going to be born with a dented head and I'll have to answer questions about it for life."

I shake my head. "Dakota."

My thumb whisks over her ring finger. Christ, I love the way that diamond looks. Love what it means. That she's mine.

Marrying Dakota is like boarding that plane for Marine training, knowing my life would never be the same. Knowing I'd come back changed.

Dakota changed me six years ago. And she's still doing it.

"Worries are normal, okay? But we can solve every single one of them."

"What about a crib?"

"Already ordered."

She nuzzles her cheek against my hand. "Squish needs a name."

"How about Stede's middle name?"

She arches a brow in quiet contemplation, then says, "He needs a room."

"He'll have one," I promise her. I kiss her tiny lip freckle, her cheek. "Soon."

Her eyes widen. "Really?"

"Really." I help her sit up. "Come with me. I want to show you something."

37

Dakota

I BOUNCE ALONG IN THE PASSENGER SEAT AS DAVIS drives his truck behind the ranch and into the mountains. We bump along a rutted path in the green forest. Soon, our surroundings become familiar to me.

Eden.

The small cabin sits in the middle of a clearing. Dappled sunlight falls through the aspens onto the matted grass in front of the entrance. Off in the distance, the sound of Crybaby Falls.

I quirk a brow. "Davis Montgomery, you bring me up here for another quickie?"

A hint of a smile plays on his lips. "Not yet." He leans over to unbuckle my seatbelt below my belly.

We get out of the truck and he slides his arm around my waist. I inhale the crisp spring air, let the bright sunlight bathe my skin.

Davis takes five paces from me to stand in front of the cabin. He looks down, frowns at something, picks it up, puts it in his pocket.

Gaze lighting on me, his face softens. "What about here?" he asks, spreading his arms.

"Here for what?"

"We build our home."

I let out a strangled laugh. "What?"

"A place to live," Davis says. "For me, you and Squish."

His boots crunch twigs as he wanders around the space. "I see a wraparound front porch here. And back here…a kitchen. As big and as messy as you want."

Unable to speak, I bobble-head nod. Tears warm the backs of my eyes.

As if he knows I'm a hot mess of tears, Davis smiles and keeps talking. "Bedrooms. For friends and family. And this…" He stops at the corner of the cabin, a spot that overlooks a field of wildflowers. "This is our son's room."

My heart cracks open. Absolutely shatters.

I marvel as I stare at him in the late afternoon light. Handsome and hard, but soft and kind. I get to love this man. I can imagine me and Davis in the mornings, waking with the sun, a big eat-in kitchen with skylights, and a playroom for our son.

"What about the lodge?" I ask, my heart hammering.

"I'll still be at the ranch. We'll just have our own space." His eyes trace over my face as he comes back to me. His hands go to the curve of my hips, my stomach. "What do you think, Koty?" Davis's gruff voice betrays his nerves. "Do you like it? Could you make a home here?"

I slide my hands up his chest and smile. "Wherever you are is home, Davis. You just tell me where to plant roots."

With a grin, Davis pulls me in for a mind-scrambling kiss.

A wave of joy blooms over me. The world is my oyster and I get to decide where to go from here. And I choose Davis. A beautiful home with a man who never raises his voice or his hand. A man who loves a child he didn't make and has healed trauma he didn't create. This man is a miracle. He is my miracle.

Because of him, I found my voice again. Aiden can't

silence me. I can kiss Davis with wild abandon. I can laugh with my sister. Spend time with my father. Love my child. And I do love him. The biggest rope-the-moon love in the world, and for once I understand my mother.

I don't forget or forgive, but I understand.

"We'll build it as soon as we can." Davis glances around the forest. "We might have to raise the baby in the lodge for a few months, but we'll get it done." He curses, and I swear I can see the long list of to-dos running through his laser-sharp brain. "I need to babyproof."

I laugh, then kiss his scruffy cheek. "You're going to be a wonderful father, Davis."

He closes his eyes. "Koty—"

I hold on tighter to him. "Thank you for keeping me safe all these nights. Thank you for loving me. And him."

A muscle in his jaw jerks. He looks down at my belly. Palms it. "We'll make it official," he says, his voice thick with emotion. "After he's born."

I nod. "Yes," I whisper.

My son and I will live the great life we deserve with Davis Montgomery.

I cup his cheek, feeling the scratchy stubble beneath. "I love you," I say, wrapping my arms around his neck and beaming up at him. "And I know I'll love being your wife."

"I love you, Cupcake," Davis growls, his eyes misty.

I poke his chest. "Tonight, we tell my father." Nerves crash over me, and I look at the ring glittering on my finger. "And I have to tell him I want The Corner Store."

His big fingers fiddle with the dog tag around my neck. "You got this, Dakota."

I laugh. "Am I crazy for taking on a bakery and having a baby?"

He chuckles. "No, because I'll be right here with you."

He kisses me again, then takes me by the hand. Halfway back to the truck, I stop and turn around. I survey the forest. Stare up at the bright spring sky. I used to think it overwhelming and frightening. But not anymore.

It's wide and open, like my future.

I hold my stomach. Squish kicks.

A rustling has me looking off to the right. I see the flicker of the wolf's tail and I smile.

Go, I think. *Be free.*

Because I am.

38

Dakota

ALLON LIVES IN BETWEEN RESURRECTION AND Runaway Ranch, far enough out of town that her cute cottage still feels like it's out in the country. The weather tonight is perfect, warm enough, yet in true Montana style, breezy. Everyone's assembled for Family, which Davis has told me is a get-together to bullshit and rally around Stede. It makes me love him and his brothers even more. They took care of my father when I was gone.

And Family's especially important tonight. Fallon and I were both with Stede earlier this week when our father rang the bell at chemo. After nine months, he's finally done with treatment. Another light at the end of the tunnel.

Everyone sips beers and sits around on the mishmash of patio furniture. A picnic table, two Adirondack chairs and a dusty old sofa. The air hangs heavy with the scent of cornbread and chili.

Keena, her nose resting on my leg, watches enviously as Davis takes a bite of chili. She whines and I sneak her a hunk of cornbread. I'm a sucker for her and she knows it.

I shift and rub my belly. The old Adirondack chair's violent slope backwards isn't doing a thing for my center of gravity.

Davis leans in, an amused smile on his face as he watches me wiggle. "You okay?"

"Yeah, just rallying." So far, Davis and I have been

chickens and let the night pass without talking to my father. I stick a hand out to Ford who's passing by. "Help."

Ford chuckles and pulls me to standing.

Davis makes a move to follow, but he gets caught up in a conversation with my father about the calving season.

Holding my belly, I pace the small backyard and wonder if Squish can feel my anxiety.

I look up at the moon, full and bright in the dusky evening sky. The flames from the fire cast an ominous gray glow across the fence. Something pricks at the back of my neck as I stare out into nothingness.

Something's out there.

I jump at the hand on my arm.

"We have to tell, Dad," Fallon hisses. "Now."

I chuckle and give her a shove. "Okay. You first."

"Christ, I need a beer," Fallon says.

Charlie, stomping past, makes a growl of consternation as she yanks his from his hands. She slugs it down.

"C'mon, you little chicken." I loop my arm through hers. Slowly, we approach our father.

"You here to ambush me, girls?" Our father gestures at the couch and we sit down beside him. He's grown his mustache out, nearly to the end of his chin, in true cowboy style.

"Something like that." I glance at Davis. Everyone's eyes are on me like a spotlight. "It's time for secrets." At the mention of our old game, my sister smiles. "We have something to tell you."

At the dart board, Ruby and Charlie still.

"I may be an old man, daydreamer, but I don't miss much." My father grins at the ring on my finger. "It's about fucking time you two stopped dancing around it."

Davis clears his throat and nods.

"A real good life is hard to find. A good love is even harder." Stede's eyes bounce from me to Davis. "But you two got it. And you hang tight to that."

"Here, here," Ford calls and lifts his beer.

"And…we're moving to Eden," Davis says, pride resonating in his voice.

Hoots come from all around.

"But that's not all." Fallon's voice comes out strained. "I have to tell you something, too."

Across the yard, Wyatt stares into his beer.

"I…" For once in her life, words fail her. Fallon's panicked eyes dart to me.

I take pity on my sister and go first.

I slip my father's hand into mine. "I want to buy The Corner Store, Daddy. I want it to stay in the family, but I want…I want to turn it into a bakery."

"A bakery, huh?" My father wears his surprise well, stroking a finger down one side of his mustache. His gaze drifts to Fallon. "I don't know how Fallon feels about that."

Fallon inhales. "Let Dakota have the store. I don't want it." She bites her lip and takes my father's other hand. "I've been training with Pappy Starr."

Our father's breath hitches.

"I'm riding bulls," Fallon says. Every muscle in her body is rigid. "I'm going to enter the PBR."

Silence. For two straight minutes.

"Give me your blessing, Daddy. Please." Fallon's lower lip trembles. If there's one thing that will get her to cry, it's our father.

After a pause, he nods at Fallon. "I give you mine, baby girl," he says, but I don't miss the concern in his eyes.

"Thank you." Two bright spots of color appear on Fallon's cheeks. She looks at Wyatt and juts her chin out in that defiant way of hers. "Give me yours."

The brothers swing their heads to him.

"No." Wyatt stands and chucks his beer into the yard. Seconds later, he exits the side gate. The roar of his truck has Fallon looking down at her hands.

"Tomorrow ain't promised, girls," our father says, and Fallon's head snaps up. It's like we're the only three people in the world when he looks at us. "You two shine as bright as you possibly can. I've never been more goddamn proud of you both."

I sniffle. Fallon's eyes glow.

It's the strongest, strangest, most magical thing my sister and I have ever done. Telling our father the truth. Showing him our feelings. It feels like I've defeated a large beast that's been holding me down for so long.

"Now..." Dad looks around the yard and grins. "We got shit to celebrate, don't we? Babies, bakeries, bulls. Let's put the wild in this west."

~

While the crickets chirp in the night, I lift a hand to Ruby, Charlie, and Ford, who head across the gravel drive to their trucks. My father and Davis stand in Fallon's front yard, deep in conversation. After many drinks and rounds of cornhole, the party's breaking up.

"Stay the night," Fallon says, exiting her front door. She smiles. "Let's plan your baby shower."

"Seriously?" Fallon's the last person I expected to channel a maternal vibe.

She gives me a don't-be-dumb look. "Yeah, seriously. You're gonna pop in a month and we don't have shit planned."

"I don't know." I cast a glance at Davis.

A shrill ring cuts the peace of the night.

"Shit," Davis says, abruptly breaking away from my father.

I watch him pace the yard, phone pressed to his ear.

"What's wrong?" I ask when he bounds up the porch steps. He looks grim, and panic expands inside my chest.

His shoulders deflate. "It was Richter. A little boy's missing over in the Briar Gorge."

I clutch my belly. My heart hammers. "Oh no."

"I have to go," he says, sweeping a hand over his close-cropped hair.

I nod. "Of course. I understand."

Frowning, he puts a big hand on my waist and scours the yard. Everyone else is already gone. "I'll take you back to the ranch, drop you there, then head up."

"She can stay here." My sister slips in beside me. Davis opens his mouth, but Fallon's faster. "Baby shower talk," she adds obstinately. "Dakota's gotta have one."

Davis's brow furrows. "I don't like you unprotected."

"I have knives," Fallon sing-songs, slipping away to help our father up the porch stairs and into the house.

"Call in your tail." I smile. "I know you still have one."

A muscle in his jaw works. I can see him refusing to leave.

"Davis." I palm his cheek. "It's been months now. I want to enjoy life. Normality."

He blows out a deep breath and pulls me closer.

I grip his shirt, looking into his worried eyes. "What if it were Squish? Go, Davis. You have to find him."

"You don't leave this house," he growls.

"I won't," I promise.

"I love you," he says fiercely, cupping my face in his hands. "So goddamn much."

I kiss him, love spreading through my bones like wildfire. He gives me one last look, then, phone already to his ear, I watch his broad-shouldered form jog toward his truck. Keena follows at his heels.

"Oh my God." Fallon peers at me through the screen door. "Is he always so rigid?"

I smile. "Uncompromising."

"Look at that stance," Fallon says, propping open the door for me. "He's going full Liam Neeson."

I choke out a laugh. "Stop checking out my fiancé's ass."

"Gross," she says.

Her nose wrinkles as a white police cruiser pulls up alongside her street. Police lights flash blue and red. I roll my eyes. Davis works fast.

"Double gross. Topper's here," Fallon says, and I know she's thinking of that time he got Gak in her hair in third grade. "It's the fucking Keystone Kop cavalry."

I follow her inside and back into the kitchen. We say goodnight to our father and finish cleaning up. Hunger pains get the better of me, and I make a cheese plate and popcorn. Fallon brews a pot of tea, opens a bottle of wine, and after changing into terry-cloth shorts and hoodies, we plop onto her big couch, cozy in blankets and a pillow fort.

At a rising swell of nervousness, I remind myself it's fine. Everything's fine. We're safe. Davis is out there slaying dragons and savings babies and I'm warm and safe with my sister.

"We haven't done this in years." At Fallon's eyebrow raise, I elaborate. "Girl talk."

She yawns, takes a sip of wine. "More like baby talk, but I'm okay with it."

I stare at the hoodie stretched tight over my stomach. My son is coming soon. A thought that once filled me with terror is now the brightest light in my world.

With the cheese knife, Fallon scoops brie onto a crisp cracker. Her unbound caramel hair waves around her shoulders. "For your shower, I was thinking the arcade, pizza, and dessert. We can get a cake from Costco."

I scoff. "That's like eating radioactive plastic."

She nudges me with her foot. "Snob."

"I can—"

"No," she interjects. She clicks her tongue at me like I'm one of her nags. "You're not making your own cupcakes, Dakota."

I laugh and chop a wedge of cheddar. "What about games?"

"Games?"

"You know, baby games?"

She wrinkles her nose, then groans. "I'm not good at this shit."

"Bulls, not babies."

"Right," she says, a glint in her hazel eyes.

Tonight, for the first time in a long time, we're back to how it used to be. How it should be—sisters.

I sip my tea and sit up against the cushions. "What about boys?"

She shakes her head. "What about boys?"

One of my brows wings up. "Are we going to be real or bullshit?"

She groans again. "Ugh. I hate it when you use my threats against me."

"Your new guy…you like him?" I ask as I finish the last of my tea.

"He's handsome, nice, rich." She chuckles. "Good in bed. Perfect package. But…"

"But what?"

"It's the little things. Like he's never remembered Lawless's name. He kept calling her Lucky." She bites her lip. "And… this is stupid, but… he makes me walk on the outside. I know it's small, but—"

"No." I squeeze her hand. "That isn't small. It's everything. Little things matter."

A one-shouldered shrug. "It's been fun, but I doubt we'll last through the summer. I don't have time for a relationship, anyway."

"Then why are you doing what you're doing with Wyatt?"

Tension settles into her shoulders. The flare in her nostrils tells me I'm pressing a red-hot button. "What am I doing with Wyatt?"

I keep a steady gaze on her until she drops eye contact. "Don't bullshit me. You're rattling him on purpose."

She swallows. "Because it's easier." The tips of her ears turn pink. "Because it's what we do."

"And what's that?"

She takes a bracing gulp of her wine. "When we're on the circuit…he's a—a good way to work off tension."

I cover my eyes with my hand and groan. "Oh my god, Fallon."

"We both understand what it is."

I look at her through parted fingers. "And what's that? That your constant need to outdo each other either has you fighting or tearing your clothes off?"

Face sour, Fallon refills her wine. "I regret saying a word to you."

"Are you still mad about what he said? That you—"

"Don't, Dakota," she warns, giving me a chilly glare. "I remember."

I bite my tongue, seeing what my sister's doing. Fallon's the definition of *keep your enemies close*.

She used Wyatt to get better, took his lessons to change the course of her career, and now...

It's a vicious long game. Make Wyatt Montgomery eat his words.

"You know what I remember about that day?" I say, shifting on the couch to look at her. "You were hurt, Fallon. I remember your face when you got home." I remember her crying in my arms too and cursing Wyatt Montgomery to hell and back, but I think it's wise not to bring that part up.

She tosses the cheese knife onto the tray. "Yeah, well."

"It's not for him, is it?" I ask softly. "Riding bulls?"

She laughs, a sharp blast of sound that has me wincing. "And give him that satisfaction? No. It's for me. Getting under his skin is just a bonus."

I want to tell her you don't do this with someone you don't care about, but I bite my tongue. There's a thin line between love and hate, and Fallon's walking a tightrope with Wyatt. It's only a matter of time before they both get burned.

The doorbell rings.

I gasp and jump. My heartbeat pounds in my ears.

"Jesus." Eyes wide, Fallon slaps a hand to her chest. "If they wake Dad, I'll kill them." She hops off the couch and rushes to the front door.

"Shit," I hear her hiss.

I rub my arm, still achy from the cast. "What is it?"

"It's Danny." She pokes her head around the corner and makes a face. "Sorry, I didn't know he was in town. Topper's asking if we want to let him in."

"It's up to you." I'm partly curious to meet the guy, even if I know Davis will be ready to murder me.

"We'll keep it quick, then kick his ass out." Fallon disappears, and I hear the crack of the screen door. "Jesus, Topper, get out of the fucking way. C'mon in."

Fighting a yawn, I stand and pick up the bowl of popcorn. Low conversation sounds behind me.

"Danny, this is my sister—"

"Dakota."

I freeze at the familiar voice. The hair on the back of my neck stands up.

No. It can't be.

Slowly, I turn around.

Aiden King stands beside my sister with a triumphant grin.

He looks like the picture-perfect golden boy, mussed blond hair and rough stubble, casually dressed in jeans and a tight Henley. There's a hard candy tucked in his cheek as he stares at me with those intense green eyes.

The bowl of popcorn hits the ground. The world roars in my ears.

Fallon frowns. "Koty, what—"

"Fallon," I say in a low voice, reaching for my sister. "Get away from him."

"What?"

"It's Aiden."

My sister goes ghost white. "What the fuck?" Fallon bites out. The raw shock and rage on her face gut me.

I grab her wrist and yank her behind me.

Aiden grins menacingly. "Hi, Dakota." He jerks a gun from his waistband and points it at us. "Nice to see you again."

My stomach twists.

Fear coils in my chest.

Davis.

The tracker.

Spurred by adrenaline, I reach for the tracker around my throat, but I'm not fast enough. A rough hand darts out and Aiden tears the dog tag from my neck.

I cry out.

He looks at the dog tag and sneers. "You came back for this. Couldn't stay away, could you?"

I watch as he drops the dog tag and tracker in the cup of tea.

I choke down the scream building in my throat. "Aiden," I say calmly. "I'll do whatever you want. Just leave my sister alone."

He scoffs. "Let you off that easy when I've played the game for so long? I don't fucking think so."

His handsome face is composed, but I see the cracks. The shaky hands. Those cold, stark eyes. Aiden looks sick, like he's coming down with something, but it's not the flu. It's madness.

Revenge.

"I'd ask you if you missed me, but I see you've been doing fine without me." His eyes drop to my stomach. "You've *both* been doing just fine without me."

I press my palms to my belly, backing up into Fallon. Her hand clamps down on my arm.

"If you're wondering, I've been doing just fine without

you, too, Dakota," he says conversationally. A grotesque smile twists his mouth. His gaze bounces to Fallon. "I've been having fun playing with your sister. Your pussy was nice, but hers is nicer."

"Fuck you," Fallon snarls.

Aiden steps closer. "I jerked off to you every night, Dakota. Jerked off after I fucked your little sister."

"Stop," I say on a sob. I want to clap my hands over Fallon's ears. Block out the bastard's voice. My sister will never get over this. "Stop it."

I don't want this awful memory for my sister. This guilt. I reach for her. "It's okay."

"Don't touch her," Aiden orders. The gun bobs in his hand. "He's good. I'll give him that. He kept you on that ranch. I couldn't get to you, so I had to find other ways."

Fallon swears under her breath.

A chilling rage stains his voice. "I told you that I always win. I get what I want. And I want to take everything away from you, like you did to me. My money. My bakery. My *baby*."

No.

His vile words are terrifying, and I wrap my arms around my belly. "Never," I rasp. "He'll never be yours."

Aiden's mask drops. "Tonight, you're going to see just what exactly is mine."

A noise down the hall freezes us all.

Fallon and I lock eyes.

Fear for our father.

Dad ambles into the living room and squints into the bright light. "What's going on out here?"

Terror grips my heart.

"Daddy," I gasp.

Fallon and I watch in horror as Aiden raises the gun and aims it at our father. A shot pops off, the silencer muffling the noise.

Stede crumples to the floor.

"No!" Fallon cries out.

"You bastard," I hiss as I race across the room to our father. "Daddy," I whisper, crouching beside him. Blood seeps through his pant leg.

Across the room, Fallon stands frozen.

Stede moans.

"Stay still." I grab a towel from the coffee table and press it over the wound, hoping to staunch the blood. I can't tell if it's deep or a graze, and it terrifies me.

Relief fills me when Stede's hand finds mine. His grip is strong.

"Run," my father rasps.

I can't, I mouth. Tears fill my eyes as I look up at Aiden and take a steadying breath.

"So you what, waited?" I ask, trying to draw his attention away from my father. Trying to get one good chance to go for the tracker. Trying to understand his strategy so I can fight for a way out. "Now what? What are you going to do with me?"

"I have plans. I didn't work this hard with this one"—he jerks the gun at Fallon and she flinches—"to not have a plan. You know that, Dakota. Don't be so fucking stupid. You know you're mine. You know I win."

"Can you let her go? Please," I beg.

"Dakota, shut up," Fallon hisses.

I ignore her. "Fallon has nothing to do with this. Or us." My eyes land on the cheeseboard. The knife, in particular.

"Doesn't she now? She's family." Aiden circles Fallon. "Why would I leave your pretty little sister out of this?"

He traces a hand down her arm.

Fallon snaps. "You motherfucker," she shrieks, suddenly charging Aiden.

He backhands her with the gun, snapping her head back and stunning her. Eyes wide she stares at me, makes some sort of tiny, exhaled groan, and collapses to the ground.

A scream rips through my throat.

Choking on sobs, I crawl from my father to my sister. Her breathing's hitched and her body convulses. "No," I cry out, digging my nails into her shoulders to hold her steady.

Our father calls to us, his voice anguished.

There's the crunch of popcorn as wing-tip loafers settle beside us.

I squeeze my eyes shut. "Please don't do this. Don't hurt her. I'll go with you. Please."

"That's right. You're going to pay for taking what's mine, Dakota," Aiden says, bending to lift Fallon's limp body.

When he's distracted, I slip the cheese knife into the large front pocket of my hoodie.

"Davis will kill you," I growl, watching as he tosses my sister over his shoulder.

She flops against his body like a rag doll.

Aiden's gaze snaps back to me.

"If he makes it in time. Which seems unlikely, seeing as how he's on the other side of town saving little boys from deep dark forests." Aiden jerks the gun at the front door. "Now get the fuck up and let's go."

39

Davis

MY BOOTS CRUNCH GRAVEL AS I HOP OUT OF MY pickup truck and head toward the bright lights of the Bullshit Box. Keena prances proudly beside me, even if tonight was a waste of time and manpower.

It took an hour to get over to Briar Gorge, only to discover there was no one there. No parents. Definitely no kid. Richter and the deputies stayed behind in case they showed. Maybe the parents found their son. Maybe they forgot to call it back in.

Regardless, I needed to get back to Dakota.

As I enter the Bullshit Box, I let out a tense breath. *Home.*

"You find the kid?" Charlie asks, angled into the dartboard, scrutinizing his target. Aiden King's photo has a dart sticking in the middle of his forehead.

"Nope." I settle in at my desk, unholster my gun, and take a quick breather. My gaze scans Wyatt, who's reclined in a busted folding chair. Keena goes to her water bowl as I open my phone and check the tracker. The GPS still shows Dakota at Fallon's.

"No one was there. Think it was a prank call," I say, rolling out my shoulders. "I'm dropping off Keena, then I'm headed back out."

"That's real shitty, man," Wyatt drawls, standing. "Who'd lie about a goddamn kid going missing?"

Something cold settles in my gut.

Wyatt plucks his beer off the desk, takes a long swig, and flings a dart at King.

He hoots in victory. "Right between the fuckin' eyes."

The door opens, and Ford enters. He leans back against the wall and stares the dart board for a long second, then looks at Wyatt. "Really takin' it all out on Fallon's guy, ain't you?"

My head snaps up. "Say that again."

Ford frowns. "That ass-face on the dartboard." His amber eyes flick apologetically to Wyatt. "Saw him and Fallon the other day at the Legion." He holds up his hands. "Don't shoot the messenger."

The room spins. My stomach's turned into an iceberg.

I launch myself out of my chair. "Fuck."

"Davis?" Charlie's voice cuts through the red fog in my head.

My brothers are staring at me like I'm a madman.

"Fallon's boyfriend—it's Dakota's ex. It's Aiden." I barely recognize my voice.

Wyatt and Ford share a wide-eyed look.

I grab my gun off the desk. Whip my head to Charlie. "Stay with Ruby. Don't let her out of your sight."

And then I run. Dread and desperation searing my chest like a red-hot iron.

The missing kid—it *was* a prank call. A decoy to get me away from Dakota. I fell for it. I left her there alone. Unprotected.

I fucked up.

Fuck. Fuck. Fuck.

The world's a dark blur of fury as I race across the ranch and hop into my truck, dialing Dakota at the same time. She doesn't pick up. I fly down the highway, praying I'm not too late. Praying I'm wrong.

I'm not.

Fallon's cottage comes into view, and my stomach tumbles. I pull up to the curb and brake hard, sending up dust and gravel, staring at the scene that greets me.

Red and blue lights illuminate the night. Richter's out front, along with half the damn town. Buzz Topper lies on the front lawn. Dead. Glassy eyes wide, a deep pool of red beneath him.

Out of the front door of the cottage comes a stretcher.

"Stede!" I yell, blasting out of my truck. No one tries to stop me as I race up to him. His hand lifts to me and I grip it. "What happened?"

"Bastard came to the house. The girls didn't know—" He breaks off in a cough. "Shot me in the damn leg. He took them," he says, voice stricken. Tears line his eyes. "That motherfucker took my girls."

"We'll find them."

"I'm sorry," he groans. "I didn't protect them. I couldn't—"

"This is my fault. I never should have left." I close my eyes and let panic wash over me.

Dakota's words of warning wreak havoc on my mind. *Aiden plays the long game.*

And he did. Bided his time. Waited. And now…

Time's up.

"He's going to hurt them. I heard what he said." Stede struggles to sit up. "You find my girls, Davis."

"I will," I grit out. Guilt has me in a stranglehold. I promised Stede I'd protect Dakota and Fallon. Now both his daughters are missing.

If I have to tear this entire fucking town apart to find them, I will.

Tires squeal on the street and car doors slam. I turn in time to see Wyatt leap out of his pickup and bolt up the steps to Fallon's cottage. Ford on his heels.

"Wyatt, wait!" I roar after him. The house isn't secure. Christ.

I leave Stede with the paramedics and race after my brothers who are already inside.

"Fallon!" Wyatt shouts, his voice raw and ragged. He looks desperate as his panicked gaze scans the living room.

"Stay the fuck back," I snap, grabbing him by the shirt collar and moving him away from the crime scene. My mind's a mess, and the panic on my little brother's face isn't helping.

The color drains from Wyatt's face. His gaze falls to the rug. "Fuck. Is that—"

Ford grabs him and spins him around before he can see more.

I take in the carnage. Broken glass. Popcorn. The tracker in a cup of tea. A pool of blood spread across the rug.

Fuck.

Time stops. The only sound I hear is my heart pounding in my ears. Nothing else.

Dakota.

I can't breathe. Can't focus.

I didn't protect her. I failed her. I fucking let him take her.

"Montgomery!" Richter's voice booms like a grenade as he stomps inside the cottage.

I spin around. Fight through the fog in my head to focus. "Tell me what's going on."

"We got a witness. Gertie Dump, two houses over, said she saw a man leaving the residence about twenty minutes ago. He was carrying one. Made the other walk. Looked like he had a gun."

"Fuck," Ford hisses.

Wyatt drops onto the couch, hands permanently glued to his hair.

Richter continues. "Guy got in a dark blue Mercedes and drove off in a southerly direction. No plate numbers yet."

Alive.

For once in my life, I've never been so happy for small town gossip.

"King's been here all along," I say, piecing together what I've gathered so far. "Flying in on the weekends to date Fallon. To watch Dakota. He couldn't get on the ranch, so he waited."

Richter stares at me like I've announced aliens have landed. Then he shakes his head. "We'll find her, Montgomery. Now, out."

With that, I reach down and slip the dog tag into my pocket. I walk out of the house and onto the porch. Humid air mists my skin, the sleepy street of Resurrection cast in shadow.

Bending over, I put my hands on my knees and concentrate on breathing. On not burning the entire goddamn world to the ground.

My son and the woman I love kidnapped. Taken.

The thought of losing both, an all-encompassing nightmare.

I squeeze my eyes shut.

I won't be too late. This won't be like Sully.

Footsteps behind me have me exhaling and straightening up.

"Deep breath, brother." Ford puts a hand on my shoulder, squeezes. "Don't fall apart. Dakota needs you."

Wyatt stares at me. His face so pleading, I fucking hate myself. "Where are they, Davis?"

"I don't know. I don't know fucking anything." My voice is ragged, my heart on its last fucking thread.

Where would King take them? Where has he been staying this entire fucking time where there aren't eyes on him?

As I stomp down the front porch steps, my attention zeros in on the rock path. A candy wrapper. I frown, sinking down into a squat to pick it up. Red hot cinnamon candies.

"Yours?" I ask Ford.

"Nah, man."

My heart stops.

I've seen these before. The same place I told Dakota I loved her. The spot we picked to raise our son. Build our future.

I reach into my pocket and pull out the trash I picked up earlier today.

A goddamn fucking candy wrapper.

Eden.

My heart starts.

I launch myself up. "I know where they are."

I'm moving fast for my truck. I need to get there and find my girl, my son, and kill the motherfucker that took them.

"I'm coming with you," Wyatt announces.

I stop and glare at him. "You get your ass back to the ranch and stay there." The last thing I need is my idiot brother playing hero.

Wyatt crosses his arms and squares off with me. "Fuck that, Davis."

Ford gives a nod of solidarity. "He's right. Fuck that. And if I can add, fuck you."

I stare into my twin's blazing eyes. He won't take no for an answer and he won't leave me.

"For fuck's sake," I mutter. I scrape a hand over my scalp. "Let's go."

Ford grins. "Looks like the three of us are playing cowboy mafia."

I don't waste time arguing. My boots hit the ground as I break into a jog.

Ford appears beside me. His voice is low, dangerous. "You find him, this ain't going to court."

A lawlessness, cold and unforgiving, rises in me.

"No," I growl. "It's not."

40

Dakota

I TRY TO MOVE BUT CAN'T.

My head throbs. Memory crashes over me like a wrecking ball. Aiden walking me to his car and tossing Fallon unceremoniously into the backseat. The second I was inside, he hit my head with the butt of the gun and my vision exploded into darkness.

Slowly, I force my eyes open.

I'm in a cabin. Eden. The bedroom. The tableside light is on, casting the wooden room in an eerie glow. Davis's coffee mug is still on the nightstand, but the bed is unmade. There're strange blankets that weren't here before.

Aiden's been staying here. All this time. The thought is enough to make me want to puke.

I turn my head to the right and the entire room swims.

Fallon's tied to a chair beside me. Her chin hangs to her chest. Dried blood streaks her temple. She has a concussion, or worse.

Please be okay. Please be alive.

"Fallon," I hiss. "Wake up."

Please wake up.

Silence.

My heart hammers in my chest. We are trapped. He's going to kill us. Make us suffer. That much is clear.

A shuddery breath tears out of me.

Breathe, Koty.

I fight the rising panic and instead focus on escape. I did it once. I can do it again. First step—get free.

Back and forth, I rotate my wrists. They're tied behind me, but my legs aren't. The cheese knife is heavy in the front pocket of my hoodie, a reminder that I still have a weapon up my sleeve.

A low groan.

I look over as Fallon's eyes flutter open, cross, then focus on me. "And you were worried about me riding bulls," she murmurs.

I choke on a sob-laugh.

"Koty. What do we do?" She stares at me with the most terrified eyes I've ever seen. A sudden surge of protection zips through my heart.

I jerk against the ties, expand my chest, lengthen my arms. "We're getting out of here."

"Fucking great idea," she grunts, following suit. "Why didn't I think of that?"

I smile. I've never in my life been so glad to hear sarcasm from my sister.

That's when Fallon stiffens. Her eyes widen, and I follow her gaze to Aiden in the doorway. Always so quiet. A lurking ghost.

"Bout time you woke up," he says to Fallon. "You couldn't miss the show."

"Fuck you," she growls.

Smirking, he drags a chair from the corner of the room to sit in front of me. Gone is the gun. In its place, a butcher knife. My mouth goes dry.

"Always trying to escape, Koty. Even when it's hopeless. Even when there's no running. Not from me." His voice is rational, controlled.

"You're in control," I say, still jerking at the ropes. "That's what this is all about, isn't it?" I can't keep the hate out of my voice.

With one hand, he grabs my hair, jerking my neck sharply. I cry out. Fallon screams. Aiden leans in, his face an inch from mine. The scent of cinnamon is overpowering, and I fight the urge to vomit. I fight the urge to go back to the night he broke my arm. To relive that life. To be beaten. Broken. I am stronger than that.

Davis will come. He will find me. I will beat Aiden.

"You little fucking bitch," Aiden growls. "Why do you have to open your fucking mouth?"

"Hey, asshole," Fallon shouts. "You sociopathic rat-fuck! You little bitch-ass motherfucker!"

I watch the rage simmer on Aiden's face as my sister hurls her insults. Icy terror grips me when he turns her way. I shake my head at her, wanting her to shut up. Wanting her to remain invisible.

On a sigh, he stands and stalks across the room. He slaps Fallon across the face. Hard. She slumps forward.

"This one never stops talking," he says in exasperation, jabbing the knife her way. "Pains in my ass, the both of you."

Tears stream down my cheeks as I stare at my sister.

Lip curling in distaste, he sits across from me. "You're a chef. You work with knives, right?"

I shiver as he rests the flat edge of the knife on his thigh. The binds dig into my wrists as I frantically work them.

"So it makes sense to use one on you."

My eyes pop in terror. "Don't."

A wicked smile spreads across his face. "You want to know why I waited so long to have our little reunion?"

Nausea constricts in my throat. I feel faint. "No," I plead.

"I almost gave up, you know. I almost let him have you, but then I saw that you were expecting. I saw how happy you were, and I thought…why not wait until you have almost everything you ever wanted in life and then take it all away?" He leans in and lifts my shirt, baring my belly. "I told you I'd take everything from you, Dakota. I'll take this."

"Please, not my baby," I weep. I cringe as his clammy palm rubs a circle on my stomach. "Not my son."

His hand wraps around my jaw. The knife dances in my periphery. "*Our son.*"

"He will never be yours," I rasp.

Aiden shoves my face away and sits back down, trembling with rage. There's a distant look in his eyes. This blank look of hatred. "You could have come back. We could have been a family. But no. You made me chase you."

Behind me, one hand slips loose.

"Now, this is where we land, Dakota. I'm going to cut you apart. Take your baby. And as you bleed out, you can watch me kill your little sister." He rests the sharp edge of the knife low against my belly. I flinch as the blade breaks the skin. Hot stinging pain crests over me as blood trickles down toward my waistline.

I hiss a breath and wait for it.

Pain. Death.

Only a screeching, clattering sound has Aiden freezing. Fallon.

Her muscular body rocks her chair forward, backward. Its wooden legs skid and skitter across the hardwood floor.

One binding has slipped off her wrist, and my sister jerks at the ropes.

She wears her fury like a halo. It's everywhere. There's no doubt if my sister gets out of those ropes, she'll burn the world.

"Stop," Aiden orders.

But she doesn't. Over and over again, her body tee-ter-totters the chair.

And then she opens her mouth and screams. Great howling screams that I'm sure will crack every board in the cabin.

"Fucking fine." The knife leaves my belly, and Aiden stands. "She dies first."

"No," I cry. I twist and wrench my once-broken arm at an impossible angle. It screams at me. "Don't fucking touch her."

The last bind snaps.

Aiden pauses halfway to Fallon. "She'll bleed out before anyone finds you."

"You don't know my family. You don't know him." I smile. "You're dead. He will find you and he will kill you."

Fallon's eyes flick to me.

"He's already on his way." I lower my voice. "In fact… he's right outside the door."

Aiden nervously glances over his shoulder.

That millisecond of doubt is enough.

With a vicious scream, Fallon rocks the chair back-ward, and it smashes into pieces.

The second Fallon pops up, I tear out of the binds and surge forward. I whip out the knife from the pocket of my hoodie.

"Run, Koty!" Fallon screams, charging Aiden. "Go!

He lunges toward her. The knife slices across her ribs. Fallon screams in pain, but still, she flings herself at Aiden.

Aiden rears back to stab her again.

A primal protection overtakes me. I'm not going to die today and neither is my sister.

I spring onto his back, reach around, and stab the cheese knife into his chest.

"Mother. Fucker," I enunciate, digging it in with the heel of my palm.

"You fucking bitch," he howls, thrashing violently.

Fallon collapses to the floor.

Knocked off balance, Aiden hits his knees, smacking his head on the corner of the nightstand. The lamp smashes to the ground. The light goes out.

I leap across the floor, adrenaline coursing through my veins. I've never moved so fast, pregnant or otherwise. "Come and get me, asshole," I hiss.

My only thought is to draw him away from Fallon. Get help. Stay alive.

With blood roaring in my ears and Aiden's ragged screams at my back, I stagger and weave through the cabin. And then I'm outside.

Free.

41

Davis

THE PICKUP'S HEADLIGHTS ILLUMINATE THE forest. I get out and close the door, doing a quick sweep of our surroundings. The full moon above. The cabin a hundred yards in front of us. And one set of footprints—aimed for Eden.

There was no time to get Keena. I used the access route from the ranch up to Eden, saving me a thirty-minute drive via Dead Fred's Curve. I called for backup the second we hit the forest. This way, I get a head start on the cops.

Fuck this holding up in court. It won't get that far. I'm putting King down. Tonight.

I draw my gun and inch forward. Ford and Wyatt follow behind me. There's a nervous energy in the air. I haven't felt this kind of pressure since that night overseas. This counts for everything.

It would take a grave to drag me away from Dakota. But even then, I'd find my way out.

Because my reason for living is on the other side of that dirt and I don't go anywhere without her.

We cover the distance to the cabin easily, moving over soft soil and loam. My heart pounds in my chest as we approach. If this is a trap, so fucking be it. Dakota's here. I can feel it.

When I find that girl, I'm marrying her. No way in hell I'm letting her out of my arms, let alone my sight, again.

I freeze a foot from the cabin.

The door is open.

A rasp beside me. "Fallon." Wyatt's complexion resembles the color of chalk.

Ready for it, I throw an arm out, cutting off Wyatt before he can barrel past me. His lean body is tense, poised for battle. He whips to me, his jaw set in a tight line. Anger radiates from him.

"Stay the fuck back." I point at the cabin, look at Ford. "I go in first. He's armed."

"Don't get your ass shot," Ford hisses. "Again."

"Remind me to tell you that story," I promise, inching forward. "We make it out of here."

"Hold you to it, brother." Ford nods, grabs Wyatt by the neck. "Go. I got him."

I step through the open door and do a quick scan of the kitchen.

Empty.

I continue down the hall until I find the bedroom. The door is open, the room dark. I smell the metallic tang of blood before I see it.

God, no.

My brain empties. I feel along the wall for a light switch and when I flick it on, my heart stops.

There's a body in the middle of the room.

"Dakota," I rasp.

Dread curdles my stomach. I drop to my knees and roll her over.

Except it's not her.

"Fuck."

Fallon's pale, unconscious face stares up at me. A nasty bruise paints her cheek and temple. Crimson blooms across her torso. It seeps through the fabric of her thin tank top to creep across the floorboards beneath her.

I press my fingers to her neck. Relief floods me. There's a pulse.

Sluggish, but it's there.

"Ford," I shout, grabbing a sheet off the bed. "I need some fucking help."

Boots rattle the floorboards. Seconds later, my brothers are on their knees beside me.

"*Fallon.*" Her name tears from Wyatt's lips. He's pale as he lifts her into his arms. "No," he gasps. His hands run over her body like he's trying to find the hole and plug it.

I ball up the sheet and press it to her side, trying to stifle the spread of blood. Ford's hands shoot out to grip it. I can't tell how deep the cut, but it doesn't look good.

"She's alive," I say, "but she needs a hospital."

With trembling hands, Wyatt cups her face. "Fallon, wake up." He gives her a shake. "*Wake the fuck up.*"

"She's out cold, man." Ford's voice is gentle as we watch our younger brother slowly lose it.

Frustration and fear build in me. I scan the cabin— smashed chair, a coil of rope, gun on the nightstand.

Where the fuck is Dakota? She's close. I can feel it.

A sharp gasp has all of us tensing.

Fallon groans. Her eyelids flutter. "It's about damn time you assholes got here," she says weakly.

Relief shoots through me. She's still talking shit, which means she's okay. For now.

"Goddamn left my soul for a second," Ford breathes, increasing pressure on her wound.

Wyatt chokes out a laugh. "You ain't lookin' too good, cowgirl."

"No shit," she mutters.

"Fallon," I say, leaning down. "Do you remember what happened? Where's Dakota?"

"She ran." Fallon whimpers, but her lips curl in a smile. "She stabbed the asshole in the fucking heart and ran into the woods."

Pride pushes against my chest. That's my girl.

"Where's Aiden?"

"He went after her." When she looks at me, my stomach turns. Her pupils could rival the moon. "I tried to stop him, but…he stabbed me like a little bitch."

Wyatt winces as she lets out a cry of pain.

"Fuck, it hurts." A harsh shudder wracks her frame. She turns glassy eyes up. "It hurts, Wyatt."

"Yeah, it does, but you got this, don't you?" Wyatt shifts her in his arms. "You're tough."

"Tough," she pants.

"The toughest."

Her hazel eyes close. Open. "I meant it when I said I hated you."

"I know you did," he murmurs, a hitch in his voice. His hands shake. "Stay with me, okay? You can hate me tomorrow."

"I…will." Head lolling in Wyatt's lap, she looks pleadingly at me. "He has a knife. You have to find her."

I smooth back her hair. "I will," I promise.

I look at my brothers. Hand Ford the keys to my truck. "Get Fallon to the hospital. Fast," I say grimly. "I'm going after King."

42

Dakota

ROPE THE MOON, KOTY. ROPE THE MOON AND RUN *your pregnant ass off.*

I'm on autopilot as I slice through the woods. There's enough moonlight to illuminate my way. To give me hope.

My bare feet sweep over small rocks, grass, pine needles. Long, spindly branches scrape my bare legs. But I barely feel it. My entire focus is on escape. Get Aiden away from my sister. Keep Fallon and my baby safe.

"Poor little lost Dakota!" Aiden screams in the dark. I can hear him crashing behind me. "Always running! Just wait until I find you!"

Nausea constricts in my throat. I hold my belly as I run, like I can keep Squish in. I feel him in there, squirming around. It gives me fight. Makes me move.

If I can keep away from Aiden, hide in the woods, Davis will find me. All I have to do is survive.

I climb a small rocky hill that in my pregnant state feels like I'm scaling Everest. My belly feels like it weighs a hundred pounds. Still, I press on. My body won't let me fail. And I won't fail my son. I won't fail myself.

Back to the ranch. It's the sole mission in my mind.

There's just one little problem.

I don't know where the fuck I am.

Chest heaving, I stop and scan my surroundings.

There are two paths. Right or left. The ranch and the road are below me. Somewhere. But so is Aiden.

Twigs crunch behind me as Aiden closes the gap between us.

Fuck. Fuck.

My heart trembles in my chest.

Think, Dakota.

I close my eyes. Davis's words echo in my head.

Meadow Mountain and Eden is to the west. The hiking trail near the cabin leads back to the ranch.

I open my eyes and frantically scour the ground.

Hiking trail. Hiking trail.

I note a rugged dirt path to my right. Unmarked, but that has to be it.

I turn to run, but my foot catches on a root and I'm sent sprawling. I hit the forest floor, covering my belly protectively. Excruciating pain radiates through my leg.

I cover my face with my hands in anguish. My cheeks are wet and I don't remember when I started crying again.

"Fuck," I moan into my palms. I'm exhausted. Numb. But I can't afford to stop.

I have everything. Everything to lose.

Soft dough in my hand. My fingertips gripping the sheet corner, Davis's mouth on mine. The squirm of my baby in my belly. Fallon's sharp laugh in the morning at The Corner Store. My father telling me he's proud of me.

Mine. All mine.

I fought for this life, and I am not losing it now.

Sucking in a sharp breath, I look up at the moon.

"Don't stop," I tell myself. Squish kicks like he's telling me to move my ass. "Get up. Don't stop."

A snuffling noise cuts through the night. Something

dark and swift barrels over my side. The scent of musk and dirt lingers in the air.

I flatten against the ground and feel for a rock. My heart's going to explode out of my chest. I close my hand over the rock and hold my breath, ready to spring. Attack.

That's when a warm, wet nose hits my elbow.

"Keena?" Hope springs. Davis is close. He found me.

Palms flat against damp earth, I press myself up and gasp.

The wolf.

Inquisitive yellow eyes stare back at me. Her fur's silver tipped with black. We're inches apart.

"Dakota!" Aiden's voice echoes in the night.

At the noise, the wolf's ears prick dog-like, and she glides past me. Pauses and looks back. Waits.

For me.

On shaky legs, I stand. My gut says to follow her, because the righteous wild of Montana has never let me down.

She goes right, and I follow, careful and deft on the trail. We rush through the woods, swift as wind. Now and then, the wolf glances back to watch me with dark eyes. She leads me through the forest, over loam and mulch and wet sand.

We head down a steep slope. The wolf weaves around a tree and comes to a stop in front of a massive, jagged wall of rock. It juts from the earth like a spire. In the center of it is a crack, barely wide enough to fit a person, but when I pass the mouth of the cave, I gasp.

Two wolf pups.

With a flick of her tail, the wolf disappears inside.

When I turn my head, I see the glittering bright lights of Runaway Ranch. Fifteen minutes away, if not less.

"Thank you," I whisper.

Hope glows in my chest, and I move. Fast.

I never see him coming.

A fist lashes out and catches me in the face. The impact sends me to my knees, nearly jars my teeth loose. My head swims, stars blink in and out of my vision.

Aiden wraps his hand in my hair, yanks me to standing. "Get up, you fucking bitch." Icy rage burns in his eyes.

The slash of the knife shines silver in the night.

"No!" I scream and twist in his grip.

Aiden drags me back against him. One arm wraps tightly around my neck, the other dips to press the knife against my stomach. "Welcome home, Dakota."

A split second later, a growl cuts through the night. "Don't fucking move."

"Davis," I whisper.

My heart races as a shadow moves in the woods. Davis comes into view. The barrel of his gun trails Aiden, but I can sense his hesitation. He can't get a good shot. Ever the asshole, Aiden uses me as a human-shield.

"Put the knife down and let her go."

"Don't come any closer," Aiden warns. "I'll stab her. Right in the belly."

I make a sound of panic as the knife rests against the curve of my stomach.

To anyone else, Davis looks emotionless, but I see the pain etched across his face. It's killing him to point the gun at me.

It's okay, I mouth.

That strong muscle in his jaw tics. He advances, leaving six feet between us. His finger hovers over the trigger.

A twig snaps in the woods.

Davis's eyes flick to the left. Then he zeroes in on Aiden. The gun steadies.

"Do it," he commands, his voice clear and cool.

"Hey, asshole." Ford's drawl cuts through the black night.

Something round and black whips through the air, barely missing my cheek.

The rock hits Aiden smack center in the forehead, catching him off guard.

It's all I need.

I slam an elbow into Aiden's stomach and twist out of his arms.

I sprint blindly toward Ford.

He pulls me into a tight hug that shields me. "Don't watch," he says, low in my ear.

Davis fires.

Gunshots ring out.

I flinch against Ford's chest.

Silence. My heartbeat throbs in my temples.

I stay still for a long second, curled into Ford, barely able to breathe, to believe, and then—

"Dakota?"

Davis's whiskey-soaked voice is heaven to my ears.

A cry leaves my mouth. I practically fly the distance between us, so fast my feet barely touch the ground. I throw myself into Davis's arms.

"Dakota," he mutters desperately. Cradling me tight against him, he kisses my jaw, my hair, my cheek, my lips. "Christ, I have you. I have you."

I let the last thread of calm holding me together snap. A terrible sob rocks my body, but Davis only holds me tighter. I melt into him—soak in his steadiness, breathe in his strength.

"It's okay," he husks, rocking me back and forth. "You're okay. I got you."

He does. He always has. The lengths he's gone to for me steal my breath.

"Aiden?" I look up at him.

"Don't look," he orders, crushing me to his chest.

But I have to.

I have to see that he's gone.

When I look over, I see Aiden King face-up, unmoving on the forest floor. Two perfectly placed holes right between the eyes.

"He's gone," I whisper. Tears slide down my cheeks.

"It'll never be enough," Davis says, crushing me closer. "For what he did to you." His dark brown eyes burn with icy fury, wild and intense. Too much rage for the man I love.

I reach up and cup that strong, whiskered jaw. "I knew you'd come. I knew you'd find us."

"Baby, I was ready to tear down the entire fucking world the second he took you."

Behind us, sirens cut the night air.

Footsteps. Ford.

"How in the hell you find us?" Davis gruffs over the top of my head.

"Woo-woo shit, man," Ford drawls. I hear the soft lope of his boots, see the smile on his face as he passes us by in the forest. "It's that woo-woo shit."

Davis chuckles, then takes my chin between his fingers. He tilts my gaze to his and scours my face with an intensity I've never seen from him. "Are you hurt?" His massive hand palms my belly. "Squish?"

"We're fine." A knot of emotion forms in my throat. "My dad. Fallon." Tears blur my vision. "She's hurt. Aiden stabbed her. And my dad—"

"Stede's alert and at the hospital by now. Bullet only grazed him. Fallon's a little worse for wear, but she'll be okay. Wyatt's with her."

I smile. "She'll love that."

"Let's get you there, too. So we can get you and Squish checked over."

"And then what?"

A grin tips his lips. "Didn't you hear, Cupcake? We're getting married."

43

Davis

DAKOTA AND THE BABY GET POKED AND PRODDED until I'm reassured by the doctor that everything is okay. Dakota has heavy bruises and a cut on her abdomen, but she's fine. Squish is okay too.

Thank God.

Thank God for Dakota.

She's sore, but she's alive.

A pissed off woman, a hurt woman, turns into one hell of a warrior. She got herself and our son out of there. Protected her sister. Saved my goddamn life.

Because if anything had happened to her...

Terror rakes its claws down my spine.

Fucking unfathomable.

With my hand guiding her out of the exam room, I turn to the doctor, unconvinced. "Are you sure they're okay?"

Dakota grips my arm and rolls her eyes. "We're fine." She takes my hand and pulls me down the hallway. "C'mon, Hotshot. I want to see about my family."

It's commotion when we enter the waiting room. Half the damn town has come out to see about the McGraws. Keeping a tight grip on Dakota's hand, I pull her through the ring of people. She's covered in mud, her dark hair a wild snarl of forest, her faced bruised, but she's never looked more beautiful.

Fierce.

When she sees us, Ruby bursts into tears, throwing her arms around both me and Dakota. Charlie passes me a flask and I take a nip and send it on down the line to Ford.

Richter arrives, a parade of cops flanking him. "What part of 'you don't have a badge' did you not understand?" he asks, shaking his head as he takes my statement.

It's short and simple. Aiden King kidnapped Dakota and held her hostage. I shot him to save her life.

No remorse. Bastard tried to take my family from me. He got what he deserves.

Soon the doctor arrives. He informs us a bullet grazed Stede and he should recover in two weeks. Fallon, on the other hand, has a nasty concussion. The cut was shallow. Nothing life-threatening, but because of the concussion, she'll need months to recover.

We see Stede first.

Dakota flies into his arms. "I'm so glad you're okay."

Stede reaches out and grips my hand as I approach. Tears line his silver eyes. "You brought my girls back to me. Thank you, son."

I clear my throat of emotion. "I told you I'd protect them. I meant it."

Dakota fusses with his blanket. "You feel okay, Daddy?"

Stede barks a laugh. "Hell, I could lead a parade right now."

Dakota scowls. "Don't even think about it."

By the time we make it to Fallon's room, Wyatt's already there.

Fallon sits upright in the hospital bed in a white gown, thick caramel hair hanging past her shoulders. It looks like she went eight seconds on a bull. She's bruised from head to toe, and a nasty shiner paints her right eye. Wyatt stands next to her, a tight expression on his face.

Dakota cries as she rocks her sister in her arms, and though Fallon's dry-eyed, she's shaking.

"Are you okay?"

"I'm okay."

"Really?"

"Really."

Dakota searches her sister's face. "You don't have to pretend."

"I'm fine, Koty," Fallon insists. But I don't miss the tremble of her lower lip, warring with the stubborn jut of her chin.

"How do you feel?" I ask, reaching down to squeeze her leg through the blankets.

She stares at me with glassy, drug-laced eyes. "I'm higher than a fucking choir," Fallon slurs, sticking an arm up in the air like a jazz hand. She yanks at her IV tubing and Wyatt lunges to steady it.

Fallon barks a harsh laugh. "Down to three lives now."

"Don't say that," Dakota scolds, helping her settle back into the bed.

"Tougher than me, that's for sure," Wyatt drawls. He takes a long last look at Fallon, whose eyes are slowly closing, then crosses the room.

I follow him out into the hall.

"Hey." I snag his arm before he can duck out. "You okay?" He looks shell-shocked as the adrenaline wears off and the hard reality of the night sinks in.

The muscles in his jaw and throat work. His shoulders slump. His eyes stay glued to Fallon's hospital door as he runs a hand through his shaggy hair to grip the back of his neck. "He hit her, D," he says, his voice breaking. "He could have killed her."

"You go back to the ranch. Ride it off."

"Nah." He shakes his head. "I'm gonna head to Fallon's and clean up her place. I don't want her to see it like that."

"You have time," I tell him, wanting him to rest. "It'll be a few days before she goes home."

"I just…" He clears his throat. "I have to get outta here. Do something."

I watch him stride down the hall.

We'll all have to wrestle with the weight of tonight, but maybe none more than Fallon.

A noise behind me has me turning. Dakota stands in the doorway. Her smile is the brightest light I've ever seen. "Fallon's asleep. Let's go home."

Dawn's breaking on the horizon by the time we get back to the ranch. Without words, I carry Dakota upstairs, strip her bare, and kiss every inch of her skin—every bruise that bastard inflicted on her. I show her *I love you* with my mouth between her legs, then I pull her on top of me and fuck her until we're both prepared to detonate.

After, my hand strokes slow, lazy circles over her belly as we lie in bed. I'm careful of the bandage on her belly. It makes me want to kill the bastard all over again for marking her.

"I don't think this is what the doctor meant when he said rest and relaxation," she whispers.

I give her a devilish grin, push up on my elbow and snag my jeans. From my pocket, I bring out her dog tag. Dakota watches as I remove the tracker, then slip the chain back over her neck. Where it's always belonged.

Her beautiful brown eyes are glassy with tears. "I never

had any doubt that you'd come for us," she says, rubbing her thumb over the tag.

"I'll always come for you," I murmur, my lips dropping to hers. I breathe her in. "Five seconds, five minutes, five lifetimes."

She laughs lightly. "That's what tonight has been. One long lifetime."

I tuck her against me. "Get some sleep, Cupcake."

"Can't. I'm afraid it's all a dream and if I fall asleep, I'll wake up and it won't be true."

"It's true," I tell her, running a fingertip over her ring. Dakota, safe and sound in my arms, wearing my ring, is all I've ever wanted. "No matter where you are. I'll be there. I'll find you. Even in your dreams."

Her eyes soften. "Even on the moon, Hotshot?"

I cup her face and lower my brow to hers. "Forever on the moon."

Epilogue

Davis

T HE FIRST WEEK OF SEPTEMBER IS WARM AND bright. The sky is a piercing blue. It's like Montana herself called in a favor for the good weather to last. At least long enough for this wedding.

Even though the season is over, Runaway Ranch is full. Dakota and I decided to have a simple ceremony at the ranch. Fitting, considering it's the place where we first began. Friends and family have flown in. My mother and father sit in the front row. Mama Belle fans her hands in front of her face. Laughter rings out from the sidelines. My little sister and her husband chase after their twins. Ferraro's flown in for the special occasion, bringing with him a handful of top-secret government devices for us to—in his words—test out later.

The pasture is full of white chairs. The aisle covered in rose petals. Marvin, a local from town, sits with a guitar and strums a simple rock 'n' roll melody. A rustic triangle-shaped wood arch decorated with fragrant flowers completes the setup.

But I couldn't give a shit about any of that. All I care about is Dakota. I've waited six long years for this moment. I can wait five more minutes.

Clearing my throat, I nervously run a hand down my tie.

A snort floats my way. "Still can't believe you got me into a tux."

I side-eye Wyatt. "Believe it. And shut it."

Grady, the youngest, smirks and leans in. "Think she changed her mind?"

Charlie rolls his eyes. I grin down at them.

Beside me, my brothers line the front of the aisle. Next to me. Where they always have been and always will be. It was last week at a riotous and drunken bachelor party at Nowhere that I finally spilled the truth to my brothers about my time in special ops. What I went through to get back to Charlie.

Another long due secret unburied. Another step to getting closer to my brothers.

The music swells, and the knot of nerves in my stomach doubles.

Keena trots down the aisle with the rings tied to her collar.

"Good girl," I tell her, leaning down to retrieve them. The crowd lets out a murmur of *aw* as I give her a big hug and then she settles beside Charlie.

Ruby appears at the end of the aisle. She bounces toward us in a flowy one-shouldered gold dress. Her rose-gold hair is long and loose. A small crown of baby's breath halos around her head. She gives Charlie a flirty wink before standing at the front of the aisle opposite us.

Next is Fallon.

I grin when I see her cheeks are flushed a pretty pink. She looks unlike herself, soft and feminine in a long sage dress of chiffon. On her arm is Ford. They take slow steps as they walk down the aisle.

Three months after her attack, Fallon's almost fully

recovered. She's back on a horse, but the lingering concussion symptoms have taken a toll on her riding. She still won't talk about Aiden. There's a cloudiness in her eyes that unsettles both Dakota and me.

When they reach the end of the aisle, Ford settles by my side, Fallon across from me.

She narrows her eyes and mouths, *Don't fuck it up.*

The music changes to an acoustic version of the Rolling Stones "Wild Horses."

My nerves skyrocket and I barely have any time to wonder how in the hell I'm going to keep it together, because there she is.

Dakota appears at the end of the aisle with Stede by her side.

"Fuck," I croak.

She's the most beautiful thing I've ever seen.

She looks stunning in a draped gown with a bow at the waist. Her black hair is sleek and shiny, spilling around her slender shoulders. The smile on her face is devastating.

I love seeing her like this. Free and beautiful and happy. Everything Dakota deserves. Everything I will give her for the rest of our lives.

And in her arms, our son Duke.

Three weeks after the nightmare with Aiden King, Dakota went into labor. It was a middle of the night drag race to the hospital. With seconds to spare, our son was born in the lobby of Bear Creek Clinic. But it's what I've come to expect. The unplanned—the chaos—in this life with Dakota. I'll take it all. Every second, every unexpected moment with this woman and our son.

"Hey, Hotshot," Dakota says softly as Stede hands her over to me.

A muscle in my jaw tics. "Hey, yourself."

Chest tight, I look down at Duke. The baby is all Dakota. Tufts of dark hair, jet-black eyes. But he's as much mine as he is hers. When I met him for the first time, and he wrapped his tiny finger around mine, I was done. He claimed my heart as much as his mother has, and we made it official when Dakota put my name on the birth certificate as his father.

Dakota gives me a watery smile, then turns to hand Duke to Fallon. Instantly, Keena swaps sides. She noses beside Fallon to stare up at Duke. Ever since the baby was born, Keena has been a loyal protector.

I can't wait anymore. Hands shaking, I reach for Dakota and haul her into my chest, earning chuckles and sighs from the guests.

A clog of emotion settles in my throat. She's locked in my arms, her heart against mine. "You look beautiful."

She palms my chest. "Not too shabby yourself."

"Last chance to run," I gruff.

Tears well in her eyes dangerously fast. She curls her fingers around mine. "Never," she says on a broken whisper. "You're stuck with me."

In Fallon's arms, Duke begins his tiny whimper.

Dakota's wide eyes slice to mine. Fuck. By now, we're well accustomed to our son's demands. We have minutes until he nears meltdown status.

"Marry us now," she commands the justice of the peace.

He does. No dry eyes in the house. The ceremony goes on even when Dakota nurses Duke mid-vow. We're not waiting. Not any longer.

After we say "I do," Mama Belle wails in the front row. Stede blows his nose into a big white handkerchief, breaks out a flask, and passes it around the guests. Duke screams his tiny head off and it's everything I've ever wanted.

Then it's time for the real party. Everyone crowds into the lodge for the reception and drinks. Music pumps out over the newly installed speakers.

I glance over my shoulder to where loud cackles float from the lawn. My brothers, sister, and Ruby are trying to two-step across the front porch of the lodge, blitzed out on moonshine from Stede's stash. Fallon is suspiciously absent.

I use the distraction to snag Dakota's wrist and pull her back behind the lodge. "Peace and quiet."

She falls into me and loops her arms around my neck. "No more peace. We have a baby and my boobs are about to burst."

I cup her breast. "Where is the baby?"

"With your mother." Dark eyes laced with lust, she giggles and grips my tie. "I have to say... Marine mode is hot, but daddy mode is hotter."

I kiss her shoulder, the tiny freckle on her lip. Dakota's gaze drifts as she watches Fallon, cigarette in hand, bound down the front steps, headed for God knows where.

"What if he broke her, Davis?" she murmurs.

"Not Fallon." I tip her chin to meet my eyes. "She'll be okay. We won't let her break."

Dakota's cloudy eyes clear. I press her back against the side of the lodge and hook my finger through her dress strap. A fire builds between us.

"Since we got a babysitter, think it's time we go back to sneakin' around."

A magnificent smile stretches across her face. "Oh, you do, do you?"

I'm already leaning in. I need that full mouth on mine. Need her against me. "I do."

I clasp her neck and bring her in for a kiss.

We pull back, panting, and I keep her against me. I don't dare let her go.

A warmth spreads in my chest, behind my eyes. "I love you, Koty," I rasp out, my voice thick with emotion.

Dakota lets out a sigh of contentment. "Thank you." She tilts her face to look up at me. "You changed my heart, my last name, my entire world, Davis.

"Every day," I promise. "Every day, I will change your life."

Years ago, when Dakota left Resurrection, she left me dreaming of the day she would be back in my arms. And here she is. So much joy I never thought I deserved. But now, I know I do. My wife. Our son. Our life.

Our home on Runaway Ranch.

Bonus Epilogue

Dakota

"LIKE THIS?"

"Perfect," I say and step aside to watch Duke roll the rolling pin over the dough. I smile and note the cute quirk of his tongue. Solemn, quiet intensity is my seven-year-old son.

Duke frowns as the rolling pin sticks to the dough. "Shoot."

I dip my hand in the silky flour and dust some over the surface. "There. Try that."

"Okay."

This is our Friday after-school tradition. The scent of freshly baked bread. The set of the coral sun. The plumes of flour cascading in the air.

Just us, prepping at the bakery for the weekend. And we always get in a game of Cowgirl Coven. I moved in the pinball machine not long after we opened. I want my son to love what I love. Even if it doesn't last, some part of him will always know what makes his mother tick.

I ruffle his dark, fluffy hair. "What kind of pie are we making today?"

He wrinkles his nose. "Peach."

"Good choice."

After smacking a kiss on the side of his head, I leave

him to it and disappear into the front. With a sigh, I run my eyes over my dreamy little world.

The Huckleberry. My bakery, adorned in hues of lilac and lavender. The bakery has been open for almost six years and is beloved by locals and food critics alike. After a write-up in *Food & Wine*, it's been an extreme sport to keep up with the demand of tourists.

Cowboy Cupcakes. Ruby's Bucket List Carrot Cake. And, of course, my iconic huckleberry and lemon cinnamon rolls.

The chimes above the door jingle. I smile at the familiar stomping stride and the sound of little feet.

"Mama!"

I swipe my five-year-old, Lainie, up in my arms. "Hey, dirty girl." I dab at the mud on her cheek. There's grass in her wild chocolate-brown curls. "What happened to you?"

My husband stands there grinning. He never fails to set my heart aflame. He wears his Warrior Heart Home T-shirt. The ranch has taken up even more of Davis's time. Two years after I had Duke, it became an official sanctuary for dogs. And it's grown bigger than it's ever been, which means we've hired instructors and military veterans to train the dogs. Each dog finds their forever home, thanks to Davis. Though Keena's old and grouchy, she's still our best girl at the Warrior Heart home.

Lainie's chocolate-brown eyes sparkle. "Uncle Ford took me down into the canyon." She lifts and waves her dirty fingers. "You know, the one with the skeletons."

"Mm-hmm." I give Davis a flat look. "Ford needs his uncle's license revoked."

Davis chuckles. "He needs the practice. I'll hose her down when we get back to the ranch."

The kitchen door swings open.

"Dad!" Duke rushes toward Davis, eyes alight.

Davis wraps his arm around Duke and brings him in for a hug. "Hey, kiddo. Keeping your mama busy?"

"We're making peach pie."

"Save me a slice."

Duke beams. The way he's holding onto Davis and looking at him with pure love and adoration makes my heart squeeze.

Their connection is undeniable. Since the day Duke was born, Davis has been there for every "first." First step, first tear, first baseball game. The best role model, he's taught our son about the things in life that matter. Being a good man. Integrity. Honor. Respect for women.

Now and then, I'll think of Aiden. Some small memory. But it doesn't get far. Not with Davis around. He's Duke's father.

In every way that matters.

"Down, down, down." Lainie wriggles and kicks her legs impatiently.

With a huff, I set her on her feet. Duke takes her hand and the two of them run, giggling, for the pinball machine.

The best big brother. He's an even bigger protector than Davis.

Davis shoots me a smoldering look and corners me behind the register. I shiver as a big hand cups the curve of my ass. The other lifts the edge of a lavender pastry box.

"Not yours," I scold and palm his steel chest. "These are going to Ruby's for her flower arranging class."

"Playing favorites, Cupcake? Don't make me take you back into the kitchen." I shudder at the husk in his voice.

Goosebumps break across my skin as he tugs me tighter into his arms.

I scoff. "You wouldn't dare," I say right before his mouth crashes down on mine. Everything falls away. I loop my arms around his neck and drink him in.

The man of my dreams.

A dark shadow passing by the window catches my eye.

"We have company," I murmur against his lips.

Davis growls at the jingle of the door chimes.

I twist in his arms to see Charlie standing in the doorway. On his shoulders, his two-year-old daughter, Meadow. Though Ruby and Charlie weren't able to have children on their own, Ford's wife offered to be Ruby's surrogate. No gift could ever compare to what she gave them.

"Da-dee! Da-dee! Da-dee!" Meadow smashes her hands to Charlie's dark beard, and he merely grins as he takes the abuse.

"Got the stash?" he asks.

"There," I say, pointing at the box. "Twenty eclairs that your brother almost got ahold of."

He gives me a grin, hefts the box in his hands. "You're a lifesaver."

I tug on Meadow's chubby little foot, and she squeals in delight. She's a strawberry blonde beauty like her mother. "Anything for Ruby."

After ruffling Meadow's hair, Davis points a finger at his brother. "Wyatt's in town. We got poker tonight. Nine p.m. Bullshit box."

Charlie rolls his eyes and bounces a squealing Meadow on his back. "Bossy bastard." With a grin on his face, he ducks his broad-shouldered frame and disappears out the door.

Davis tugs at my apron strings. "You ready to come home with your husband and take it easy?"

I simply laugh and glance over at Duke, who is hefting Lainie onto a stool so she can expertly smash the plungers. "When have I ever taken it easy?"

His smile is wicked. "Got two reasons to," he says, his broad hand splaying across my rounded stomach as he leans down to sweep his lips across mine.

Twins.

It was the best, most shocking surprise of the entire year. If Davis has his way, we're going to have a baker's dozen of babies. But I love it. Love the world Davis and I have created. Filled with love and chaos and babies and bottles, the way we both want it to be.

I never imagined this would have been possible. The darkness in my life so many years ago, sucker punched by sunshine and joy. Davis has devoured my heart and soul and has only given me happiness.

A year after Duke was born, my dream home at Eden was completed. A massive two-story modern farmhouse with a gourmet kitchen and a wraparound porch. Just like the setting sun, Davis is dependable. Every day, he rises, tearing up the gravel drive to start his days at Runaway Ranch.

And in the evenings…it's a sight I never get sick of.

My husband coming home to me.

Weekends are for fun and bonfires down at the ranch. Our family's close. We fight and argue and love fiercely. It seems like I can't take a step around Resurrection without running into nieces, nephews, and sisters- and brothers-in-law I adore. Our compound at the ranch is growing by the day—especially with our twins and the recent news that Ford's wife is expecting.

Now I know what love is. The golden light of Runaway Ranch. A flour dusted apron on Sunday morning and Davis Montgomery's hand in mine. It's bliss.

The greatest love story I could have ever dreamed up.

Davis frames my face with his hands, his brown eyes gleaming. "Home, Cupcake?"

A slow smile spreads across my face. "Home."

The Runaway Ranch series continues with
Burn the Wild.

Thank you for reading!

If you enjoyed the book, please consider leaving a review on Goodreads and the site you bought it from. Every review means the world to indie authors.

Don't miss out on Ava Hunter's upcoming books! Sign up at www.authoravahunter.com to be the first to get the latest book news and bonus content.

Acknowledgments

A huge thank you to Echo at Wildheart Graphics for bringing this discreet cover to life! As always, thank you to Paula at Lilypad Lit for working magic on my words.

Thanks to my amazing beta readers—Anna P., Chelsea, Yolanda, and Rachel—for your endless support and feedback. You always give me the confidence to make the book better and then go forth and publish.

Next, thank you to Tabitha for popping into my DMs and then taking the time to fact/sensitivity check all the trauma/medical related sections. I'm so thankful we connected.

Thank you to Mary, my wonderful PA, for proofreading.

As always, thank you to my readers. Every post, every review means so much. I could not do this without you.

About the Author

Ava Hunter is an Amazon top 50 bestselling author. She writes romance with heart, humor, and heat. Her bestselling books include *Babymoon or Bust*, an accidental pregnancy rom-com, and *Tame the Heart*, a grumpy/sunshine cowboy romance with Yellowstone-vibes. When she's not at her computer with a hot cup of coffee, you'll either find her reading the latest true crime book or traveling with her family. Otherwise, she'll be behind her desk, plotting out or typing up her next dreamy love story.

CONNECT WITH AVA:

WEBSITE: www.authoravahunter.com

NEWSLETTER: www.authoravahunter.com

FACEBOOK: facebook.com/authoravahunter

INSTAGRAM: instagram.com/authoravahunter

TIKTOK: tiktok.com/@authoravahunter